Mercy reached one reddened hand out to take Abigail's, threading their fingers together.

Her skin was still cool and pleasant in spite of the burns – and again, Abigail found herself thinking about how long and fine Mercy's fingers were. There shouldn't have been anything improper about touching another woman's hand – but somehow, Abigail was sure that if she'd had a chaperone nearby, she would have been scolded for touching *Mercy's* hand.

Magic tingled lightly across Abigail's skin. Even as she watched, the shadows of the forest parted like a curtain. Colour crept across her vision, replacing the ambient moonlight with splashes of vibrant twilight. The trees glimmered with blues and pinks and yellows, all mixed together like a painter's canvas.

By Olivia Atwater

REGENCY FAERIE TALES

Half a Soul

Ten Thousand Stitches

Longshadow

LONG SHADOW

Regency Faerie Tales: Book Three

OLIVIA ATWATER

orbitbooks.net

This book is a work of fiction. Names, characters, places, and incidents are the product of the author's imagination or are used fictitiously. Any resemblance to actual events, locales, or persons, living or dead, is coincidental.

Cover images by Shutterstock

Orbit
Hachette Book Group
1290 Avenue of the Americas
New York, NY 10104
orbitbooks.net

First Orbit Paperback Edition: August 2022
First Orbit eBook Edition: April 2022
Simultaneously published in Great Britain by Orbit
Originally published by Starwatch Press in 2021

Orbit is an imprint of Hachette Book Group.
The Orbit name and logo are trademarks of Little, Brown Book Group Limited.

Library of Congress Control Number: 2022933334

ISBNs: 9780316463126 (trade paperback), 9780316463225 (ebook)

Printed in the United States of America

LSC-C

Printing 3, 2024

Dramatis Personae

Miss Abigail Wilder – Dora and Elias Wilder's fostered ward; apprentice magician

Hugh Wilder – Abigail's ghostly adoptive brother; often longs for tarts

Lady Theodora Eloisa Charity Wilder – Abigail's adoptive mother; the better half of the Lord Sorcier; possesses half a soul

Lord Elias Wilder – the uncouth Lord Sorcier and court magician of England; performs three impossible things before breakfast each day

Miss Vanessa Lowe – Abigail's aunt; a socialite and charitable soul

Lady Mulgrew – a tea lady and an incorrigible gossip

Miss Esther Fernside – Lord Breckart's daughter; a recent addition to the tea ladies

Miss Langley – Abigail's old governess; still employed by the Lord Sorcier's household

Mr Hayes – magical scarecrow and bane of the sluagh

Lady Pinckney – Miss Lucy Kendall's grieving mother

Mr Swinton – Lady Pinckney's butler

Mercy – a magically gifted laundress who often speaks to ghosts

Miss Lucy Kendall – ghost of a recently deceased debutante

Miss Bridget Gillingham and Miss Phoebe Haddington – debutantes; once in Miss Lucy Kendall's inner social circle

Mr James Ruell – an eligible bachelor; also known as "Mr Red" for his favourite red cravat

Lady Hollowvale – faerie marchioness of Hollowvale; Hugh and Abigail's Other Mum; possesses half an English soul

Lord Longshadow – lord of the sluagh, with dominion over the dead; placed under three magical bans by the Lord Sorcier

Mrs Euphemia Jubilee – wife of Mr Juniper Jubilee; possessed of excellent common sense and a healthy surplus of anger

Mr Juniper Jubilee – formerly Lord Blackthorn; faerie and husband to Euphemia Reeves; English enthusiast and temporary governess

Black Catastrophe and Lightless Moon – faeries of the sluagh

Prologue

Miss Abigail Wilder was not supposed to use her magic in front of the tea ladies. *Never use your magic in front of the* ton, her father had told her. *Once you do, they'll never let you rest – you'll be doing useless magic tricks until you're old and grey.*

Eighteen-year-old Abigail greatly suspected that the tea ladies were exactly the sort of nobility her father had warned her about. Once every month, the tea ladies met in her Aunt Vanessa's sitting room for tea. Ostensibly, the ladies were there at Aunt Vanessa's invitation in order to discuss the charity she intended to set up – but in practice, they rarely did much other than take their tea and gossip about the rest of the *beau monde.* Often, in fact, their conversations turned to the subject of Abigail's father, Lord Elias Wilder – England's court magician, sometimes known as the Lord Sorcier.

"Won't you tell us at least a *little* bit of what your husband is up to, my Lady Sorcière?" Lady Mulgrew asked. She was a thin, pinched-looking woman with a high, reedy voice – Abigail sometimes thought she looked a bit like a horse. Lady Mulgrew had been a tea lady for months now, ever since Aunt Vanessa had started their meetings. As one of the few ladies who had donated any real money so far, Lady Mulgrew carried herself with a certain air of importance, enjoying Vanessa's increased attentions. She always sat in a spot of honour at tea, just next to Vanessa herself.

Abigail's mother, Lady Theodora Wilder, did not respond immediately to the query. In fact, she continued sipping at her tea for a long while, as though she hadn't heard the question at all. Abigail knew that her mother *had* heard the question, despite her lack of reaction – she was simply thinking through the implications, trying very hard to formulate an appropriate response. Lady Theodora Wilder had only half a soul, which skewed her social acumen somewhat. Long silences never bothered Dora in the way that they bothered most other people – and since Dora's first instincts always suggested that she should be utterly honest and forthright, she often required those long silences in order to engineer a more appropriate, diplomatic reply.

Lady Mulgrew blinked over her tea. "I'm not certain if you heard me, my Lady Sorcière," she observed very slowly, as though she were talking to a deaf woman. "I said—"

"Oh yes, I did hear you," Dora assured Lady Mulgrew. She set her teacup down on the table in front of her, buying herself further time to think. Dora turned her mismatched green and grey eyes upon Lady Mulgrew, considering her gravely. "I know much of my husband's business," Dora said finally, "but I do my best to keep it to myself. It is his duty to protect England from black magic – and from worse sometimes. One never knows when a stray word might have unintended consequences."

This was not, of course, what Lady Mulgrew wished to hear. She leaned forward in her seat of honour. "But surely," she insisted, "nothing terrible could come of sharing some small news of interest with *us*. We are hardly the sort of people from which the Lord Sorcier must protect England!"

Abigail snorted into her teacup. Dora shot her daughter a sideways look – and though Dora rarely showed emotion on her face as other people did, Abigail knew that they were sharing the same thought: Lord Elias Wilder *often* implied that the aristocracy were worse than any black magicians.

Aunt Vanessa probably had the best of intentions asking Abigail and her mother to tea. Abigail was, herself, the product of Good Charity – as anyone could surely tell. For though Lord Elias Wilder *called* Abigail his daughter, and though he had loaned her his surname, he was truly just fostering her as his ward. And while Lady Theodora Wilder had dressed Abigail in creamy muslin and done up her hair with a green taffeta ribbon, Abigail's skin was still covered in old pockmarks, and her blonde hair was lank and straw-like. Abigail had made half an effort to improve her accent, mostly just to please her old governess – but she had to speak very slowly and with great concentration in order to manage her elocution.

Aunt Vanessa thought that the tea ladies would be more willing to help other children if they saw how much Abigail had benefitted from similar charity. Abigail was . . . less convinced. But Aunt Vanessa had asked with such lovely, naive sincerity that it was difficult to turn her down.

Which all went a very long way to explaining why Abigail Wilder was currently settled in her aunt's sitting room deflecting attempts at gossip, rather than practising magic with her father as she would have preferred.

Dora picked her tea back up – and Abigail realised that her mother didn't intend to respond to Lady Mulgrew's comment. Abigail sipped at her own tea, contemplating a reply. She had found Dora's tea-sipping strategy to be terribly helpful herself – for Abigail often felt tempted to say very *honest* things aloud just to see how people might react. The tea, she found, stifled that impulse somewhat.

What Abigail thought was: *You will spread the slightest bit of gossip all over London regardless of the consequences, and my entire family knows it.*

But Abigail swallowed down the words along with her tea.

What she said aloud was: "Magicians can scry upon people and conversations from a distance. Naturally, everyone here can be trusted . . . but I don't believe that Aunt Vanessa has any magical protections cast upon her sitting room."

Abigail worked to keep her vowels crisp and rounded – but she knew from the way the other women shifted in their seats that something was still subtly *wrong* with her diction.

"I have no such protections, of course," Aunt Vanessa said with a smile. "I have never felt the need to hide my social gatherings from strange magicians." Vanessa reached up to tug self-consciously at one of her blonde curls, however, and Abigail suspected that her aunt found the topic of conversation a bit discomfiting. Aunt Vanessa was a very proper woman, and she disliked the idea of prying into other people's business. Lady Mulgrew was the only tea lady to have shown genuine interest in Vanessa's charitable endeavours so far, though, and so Vanessa's attempts to deflect Lady Mulgrew's gossip were often half-hearted.

"You must know much of magic yourself, Miss Wilder?" Miss Esther Fernside piped up. At seventeen years old, she was the youngest lady present. Miss Fernside was a recent addition to the tea ladies. She had only joined them for last month's tea – and even then, Abigail couldn't remember her having said a word. She was a young, mousy woman of quiet demeanour and large, dark eyes; her curly brown hair had already mostly escaped its neat bun after only an hour of tea, and her smile was dim and hesitant.

"It would be strange if I didn't know *anything* about magic, wouldn't it?" Abigail replied carefully. The last thing Abigail needed was for Miss Fernside to realise that she could do magic – the resulting conversation would probably derail the entire tea.

"Oh yes, I suppose that would be strange," Miss Fernside admitted sheepishly. She looked so embarrassed by her own question now that Abigail felt a moment of pity.

"I've read many of my father's books," Abigail elaborated. "We talk about magic an awful lot. There are two kinds, you know – mortal magic and faerie magic. Almost all magic done in England is mortal magic, but faeries work the strangest spells by far."

This distinction was one of the very first things any magician learned – but it tended to impress people who knew nothing about the subject. Miss Fernside brightened at the discussion, sitting up in her chair once more.

"I knew that!" Miss Fernside assured Abigail. "My mother used to read me faerie tales. She said that faeries are wild and dangerous and wonderful. She said they can do just about *anything* if you pay them the right price."

Abigail shivered with sudden unease. Miss Fernside had no way of knowing that Abigail herself had been stolen away by a faerie – it wasn't precisely common knowledge. But the reminder did little to improve Abigail's already lacklustre enthusiasm for tea.

"Faeries *are* dangerous," Dora said softly. "And . . . yes, wild and wonderful. Which is why you should hope never to catch their attention."

Dora, too, had been stolen away to faerie. Abigail could still remember the day they'd met, in the awful halls of Hollowvale's Charity House. At the time, Abigail had been convinced that they would never leave again. But Dora had assured her that they would escape . . . and then, of all things, Dora had killed their cruel faerie captor.

No one in the sitting room – Aunt Vanessa included – would ever have imagined that mild-mannered Dora was capable of murdering a faerie. But Abigail *did* know . . . and in fact, it was one of the things she loved most about her mother. None of the other women here, Abigail thought, would have dared to do what was necessary to save her from Charity House.

"Faeries are *terribly* dangerous," Lady Mulgrew interjected, in an attempt to regain control of the conversation. "Why, I've heard other ladies and gentlemen of our acquaintance speculate that the recent deaths in London are to do with a faerie. I assured them that the Lord Sorcier was surely looking into the matter... but of course, no one here could possibly confirm such a thing." Lady Mulgrew smiled specifically at Dora, with only a hint of annoyance.

"What recent deaths would those be?" Abigail asked worriedly. She fixed her gaze upon Lady Mulgrew, discarding her other thoughts.

Lady Mulgrew raised her eyebrows. "Why, I assumed that you would know, Miss Wilder," she said. "Such awful business. We have lost several fine ladies in the last few weeks. They pass overnight, in their sleep – with the western window open."

This last statement should have meant something to Abigail, perhaps. But she didn't dare admit that it had gone entirely over her head. Abigail glanced at her mother – but Dora's expression was, as always, blank and serene.

"Is it possible that the Lord Sorcier is *not* investigating these tragedies?" Lady Mulgrew asked Dora archly.

Dora looked down at her empty teacup with vague surprise. "Oh," she said. "I have finished my tea."

And then – with absolutely no preamble – Dora stood and smoothed her gown. Abigail hurried to follow suit, just as her mother turned to leave the room.

"We have an appointment," Abigail lied. It was barely an excuse – but it was something, at least.

Aunt Vanessa smiled ruefully at Abigail. She knew, more than anyone, how different Dora's social perceptions were. "It was lovely having you both here," she assured Abigail. "I appreciate that you came."

The words held more meaning than most of the tea ladies likely appreciated. Aunt Vanessa had almost surely noticed Abigail's discomfort today.

Abigail curtsied awkwardly, and left to join her mother.

Chapter One

Abigail hurried after Dora, hiking up her skirts over her half-boots. Aunt Vanessa's servants winced and looked away as she sprinted through Crescent Hill's entryway, no doubt scandalised by the sight of Abigail's calves.

"Mum!" Abigail gasped breathlessly. "We have to wait for Hugh!"

Dora paused in the doorway. She turned back towards Abigail with a look of mild recollection. "Oh yes, Hugh," Dora murmured. "I begin to fear that I am very terrible at this mothering business. I am sure that none of the other ladies would forget their own son."

Abigail smiled ruefully. "You can't see him, Mum," she said. "I know you try to remember when he's with us, but it makes sense you'd forget sometimes. Anyway, it's all right. I bet he's down in the kitchens again. I'll go fetch him if you'll wait in the carriage."

Dora smiled distantly back at Abigail. Most mothers probably smiled more broadly at their children – but Abigail wouldn't have traded her awkward mother for all of the brilliant smiles in the world. "Thank you, Abigail," Dora said softly. "I'll wait for you both."

Abigail turned for the green baize door which led down to the kitchens. Servants darted out of her way as she descended, faintly alarmed ... but it couldn't be helped. Most people didn't notice Hugh Wilder, which meant that he could wander rather anywhere he pleased. Abigail had no such advantage – though she technically knew of spells to make herself seem less interesting to look at, she was not very good at actually casting them.

Abigail came out into the kitchens, where Mrs Montgomery currently worked to plate more sandwiches. Aunt Vanessa's cook was a short, brown-haired woman with broad shoulders and a military sort of bearing. Mrs Montgomery did not particularly enjoy the idea of ladies entering her kitchen uninvited – but she had always forced a certain politeness towards Abigail regardless, during the few times that she had visited.

"Good afternoon, Mrs Montgomery," Abigail said carefully, as she slipped through the doorway. "Sorry to trouble you again."

Mrs Montgomery glanced sharply towards Abigail, but she kept her tone even. "You're no trouble, Miss Wilder," the cook assured Abigail.

Abigail snorted. "Many people would disagree with you, Mrs Montgomery," she said. "But I appreciate the sentiment. Mum and I are just headed off, and I was hoping we could take with us one of your lovely ..."

"Apple tarts," a young boy's voice cut in very quickly.

" ...your lovely apple tarts," Abigail finished obediently.

Abigail glanced towards the corner of the room, whence the voice had originated. Her younger brother Hugh stood there, staring longingly at a plate of apple tarts which had been set aside on the counter.

Hugh was dressed for the occasion today, though Abigail was probably the only person who would ever see him. He wore a neatly tailored blue waistcoat and trousers, and freshly polished shoes. A black silk kerchief hid Hugh's missing eye; Abigail often told him that the kerchief made him look like a pirate. Hugh looked in most respects like a well-mannered eight-year-old boy … but the truth was that he had been eight years old for ages and ages now, ever since the day that he had died.

"Of course, Miss Wilder," Mrs Montgomery said. "Take as many tarts as you like. And please give your mother my best."

"Those tarts look so good," Hugh sighed. "You could take two an' give one to Mum."

Abigail dropped into a clumsy curtsy. "Thank you kindly, Mrs Montgomery," she said. She gathered up two of the apple tarts in her handkerchief. Abigail nearly tried to stow the handkerchief in her pocket – but since she was dressed as a lady today, she didn't *have* any pockets. As such, she had to hold the handkerchief awkwardly to her chest as she turned to flee the kitchens.

Hugh followed Abigail back up the servants' stairs. "I haven't seen those sandwiches before," Hugh said. "Are they delicious?"

Abigail hid a small smile. "I think they're cucumber sandwiches," she said. "Mum likes 'em, but I think they're squidgy." Talking to Hugh always lured out Abigail's normal, lower-class accent. Being dead, Hugh had never needed to polish his elocution.

"Other Mum lets us eat all kinds of things," Hugh murmured. "But faerie food doesn't taste the same. Wish I could have *one* real apple tart – just so I know what it's like."

The other half of Lady Theodora Wilder's soul currently lived in faerie with all of the children who *hadn't* made it back from Hollowvale alive. Hugh and Abigail called the other half of Dora's soul Other Mum whenever they were in England – but most people who knew of her at all called her Lady Hollowvale.

Abigail heaved a sigh. "I'm sorry, Hugh," she said. "I haven't found a way to let you eat food yet. But I'll keep lookin', I promise."

Hugh quickened his steps – it was a bit eerie having him around, since his shoes made no noise upon the stairs. "You already figured out how to get me out of Hollowvale," Hugh said. "It's more'n you should've done. I'll just watch you eat the tarts, if you don't mind. You can tell me how they are."

Abigail walked through the green baize door once again, turning to hold it open for Hugh. Her younger brother giggled as he walked past her. "I can walk through doors, you know," he said. "Walls too."

Abigail rolled her eyes. "It's only polite to hold the door," she said. "An' I'm well aware you can go wherever you please. You got bored with the tea ladies quick enough. Five minutes in, and you were already gone."

"They were just tellin' the same old stories an' talkin' about people they don't like again," Hugh said with a yawn. "Mrs Montgomery's more interestin'. I like watchin' her cook. An' *she* was talkin' about dead girls an' faeries with Mr Notley."

Abigail had been holding the front door for Hugh . . . but at this observation, she paused. "Dead girls an' faeries?" she repeated slowly.

Hugh straightened his tiny neck cloth, striding out the door in a comically dignified manner. "Three well-bred young ladies have died this Season, in the very prime of their lives!" he proclaimed, mimicking a more adult tone of voice as he spoke. "Rumours say they were found in their bedrooms the next morning with their western windows open!"

Abigail knit her brow, following after him. "Why *does* everyone keep talkin' about western windows?" she asked.

Hugh glanced back towards Abigail, waiting at the foot of the carriage. "You don't know?" he asked. "Oh . . . I guess that makes sense. You spend less time with Other Mum than the rest of us." He locked his wrists behind his back. "Sluagh use the western window. They're, you know . . . the *creepy* faeries. They look like ravens most times. If you leave your western window open at night, they might fly through an' kill you in your sleep."

Abigail shivered uncomfortably. Hugh had an understandably cavalier way of discussing death, given his current state – but her own heart still beat within her chest, and she found the subject far less comfortable. Worse by far was the suggestion that cruel faeries had once again decided to meddle in London. The idea was very personally horrifying; it came with a surge of fury, fear and righteous indignation.

Abigail swallowed these emotions with great effort. She knew that Hugh, of all people, did not deserve for her to vent her anger upon him. "Have you ever met a sluagh, Hugh?" she asked carefully. "I don't remember any of 'em comin' to visit Hollowvale . . . but you're more often there than I am."

Hugh shook his head. "Other Mum won't let the sluagh into Hollowvale," he said. "She doesn't like to talk about it much."

Aunt Vanessa's carriage driver hopped from his seat to pull down the steps and open the carriage door for Abigail. It was an odd feeling, being waited upon so insistently. Abigail could still remember sleeping three to a bed in the Cleveland Street Workhouse, wearing the same dirty clothes every day.

"Thank you," Abigail mumbled at the carriage driver. Hugh clambered up the steps ahead of her, and she followed after him, settling into the carriage with her mother.

Hugh had tucked himself in next to Dora, smiling broadly. "– an' Abigail's bringin' you an apple tart!" he was saying. "You have to eat it for me, Mum; them's the rules!"

Hugh had a habit of talking to the living as though they could hear him. Abigail had always found it a bit painful to watch, but Hugh assured her that it made him feel better about the *being dead* situation. Alas, Dora could not hear Hugh any better than most – though her small talent at scrying meant that she could see his reflection in mirrors if she exercised herself.

"You've found Hugh, then?" Dora asked Abigail pleasantly.

Abigail glanced towards Hugh, still leaning against Dora's side. "I did," she said. "He was in the kitchens, like I guessed.

He's right next to you, tellin' you how you've got to eat the tart I'm about to give you."

Dora turned a distant smile upon the empty spot next to her. "Oh, my apologies, Hugh," she said. "I didn't see you there. You are *very* good at hiding. Thank you for thinking of me. I do love tarts."

Hugh beamed at Dora's response. "I watched Mrs Montgomery make 'em," he said. "If Abby ever finds a way to let me bake, I'll make some for you myself!"

Abigail passed one of the apple tarts to Dora, who took it obligingly. "Hugh says he'd like to bake some tarts," Abigail repeated dutifully.

Hugh scowled at Abigail as Dora nibbled fondly at the tart. "That's not *exactly* what I said!" he told her, with a pout. "I said—"

Abigail repeated his words again – more precisely this time – and the peeved expression on Hugh's face melted away. It was hard to keep up with Hugh's breathless chatter sometimes, and he was normally understanding when Abigail had to shorten his sentences. But while Dora could not see Hugh, she had still done everything in her power to make him feel loved and included, and the effort had touched him deeply. As a consequence of this, Hugh craved every last scrap of connection he could manage with their mother.

"This *is* delicious," Dora said gravely, addressing Hugh's spot. Somehow, she made the conversation seem utterly natural. "I think it must be spiced with cinnamon."

"I thought so!" Hugh said eagerly. "I kept track of all the ingredients—"

"I don't want to interrupt," Abigail said, in between bites of her own tart, "but Hugh heard somethin' in the kitchens, an' I wanted to ask you about it, Mum."

Hugh frowned. "You mean the bit about the dead girls an' the sluagh?" he asked Abigail.

Abigail nodded. "Can you repeat what you heard, Hugh?" she asked. "I'll tell it all exactly, I promise."

Over the next few minutes, Hugh and Abigail related the conversation he'd overheard. Dora gave no indication of her feelings on the matter either way, of course.

"I'm not Lady Mulgrew," Abigail said finally. "If Dad is lookin' into the sluagh, he ought to have told me. He *knows* how I feel about faeries hurtin' people. He said he'd teach me magic so I could help him with things just like this – but I can't help him if he never *tells* me anything!"

Dora remained silent for a long moment. It was sometimes hard for Abigail to remember that her mother was probably thinking hard and not just ignoring her – but long experience had taught her to be patient.

Finally, Dora said, "Do you know . . . much as I am terrible at reading people, I think I must be the closest thing to an expert at reading Elias. I suspect that he is worried about endangering you, Abigail. I know that does not much improve matters, but it is a place from which to begin."

Abigail scowled darkly. "How does that make any sense?" she demanded. "Does he really think he's protectin' me by keepin' secrets?"

Dora sighed. "I do not know how it makes sense," she admitted. "But if I ask him to explain, then I am sure that he will do so. I promise I will speak to him on the matter."

The carriage slowed to a stop shortly thereafter. The carriage driver opened the door, and the three of them climbed out.

At any given time, England's court magician was afforded a generous living, which included a set of apartments off Hyde Park. England's current court magician, of course, was deeply contrary in temperament, which had led at times to a diminishment of his living standards when the Prince Regent became irritated with him. Currently, Lord Elias Wilder had been moved into apartments which were smaller and less opulent than a man of his stature and achievements ought to deserve – a circumstance which bothered him and his family not one whit. Elias had spent his young life in workhouses and his later life at war across the English Channel; any bed, he had often related, was better than cold mud.

As Elias was not overly fond of titles, they had all taken to referring to the tall, narrow building as "the House." The previous House had smelled incessantly of flowers due to its place above a perfumery. The new House did not smell quite so lovely, given its place above a butcher's shop – but the butcher was exceedingly polite, and he always saved them excellent cuts of meat for their supper.

The House came with several servants, which had always seemed a bit of a waste given how little time Elias truly spent there. Eventually, however, Abigail's interest in magic had required her to take a room in the House, rather than at the private orphanage which their family still sponsored. At this point, Dora had decided to hire a governess. And since a governess for just one child had seemed a terrible sort of waste, *further* children had been moved into the House, until it was difficult to tell the place from yet another orphanage.

The servants had not wanted for work ever since.

As they climbed the stairs to the main floor, just above the butcher, Abigail became aware that there was an odd feeling to the House today. Several of the children had gathered in the dining room. This was not uncommon in and of itself – but they were all very quiet and serious, which *was* uncommon. The governess, Miss Langley, had settled herself at the end of the table – but as the three of them entered, she rose from her seat, hurrying over towards Dora.

"Thank goodness you're here!" Miss Langley breathed. "I'm certain there's been a disaster!"

Miss Langley was half a head taller than Dora and several years her senior. Her brown hair had just started fading in places to grey, and wrinkles had started coming in at the corners of her eyes. She was normally quite calm and composed – but even her stoic demeanour was not enough to hide the tension which currently poured off of her in waves.

Dora frowned dimly. It was a good thing, Abigail thought, that her mother was rather incapable of panic. "Do explain, Miss Langley," she said. "What has happened, and how can I help?"

Miss Langley glanced back towards the children, all of whom were now pretending very fiercely and very unconvincingly that they were not listening to the conversation. She lowered her voice as far as she dared. "His Lordship went up to the third floor more than an hour ago. He said that I should keep all the children down here, and that none of us should disturb him on *any* account. I did as he asked, and . . . well, there was an *awful* noise, like nothing I've ever heard before. It's all gone silent now, and I've started to fear the worst."

"I see," Dora said. "I shall go and check on him, of course. Thank you for keeping the children calm, Miss Langley."

Privately, Abigail thought that it was the *children* keeping Miss Langley calm, and not the other way around. Most of them were well used to dealing with emergencies, given the rampant sickness in the workhouses. Even as Abigail watched, fourteen-year-old Roger limped over to pull a chair out for Miss Langley, who collapsed into it gratefully.

Dora headed for the stairs. Abigail glanced towards Hugh. "We're goin' up, of course," Abigail muttered at him. "What do you want to wager this has somethin' to do with Dad's work?"

"I'd wager a tart," Hugh said, "but I'd only have to give it to you to eat for me anyway." He shot her a half-grin. "I'll race you there."

"That might not be safe—" Abigail began.

But Hugh had already vanished up the stairs after Dora.

Abigail hiked up her skirts once more and scurried to follow him. It was a sign of Miss Langley's current distress that

Abigail's old governess did not think to rebuke her for it. By the time Abigail reached the door to the third floor, Dora had already opened it and walked through.

The third floor of the House was supposed to have been a ballroom – but it had never once been used for that purpose since coming into the Lord Sorcier's possession. In fact, Elias had turned it into a place for his work. As such, Abigail was rather used to seeing the place in disarray ... but today, it seemed, Elias had far outdone himself.

The giant silver chandelier which normally overlooked the old ballroom had crashed to the floor, splintering the wooden floorboards beneath it. Bookshelves had toppled from the walls, spilling their precious contents. Scorch marks and strange gouges marked the walls.

Strewn everywhere across the room were several large black feathers.

Abigail spotted her mother near the open western window – and for an instant, her heart lurched in her chest. Elias was crumpled just beneath the window, leaning heavily against the wall. His white-blond hair was oddly windswept, and his eyes were currently closed. His brown waistcoat was partially undone, and his cravat was barely knotted – though, to be absolutely fair, this was the normal state of affairs when he was not required at some official function. His face was so pale, and his form so still, that Abigail nearly mistook him for dead.

But even as Abigail watched, Elias murmured something to Dora, and her chest unclenched again.

"Abby!" Hugh called. "Come look at this!"

Hugh was standing in the centre of the room, staring down at a set of circular chalk marks on the floor. Abigail gave her father one last glance before she walked over to join Hugh, looking over the markings. The shape and the writing were familiar to her – though far more complex than anything she had ever attempted for herself.

"A summonin' circle," Abigail murmured. "A real powerful one. What's he been summonin', then?" The black feathers were particularly thick on the ground just next to the circle, and a terrible suspicion started to grow within her mind.

Abigail whirled to stalk towards her father. Dora had helped him up from the floor – Elias leaned heavily upon her, looking ragged and weary. There was a strange dignity to him all the same, which he never quite lost. At the moment, that dignity infuriated Abigail for reasons that she could not quite explain.

"You summoned a sluagh!" Abigail accused him. "All on your own, as well! I know you're used to doin' dangerous things, but I still could've helped you if you'd asked!"

Elias drew himself up. His golden, ember-like eyes focused upon Abigail – but when he spoke, it was to Dora. "You told Abigail about the sluagh, then?" he asked.

Dora blinked at him. "I did not," she said. "But I think that perhaps *you* should have done."

Abigail narrowed her eyes. "I'd have liked to hear it from you instead of from Hugh, who heard it from *Mrs Montgomery*," she said spitefully.

Elias took a deep, steadying breath. Slowly, he straightened his posture. "Hugh is here, then?" he asked. "I thought he'd gone back to Hollowvale for a time."

Abigail answered this question by tugging at a chain around her neck. This gesture produced the silver, heart-shaped locket which anchored Hugh to the mortal world and allowed him to wander freely away from Hollowvale. It had taken both Abigail and her Other Mum several months of work to create the locket, which contained a lock of Hugh's real hair.

Elias rubbed his face. The sight of the locket seemed to distress him. "You shall both have to return to Hollowvale," he told Abigail. "You *and* Hugh. London isn't safe for you right now, and I'm no longer certain that I can protect you."

Abigail let out a loud, frustrated noise. "I don't need

protection!" she said. "I've had years an' years of magic lessons now so I can protect *myself*."

Elias closed his eyes, and Abigail knew that he was working to contain his famous temper. "You are still an amateur magician, Abigail," he said. "I have many years of wartime experience, and even *I* have barely managed to handle the matter. If you are here, then I will continue to worry for your safety. Neither of us can afford that."

Abigail scoffed and crossed her arms. "Look at all this mess," she said. "You really think I'm goin' back to Hollowvale to hide behind Other Mum's skirts with you in this state? I'm *surely* not leavin' until you explain what I'm lookin' at."

Elias groaned. He opened his eyes to look at Dora appealingly – but Dora had an expression of reasonable expectation upon her own features, such that he soon realised how outnumbered he was. He raked his fingers back through his hair.

"I did not summon a sluagh," Elias said stiffly. "I summoned the *first* among sluagh. I called Lord Longshadow, and he answered. I had hoped that we might have a reasonable conversation . . . but that did not occur."

Abigail frowned darkly at the black feathers which still littered the room. "Clearly," she mumbled. She didn't know very much at all about Lord Longshadow, she realised – most of her knowledge of faeries came from either her father or else her Other Mum, and neither one had ever mentioned the faerie before. That, Abigail thought, was somewhat strange.

"I asked Lord Longshadow if one of his sluagh had murdered those girls," Elias continued, "but he would not tell me so, no matter how I pressed him. Faeries, you recall, cannot lie. Instead, he told me that he did not recognise my authority in any way. He said that he would do as he pleased within London, and that the only way I would ever stop him was by force." Elias's expression grew very dark at this, and the scattered feathers suddenly took on new meaning. "I took him up on his invitation. It was a terrible conflict . . . but I believe that I came out the better of the two of us."

Dora frowned. "Have you killed Lord Longshadow, then?" she asked.

Elias shook his head. "I have not," he said. "He is far darker and more powerful than even Lord Hollowvale was. If I had known Lord Longshadow's true name, I could have killed or commanded him – but in the absence of his name, I have used his own feathers against him to bind him with my magic." So saying, Elias raised one hand – and Abigail saw that he had clenched his fingers around three particularly large black feathers. They had an oily, iridescent shimmer to them which shifted in the light of the open western window. "I have laid three bans upon him. Until the feathers are destroyed, he shall not harm anyone with his magic – nor shall he steal away any unwilling beings, nor speak to his sluagh."

"Those are very powerful bans," Dora observed carefully. "You have bound your own magic up within them, I expect." Dora had no magic of her own, other than her tendency towards scrying – but she had learned quite a lot about magic since marrying the Lord Sorcier.

Elias's grimace suggested that Dora had assessed the situation correctly. "I have leverage over the faerie now," he said, by way of reply. "He will eventually realise how little fun it is to be so bound. I am sure that he will come back and negotiate for the return of his feathers. Life shall be very boring for him in the meantime."

Abigail straightened. "If you're tryin' to convince me to run away to Hollowvale, then you're doin' a poor job," she said. "I'm hardly leavin' you to face the lord of the sluagh while you're all alone an' powerless, even if he *is* under all those bans. You can't have more'n a thimbleful of your magic left after all of that."

Elias narrowed his eyes. "This is not up for discussion," he said. "It is my job and my responsibility to protect England from black magic – not yours. I rarely ask anything of you at all, Abigail, but I am asking you now to take Hugh back to Hollowvale and to remain there with him until I can resolve this."

Abigail opened her mouth to protest – but Dora raised her eyebrows, just behind Elias's shoulder, and shook her head minutely.

Slowly, Abigail closed her mouth again.

"Fine," she said. "I'll take Hugh back to Hollowvale."

Elias relaxed his shoulders. He wavered visibly on his feet again, before Dora caught him by the shoulders. "Thank you, Abigail," he said. His voice was tired and relieved. "I'll send word as soon as this is sorted. I have hope that it won't be long."

Abigail clenched her jaw – but she forced a nod. "Mum," she said, "can we talk outside for a moment?"

Dora nodded. "Would you find your father a chair first?" she asked. "I think it's best if he rests for a bit longer."

Abigail turned to head across the room, towards a desk and chair at the far wall. Hugh followed at her heels, scowling.

"I don't *want* to go back to Hollowvale," Hugh said. "I know you don't either, Abby. Why'd you say yes?"

"We're not *actually* goin' back to Hollowvale," Abigail muttered beneath her breath. "There's just no use arguin' with Dad when he's like this."

Hugh blinked. "So you lied?" he asked.

Abigail smiled humourlessly. "Dad's the one who started keepin' secrets," she said. "I'm just followin' his lead."

There were notes still scattered across the desk. Abigail glanced them over quickly, picking out her father's slightly messy handwriting. Her eyes caught upon the name *Miss Lucy Kendall*, and she blinked in surprise, filing it away for later.

The desk chair was a bit too large and bulky for Abigail to pick it up herself. There was a stool next to one of the toppled bookcases, however, and she picked this up to bring it back towards the window. Dora helped Elias to sit down, and she nodded at Abigail.

"Let's speak before you leave, then," Dora said. "I'll return shortly, Elias."

They headed back onto the stairs just outside the ballroom. Once the door had closed behind them, Dora turned towards Abigail.

"You want me to go to Hollowvale too?" Abigail asked her mother sourly.

Dora sighed. "I promised to speak to your father," she said, "and I will do that. I believe that I can puzzle through whatever is making him act this way. But, in the meantime, it is not the worst idea for you to visit Hollowvale. It has occurred to me that Lady Hollowvale probably knows much more about Lord Longshadow than any of us would know. Perhaps you could ask her if she has any useful information while you are there."

Abigail pursed her lips. "We could just as easily summon her," she said. "Other Mum would come, if it was one of us callin' her."

"Lady Hollowvale only leaves her realm under the gravest circumstances," Dora said. "She is very protective of the other children there. The matter does not yet seem that urgent, I think." She smiled dimly at Abigail. "I will bring your father around, I promise. I think you would be a great help to him, if he would only admit it. You shall only be in Hollowvale for a little bit."

Abigail heaved a put-upon sigh. It felt worse, she thought, to lie to her mother. Dora was always so painfully sincere, and Abigail knew that it was *easy* to lie to her because she so poorly understood people.

But when Abigail spoke, it was indeed a lie which spilled from her lips.

"I'd best get goin' to Hollowvale then," she said.

Chapter Two

Abigail had not particularly liked Miss Lucy Kendall. It was a strange circumstance, therefore, to be investigating the other girl's death.

"Should I feel bad that Lucy's dead?" Abigail asked Hugh, as they stepped out of a hired hackney. "Am I allowed to be relieved she won't be at the next stupid party instead?"

Hugh considered this as he walked behind her. "Wasn't Lucy the one who made fun of your pockmarks an' called you a leper?" he asked.

"That was her," Abigail said grimly. "As if I'd ever forget."

Miss Lucy Kendall was – *had* been – a true beauty, and she had rarely let anyone forget it, even for a moment. Lucy's mother, Lady Pinckney, was a woman of sharp tongue and great social standing, and Lucy had done everything in her power to emulate her. Lucy had technically come out into society several years ago, while she was still quite young – but everyone truly expected her to start selecting a husband this Season, now that she had reached the age of majority.

Abigail hadn't really expected a fanfare when she came out into society herself – after all, she was not truly related to either her mother or her father, and very few of the *bon ton* wanted a workhouse brat at their functions, no matter how well Abigail dressed or spoke. But Aunt Vanessa had decided that Abigail ought to enjoy at least one Season of parties and gowns, and it was always so difficult to say no to Aunt Vanessa.

For some reason, Aunt Vanessa's enthusiasm had convinced Abigail that the idea might *not* be an unmitigated disaster. But of course, it had been. Much as Abigail liked to consider herself thick-skinned, Lucy Kendall had made her run home crying at least once – and the older adults at those parties had at times been even worse.

Only the possibility that Elias might be blamed had prevented Abigail from cursing the awful girl with warts. It had been a terribly close thing, however.

Now here Abigail was, standing in front of Lord Pinckney's townhouse with a black mourning ribbon on her bonnet, intent on learning more about his daughter's murder.

"I think you're allowed to be relieved," Hugh said solemnly. "If Lucy wanted you to miss her, she could've treated you more nicely." He paused. "An' it's not like *you* killed her."

Abigail sighed. "No one would've missed *me* if I'd died in the workhouses," she said. "Well – Mum an' Dad would've missed me, even then. I want to miss anyone who dies, I guess, just on principle. But it's harder'n I thought it would be."

"I think Lucy's got plenty of people to miss her," Hugh said. "But none of *those* people can figure out why the sluagh killed her an' stop 'em from doin' it again – so you can do that instead of missin' her."

Abigail grimaced. "You'll have to talk to Lucy for me if her ghost is hangin' around," she warned Hugh. "I can only see *you* because I've got your locket."

Hugh twisted up his mouth as though he'd eaten a lemon. "If I have to," he said. "It's better'n goin' back to Hollowvale, I guess."

A flutter of black at the edge of Abigail's vision distracted her, drawing her eyes. She turned and saw two large ravens settled upon the overhang of an opposite townhouse. Both of the birds were watching her far too intently. Abigail narrowed her eyes at them.

"If you're normal birds," she called over to them, "you'd best get gone! An' if you're *not* normal birds . . . well, same thing!"

The two ravens continued staring at her, unblinking.

"You think they're sluagh?" Hugh asked Abigail worriedly.

"I think it'd be an awful coincidence if they *weren't* sluagh," Abigail replied darkly. "Either they're watchin' the scene of their crime, or else . . ." She trailed off as a nasty thought occurred to her.

"Or else?" Hugh prompted carefully.

"Or else they're followin' *me*," Abigail said. "Lord Longshadow can't talk to his sluagh, but they might still have figured out it was Dad who bound him. Maybe they think I'll lead 'em to Lord Longshadow's feathers."

Hugh shifted on his feet. "You think you could handle a pair of sluagh?" he asked Abigail warily.

Abigail straightened her back. "Let's find out," she said.

Technically speaking, Abigail had learned mortal magic from her father and faerie magic from her Other Mum. Most normal people shouldn't have been able to use faerie magic at all – but ever since Abigail had returned from Hollowvale the first time, she'd exhibited a talent for both magics at once.

Of the two, mortal magic *should* have been more difficult; it required strange props, careful study and sometimes very specific incantations. But Abigail had always found faerie magic to be far more trying. *Faerie* magic, Other Mum had told her, required only that you utterly believe that what you were trying to accomplish would happen. Faeries, she'd said, were experts at believing in ridiculous things.

Abigail was *not* very good at believing in ridiculous things. For much of her early life, she'd been incapable of changing the world around her, no matter how hard she tried. When Abigail's first mother had grown ill, she'd tried very hard to nurse her back to health – but obviously, that had not worked very well, and her mother had died instead. At the Cleveland Street Workhouse, the workhouse master had controlled every aspect of Abigail's life, from the moment she woke and ate her miserly breakfast to the moment she finished picking oakum and staggered her way to bed.

The first time Abigail had truly managed to change anything had been that moment in Hollowvale when she'd lied to her faerie captor and helped to hide Dora from him. She hadn't expected *that* to change much of anything either . . . but thankfully, it had.

It now seemed insulting to Abigail that she was so terrible at believing in things. And so she often ended up *trying* to use faerie magic, even when it wasn't terribly advisable.

Abigail dug down into her soul for the cold seed of power which Hollowvale had planted within her. Hollowvale's power numbed her fingers and tickled at her insides, searching eagerly for an outlet. Abigail concentrated hard, doing her best to *give* it that outlet.

She stared down the two ravens and tried to imagine them being blown away by a stiff wind. That was plausible, she thought, and therefore easier to believe.

Hollowvale's power lurched within her, clumsy and uncertain. The magic tried to shape itself to Abigail's imagination – but her belief in that stiff wind was nearly as squidgy as the cucumber sandwiches from that morning. Abigail scowled and swayed on her feet, shoving the faerie magic hastily back down inside herself.

Silence settled in upon the street. One of the two ravens cocked its head at her curiously. For a second, Abigail thought she could feel a tiny breeze . . . but perhaps that was just nature's way of trying to make her feel better.

"Fine," Abigail snapped frustratedly. "We'll do it the other way."

Abigail still wore her very proper pocketless muslin – but she had brought with her the largest reticule she could find, full of her most important magician's tools. From this reticule, she extracted a small bundle of straw and a ball of twine. She tied off bits of straw with the string until she'd formed a clumsy human figure.

Hugh watched with interest. "Is that supposed to be a doll?" he asked. "Looks a bit funny."

"Hush, you," Abigail muttered. "It'll do in a pinch." So saying, she spat once upon the straw doll and set it down on the ground in front of her feet. Abigail paused as she looked at it. "Curses," she said. "I have to name him now. Anything you want to walk around on its own really *ought* to have a name."

Hugh grinned. "You could call him Mr Hayes," he said.

Abigail groaned softly at the pun. But since her mind had yet to offer up a better name, she shook her head in resignation. "Doll!" she declared. "I name you Mr Hayes! Go forth an' scare the birds, as you were made to do!"

This time, Abigail called the magic from all around her instead of from inside herself. It beaded invisibly upon her skin like dew collecting on grass, trickling into her consciousness and shaping itself into a form that centuries of English farmers found so very familiar. Finally, as she became convinced that she had collected enough power, she forced the image of the scarecrow upon the doll just in front of her.

At first, Abigail worried that even this bit of mortal magic had failed. But a second later, the little straw doll wiggled itself onto its feet. It did not have a head, so much as a short stub of straw – but she still had the impression that it was looking up at her.

Mr Hayes lifted one clumsy arm of straw and saluted her.

The tiny doll turned around and marched across the street towards the curious ravens on the other side.

Mr Hayes was far from the most terrifying creature in the

world – but that didn't much matter. Many thousands of people *believed* that scarecrows did indeed scare crows – and ravens were close enough as made no difference. As the doll marched closer and closer to the foot of the building where the birds perched, they began to shuffle in alarm.

Mr Hayes paused beneath the awning with the birds, staring up at them with his head made of hay. Then – very seriously – he began to dance from foot to foot in what was surely meant to be a threatening manner.

The ravens croaked with terror. One of them took off instantly, bolting into the air. The other one inched backwards, cowering from the sight of the doll.

"Good job, Mr Hayes!" Hugh called out – though it was unlikely that the doll could hear him. "Go get those sluagh!"

The doll continued its strange dance; now, it waved its arms like fronds. The raven that still lingered croaked pitifully, and fled.

Mr Hayes watched the two ravens go with mute satisfaction. Eventually, he marched back towards Abigail and then settled in front of her, as though awaiting orders.

"Stay out here an' guard against more birds," Abigail ordered him. "They might try to come back."

Mr Hayes saluted once more – and Abigail turned back towards Lord Pinckney's townhouse.

Slowly, she headed up the steps in front of the building, pausing in front of its bright red door. Abigail eyed the wrought-iron door knocker there with distaste – for though her time in Hollowvale had granted her some measure of faerie magic, she had also found that iron now burned her in the same way that it burned faeries. She rapped her knuckles against the thick wooden door, avoiding the door knocker entirely.

A little while later, the butler opened the door. His clothing was sharp and neat, but Abigail was unsurprised to see dark circles under his eyes. "May I help you, miss?" he asked politely.

"Would you please let Lady Pinckney know that Miss Abigail Wilder has come to call?" Abigail asked. "I am here to offer my condolences, among other things." She fished out a calling card and passed it over. Abigail hadn't expected ever to require her own calling cards, but thankfully Aunt Vanessa had insisted on having them made for her when she'd turned eighteen. Sometimes, Abigail thought, her aunt was a bit more foresighted than she liked to admit.

The butler nodded and took the calling card. "I will inform Lady Pinckney of your visit," he said. "If you could please wait here?"

He framed this as a question – but of course, Abigail was not interested in waiting awkwardly on the doorstep. She nodded and followed him into the entryway, where she sat down on a stool to wait.

It took only five minutes before Hugh began to squirm. "How long d'you think we're goin' to wait?" he asked Abigail anxiously.

"Probably quite a while," Abigail mumbled quietly. "Lady Pinckney hates our whole family, I hear. Lucy got it from somewhere."

Hugh rolled his eyes. "She can't have even *met* our whole family," he said. "Mum an' Dad barely socialise at all."

"Yes," Abigail said ironically. "We all make very fine fodder for gossip that way."

Hugh groaned. "I'm tired of waitin'," he said. "I'm goin' to take a look around for ghosts."

Abigail bit her lip. Hugh's ability to wander *was* very useful, and she'd begun to worry that Lady Pinckney wouldn't allow her to investigate matters at all. "As you like," she said softly. "Just let me know if you find anything."

Hugh grinned. "If I find Lucy's ghost," he said, "you're goin' to get a *whole* earful, I promise." So saying, he waltzed for the far end of the entryway and disappeared deeper into the townhouse.

After about a half-hour more of waiting in the entryway,

Abigail knew for certain that she was unwelcome. But she was far too stubborn to leave – and eventually, the lady of the house must have become at least mildly curious, because the butler finally returned.

"The lady is just finishing her morning meditations," he advised Abigail, "but she has agreed to see you." There was a faint superiority to his voice now, and Abigail knew that Lady Pinckney had expressed to him her personal dislike of Abigail's family. Nevertheless, she rose to her feet and followed him into the drawing room.

Lady Pinckney was in every way an older version of her late daughter: her porcelain skin had only a few aged wrinkles, and her fine blonde hair was neatly swept atop her head. She wore a full black mourning gown and a shawl – and, just as with the butler, she had large black circles beneath her eyes, which she had not bothered to hide in any way.

Currently, the lady sat in a chair at the table, reading her Bible. She did not look up as Abigail entered the room, though there was at least a fresh pot of tea on the table along with two teacups. The only other available seat was a hard-backed wooden chair, which faced the wall and not the windows. A maid stood silently to one side, just behind the lady's table.

Abigail inclined her head. "Thank you for seeing me, Lady Pinckney," she said. "You have my condolences with regard to recent events." Abigail spoke very slowly, trying for a crisp, elevated accent.

Lady Pinckney did not set aside her Bible. Nor did she look directly at Abigail. "Thank you for your sentiments," she said. Her tone was flat and cold. "Will that be all, Miss Wilder?"

Abigail responded by taking the hard wooden seat which had been provided. "I won't take too much of your time," she said. "I was told that strange circumstances were involved. With your leave, I would like to search for any clues that might help stop this from happening again."

Lady Pinckney's lips curled with obvious distaste. "Was it not enough that the Lord Sorcier must tramp about my home casting spells?" she asked. "He has already come and gone, with or without my permission. Lord Pinckney said that it was a matter of the Crown, and that we had no standing to send him away." She narrowed her eyes at her Bible. "You are *not* the Lord Sorcier, and I will not allow you to play at court magician in my home. You may leave."

Abigail clenched her jaw. The harsh superiority in the lady's tone jangled at her nerves, tempting her to lash out. But Abigail had known that this conversation would not be easy – and so, rather than respond immediately, she reached for the teacup and took a long, lingering sip. It was a soothing lime-flower tea, and it calmed the raw edges of her emotions.

I am not here for my own well-being, Abigail reminded herself.

Faeries are hurting people again, and I was the one who decided to try and stop them, she thought next.

Lady Pinckney is never pleasant to me, she thought finally, *but she is grieving right now, and I must be the better person.*

Abigail set the teacup down.

"My father is often very brusque," she said. "I am sorry if he caused you further grief. But I am not here to play at court magician, Lady Pinckney. I want to help make sure this doesn't happen again. I swear that is my only intention."

"You despised Lucy," Lady Pinckney said simply. "I do not want you looking through her things."

Abigail clenched her fingers on the teacup. What she *wanted* to say was, *Lucy despised me first, and I never gave her reason to do so.*

But she took another swallow of tea instead.

"I will not pretend that Lucy and I were good friends," Abigail said, "but she did not deserve this." She summoned up her breath. "You may believe that we are very different, and that I cannot possibly understand what you are feeling. But I lost my first mother, Lady Pinckney – and while I love my current mother dearly, there is no such thing as a replacement. I will have an awful hollow spot in my chest where she once was until the day that I die. And I am compelled to do any little bit that I might do in order to prevent other people from knowing that feeling. I believe that you would do the same."

Lady Pinckney stared at her Bible. The cold, hard expression on her face fractured – and for a moment, Abigail caught sight of the unspeakable misery beneath. Tears threatened at the older woman's eyes, and she hid her face more fully behind her book.

"You are no magician," Lady Pinckney said in a hoarse tone. "What could you possibly find which the Lord Sorcier did not?"

Abigail bit her lip. Her father's warnings about magic echoed in her ears . . . but she did not grudge Lady Pinckney the question. Abigail knew very well that she had made a tall request.

I shall have to be known as a magician someday, after all, Abigail thought.

Abigail sipped once more at her tea, letting the lime flower rest upon her tongue. It made sense, of course, that Lady Pinckney would drink lime-flower tea at a time like this; the flavour was known to soothe one's nerves.

Slowly, Abigail collected up the magic around her again, focusing on the sweet scent and taste of the lime flower. She rose from her chair and reached out to touch the teapot on the table, letting that magic trickle through her fingers like water. A soft golden glow lit the teapot from within, casting ripples of sunlight across the table.

"Have another cup of tea," Abigail told Lady Pinckney gravely. "It won't dispel your grief – but it will soften the edges for a while, and maybe let you rest."

Lady Pinckney let her Bible fall from her face. She stared at the teapot for a long moment. Slowly – with a sideways glance at Abigail – the lady reached out to place her hand hesitantly upon the pot.

Some of the tension drained from her body. She closed her eyes and sighed in weary relief.

Abigail's heart twinged at the sight. Though she held no love for Lady Pinckney or her daughter, she knew that she had lessened an awful pain for just a little bit. That, Abigail thought, was worthwhile – and it was not the sort of magic that her father ever would have thought to perform.

Lady Pinckney opened her eyes and very gingerly poured herself another cup of tea. The potion glimmered with soft, reassuring light. The glow lit up Lady Pinckney's features as she sipped at her cup, softening her harsh expression.

They sat in silence for another minute. This time, it was an oddly comfortable, contemplative silence.

"I will have Mr Swinton show you to Lucy's bedroom," Lady Pinckney said. She hesitated uncomfortably. "You … won't disturb anything?"

Abigail shook her head. "I may need to open the window," she said, "but I will do my best to leave everything exactly as I find it."

Lady Pinckney glanced behind her at the maid. "Please find Mr Swinton and bring him here," she said. "Make certain that he has his keys."

Chapter Three

Mr Swinton was surprised and suspicious as he showed Abigail into Lucy's bedroom – but he was far too upstanding to voice any of his possible concerns aloud.

The bedroom was neat and spacious; the servants had clearly been keeping it clean in spite of its owner's absence. The western window was firmly closed – but Mr Swinton went to open it for Abigail in order to let in more light.

Hugh was sitting on top of the bed, waiting for Abigail. He glanced at her as she entered.

"No ghost," Hugh said. "It's really strange, Abby. I feel as though Lucy *should* still be here, but she isn't. I don't know why."

Abigail gave the butler a sideways look. She suspected he would not be very understanding if she started talking to thin air. "Thank you for the help," she said politely. "I will let you know if I have any questions."

Mr Swinton frowned at that. Abigail knew that he was weighing up whether he ought to protest the clear dismissal . . . but he must have erred on the side of caution, for he nodded stiffly and stepped outside of the bedroom.

"What do you mean, Lucy *should* be here?" Abigail asked Hugh softly.

Hugh hopped off the bed, frowning. "I don't know," he admitted. "It feels like . . . like she left a lot of herself behind.

She was attached enough to stay, but I don't see her anywhere around."

Abigail shook her head. "I don't like that," she said warily. "Not many things can affect ghosts." Worry gnawed at her. "Maybe Dad was right. Maybe you *should* go back to Hollowvale for a bit, Hugh."

Hugh narrowed his eyes at her. "I am *not* goin' back to Hollowvale," he stated. "If you're stayin' in London, then I'm stayin' in London." Abigail hesitated at that, and Hugh added, "Don't be like Dad, Abby. I want to stay, just like you."

Abigail sighed. For just a second, she sympathised with her father. The idea of letting Hugh walk into danger with her was suddenly terrifying. But Hugh hadn't just been abducted by a faerie – Lord Hollowvale had really killed him. It only made sense that Hugh would want to stop the sluagh from doing the same to other people like him.

"You're right," Abigail murmured. "You have the right to stay an' help. But . . . will you please be more careful from now on, Hugh? If there's somethin' around that can bother ghosts, that means we've got to stick together."

Hugh nodded reluctantly. "I'll stay close by," he promised. He turned his gaze back to the rest of the bedroom. "There's somethin' wrong here. You think you can dig around some?"

Abigail considered the room. "I don't know quite what I'm lookin' for," she admitted. "But I'll start with the obvious, I suppose, an' see if the room is hidin' anything."

Hugh bounced on his feet with excitement. "I know this one!" he said. "I've seen Dad do it before. You'll need tobacco smoke, won't you?"

Abigail scowled. "*Dad* can call fire on command," she said. "I haven't got any way of lightin' tobacco, even if I had it. Anyway, there's other ways of seein' hidden things, you know. I've got a little bit of eyebright tea, an' it works just as well."

Abigail dug into her reticule once more, producing a little

silver flask. She unscrewed the top only with a *bit* of reluctance. Eyebright tea was normally light and sweet – but Abigail had brewed this particular batch with exceptional strength in order to be sure that its magic would work, and the taste was bitterly overwhelming. Still, she screwed up her face and took a long swallow from the flask.

Slowly, the image of the bedroom grew bright and strong – as though the sun were shining in from every corner at once. Abigail cast her gaze around the room, searching for anything out of place.

Something was indeed out of place.

A black shape fled from Abigail's sight, darting away beneath the large four-poster bed. At first, she thought it must have been a raven – but a moment later, she realised that it was far too *big* to be a raven.

"Hugh," Abigail said softly, "get behind me, won't you?"

Hugh frowned – but he shuffled carefully behind Abigail, glancing around the room with curiosity.

Abigail slowly closed the silver flask and put it back into the reticule, setting the bag down onto a side table. She kept her eyes ahead of her as she reached blindly into the reticule again, searching around inside until she came out with a tiny pouch of salt – one of the best mortal remedies she had against evil spirits.

"I know you're there," Abigail announced to the bed. "You may as well come out."

The bed remained silent.

"I can *force* you out," Abigail added. "Neither of us would like that very much, I think."

Another second passed. Then a voice underneath the bed said, "You could just leave, an' pretend you never saw me."

Abigail knit her brow. The voice which had spoken was a young woman's voice. Whoever the woman was, she had an accent very similar to Abigail's – which surely meant that she had little business being in a dead noblewoman's bedroom.

"Would you *please* come out?" Abigail repeated. Her tone was a little less hostile now, and a little more curious.

The bed sighed.

Slowly, a young woman wriggled out from underneath it. Her mid-length black hair had fallen free from her simple white cap. Her face was drawn and pale – and as she clambered to her feet, Abigail saw that she had a small frame which suggested she had missed several meals over the course of her life. She wore a patched old apron over the top of a faded green frock.

The young woman was not a ghost. Rather, she was alive and well, and exactly the sort of young woman who *didn't* belong underneath a lady's four-poster bed.

"Who are you, an' what are you doin' beneath Miss Kendall's bed?" Abigail asked. She meant to use a stern tone befitting a professional magician – but the words came out less serious and more perplexed. Whatever magic had been hiding the woman before seemed gone now, though the pungent taste of eyebright still lingered on Abigail's tongue.

The young woman grimaced, wiping her hands on her apron. Abigail caught a whiff of lye mixed with some sweeter smell which she could not quite identify. Probably, she thought, she was looking at a laundress. But that fact did not feel very enlightening – rather, it only added to her existing confusion.

"I don't know that I ought to give you my name," the woman said warily. "I heard you talkin' – you're a magician, an' a *necromancer.*" She narrowed her eyes at Hugh, and Abigail blinked.

Hugh lit up with delight. "You can see me?" he asked. "No one but Abby's ever seen me before!"

The small woman frowned at Hugh. "Have you been trapped here?" she asked him seriously. "If you tell me how she's done it, I could try an' help you."

"I'm standin' right here, you know!" Abigail said hotly. "An' I'm *not* a necromancer!" She paused, and thought for a moment. "Well. I suppose I *technically* did some necromancy. But that's not the same as doin' necromancy all the time, is it? It's not like I've made a profession of it."

Hugh grinned. "I *asked* Abby to bring me to England," he said. "I'd been stuck in Hollowvale for years an' years. It's not awful there, but it does get boring after a while—"

Abigail threw up her hands. "Oh, just tell her everything then!" she said sourly. "We can surely trust strange washerwomen hidin' underneath beds, can't we?"

The dark-haired woman blinked at Hugh. "You . . . *wanted* her to bind you?" she asked. "But don't you want to finish your business an' move on to what's next?"

Hugh furrowed his brow. "I don't know what business I'd have to finish," he said, "but if I'd wanted to move on, I'd have done it." He stepped forward to offer his hand. "I'm Hugh, by the way, an' this is Abby. You can tell *me* your name – I'm not a magician."

To Abigail's unending surprise, the other woman took Hugh's hand and shook it. "Oh, fine then," she said. "My name's Mercy. I think magicians could still use a name they've *heard*, but only my first name shouldn't hurt too much."

Hugh stared down at the hand that currently gripped his. His eyes were very wide. "You can touch me too," he breathed. "No one's *ever* done that, 'less I was in Hollowvale. How do you do that? Could you teach Abby?"

Mercy cocked her head at Hugh. "Well . . . I've always just *done* it, I suppose," she said. "I've had a way with ghosts ever since I can remember."

Abigail scowled. "Step away from her, Hugh," she said. "There ought to be a ghost here, remember? Awful convenient that *she* happens to be here an' Lucy's ghost happens to be gone."

Mercy glanced at Abigail sharply – and as she did, Abigail saw that the dark irises of Mercy's eyes were tinged with shifting pink and blue hues, like windows into a twilight sky. The sight arrested Abigail so much at first that she nearly forgot that they were in the middle of an argument.

"Awful convenient there happens to be a *necromancer* here an' no ghost," Mercy challenged Abigail back. "I thought for sure I felt a ghost tied to this house, an' instead I found *you*."

Hugh dropped Mercy's hand, looking between the two girls uncertainly. "I don't think there's any need to fight," he said. "I can promise, Abby wouldn't bind a ghost who didn't want it. An', Abby, I figure whoever got rid of Lucy's ghost probably did it a while back – otherwise Dad would've noticed Lucy an' talked to her while he was here."

Abigail made a sour sort of face. "Probably so," she said grudgingly. "That doesn't mean we ought to trust her, though." She was still feeling irritable over being called a necromancer.

Mercy crossed her arms. "I didn't ask you to trust me," she huffed. "I can find a missin' ghost all on my own, thank you very much."

"But why are you lookin' for a missin' ghost at all?" Abigail pressed her.

"I've got a question," Mercy shot back at Abigail. "Why are you so *nosy*?"

"An' why *should* you go lookin' for a missin' ghost all on your own?" Hugh asked plaintively. He turned a pleading expression to Abigail. "We could use the help, Abby, couldn't we?"

"You just want her around because she can touch you," Abigail grumbled. She eyed Mercy suspiciously. "Oh, I think you *should* come with us," she added. "I'd rather have my eyes on you instead of wonderin' if you're followin' behind me. You sneaked into this house with magic – I'd have seen you without the eyebright, otherwise."

Mercy lifted her chin. "Maybe I don't want to come with you," she challenged Abigail. "I don't like bein' ordered around by stuck-up magicians who think they're better'n me."

Abigail's mouth dropped open. It was bad enough being called a necromancer – but it stung even worse to be told she was *stuck-up*.

"I am *not* a stuck-up magician!" Abigail said hotly. "I just think you're suspicious!"

Mercy rolled her eyes. "An' you've got the right to declare who's suspicious an' who's not," she snipped. "I think *you're* suspicious, but I'm not orderin' you to follow me around." She brushed the last of the dust from her apron. "Now if you'll excuse me, Miss Magician – I've got a ghost to find."

And then – even as Abigail watched – the shadows in the corner of the bedroom closed around Mercy like a broad yawn.

And she was gone.

Hugh looked back at Abigail with wide eyes. "Did you see that?" he asked in an awe-filled voice. "That was faerie magic, Abby. There's no way it was anything else! An' she did it so quick, too! You'd never be able to do somethin' like that—"

"Oh, would you be quiet, Hugh?" Abigail snapped. She didn't mean to be brusque with him – but a small part of her was feeling terribly hurt and betrayed. It wasn't enough that Hugh had found a strange woman to admire; apparently, he had to rub Abigail's face in her own lack of imagination, too.

For just a second, Hugh looked distressed – but his expression soon hardened into resentment. "Is that a *command*, Miss Magician?" he asked. "You could use that locket to make me be quiet if you wanted."

Abigail clenched her fingers into her palms. "Don't you be pert with me!" she said. "I've never made you do anything you didn't want to do, an' you know it. I'm sorry if I can't shake your hand or disappear into shadows. I only spent months makin' sure you could leave Hollowvale, an' I guess that isn't impressive enough."

Hugh opened his mouth to respond . . . but a strange look came over his face, and he closed it again.

Seconds ticked by. Finally, Hugh said, "We're both bein' very silly, aren't we?"

Abigail shifted on her feet uncomfortably. "I know *you're*

bein' silly," she grumbled. But the observation had cut through her anger somewhat, and she sighed. "I'm sorry for bein' bossy," she said. "You know how hard I keep tryin' to get the hang of faerie magic. It's just not fair seein' someone else imagine impossible things so easily."

Hugh looked down at his shoes. "I didn't mean to make you feel bad," he said. "I know how hard you worked to get me out of Hollowvale. All I meant to say was . . . if *you're* good at mortal magic, an' Mercy's good at faerie magic, then you'd be able to do a lot between the two of you."

Abigail grimaced. "I *do* think Mercy's hidin' something," she said darkly. "Imagine her showin' up with faerie magic right as we're scarin' off faeries. I meant what I said about keepin' her close. I'd chase her down if I thought I could catch her . . . but I'm not all that sure if I *could* right this second."

Hugh straightened. "I bet I can convince her to stick with us, if we manage to find her again," he said.

Abigail pursed her lips. "I'll leave that to you, then," she said, "*if* we manage to find her again." She turned back towards the bedroom. "But I doubt Lady Pinckney's goin' to let us in here again – so we'd best make the most of it while we're here first."

Abigail spent another half an hour performing spells and searching over the bedroom with a few more sips of eyebright tea. She found very little of magical note, unfortunately – but just as she was about to give up, she discovered something exceptionally peculiar beneath Lucy's dresser, right next to the western window.

"It's a little flower," Abigail said, as she pushed back up to her feet. "Look at this, though – I think it's oleander! I've only ever seen it grow in Blackthorn, in faerie. It's as poisonous as anything. I got a rash last time I touched one." Abigail offered her gloved hand out towards Hugh, with the tiny white flower at the centre of her palm.

Hugh peered at the flower. "I'm fairly sure Lord Blackthorn wouldn't poison anyone," he said. "He doesn't tend to climb through windows, neither."

Abigail frowned at her hand. "I don't think this flower's from faerie at all," she said. "Faerie stuff is always *off*, just like the tarts in Hollowvale. This is a real oleander."

Hugh crossed his arms. "Well, what's that supposed to tell us?" he asked. Hugh was far more interested in tarts than he was in flowers.

Abigail rolled her eyes at him. "None of Lucy's beaus would've given her a poisonous flower," she said. "An' she wouldn't be wearin' one, neither. I think that the sluagh that came through the window must've shed this on its way in."

Hugh cocked his head curiously. "But you just said you've never seen an oleander outside faerie," he said. "Where would you find a flower like that in London?"

Abigail smiled triumphantly. "You'd only find it somewhere like an orangery," she said. "An' I bet I know *which* orangery."

Chapter Four

Abigail nearly found them a hackney right away – it was getting late in the day, after all – but thankfully, Hugh was keen enough to remind her about Mr Hayes.

They found the little scarecrow still furiously dancing just outside the house across the street.

"Look at him go!" Hugh marvelled. "He's a hard worker, isn't he?"

Abigail pursed her lips. "I should end the spell now, shouldn't I?" she observed dubiously.

Hugh shot her an offended look. "You can't!" he said. "You already named him an' everything!"

Abigail sighed. "Technically, *you* named him," she muttered. But she too felt an odd sense of responsibility for the little scarecrow now. Abigail leaned down to scoop up the straw doll. "Just stay put for a bit," she instructed Mr Hayes. "I'm sure there'll be more sluagh for you to chase off later."

Mr Hayes slowed his wiggling in her hands. Once Abigail was sure he'd calmed down enough, she tucked him back into her reticule.

"Right," Abigail said. "Kensington Gardens isn't that far. We should be able to make it in before lock-out."

Hugh grimaced. "But you said we're not goin' back to Hollowvale—" he started.

Abigail cut him off. "We're *not* goin' back to Hollowvale," she said. "The sluagh are usin' the same paths in an' out of faerie that we do in Kensington Gardens. I think the one that came through Lucy's window must've used a path in the Greenhouse. It's not supposed to be public – but what do faeries care about visitin' hours?"

Hugh considered this seriously. "You think we'll find anything useful there?" he asked.

"I think we'll find some witnesses," Abigail said, as she whistled down a hackney.

Abigail had gone to Kensington Gardens with her mother and father quite often. Most ladies and gentlemen enjoyed walking in the gardens on Sundays during the day, while they were open to the public – but Abigail's family found the gardens both beautiful and functional. After lock-out, once the sun disappeared, dozens of paths into faerie appeared within the gardens. This was why the gardens were really off-limits after nine in the evening – for faeries of all sorts tended to stroll about them at night, no matter how much Elias tried to discourage them.

Hugh and Abigail arrived at the gardens with a few hours to spare before lock-out. Abigail probably should have been better-dressed for the occasion – but the black mourning ribbon on her bonnet must have garnered her some sympathy, for no one stopped her to remark on her very plain gown.

It was pleasant for a while, strolling along the Broad Walk with Hugh – though the well-dressed ladies and gentlemen around them saw Abigail walking all on her own. Tall green trees reached up towards the sky, casting shade along the edges of the large path. Knots of people lingered there in the last hours of daylight, laughing together as they went.

"It seems silly, doesn't it?" Hugh asked, looking around at the other people in their very best walking dress. "People come here just to walk?"

"People come here to walk *together*," Abigail corrected him. A hint of wistfulness slipped into her voice. "Couples come walkin' here especially."

Hugh shot Abigail a dry look. She knew he still didn't see the appeal. He'd never grown up enough to wonder about spending his life with someone else. Abigail *had* thought about such things – briefly, at least, before her disastrous Season had disabused her of the notion entirely. No one, she had realised then, was ever going to ask *her* to go walking with them. Long walks were for talking. Talking to other people required that you have things in common with them.

Abigail had so very little in common with any of the *beau monde*. Women like Lucy talked of French gowns and available bachelors. Men talked of things like Oxford and the Continent. Abigail could have talked about how to stretch a meal over several days – or, conversely, how to break faerie curses. Over the course of that single Season, Abigail had come to see clearly the broad gulf which separated her from London's upper crust. It was not a chasm which could ever be bridged with muslin and ribbons and careful accents.

"This is boring," Hugh declared. "I'm goin' to climb a tree."

Abigail rolled her eyes. "Oh, go ahead," she said. "I need to rest my feet a bit anyway."

Hugh spent some time picking out the perfect tree for climbing. Abigail sat herself beneath the chestnut tree he chose, watching as the world darkened around them. Soon, as the sun dipped lower on the horizon, even the most daring aristocrats began to make their way home.

One older man peeled away from the Broad Walk as he saw Abigail sitting beneath the tree. He was dressed much more finely than she was, in a speckled blue waistcoat and a severe white cravat. "Young lady," he addressed her, "it's best you depart. This is no place for civilised people once the sun goes down."

Abigail glanced up at him. "I am well aware of what happens here when the sun goes down," she assured him. "You may set your mind at ease, sir."

The man frowned deeply. He had a grey, neatly trimmed beard and moustache, which now twitched in displeasure. "The faeries of the Broad Walk are coming," he insisted, as though she hadn't heard him at all.

Abigail sighed heavily and changed her tack. "Sir," she said, "we are nearly alone right now, and I have no chaperone. I must insist that you leave *immediately*."

This statement garnered a far different response. The older man blinked and flushed self-consciously. "Yes, er," he said. But just as Abigail was beginning to wonder whether Mr Hayes could scare off nosy, meddling gentlemen just as well as birds, the man nodded at her awkwardly and turned to hurry back towards the path.

Soon, his figure disappeared into the distance . . . and Abigail was alone once more.

For the space of about half an hour, the Broad Walk was utterly empty. But eventually, Hugh leaned over one of the tree branches and called down, "Here they come!"

They looked like distant swaying lanterns at first. Each of them glowed a different colour of the rainbow, carrying their own light with them.

The faeries of the Broad Walk were all dressed like flowers this evening. The first couple to breach the horizon consisted of a violet-skinned elfin woman in a large bluebell gown and a pale pink hyacinth lady, whom she seemed to be escorting. Abigail rose to her feet and squared her shoulders, heading back onto the path to meet them.

"Excuse me!" Abigail said to the bluebell faerie. "Lovely evening, isn't it?"

The two faerie ladies ignored Abigail roundly, strolling past her as though she didn't exist.

"I simply cannot fathom it," the hyacinth faerie observed to the bluebell. "Imagine, dressing as a tulip! How gauche." At first, Abigail wondered whether the hyacinth was talking about *her* – but she saw then that the next faerie couple was dressed as an orange tulip and a yellow tulip.

Abigail stepped past the first faerie couple to speak to the tulips. "Good evening!" she said loudly. "Did you happen to see the ghost of an English lady pass by here just a few nights ago?"

The tulips ignored her completely as well.

Abigail was just starting to get *very* irritated – but before she could open her mouth to comment on the faeries' lack of politesse, someone else looped their arm through hers, such that a slim, pale hand came to rest upon her arm.

"Pardon us," Mercy said, "but have you seen the ghost of an English lady wanderin' around?"

Abigail glanced sideways at Mercy. The other woman had stepped out from the shadows in order to walk next to Abigail. Mercy was still wearing the faded green frock and apron from before; this close, however, Abigail noticed the sweet scent beneath the lye that clung to Mercy's clothing. This time, she knew for certain that it was the scent of lilies.

And who's being nosy now? Abigail thought darkly. It couldn't possibly be a coincidence that Mercy had shown up at Kensington Gardens at exactly the same time as they had done. In fact, Abigail might have wondered whether Mercy had followed them in secret, if she hadn't been watching for exactly that on their way there.

The two tulip faeries turned to regard Mercy and Abigail. One of them wore a garish orange gown, while the other wore a green shirt and trousers with a very loud yellow waistcoat and cravat.

"The ghost of an English lady?" mused the yellow tulip.

"I'm sure I haven't seen anything like *that*," the orange tulip tittered. She tilted her head at Mercy and Abigail. "But which flowers are *you* supposed to be? We are all supposed to be flowers, you know. That way, the mortals will overlook us if they wander into the gardens."

Abigail raised her eyebrows. "I don't think anyone would mistake you for—"

"We're dressed as mortals an' not as flowers," Mercy said. "I'm dressed as a laundress, an' she's a magician." Mercy shot Abigail a flat look which said, *Let's not start an argument.*

"I'm *quite* sure we all agreed to dress as flowers," the orange tulip murmured.

"But I would have preferred to be a laundress!" the yellow tulip declared with distress. "Had I known that we were allowed—"

"But you haven't seen a dead English lady anywhere?" Abigail insisted. "An' no sluagh, neither?"

"Oh, neither," the orange tulip assured Abigail. "But we don't walk here every evening. You ought to ask the crocuses – they love the gardens here more than any of the rest of us. I'm sure you'll find them dancing near the Round Pond."

The tulips bowed to them and continued onwards – whereupon Abigail turned to look at Mercy.

"I thought you didn't want to stick around me," Abigail said. She meant for the words to come out as more of a challenge – but they were strangely subdued instead. The "stuck-up magician" comment was still bothering her, whether she wanted to admit it or not.

"The faeries won't talk to anyone strollin' down the walk without a partner," Mercy grumbled. "Those are the rules this week."

Abigail nearly said, *Maybe I don't want to be your partner.* But even without a cup of tea, she managed to restrain herself and think again.

Mercy is suspicious, and we need to keep her close, Abigail thought instead.

And then there was a second, very quiet thought: *I would like to take a walk with someone who isn't related to me, just for a little bit.*

"Then I suppose we'll have to walk together," Abigail said finally. She turned her head back towards Hugh's tree, and saw that he had already jumped the last few feet to the ground.

"Hullo there, Mercy!" Hugh said breathlessly, as he hurried over to join them. "I know why *we* came to Kensington Gardens – but how'd you decide to come here?"

Mercy shifted her hand slightly against Abigail's arm. Her fingers were long and delicate, but her hands were bare; she'd gone without even the simplest gloves. Her hands were far softer and smoother than Abigail might have expected from a laundress.

"I've got my own ways of findin' things out," Mercy said – and Abigail remembered belatedly that she was supposed to be thinking about how suspicious the other woman was rather than about how nice her hands were.

"You've got faerie magic," Abigail said dryly, "and you don't seem frightened of all these funny flowers. At the very least, some faerie's taught you magic." The three of them walked down the path, nodding occasionally at the other bright faerie couples who passed them.

Mercy frowned at that. "No one *taught* me magic," she corrected Abigail. "Like I said, I've always just had it. An' I'm not sure what you mean by faerie magic, anyway. I've got inside magic an' outside magic." She glanced sideways at Abigail from beneath her messy black hair. "I don't much like outside magic. It's boring."

Abigail couldn't help the spark of interest this statement struck within her. "What, er – what do you consider inside magic an' outside magic?" she asked.

Mercy thought for a moment. "Well," she said, "inside magic comes from inside you an' you tell it what to do. You have to really believe in what you're doin', or else it misbehaves." She knit her brow. "Outside magic is where you use what everyone *else* believes. It's like borrowin' other people's imagination, so it's hard to get it wrong."

Abigail blinked. "Well . . . you've just described faerie magic an' mortal magic," she said. "Faerie magic is inside magic, by that reckonin', an' mortal magic is outside magic. Only, I've never heard them described that way before. And . . . I thought you *had* to be a faerie to do faerie magic."

Mercy shrugged. "*You're* not a faerie," she said, "but that locket you're carryin' around with you is inside magic, isn't it?"

Abigail reached up to touch the locket around her neck self-consciously. "I was stolen away to faerie for a while," she murmured quietly. "I came back with a piece of it inside me, I guess. But I don't think that makes me a *faerie*. An' I guess . . . Well, I can *do* inside magic, but I'm not very good at it."

Mercy nodded as though this was a very reasonable explanation. "Well, there you are," she said. "You're not a faerie, an' you still do inside magic." She glanced up above them – and then, without so much as a pause in their conversation, she said, "What a sky that is! Can you imagine if we fell into it, like it was a lake?"

Abigail looked up at the sky. It was now very dark out in the middle of Kensington Gardens, and she could just make out a few pin-prick stars. "That's an awful long way to fall," Abigail noted wryly.

Mercy sighed with exasperation. "See, that's your problem," she said. "You have to exercise your imagination if you want to use it for inside magic. If I tell you that sky looks like a lake, you don't say *no*, you tell me what the stars are!"

Abigail squinted upwards dubiously. "Er," she said, "I guess the stars could be fishes?"

"Sure they could!" Mercy agreed amiably. "But how'd they get there in that lake? Someone stocks the pond with fishes, don't they? Who was it who threw those star-fish into the sky?"

"A gamekeeper!" Hugh volunteered. "He must have his cottage on the moon!"

"*He* could be a *she*," Abigail told Hugh suddenly, "as long as we're imaginin' things."

"Maybe you should apply for the job," Mercy told Abigail with a slow, sly smile. A pair of cornflower faeries swept past them, glowing a vibrant violet; the colour lit Mercy's pale face strangely so that for the moment, she appeared more otherworldly than tired.

There was something at once both magnetic and distressing about it, Abigail decided. The world seemed almost to bend around Mercy, as though casting itself constantly at her feet. Part of Abigail wanted to throw herself at Mercy's feet as well – though thankfully, it was a very *small* part of Abigail, easily overruled by the rest of her rational mind.

Abigail was used to having strange feelings like that around faeries and their associates. Her Other Mum could be downright frightful at times. But for some reason, Mercy's sly smile *also* made Abigail's knees feel a little bit weak – and that had *certainly* never happened to her before.

Perhaps I'd best not exercise my imagination too much more, Abigail thought.

Thankfully, the Round Pond soon came into view – and what a view it was! Bright blue candles hovered over the lake, reflecting upon white swans and flower-dressed dancers. The faerie visitors to Kensington Gardens waltzed clockwise upon the water, twirling to the sound of a ghostly pipe.

Abigail searched the dancers carefully. "I think I see some crocuses," she said. "Those white ones over there. Perhaps we can wait until they finish dancing."

A dangerous glint came into Mercy's eyes. "Why wait at all?" she asked. "Look at that. You can't pretend you don't want to dance."

Abigail hesitated. "I don't know if I could imagine my feet into dancin' on water," she said. "An' I've got this reticule—"

Mercy waved a hand. "I want to dance," she said. "It looks like fun. I'll imagine hard enough for both of us." Whatever Mercy's opinion of Abigail might have been, the lure of the music and the temptation of the Round Pond had worked a mercurial change in her demeanour, as abrupt as a summer storm.

"I'll watch your things," Hugh added helpfully. "You've got to talk to the crocuses *somehow*, Abby."

Abigail considered Mercy for a long moment. The shadows around her had darkened, setting off the eerie twilight in her eyes; the cool blue candlelight which came from the Round Pond flickered along her pale skin and faded frock, giving her the sense of a woman who had herself been washed too many times. The laundress was *interesting*, certainly – and Abigail couldn't deny that Mercy's enthusiasm was a bit contagious. Many things were simply *off* about her, however, and Abigail still had little reason to trust her.

Though . . . the faeries here shared Mercy's brand of whimsy. Under normal circumstances, Abigail doubted if they would gracefully submit themselves to an entire bevy of boring questions from a nosy magician. Mercy's approach, Abigail thought, was probably the *right* approach.

Reluctantly, Abigail set her overlarge reticule down against a nearby tree. Mercy offered her arm again in a gentlemanly fashion, and Abigail took it gingerly. The two of them strode for the edge of the Round Pond as though they quite belonged there.

Abigail flinched a bit as her boot touched the surface of the water – but Mercy simply kept walking, pulling her confidently along. Abigail felt the subtle chill of Mercy's inside magic against her skin, dark and oddly invigorating. The water held against her boot, though it was nearly as slippery as glass. Tiny ripples expanded out from Abigail's steps as she went, like raindrops upon the lake. Somehow, Mercy's steps next to her left no trace at all.

"I don't know how to waltz," Abigail said suddenly. "Do you?"

Mercy smiled that same sly smile. "Doesn't matter, does it?" she asked. "We just need to spin quick enough to stay out of everyone else's way." She looped her arm around Abigail's waist as though to demonstrate – and then they were moving across the water with the other dancers, weaving among the swans and the faeries with dubious precision.

It was immediately clear that Mercy did *not* know how to waltz – but the make-believe dance she had pulled out of thin air was strangely graceful, nevertheless. It was far from the first time that Abigail had danced with another woman; ladies often danced together before the floor officially opened at balls, and it was sometimes difficult to secure male partners regardless. But dancing with Mercy was utterly different. Mercy had not merely settled for dancing with Abigail – she *wanted* to dance with Abigail. Her feet were sure even if her steps were bizarre, and her grip on Abigail's waist was reassuring.

"I'll wager you were better at imaginin' things when you were younger," Mercy said softly. The ghostly blue light of the candles joined the twilight in her dark eyes – and for a moment, she seemed nearly like an apparition herself.

Abigail sighed. "I don't know if I ever was," she admitted. "Maybe I was born with a broken imagination." Something about dancing out on the lake made her feel more comfortable saying things like that, where no one else could hear her.

Mercy gave Abigail a considering look. Though she was an inch or so shorter than Abigail, the magnetic darkness which clung to her made it seem as though Abigail was always looking up at her. The light which danced in her eyes now looked sad. "You say that like it's your fault," Mercy murmured.

"Maybe it is," Abigail replied. "I haven't practised my imagination like you have."

Mercy shook her head. "I didn't mean to imply you'd done somethin' wrong," she said. There was genuine sympathy in her tone now. "I don't figure anyone *chooses* to lose their imagination. Maybe you just used it all up on somethin' important."

"Mostly on survivin', I guess," Abigail said quietly. "You don't look like you've had an easy time of it either, though, an' you've still got an imagination like no one else I've ever met."

Mercy pursed her lips. "Oh, don't compare yourself to me," she said. "I've been lucky in all sorts of ways." She smiled at Abigail. "But isn't it lovely out here on the lake? Why don't you imagine somethin' up now? It's a perfect place to try."

Abigail cast her gaze across the Round Pond, taking in the sight. Faeries whirled like flowers on the surface of the water, laughing and dodging away from the sleepy swans that snapped at the hems of their gowns. Most people would have been awed by the sight, Abigail realised, rather than scheming on how to make their way towards the pair of crocuses that danced on the other side of the pond.

For just a moment, Abigail let go of that driving goal. She focused instead on the secretive smile upon Mercy's lips, and the way the candlelight threw long shadows across the water.

Almost before she could think to ask, the cool shard of Hollowvale within her offered up its magic. That frigid power trickled up into her heart, shaping itself to the thoughts in her mind. Unlike the mortal magic Abigail more often employed, Hollowvale's magic felt distinctly borrowed – alien and inhuman. But, just for now, that strangeness seemed entirely appropriate, and Abigail's mind accepted it as *normal*. She sighed dreamily; as she did, a soft plume of mist rose from her lips, hovering upon the air.

Suddenly, the dark blue shadows on the water turned about, leaving their owners behind. Shadow dancers turned counter-clockwise across the pond, whirling in perfect counterpoint to the true dancers upon the water.

One of the daisy faeries let out a delighted laugh. Abigail felt another magic answer hers like warm, honeyed sunlight. The shadow dancers then rose from the water, joining their originals upon the pond. A peony faerie gestured broadly with one hand, and soft whispers carried across Abigail's magic. The shadow dancers bowed politely to one another, then turned to offer their hands to the actual faeries on the lake.

It all happened so naturally, and in such swift succession – each spell built upon the last with wild, whimsical joy – such that Abigail quite forgot that she had been thinking about anything else at all. A smile broke out across her face, and Mercy grinned back, spinning Abigail away into the arms of another shadow Mercy, who immediately picked up their dance once again.

The shadow Mercy's arms were a bit colder, but she directed Abigail with all of the same grace and confidence as the real Mercy. Briefly, Abigail hoped that her own shadow was not trying to lead anyone else through a dance – she was not terribly good at leading. It occurred to Abigail then that this was a delightfully bizarre problem to be considering, and she shook her head at herself with another smile.

The shadow Mercy neatly spun Abigail away to a fresh partner, then – and Abigail found herself looking up at a tall, elegant lady dressed as a crocus.

"What a wonderful evening!" the crocus said. "I have not had this much fun on the Round Pond for weeks!"

"You're here very often, then?" Abigail said quickly, remembering her original intent.

"Oh, nearly every night!" the crocus faerie assured Abigail. "The swans pretend that they hate us – but I am good friends with them, and they really do enjoy the company."

They passed one of the grumpy swans, who snapped out at the crocus lady's gown as though to disprove her comment.

"Have you perhaps seen the ghost of an English lady pass through Kensington Gardens?" Abigail asked. "She might have been with a sluagh."

The crocus looked thoughtful. “Oh yes,” she said. “I do remember that. The poor dear was very distressed – but ghosts always are. There *was* a sluagh escorting her. I think they went to the Greenhouse, but I haven’t seen either of them since then.”

“Escorting”, Abigail thought, was a terribly tame word. But faeries rarely perceived abductions in the same way that mortals did.

“Pardon the question,” Abigail said slowly, “but do you know if there’s a path to faerie in the Greenhouse?”

“There is, in fact,” the crocus lady said. “I have used it once before. It leads into the wild places of faerie, in between realms. But it is the only path in London which leads anywhere near to Longshadow, and so I suppose the sluagh must use it if they wish to come and go from there.”

Abigail meant to ask more questions – but even as she opened her mouth, the crocus lady spun her away again, and she found herself dancing with a daisy’s shadow.

The dancing went on for quite a while before Abigail managed to find her way back to the real Mercy, who seemed to be having the time of her life. Her messy black hair had fallen entirely loose of her cap now, and she added new steps to her own invented dance as she took over leading Abigail across the pond.

“Lucy’s ghost went to the Greenhouse with a sluagh!” Abigail said. “We should grab our shadows and go after her!”

Mercy did not seem the least bit surprised by this revelation – but she pursed her lips and nodded. “I don’t think my shadow really wants to leave,” she said. “I’ll let it stay for a bit; I’m sure it’ll catch up with us, eventually.”

The two of them departed the pond, heading back towards the tree where Abigail had left Hugh with her reticule. He gave Abigail an expectant look as the two of them approached.

“Well?” Hugh asked.

“The sluagh definitely abducted Lucy’s ghost,” Abigail said.

"Did the crocus say that?" Mercy asked. "The abduction thing, I mean."

Abigail studied Mercy carefully. "Well . . . the sluagh was almost certainly draggin' Lucy to Longshadow," she said. "I somehow doubt they asked her nicely."

Mercy frowned, but remained silent.

Hugh seemed especially worried by this statement. "Oh," he said. "Er. But *we're* not goin' to Longshadow, right?"

Abigail knit her brow at Hugh. There was something extra shifty in his behaviour that she couldn't quite make out. "Clearly not," she said. "I *would* like to see if there's anything of interest on the path, though." Abigail eyed Hugh suspiciously. "Is there somethin' I ought to know about Longshadow, Hugh?"

Hugh cleared his throat, glancing meaningfully between Abigail and Mercy. "I don't know," he said. "Maybe." There was a question underlying the statement: *Are we speaking openly in front of Mercy now?*

Abigail frowned. "We can talk about it later," she amended.

Mercy gave Hugh a curious sort of look. But he shrugged and nodded at Abigail.

They left the dancing flowers behind and headed for the Greenhouse, while Abigail's shadow scampered to rejoin her.

Chapter Five

The Greenhouse was not open to the public, but that didn't mean it was empty. The tall windows let in just enough moonlight to illuminate the plants inside. Several orange trees spanned the inside of the long, narrow building, casting shade upon the floors with their branches. The three of them walked in silence past shelves and shelves of exotic bushes and flowers, whose scents mingled together to create a sweet, nearly cloying smell. It was a cosy place, small enough that one could dimly see from end to end, even in the relative darkness.

Normally, Abigail might have felt some trepidation at trespassing in a royal building which ought to have been off-limits – but the royal family was well aware just how actively faeries wandered the gardens in the evenings, and they had prudently decided that everyone ought to avoid the grounds at night entirely, lest the faeries run away with their staff.

"There ought to be oleander flowers here somewhere," Abigail observed quietly. "I'll wager there's a way into faerie just near them." She glanced back at Mercy and added, "You'd normally have to do somethin' special to open a way into faerie, but all the paths in Kensington Gardens are thrown open whenever the moon shines upon them. We could wander right into faerie at any moment. I s'ppose that doesn't bother you?"

Mercy blinked. "Should I be bothered?" she asked. "*You* don't seem bothered."

Abigail narrowed her eyes. "You could end up abducted," she said. "Stuck in faerie for a small eternity, pickin' oakum till your fingers bleed."

Mercy arched an eyebrow. "That seems awful specific," she said.

Abigail pressed her lips together. "You know what I think?" she said. "I think you *have* been to faerie before. I think you took a piece of it back here with you, the same way that I brought back a piece of Hollowvale."

Abigail had expected Mercy to look away and hide her expression – but instead, the other woman smiled. "Well, obviously I've been to faerie," she said. "I knew about the pathways here in the gardens. You don't need to sound so suspicious over it – I'm not stickin' with you for ever. We just happen to be headed in the same direction for now."

"But you *could* stick with us," Hugh said. "You wanted to talk more about me movin' on, didn't you?"

Mercy slowed her pace. She glanced back towards Hugh. "You said you didn't want to move on," she observed carefully.

Abigail tensed at the suggestion – but the dim moonlight revealed Hugh's sly expression, and she realised that this was how he meant to keep Mercy with them.

"I don't want to move on right *now*," Hugh said to Mercy. "But you seemed convinced that I *would* want to move on if you could only knock some sense into me. I'm all right with talkin' about it some, anyway."

For the first time since they'd met her, Mercy now looked uncertain. She crossed her arms over her chest as they walked. "You *are* supposed to move on," Mercy said. "I'm sure you would have done if you weren't bein' held by magic."

Hugh nodded agreeably, following along behind them with his hands in his pockets. "So what's great about movin' on?" he asked. "What do I get out of it?"

Sympathy flickered over Mercy's features as she looked back at Hugh. "Well, you're stuck in between, aren't you?" she asked. "It can't be fun, always watchin' everyone else do things that you can't do. There's peace on the Other Side, an' you'd fully belong there."

Mercy clearly meant every word. There was a gentle sadness in her eyes that matched the sadness in Abigail's heart. Every time Hugh talked at their mother or sighed over tarts, that sadness had grown and grown, until Abigail started thinking again how she ought to find a spell to let him talk or touch things.

"An' how do you know there's peace on the Other Side?" Hugh asked Mercy. "Have *you* ever been there?"

Mercy frowned. "I haven't," she admitted. "No one ever comes back from there once they cross the border. But it *looks* awful peaceful. You can see it from certain parts of faerie."

Hugh nodded sagely. "That is very interestin'," he said. "An' I will think about it very hard." Abigail, who had known him for quite some time, knew that this translated roughly to *I have already forgotten everything you just said*. But Mercy smiled wistfully at Hugh, and Abigail thought that the other woman must have believed him at least a little bit.

Abigail was so distracted by this conversation that she nearly passed right by the white oleanders – but Mercy stopped only a few steps after them, turning to look towards one of the tall windows which stretched from floor to ceiling.

Tonight, in fact, said window was not entirely a window. The glass there shimmered strangely, and when one looked at it sideways, the world beyond the window changed its appearance.

There was a path past the window, overlooked by large, silver trees. At first, Abigail thought that the moonlight must have made the trees *seem* silver – but as she looked more closely, she saw that they glimmered like metal beneath their tarnished bark. Each tree was laden with a different fruit: there were silver oranges, silver plums and even silver cherries hanging from the branches.

Mercy did not hesitate at all in front of the window. She hiked up her skirts and stepped onto the path beyond, with the certainty of someone who had walked it several times before.

Abigail sighed. She found herself keenly aware that she was following a strange, untrustworthy woman into faerie while wearing a thin muslin gown and carrying a bulky reticule. If she'd been able to do so, she probably would have stopped at home and packed herself some trousers to change into once she'd entered faerie. Sensible people did not normally go gallivanting around faerie in a gown, unless said people wanted thorns in unmentionable places.

Sensible people did not follow strange women into faerie, either.

But it was far too late to be sneaking back into the House for trousers, and into faerie was where Abigail's investigation had led her – and so, she hiked up her skirts once more and followed Mercy.

The window rippled around Abigail like water, chilling the surface of her skin. Metallic leaves crunched oddly beneath her feet as she came out onto the path. There was moonlight here too, but it didn't seem to come from anywhere in particular; though the way ahead was washed in silver, the dark sky held no moon and no stars.

Hugh walked behind Abigail, investigating the scenery with fascination. Though they were now in faerie, the leaves did not crunch beneath his feet; only their Other Mum's power was enough to grant Hugh something closer to a real body, and the shard of Hollowvale inside of Abigail told her that the realm was a good distance away from them. Hollowvale's power tended to wax and wane within her as the realm grew closer or further away, such that she could generally guess at its nearness.

Mercy had not walked very far ahead of them, though her

stride had seemed very confident before. In fact, she stood oddly rooted upon the path, glancing at the fruit trees around them with her brow deeply furrowed.

"Well, that's a bother," she said calmly.

Abigail frowned and followed her gaze.

Someone had nailed an iron horseshoe to the tree on their right.

Abigail blinked. "I'm sure *that's* not supposed to be there," she said.

"There's another one over here," said Hugh. Abigail turned and saw him looking up at a tarnished pear tree, where a second horseshoe had been nailed to the bark, pointing back towards them like a letter *c*.

"There's a whole circle of 'em surroundin' us," Mercy said. "Anywhere the ends of the horseshoes point towards us, we won't be able to walk past."

Abigail scoffed at this statement. "We're not faeries," she said. "I don't enjoy touchin' iron, of course, but that's no reason it should *trap* me—"

But even as Abigail started moving forward again, she found that her feet resisted her. Each step dragged as though through molasses. Eventually, the resistance was so strong that she couldn't move forward at all.

"You said you had a piece of Hollowvale inside you," Mercy observed. "It's that piece that can't pass the iron." There was an odd expression on her face as she continued looking around at the horseshoes which had trapped them. For though Mercy clearly understood the problem in theory, she was very puzzled by the *reality* of being trapped. She kept backtracking as she spoke, trying different angles to slip past the horseshoes and failing each time.

"Did you know this was here?" Abigail demanded hotly.

Mercy knit her brow, still glancing around. "Of course I didn't know about it," she said. "Why would I walk in here otherwise? There *aren't* supposed to be horseshoes here."

Abigail let out a frustrated noise. "We'll just go back to England, then," she said. "We can take a different path from Kensington Gardens …" But even as Abigail turned back towards the window which led into the Greenhouse, she saw the flaw in this plan. Whoever had set this particular trap had prepared it completely. On their way in, they had stepped over a last horseshoe which had been staked into the ground, pointing away from the window.

"Well," Hugh said, following Abigail's gaze, "I guess we won't be doin' that either."

Abigail grimaced and thought for a moment. She glanced at the surrounding foliage, searching for a stick. They were all too short to reach the horseshoe from where she was standing, however.

Mercy fixed her eyes upon the horseshoe with growing confusion and distress. Shadows gathered in ragged cobwebs around her as she reached for her inside magic.

Abigail whirled towards her. "No, don't!" she said quickly.

But Mercy had already lashed out at the horseshoe in front of the Greenhouse window. Shadows hissed towards it, cold and unfriendly; for an instant, the shadows looked like half-shrouded human forms, grasping out at the horseshoe to pry it loose from the ground.

A thunderous *crack* split the air. White-hot light tore through the shadows, shredding them like paper. Mercy staggered back with a cry of pain – and soon, there was the awful scent of something burning.

Abigail rushed over as Mercy crumpled to the ground, holding her hands to her chest.

"Is it bad?" Abigail asked urgently. "Let me see." She reached out gingerly for Mercy's wrists, tugging her hands back into view.

There was an angry red colour to the skin of Mercy's hands – but thankfully, the burns seemed mild. *Any* sort of burn was agonising, of course, and Abigail didn't grudge the tears of pain that ran down Mercy's face.

"Why would you do that?" Abigail asked her. "You must've known what would happen!"

Mercy shivered miserably. "I . . . I don't know," she said. "I'm so used to inside magic doin' whatever I want it to do, I think I just . . . believed it would work anyway."

Hugh had hurried over with Abigail; he winced as he saw Mercy's hands. "Some things are still impossible, no matter how hard you imagine 'em," he said.

Abigail sighed heavily. "Do you know," she said, "I think your imagination's a little *too* creative. You've had so long gettin' your way that you've forgotten what it's like when you don't. Faerie magic is nice an' all, but it can't solve everything."

Mercy looked down at her hands with a trembling lip. "It hurts an awful lot," she mumbled. "I think I hate horseshoes, Abby."

Abigail cocked an eyebrow. The nickname sounded strange coming from Mercy's lips. "It's Abigail," she said reluctantly. "An' I'll bet you *do* hate horseshoes. I can't say as I enjoy 'em much myself right now." She set Mercy's hands carefully down into her lap and pushed to her feet. "Well, whoever did this, we're well an' truly trapped. Even mortal magic hates iron. I'm not sure as we have a way of gettin' out of here."

The words struck them all very heavily as the implications sank in. Whoever had trapped them here would surely come by to *check* their trap – and there would be no protecting themselves at all when that occurred.

Hugh looked up at Abigail. "Well, *you* can't leave," he said. "I don't think I have any trouble gettin' past the horseshoes. It's just a shame I can't move 'em for you."

Abigail knit her brow at him. "You can't move them," she said slowly, "but maybe you could find someone *else* to move them."

Hugh crossed his arms thoughtfully. Then a sudden thought

lit up his face. "Mum!" he said. "Not Other Mum, but Normal Mum! Maybe I can get her attention in a mirror an' lead her here!"

Abigail gave him a wary look. "Your locket's in faerie with me," she said. "It might not work as well if you go back to England. What if you go too far from it an' you fall apart?"

Hugh frowned darkly. "No one *else* here can walk past iron," he said. "You need my help, Abby. Anyway, I'm not really scared of fallin' apart."

Abigail frowned at that. "You're not?" she asked. "But you said you didn't want to move on, Hugh."

Hugh shrugged. "I don't want to move on," he agreed. "Seems silly to give up everything I care about just to wander somewhere new. But you *are* what I care about. There's nothin' wrong with goin' down fightin' for that."

Abigail stared at Hugh. As she did, she realised that she had largely avoided talking to him about why he refused to move on – mostly because she didn't *want* him to move on, and some part of her had always feared that bringing up the subject would get him thinking about it.

"I don't want you to go down fightin' for me at all, Hugh," Abigail said softly. Her throat was tight on the words. The idea was suddenly very possible and very horrifying.

Hugh rolled his eyes. "That's your problem an' not mine," he said. "But anyway, you'll have to use the locket if you want to stop me. I'm goin' now, Abby. If I wait too long, I won't be able to find Mum quick enough before the sun comes up an' the paths in the gardens all close."

Abigail clenched her fingers into her palms. For just a moment, she *was* tempted to use the locket to force Hugh to stay. But she knew that was wrong. If she did that, Abigail thought, then she really *would* be a necromancer.

"I don't want you to go," Abigail said quietly, "but I won't use the locket, Hugh."

Hugh smiled up at her. "I know why I'm still here," he said. "I don't think I'll disappear as long as I know you need help. So don't worry *too* much." He sighed. "I do wish I could hug you goodbye. But you ought to know that I love you lots, Abby."

Abigail blinked away tears. It was suddenly very difficult to keep her voice level. "I love you lots too, Hugh," she said.

Mercy looked up at Abigail from her place on the ground. There was still pain on her face – but underneath that was a new and curious uncertainty. "I . . . I could strengthen your spell on the locket," she said. "I've always been good with ghosts."

Abigail considered Mercy carefully. "You don't believe in ghosts stayin' past their time," she said slowly. "You called me a necromancer for doin' the spell at all."

Mercy nodded miserably. "I don't like it much," she admitted. "But I don't want to stay here for ever with these horseshoes. And . . ." Mercy trailed off. Her dark eyes flickered to Hugh, studying him with consternation. "I don't know," she said softly. "It seems like the right thing to do just now. I never thought I'd say that."

Abigail glanced at Hugh. "It's your locket," she said. "Do you want to risk her touchin' it?"

Hugh narrowed his one eye at Mercy. "Promise you won't do anything funny to it?" he asked her. "You'll just make the spell stronger?"

Mercy nodded reluctantly. "I promise," she said.

Hugh nodded. "Go on then," he said to Abigail. "I do think she wants out as much as you do."

Abigail tugged the locket reluctantly from her shirt. She greatly disliked the idea of giving it to anyone else; she *especially* disliked giving it to Mercy given the suspicions which had started growing in her mind. But Hugh had made his decision – and so Abigail placed the locket gingerly into one of Mercy's painfully reddened hands.

Mercy flinched in discomfort. But she closed her fingers

around the locket even so. With one last worried look at the horseshoe near the window, Mercy took in a breath – and the shreds of her shadows gathered around her once more.

The magic didn't backfire this time, since Mercy wasn't trying to affect the iron – but the shadows still seemed sullen and sluggish. In England, Mercy's magic had leapt to her command whenever she pleased; here, surrounded by iron, it seemed to resent being called up at all.

Slowly, Mercy's shadows curled around the silver locket, settling into its engravings. The locket took on a tarnished look, much like the trees which surrounded them.

Perhaps it was just her imagination, but Abigail thought that Hugh's form strengthened a little bit. Certainly, he stood somewhat straighter.

Mercy let out a long, wavering breath. Abigail caught her just before she sagged forward. The scent of lilies was suddenly overwhelming – fresh and crisp and sweet, like flowers after a spring rain.

It was easier to think of Mercy as a strange and vexing presence when she was standing further away, talking in contrary tones. But as Mercy leaned her forehead wearily against Abigail's shoulder, it was suddenly difficult to ignore how very soft and fragile she could be. Much of Mercy's strength, Abigail realised, was an illusion conjured up by her stubbornness and confidence – and much of *that* was due to her belief that her inside magic would always save her.

Right now, Mercy was trembling in Abigail's arms, pained and uncertain. And though Abigail still didn't *trust* Mercy, she couldn't help an overwhelming wash of sympathy for her. For the first time in quite a while, it seemed, Mercy was entirely dependent on someone else to help her.

Though she was tired and hurt, Mercy forced some steel back into her spine and handed the locket carefully back to Abigail.

"I think that should help," Mercy said softly. "I did my best."

Abigail kept the other woman balanced against her shoulder as she looped the locket back around her neck. Something about it *did* feel subtly different – stronger, she hoped.

"I'll be off then," Hugh said – but Mercy shook her head and staggered up to her feet.

"Maybe Abigail can't give you a hug," Mercy said, "but I can give you one *for* her." A hint of that previous stubbornness had leaked back into her voice.

Hugh smiled again with a hint of relief. He launched himself at Mercy, throwing his arms around her, and Abigail remembered that it had been ages and ages since he'd been able to hug *anyone*.

Mercy floundered on her feet just a little bit, but she closed her arms around Hugh, holding him fiercely.

Abigail's heart twisted in her chest as she watched them both. So many odd, bittersweet emotions tangled up within her that she wasn't entirely sure of them all. That old sadness for Hugh had returned, several times over, but she was also deeply proud of him, and scared for him, and still pleased that *someone* could hug him right now even if she couldn't.

There was another emotion there, however, which had nothing to do with Hugh and everything to do with Mercy. However much Mercy seemed to disagree with Hugh's decision to stay in England, she clearly *cared* about his happiness. Only someone who had spent time worrying over how Hugh felt would ever go out of their way to offer him comfort. Abigail knew, moreover, that Mercy was not feeling well at all, and that it cost her something to keep her feet as Hugh held onto her.

Abigail did not want to like Mercy. It was a *terrible* idea to like her, in fact. But Abigail was beginning to suspect that she *did* like Mercy in spite of that. Abigail's heart warmed a bit as she considered the soft smile on Mercy's face. It was a lovely smile, Abigail thought – not because *Mercy* was lovely, but because the smile made her beautiful sentiments apparent.

Slowly, Mercy disentangled herself from Hugh. "Well," she managed, "*now* you can leave, I suppose." She smiled again, and Abigail's heart flickered in her chest at the sight. "Thank you for helping, Hugh. I know it's mostly for Abigail, but I still appreciate it."

Hugh cast his gaze to the ground, suddenly bashful. "It's a *little* bit for you too," he assured Mercy. "I wouldn't just leave you trapped here, even if you were the worst villain in the world." He looked past her towards Abigail. "You both take care," he said. "Don't let the sluagh get you or nothin'."

Mercy frowned at this comment, but said nothing.

Abigail shook her head. "I've still got Mr Hayes with me," she said. "Worry about yourself."

Hugh grinned at the reminder. He gave a gentlemanly sort of bow to them both.

And then he turned around to walk through the Greenhouse window, back into England.

Chapter Six

It was always terrible trying to tell time in faerie. Even simple things felt wavery and dreamlike. Night and day didn't seem to follow the usual rules, and seconds seemed to wander past rather than tick by.

Mercy settled next to Abigail against a tree, looking out over the rest of the forest. Now that Hugh was gone, the tarnished grove felt even less substantial than before – but Mercy's hands were still painfully red in a very real way.

"I wish I had somethin' for your hands," Abigail sighed. "I've only got magician's things in here, though."

Mercy leaned against Abigail. "It's all right," she mumbled distractedly. "They'll heal. Anyway, it's a lovely view, isn't it? I wouldn't mind this at all if it weren't for the iron."

Abigail was still sick with worry for Hugh – but she considered the world around them, trying to see it through Mercy's eyes. Everywhere she looked, the trees glimmered silver beneath an invisible moon, casting gentle shadows across the forest floor. Most mortals would have found the sight enchanting, Abigail thought. And for a moment, at least, she found it enchanting too.

But the moment passed as Abigail remembered their situation and her worries about the woman sitting next to her.

"I'm sure you've been all around faerie," Abigail said. "You've got a piece of it in you too. An' it's a piece of Longshadow, isn't it?"

Mercy said nothing. But her silence spoke for her.

"I thought so," Abigail murmured. She reached down to pick up one of the silver leaves on the ground next to her. "You knew the closest path to Longshadow from London – you didn't need an oleander to tell you where to look. You're all wrapped up in this too, somehow." Abigail tossed the leaf aside with a sigh. "What I can't figure out is why you were in Lucy's room at all. If you're workin' with the sluagh, then wouldn't you already know what happened to her an' why?"

Mercy pulled her knees up to her chest, resting her chin upon them. "I heard that the sluagh were bein' blamed for killin' Lucy an' those other girls," she said glumly, "but it just didn't sound right to me. Sluagh aren't normally like that."

Abigail glanced sideways at Mercy. There was real consternation on her face – as though her entire world had stopped making sense. "But sluagh *do* kill people," Abigail said. "They come in through the western window at night, an' the people inside are dead by morning."

Mercy shook her head, agitated. "Sluagh don't—" She paused, wincing, and changed what she was about to say. "Sluagh *do* kill people," she admitted. "But they only do it when someone's already dyin' an' sufferin' badly for no reason. They never kill anyone with a whole life ahead of 'em. They *wouldn't*."

Abigail frowned. "I don't understand," she said slowly. "Are you sayin' sluagh only show up when someone's *already* dyin'? But why? Just to speed things up?"

Mercy sighed. "Sluagh aren't supposed to be killers," she said. "They're shepherds. They're supposed to help ghosts to the Other Side. They can sense the dead an' dyin', so they show up when someone's about to need their help."

Abigail stared at Mercy.

It could have been a lie, of course – but everything Mercy said seemed perfectly consistent with the way she'd been behaving and the way that her magic worked. It was no wonder that Mercy hadn't liked Hugh's locket: the piece of Longshadow inside of her was meant to send ghosts on instead of keeping them longer.

"You've helped ghosts over to the Other Side too," Abigail said slowly, "haven't you?"

Mercy had spoken reluctantly so far – but at this, her manner softened, and she smiled wistfully. "Most of 'em are scared of what comes next, even if they don't realise it," she said. "They just want someone to talk to 'em an' hold their hand an' walk with 'em."

Abigail knit her brow, putting new thoughts together. "You really walk ghosts all the way through faerie to the Other Side?" she asked. "Through Longshadow, I guess?" Abigail paused and narrowed her eyes. "If I were a sluagh in London, for instance, I'd probably take a ghost right down this path on the way there."

Mercy blinked. "Well . . . yes," she said. "I was almost sure that Lucy an' the sluagh would've passed this way – an' accordin' to the other faeries, I was right."

"But here we are," Abigail said, "an' there's only a bunch of iron, an' no sluagh, an' no ghost." She looked again at the horseshoes around them. "I thought at first that my father might have set a trap for the next sluagh that came through here – but he can't touch iron any more'n I can. If this trap was his, he would've used a circle like the one he had at the House. An' obviously, the sluagh can't touch iron either, so *they* can't have left the horseshoes here."

"Your father?" Mercy interrupted. "Is he a ward of faerie too?"

"What's a *ward* of faerie?" Abigail asked, puzzled.

Mercy shrugged. "That's what you are," she said. "Hollowvale liked somethin' about you, so it decided to foster you."

Abigail blinked slowly. "Er," she said. "So you're sayin' . . . my Other Mum's *realm* is my guardian, an' not her?"

Mercy managed a faint smile at that. "Well, why not both?" she said. "I guess you've got more'n one guardian in that case."

Abigail turned the idea over in her head. Part of her didn't much like it; Hollowvale's old lord had been cruel and capricious, and he had caused an awful lot of suffering. Hollowvale had helped him do all of those terrible things, by definition – for lords in faerie were owned by their land rather than the other way around.

But Hollowvale had also accepted Abigail's Other Mum as its new lady – with great eagerness, it seemed, given the breadth of her power. Ever since, the faerie realm had helped to nurture and protect the other dead children there. Perhaps, Abigail thought, there was even a sort of affection involved.

"I wonder if faerie realms can change," Abigail murmured.

Mercy tilted her head. "What d'you mean?" she asked.

Abigail crossed her arms thoughtfully. "Lord Hollowvale believed he was bein' virtuous when he stole all of those children," she said. "He was really awful, mind you, an' I'm glad that he's dead. But I can't help but think my Other Mum must've given Hollowvale a tongue-lashing after she took over. Maybe she's teachin' it how to really care about people."

"Oh," Mercy said, in a bewildered tone. "I didn't know that was possible."

"Maybe it isn't," Abigail said. "I could be wrong." She *hoped* she wasn't wrong. The idea that Hollowvale might have fostered her as a sort of apology seemed better than the idea that it had simply taken one more thing that it wanted, without thought as to how it would affect anyone else.

Abigail tucked the thought away for now, and resolved to ask her Other Mum about it later.

"But that's neither here nor there," Abigail said belatedly. "Whoever set up this trap knew about the path the sluagh take back to Longshadow, an' they aren't a faerie or a ward of faerie. I'm afraid that leaves the obvious."

Mercy watched her warily. "The obvious?" she asked.

"I think we're dealin' with a mortal magician," Abigail said grimly. "Maybe it's just another magician tryin' to help stop the sluagh . . . but maybe not."

Even as Abigail said this, she realised that Mercy had suddenly stopped listening. Mercy's dark eyes were fixed beyond Abigail's shoulder, upon something off between the trees.

"Mercy?" Abigail asked cautiously.

"Do you know what Miss Lucy Kendall looks like?" Mercy asked quietly.

Abigail knit her brow. "I do," she said. "Lucy was around my height – blonde, and very pretty."

Mercy stumbled to her feet. "Miss Kendall!" she yelled. "We're over here! We came to find you, but you've got to come to us!"

Abigail widened her eyes, scrambling up after Mercy. "She's here?" she asked. "Where?"

Mercy shushed Abigail with a wave of her hand. "You can't see or hear her," she said. "She's in distress. She's fallin' apart some without anything to anchor her here."

Abigail looked around, though she knew that it was fruitless. Even eyebright tea wouldn't reveal a ghost to her. Normally, Hugh let her know when there was one nearby. "You can tell Lucy I'm here," Abigail said. "Though . . . that might just make her run away. She's never liked me much."

Mercy shrugged. "Tell her yourself," she said. "Maybe you can't hear Lucy, but she can hear *you*. Try an' convince her to come over to us."

Abigail winced. She hadn't enjoyed talking to Lucy when they'd both been alive – she was even less enthused about the idea of having a one-sided conversation with Lucy's ghost. But it only made sense that Abigail should *try*, since Lucy didn't know very much about Mercy.

Abigail took a deep breath and tried to readjust her accent to something slightly more upper-class. "Lucy!" she called out reluctantly. "It's Abigail! I can't see you, but I know you're here. You're in faerie right now, but I can help you get back home."

Mercy pursed her lips disapprovingly, but said nothing. She probably thought they ought to be convincing Lucy to move on instead of going home. But Abigail knew that the promise of home would likely mean more to Lucy than just a familiar, unpleasant face.

A few moments later, Mercy shifted on her feet. "She's coming this way," she said. "She *does* look the way you described." Mercy winced and held up her hands. "Oh, please slow down," she said quickly to the empty air in front of them. "Abigail can't hear you, so I've got to tell her everything."

Abigail was used to repeating Hugh's words to others; it was very strange, suddenly, to be stuck on the other side of that divide. She forced herself to wait patiently as Mercy turned back towards her to relate Lucy's words.

"Lucy says she's been wanderin' around here for a while," Mercy said. "We're the first people she's seen since she got lost." She paused and sighed. "Lucy says we're to take her home *immediately*."

Abigail suspected that Lucy had not phrased the matter even *that* politely, based on Mercy's expression. She took a deep breath.

"We're waiting on my mum," Abigail said, with carefully rounded vowels. "If you stay with us for a while, she'll come and take us back to England. In the meantime, it would be a great help if you could tell us everything you remember about how you got here."

Mercy frowned. "Repeatin' yourself isn't goin' to help," she advised the air. "We can't leave until Abigail's mum shows up. An' might I add, you're rather pert for someone who needs our help. Does that normally work for you?"

"Let me guess," Abigail said dryly. "She doesn't like your accent. Or your hair. Or your frock. Or . . . anything about you."

Mercy rolled her eyes. "Lucy thinks I'm your maid," she said. "She doesn't like my attitude."

Abigail couldn't help a small snort. "You'd make a terrible maid," she told Mercy. "I thought you were a laundress at first, but I can't imagine you washing someone else's clothing now. Maybe you wash clothing for the sluagh? But, oh . . . I imagine they mostly wear feathers."

Mercy shrugged. "I can let you talk to Abigail," she told the air, "but she already told you the same thing." She glanced at Abigail. "Do you mind if I put a spell on you?" Mercy asked. "It might speed things up some."

Abigail shot Mercy a surprised look. "You can help me see Lucy?" she asked. "Well – yes, if you don't mind. I'd appreciate it."

Mercy nodded. "You'll have to take off your gloves," she said.

Abigail didn't require much convincing on that score – if it hadn't been for her formal visit to Lady Pinckney's earlier, she would never have worn a gown into faerie at all. She peeled her gloves carefully from her hands, tucking them into her reticule just next to Mr Hayes. The straw doll wiggled emphatically as Abigail opened the bag, urgently trying to worm his way free, but Abigail closed the reticule upon him again just in time.

Mercy reached one reddened hand out to take Abigail's, threading their fingers together. Her skin was still cool and pleasant in spite of the burns – and again, Abigail found herself thinking about how long and fine Mercy's fingers were. There shouldn't have been anything improper about touching another woman's hand – but somehow, Abigail was sure that if she'd had a chaperone nearby, she would have been scolded for touching *Mercy's* hand.

Magic tingled lightly across Abigail's skin. Even as she watched, the shadows of the forest parted like a curtain. Colour crept across her vision, replacing the ambient moonlight with splashes of vibrant twilight. The trees glimmered with blues and pinks and yellows, all mixed together like a painter's canvas.

Caught between those twilight colours was a familiar woman around Abigail's age. Lucy Kendall was an inch or so taller than Abigail, with fine cheekbones and light blue eyes; her blonde hair was loose around her shoulders, nearly midway down her back. The thin white nightgown that she wore was probably not very helpful against the evening air.

Every once in a while, Lucy's form wavered with the twilight, as though she were a part of it – but she always stabilised stubbornly, clinging to solidity. Abigail wondered if this was what Mercy meant when she talked about Hugh being stuck *in between*. It was strange, seeing visual proof of the idea.

"I want to go home," Lucy informed Abigail in a curt, ladylike voice. "Either that, or else you must bring me to Lord Longshadow immediately." Lucy said both of these things as though they were orders she expected to be followed.

Abigail frowned at the second statement. "Why do you want to see Lord Longshadow?" she asked.

Lucy straightened haughtily. "I am not supposed to be dead," she sniffed. "The gentleman all in black – I believe his name was Lightless – he said that I could make my case to Lord Longshadow, and that he might bring me back to life."

Abigail raised both eyebrows at this. She was about to comment that Lord Longshadow probably would *not* bring Lucy back to life – but Mercy cut in before she could make the observation.

"Lightless?" Mercy asked Lucy. "Are you sure that was his name? I suppose he had an old, ratty coat, an' stars all in his eyes?"

Lucy glanced over at Mercy sharply. "That is correct," she said. "Do you know where it is that he's gone? Lightless said that he would hold my hand the entire way and not let go – but as soon as we entered the forest, he *did* let me go, and I suddenly felt sick and faint. I don't remember much after that."

Abigail was surprised to hear a note of concern in Lucy's voice as she talked about Lightless. Lucy had rarely evinced even a hint of worry for someone other than herself or her family while in Abigail's presence. But perhaps, Abigail thought, the fear of being left alone had knocked something loose within her, if only for a moment.

"I don't know where Lightless went," Mercy said grimly, "but I know he wouldn't leave you alone on purpose. Lightless is a sluagh – he was holdin' your hand so he could anchor you while you walked through faerie. You're still attached to your home, an' you're too far away from it to hold together without help." She paused. "The iron might've startled him. But if the iron was here when *he* was here . . . then why isn't Lightless stuck in this trap with us?"

"I don't know about any of that," Lucy said stubbornly. "What I *do* know is that I am not supposed to be dead. I was only feeling a bit ill when I went to sleep. I'm far too young to have simply . . . died! And I was going to find a husband this year. I had all manner of prospects."

Abigail held up a hand. "Wait," she said. "You were ill *before* you went to sleep? Before you ever saw the man with the stars in his eyes?"

Lucy rolled her eyes. "I was only a little bit dizzy," she said. "It was hardly a mortal illness."

Abigail glanced sideways at Mercy. More and more, she was beginning to suspect that Mercy was correct, and that the sluagh had *not* killed Lucy at all.

"I thought sluagh looked like ravens," Abigail said to Mercy.

"Sluagh *sometimes* look like ravens," Mercy corrected Abigail. "Sluagh are shapeshifters. Ghosts who make it to the Other Side leave sluagh with their smile or their laugh or their curtsy as a kind of thank you. The sluagh collect it all up an' make new faces for 'emselves."

"Well, whoever gave Lightless his smile had a very *handsome* smile," Lucy said distractedly. "I am very upset with him for leaving me here, but perhaps he will come back and apologise." Her form wavered again in the twilight, and she caught herself against a nearby tree. "Oh, drat. I am feeling faint again."

Mercy reached out her other hand to take Lucy's. As she did, the wavering stopped abruptly, and Lucy straightened with a sharp breath.

"You really can't remember what happened to Lightless?" Mercy asked Lucy seriously. "I suppose everything got jumbled up when you lost his hand."

Lucy glanced down at the hand in hers with a slight curl of her lip. "Your hands are dirty," she said sullenly.

"Her hands are *not* dirty," Abigail said, with a hint of testiness. "She's *hurt* her hands, an' she's still tryin' to help you for some reason." Abigail realised belatedly that her normal accent had slipped out, and she felt her cheeks colour with embarrassment.

Lucy jerked her hand away from Mercy. Her outline had strengthened significantly – but it wavered anew at the edges, and she sank to her knees. "This is all very serious," Lucy snapped at Abigail, as she leaned her shoulder against the tree. "I have no intention of trusting my life to either of you tatty urchins. If you intend to help me at all, then you should go and get your father, Abigail. I dare say the Lord Sorcier will have an interest in this – if he ever *actually* performs his duties, that is."

Anger flashed through Abigail's body. "My father's busy tryin' to stop *other* people from dyin'," she said. "Anyway, I'm startin' to think no one ought to help you at all. Maybe when Mum gets here, I'll give you what you want an' leave you wanderin' around faerie all alone."

Lucy balled her hands into fists at her sides. "I wish you *would* go away," she said. "At least it was quiet before you got here."

Mercy let out a soft hiss of pain – and Abigail realised that she had tightened her fingers on Mercy's burned skin. She released Mercy's hand quickly with an apologetic look; as she did, twilight flashed back into moonlight, and Lucy's form disappeared abruptly.

"I'm sorry," Abigail told Mercy miserably. "I didn't mean to hurt you."

Mercy shook her head, cradling her hand to her chest. "It's all right," she said. "I don't think we were gettin' anywhere, anyway." She glanced back towards the base of the tree just next to them. "Have it your way," she told the air there. "We'll be here when you want to talk. I'm sure it'll be an awful boring wait, otherwise."

Abigail helped Mercy back towards another tree, and she settled down next to her once again.

Chapter Seven

"Lucy's wanderin' again," Mercy said to Abigail, sometime later. "She keeps makin' sure we're still here, though."

Abigail leaned her head back into the tree, still stewing in anger. "You don't seem upset," she said. "Lucy said some awful things to you too."

Mercy settled her head idly onto Abigail's shoulder. "It's hard to be upset with a dead person," she said. "Anyway, she'll come around. They always do eventually."

Abigail tilted her head to look at Mercy. "You've helped a *lot* of ghosts, haven't you?" she asked.

Mercy nodded lightly. "They're always upset," she said. "People don't tend to leave ghosts behind unless they died too suddenly, or with too much left to do." She paused. "Powerful people take the longest to figure it all out. They're so used to gettin' their way in life, they just don't know what to do once no one is listenin' to 'em any more."

Abigail ruminated on this for a moment. "But they do come around?" she asked. "Always?"

"Mm . . . *most* always," Mercy said. "You can't be too nice to 'em too quickly, though. I figured that out early on. You can't get through to someone as long as they still think they're powerful. When you talk back some an' let 'em go off an' flounder, they start to realise they're not in charge any more. Once it really sinks in, you can afford to be a little nice."

Abigail managed a small smile at this. "I see," she said. "I was wonderin' why you were actin' so patient about it."

Mercy eyed Abigail consideringly. "Lucy said your father's the Lord Sorcier," she observed. "That's true, then?"

Abigail's smile vanished, and she looked away. "That's right," she said. "I won't tell you anything about his business, though."

Mercy heaved a sigh. "I heard he's awful," she said. "You're far too nice to be his daughter."

Abigail blinked. "*Awful?*" she repeated incredulously. "He's wonderful! I couldn't ask for a better father."

Mercy raised her eyebrows. "Well, he's just a bully, isn't he?" she said. "Always tellin' faeries what to do, an' threatenin' 'em if they don't let him have his way. I heard he killed *two* lords of faerie."

Abigail crossed her arms over her chest. "Oh, he tells faeries what to do," she said. "Mostly when they've been hurtin' people. Maybe the sluagh have been nice to *you*, but faeries meddle with people in England all the time, an' they haven't got a care how those people feel about bein' meddled with." She narrowed her eyes at Mercy. "Lord Hollowvale bought me from a workhouse master like I was a slave, an' he stole me away to faerie. He worked me all day, without letting me sleep. Said he was doin' me a *favour*, an' he wouldn't hear otherwise."

Mercy winced. "Well . . . maybe Lord Hollowvale deserved it, then," she allowed.

"Not that *Dad* killed Lord Hollowvale," Abigail added. "It was Mum that stabbed him with her scissors." She smiled grimly. "I wish *I* could carry some iron scissors, but they'd just make me sick."

Mercy *did* seem surprised by that revelation, though she tucked it away very quickly. She studied Abigail's face carefully. "Lord Longshadow isn't Lord Hollowvale, though," Mercy said. "I can tell that you think they're alike, but they're not. Faeries aren't all the same."

Abigail pursed her lips. "They *are* the same in some ways," she said. "They're all so powerful, they can do almost whatever they want. An' even when they *want* to be good to people, they just don't know how. If they do get it right, it's nearly by accident." She gestured generally towards the other tree where Lucy had once been. "Faeries are like Lucy. You'll never convince 'em they're wrong about anything most days. Dad just knows you can't be too nice to 'em too quickly, exactly like you said."

Mercy opened her mouth to respond . . . but she paused with a sudden expression of consternation. Abigail could tell that she was thinking very hard about the comparison.

"You're like that sometimes, too," Abigail told her. "The sluagh told you that ghosts ought to move on, an' you decided to *make* ghosts move on. You never even considered otherwise, until you were in trouble an' you needed help from a ghost."

Mercy's eyes flashed with irritation. "I *care* what happens to ghosts," she said. "There's nothin' but pain for 'em when they stick around past their time. They all figure that out eventually, you know."

Abigail shook her head. "Carin' what happens to someone doesn't make it all right to make decisions for 'em," she said. "Sometimes we choose our pain because it's for somethin' we believe in. If no one ever chose pain, then it'd be awful hard to get anything done, wouldn't it?"

Mercy made an expression like she'd tasted something sour on her tongue. "It's natural for ghosts to move on," she said stubbornly.

Abigail snorted. "Humans *exist* to be unnatural," she said. "Nature's cruel an' unfair, an' we decided to fix it. That's why we've got clothes an' houses an' medicine. What's natural isn't always good. An' as for me . . . I think I like what's good an' fair an' kind better'n what's *natural*."

Mercy pressed her lips together. "An' what if there's consequences to that?" she asked. "Do *you* know what happens if a ghost stays too long?"

"I don't," Abigail said. "I'd be willin' to change my mind if I knew it was bad – but no one's told me anything like that just yet." She met Mercy's eyes. "Maybe the sluagh know somethin' the rest of us don't. But if that's the case, they'll have to say it to my face."

Mercy let out a breath. There was frustration there, and a small hint of confusion. But even as she paused to search for an adequate response, a voice spoke from behind them.

"Is that a horseshoe?"

Lady Theodora Wilder stood just in front of the window that led back into the Greenhouse. Dora wore a hastily donned pelisse and half-boots; her rusted red hair was barely pinned, and her cheeks were flushed with exertion. She held a small pocket mirror in one hand.

Hugh stumbled in just after Dora. He looked awfully pale and ragged at the edges; his form wavered urgently, as though he was barely holding together. But just as he set foot in faerie, the silver locket against Abigail's chest chilled with recognition, and Hugh's image became steadier.

"Mum!" Abigail managed. "You made it!"

Dora blinked mildly. "Of course I did," she said. "You would never have let Hugh out of your sight unless it was a very serious situation."

Hugh grinned wearily. "You should've seen her!" he said. "We got to the gate into the gardens, an' there was no one there, an' Mum just climbed right over it!"

Abigail smiled in relief. "I'm glad you're all right, Hugh," she said. "I'll find a way to make it up to you, I promise."

Dora nudged at the horseshoe on the ground with the toe of her boot. "Should I move this?" she asked. "It seems rather in the way."

"Please do," Abigail said. "Feels like we've been stuck in this trap for ages."

Dora sat herself down in the dirt, examining the horseshoe. "It's been staked here," she said, "but the ground is soft. I should be able to pry it free." She rolled up her sleeves and reached for a short, stubby stick, nudging it beneath the edge of the iron. "You have a friend with you," Dora observed absently, as she worked at the horseshoe. "I don't believe that we have met before."

Abigail glanced at Mercy, still weary and red-handed where she leaned against the tree. "Mercy, this is Mum," she said. "Mum, this is—"

"Oh, I didn't mean for you to introduce me," Dora interrupted. "You might as well wait until we join your father. The garden gate is made of iron, obviously, and he could not climb it as I did."

Abigail groaned. "Dad came with you?" she asked.

Dora glanced up at her. "Well, naturally he came with me," she said reasonably. "We thought you were in danger. He is very agitated. It's really best if we don't leave him for long."

Mercy eyed Dora sceptically. "*You* killed a lord of faerie?" she asked.

Dora leaned one last time upon the stick, popping the horseshoe neatly from the ground. She pushed up to her feet, dusting the dirt from her pelisse. "I did," said Dora. "How curious of you to bring it up." She leaned down to retrieve the horseshoe, removing it from their path. As she did, a faint tension eased from Abigail's spine, and she sighed in relief.

"Yes, hush!" Mercy muttered – and Abigail saw that she had turned her attention behind them to a particular spot of empty air. "We're not leavin' you here, no matter how bad your manners are."

Hugh glanced sharply past Mercy. "Oh," he said. "You *did* find Lucy." He made a sour face. "Do we *have* to bring her with us?"

"We have to bring her with us, Hugh," Abigail said with a sigh. "It's not right to leave her. An' besides which, we might want to ask her more questions."

Dora, meanwhile, had stepped aside to inspect another of the horseshoes which had been nailed to a tree. Her lips pursed with interest. "These horseshoes are quite loose as well," she said. "I think someone has pried them down and put them back up a few times now. Should I try to remove them?"

"I don't think so," Abigail said. "We really want to get back to Kensington Gardens before the sun comes up an' the path closes. At least any other faeries who wander in here will be able to go back the way they came now." She pushed to her feet and reached down to help Mercy up gingerly by the arm.

"Hold my hand," Mercy murmured to the ghost next to them. "You look as though you need it."

Abigail couldn't see Lucy any more – but there was a hint of sympathy in Mercy's voice now, and she had to assume that Lucy had finally taken on a more conciliatory tone.

They stepped back through the window into the darkened Greenhouse. Suddenly, there was a real moon in the sky once more, shining through the glass. Part of Abigail relaxed at being once more in England, though another part of her missed the strange effervescence of faerie.

They passed very few flowered faeries on their way back to the gate – only a sleepy pair of hollyhocks and some foxgloves remained, chatting amiably with one another as they wound their way back to a faerie path. One of the foxgloves nodded and smiled at Abigail; she realised then that she was still holding onto Mercy's arm and was therefore worthy of acknowledgement.

A tall, agitated figure paced just in front of the iron gate. Lord Elias Wilder had not grown any less dishevelled since the last time Abigail had seen him on the floor of the House's ballroom; his hair was still an awful mess, and his cravat was now nowhere to be seen. Abigail felt a brief pang of guilt, knowing that he and Dora had probably rushed out to her aid without much pause.

Elias fixed his eyes upon them as soon as they came into view. He took one step closer to the gate before flinching at the sensation of nearby iron. "Are you all right, Abigail?" he asked. "What on earth is going on?"

Abigail winced. "I'm fine," she said. "Mercy's hands are burned, though. The rest is an awful long story." She eyed the gate in front of them. "I suppose Mum could climb the gate again, but I won't be able to touch it."

Elias grimaced. "I roused someone to fetch the key," he said. "I have told them there was faerie business here, and that is all that anyone ever wants to know." He turned his golden eyes upon Mercy, inspecting her keenly. "I don't believe that we have any ladies named Mercy in any of the orphanages," he said doubtfully.

Abigail shook her head. "I met Mercy just today; she's got a piece of Longshadow in her, the same way I've got a piece of Hollowvale in me. I think you'll want to hear some of what she has to say." Abigail turned to Mercy. "This is my father, Lord Elias Wilder. You can see for yourself: he's very kind, an' not terrible at all."

The mention of Longshadow had raised a flicker of suspicion in Elias's eyes. But he blinked at Abigail's next words. "Terrible?" he repeated. "Well, I like to believe that I am *sometimes* terrible." The statement was oddly defensive, and Abigail knew that Elias was feeling sheepish about his current, not-very-terrifying state.

"You are not generally terrible to young women with injured hands," Dora said patiently, "which is all that anyone here needs to know for now." Dora attempted a reassuring smile at Mercy, though the expression was as always slightly flat.

Mercy, for her part, was now studying Elias with great

wariness. Abigail's and Dora's words had clearly done little, if anything, to reassure her. "I'm no danger to anyone you care about right now, Lord Sorcier," Mercy said carefully. "I know you don't get on with Longshadow, but I'm just tryin' to figure out what's goin' on."

Elias frowned at Mercy through the iron gate. "I do not, as a rule, bully young working women," he said. "If you were a noblewoman or a faerie, of course, it might be a different matter. But as long as you are uninvolved in pesky things like murder, I am sure that we can find some common ground."

This did not entirely mollify Mercy's unease – but she nodded reluctantly nevertheless.

Eventually, one of the groundskeepers returned to open the garden gate. By then, the sun had just started to peek above the horizon. The groundskeeper gave their small group quite the strange look – but all he asked Elias was whether the gardens were safe again, and faerie-free. Elias assured him that they were, and this seemed to bring the matter to an abrupt end.

The walk from Kensington Gardens to the House was short enough that they could make it without a carriage. It was a weary trek, nevertheless, as they had all been awake the entire evening.

The dining room was still empty except for a single maid, who sighed at their bedraggled state. Elias took the woman aside briefly, and she soon disappeared down the stairs.

"I expect that we will require tea for this conversation," Elias said ruefully.

Abigail stifled a yawn. She was not terribly keen on admitting everything to her father – but there seemed to be little getting around the matter, if she was going to tell him anything useful about the dead girls. First, however, she glanced at Mercy.

"Will Lucy be all right for a bit?" Abigail asked her tiredly. "It can't be nice havin' to hold her hand all this time, what with your hands like that."

"Lucy should be fine now that we're back in England," Mercy mumbled. "I've held her hand till now because she's scared. But we're close enough to her home that she shouldn't fall apart."

Abigail nodded. The maid soon returned with a tray of tea and a cool bowl of water, which she placed in front of Mercy. Mercy submerged her hands with a grateful sigh of relief as Abigail took a few long sips of her tea and started her story.

Elias was predictably displeased to hear that Abigail had lied to him so directly about returning to Hollowvale. But he did not interrupt her as she explained her visit to Lady Pinckney, her meeting with Mercy and her investigation at Kensington Gardens.

"All of this is just to say," Abigail finished slowly, "I'm startin' to think Lord Longshadow an' the sluagh *aren't* the ones killin' the girls. Lucy said that she was already feelin' ill when she went to bed, an' I don't imagine you *or* the sluagh had anything to do with those horseshoes."

Elias frowned darkly. "I do not know where those horseshoes came from," he said. "I am inclined to agree with the rest. I thought I caught a hint of black magic when I investigated Miss Kendall's bedroom, but a priest had already been there and performed his blessings, which made it difficult to tell."

Abigail shifted uncomfortably in her chair. "Then shouldn't you destroy those bans on Lord Longshadow?" she asked. "If he's not responsible for all of this, then aren't they just tyin' up your magic?"

Elias looked away, rather than responding . . . and Abigail narrowed her eyes.

"You're still keepin' somethin' from me," Abigail said. "An' Hugh is keepin' somethin' from me too, now that I think about it." She turned her gaze upon Hugh, who had settled himself on Mercy's other side, presumably opposite to Lucy. "You were worried about goin' too close to Longshadow in particular, Hugh. I think *someone* ought to tell me the truth at this point."

Hugh looked down at his hands on the table. "When you first gave me the locket," he said, "Other Mum told me I should be careful not to wander near to Longshadow. I wasn't keepin' it from you on purpose, Abby. It just never came up before now."

Abigail scowled at her father and crossed her arms over her chest.

Elias sighed heavily. "I have a history with Lord Longshadow," he said. He glanced at Mercy as he spoke, and Abigail had the feeling he was reluctant to discuss the matter in front of her. But he forced himself to continue nevertheless. "I was raised in faerie by Lord Swiftburn. As I grew older, however, Lord Swiftburn turned upon me and tried to kill me. At the time, I didn't understand why . . . but since seeing the way that Hollowvale has treated you, Abigail, I think it must be that Swiftburn – the realm – took a liking to me, and Lord Swiftburn considered it an insult."

Elias ruminated over his tea rather than drinking it. "I was forced to kill Lord Swiftburn. I still suspect that I only managed to do so because the realm was upset with him. I knew that Swiftburn wanted me to take my father's place, but I was . . . grief-stricken, in a way. I had convinced myself that I loved him, though he was terribly cruel. I only wanted to leave, to find somewhere kinder than faerie." Elias leaned back tiredly into his chair. "The other faeries were afraid of me. But Lord Longshadow offered to lead me back to England. He said that I belonged in England. He was wrong, of course. But then, I have come to understand that I don't quite belong anywhere."

Abigail knit her brow. "But none of that seems too terrible," she said slowly. "Why would you fight with Lord Longshadow if he helped you?"

Mercy was now looking every bit as uncomfortable as Elias, and Abigail began to suspect that she also knew the answer to this question.

"Lord Longshadow came to visit me again not long after

Lord Hollowvale's death," Elias said. "He told me that I owed him a debt, and that he had come to collect it." He tightened his jaw. "Lord Longshadow demanded that I give him the children who had died in Hollowvale so that he could send them on to the Other Side. Sending ghosts on is something which he exists to do, for whatever inhuman purpose, and I could not placate him with either sentiment or reason. Naturally, I refused to give him the children. But he has not let the matter rest – not even for a moment. Lady Hollowvale must therefore remain in Hollowvale to watch over the children as much as possible, so that the sluagh do not steal them away."

Hugh looked at Mercy. "You knew about this?" he asked her in a small voice.

Mercy shrank down into her seat, pulling her hands from the bowl of water. "They're . . . the children are past their time," she mumbled. "It's not fair to make 'em linger like that."

Hugh's eyes flashed with anger. "No one's *makin'* us linger," he said. "I never got to have parents before I died, you know. Other Mum's the first mum I ever got, an' I *love* her. An' I love Mum an' Dad an' Abby, too. What's not *fair* is me never gettin' a family until I can't really have 'em. But you an' your sluagh don't think about that part, do you, cos you don't think it matters."

Mercy pressed her lips together. Hugh's anger had struck her tangibly, and Abigail could tell that she was miserable over it.

Elias couldn't hear Hugh's response. At first, he fixed Mercy with a dark expression – but guilt and weariness overtook him, and he looked away again. "I *did* summon Lord Longshadow to ask about the dying girls," Elias admitted. "But he evaded all my questions, and we argued about the children in Hollowvale yet again. And so I set three bans upon him: that he shall not harm anyone with his magic, nor steal away any unwilling beings, nor speak to his sluagh." This, Elias seemed to add for Mercy's benefit, though Abigail noticed that he did not mention that the bans were tied to Lord Longshadow's feathers. "Now that I have finally bound him, I do not know if I dare to give him back his power."

Elias pressed his hands against his face. "I didn't want to tell any of you because . . . I think I worried, on some level, that Lord Longshadow was right, even if his reasons were inhuman. That I was being selfish, holding all the children back from something better."

Abigail had been terribly angry with her father over his secrets . . . but somehow, as he admitted this aloud, all of her anger melted away into sadness. She'd had such similar thoughts herself more than once. Hadn't she avoided talking to Hugh about moving on for exactly the same reason?

"It's Hugh who needs an apology," Abigail said quietly. "I know you just wanted to protect him. But all of us have had enough of people makin' decisions for our own good. That's how Lord Hollowvale wrecked our lives in the first place."

Elias ran his fingers back through his hair. "God save me from my own arrogance," he muttered. The comparison had shocked a genuine sense of contrition onto his face. "You are right – and I am sorry, Hugh. It is your soul most on the line."

Abigail glanced at Mercy with grim expectation. Mercy looked down at her reddened hands.

"I'm sorry," Mercy said softly. "Really, I am. I know Lord Longshadow meant it for the best, but . . . I guess that doesn't help things much."

Hugh looked between them. The apologies seemed to surprise him more than anything. In fact, he now looked embarrassed. "Well, we . . . we still don't know what's goin' on with the dyin' girls," he mumbled, moving swiftly past the matter. "I'm not sure this changes anything until we're sure the sluagh aren't killin' people." He glanced apologetically at Mercy. "I know you think they *wouldn't*, but we still could use some proof one way or another."

Abigail related his words exactly for once, and Elias frowned.

"You seem to know Lord Longshadow better than I do," he addressed Mercy. "I can't say that I'm willing to take you at your word, but I *would* like to hear your thoughts. What do you think of these deaths?"

Mercy shifted uncomfortably. "I *want* to say no sluagh would ever do this," she said. "Everything I know an' every instinct I've got says they wouldn't. I *want* to find you proof of that. Anyway, Lightless is a kind sluagh, an' I'm more worried for him than I am *about* him. Maybe . . ." She hesitated and looked at Abigail. "I'm not in a state to summon Lightless. But *you* could if I gave you his name."

Abigail blinked. "You mean his *full* name?" she asked. "I didn't realise you knew it. Are you sure you want to trust me with somethin' that important?"

Mercy grimaced. "I don't love the idea," she said, "but I trust you more'n I trust the Lord Sorcier." She glanced at Elias sideways. "No offence intended, Your Lordship."

Elias waved Mercy off. He turned his gaze upon Abigail. "My magic is still weak," he said slowly, "but I can chalk a summoning circle for you if you feel that you are up to the task."

Abigail straightened in her chair. It was the first time her father had ever explicitly invited her to help him with his work. "I'm a bit tired," she said, "but I should be fine for it."

Mercy glanced sideways at the empty chair next to her. "No, you *can't* be there," she told Lucy. "I'm only tellin' *Abigail* his full name. I don't want anyone else in the room when she uses it."

Hugh rolled his eyes. "I'll keep Lucy company for a bit," he said, in a long-suffering tone.

Dora smiled vaguely in Lucy's direction. "I know we can't offer you any tea or biscuits, Lucy," she said, "but I do want you to know that you're welcome here. I promise we will do our best to help you."

Hugh looked between Dora and the empty chair. "Lucy says thank you," he informed Dora helpfully.

Abigail winced. "Mum can't hear you either, Hugh," she reminded him.

Hugh blinked in realisation, and Mercy giggled at him.

"Lucy says thank you," Mercy repeated.

Abigail wondered briefly whether the words were exact. She had never heard the words *thank you* cross Lucy's lips before.

Elias rose tiredly from his seat. "I suppose you are staying to help with this investigation, after all," he murmured to Abigail. "I do not like it. I had hoped . . . well, I had hoped that you would have a more peaceful life than I have had."

Abigail smiled ruefully at him. "You never chose a peaceful life," she said. "What made you think I'd choose any different?"

Elias winced. "I have only myself to blame," he muttered. But he shook his head and rounded the table to pull out Abigail's chair. He took her hands in his, looking down at her seriously. "I am not pleased at the idea of putting you into danger," he said. "But I am proud of you. I can be both at once, I suppose."

Abigail flushed with unexpected pleasure. She had never once questioned that her father loved her. But he had never said before that he was *proud* of her.

She smiled up at him affectionately and squeezed his hands in hers. "Well," she replied cheekily, "I'm proud of you too."

Chapter Eight

It was depressingly late in the morning by the time Elias finished chalking a brand-new summoning circle in the ballroom upstairs. Abigail could hear the children rising for breakfast downstairs, and her stomach gurgled plaintively at her.

"Hush, you," Abigail muttered to herself. "We'll eat when we're done."

"I'll be just outside if anything goes awry," Elias said warily. He glanced suspiciously at Mercy, who wrinkled her nose at him.

"I'm hardly in a state to hurt anyone," Mercy said. She held up her hands, which Dora had gingerly bandaged.

"Even so," Elias murmured, "I *will* be just outside."

"I'll be all right," Abigail told him. "I've still got Mr Hayes if anything goes wrong." She patted the reticule on the floor next to her.

Elias blinked at her. "Who is Mr Hayes?" he asked.

Abigail snorted. "Don't worry about it," she told him. "It's not important." She waved Elias away, and he turned reluctantly to head back through the door, closing it behind him.

Abigail shifted to cross her legs, turning herself to face the front of the circle. She'd left a cup of milk and honey at the centre to help lure in the sluagh. Mercy had scoffed and muttered what a silly superstition *that* was – but all of the spells that Abigail had read required milk and honey, and she was not nearly foolish enough to try making up her own spell.

"Lightless won't bite," Mercy told Abigail. "He's really a proper gentleman. I mean to say, er . . . a proper gentleman gave Lightless his manners, an' he's very fond of 'em."

Abigail nodded, trying to pretend more confidence than she really felt. She'd never actually *tried* to summon anything before. "Are you still willin' to give me his name?" she asked Mercy. "I think I'd have trouble doin' anything without it."

Mercy sat down next to her, looking reluctant. "I did say that I would," she mumbled. "But . . . you promise you won't give his name to anyone else? An' you won't use it to hurt him?"

Promises were a serious matter for both faeries and magicians – magic tended to start misbehaving when one had a history of broken oaths. But Abigail nodded solemnly.

"I promise I won't give his name to anyone else," Abigail repeated. "An' I won't use it to hurt him unless he tries to hurt someone else first."

Mercy took a deep breath. "His full name is Lightless Moon," she said. "He has other names an' titles, but that's the one he prizes most. He'll come for sure if you call it." She paused. "It'd be best to call his name three times, actually."

Abigail turned her attention back to the circle. She reached out for the magic around her, hooking it upon the chalked symbols before her as well as the milk and honey. "Lightless Moon!" she called out firmly. "Lightless Moon, Lightless Moon! I am here with Mercy, an' we require your presence."

The name rang through the air like a clear bell, echoing oddly. The magic in the circle surged, searching for the name's owner . . .

. . . but nothing happened.

The magic of the circle slipped away from Abigail's grip and slowly died.

"Did I do it wrong?" Abigail whispered.

Mercy stared at the circle, ashen-faced. "No," she said. "You did it right. But he . . . he's not answerin'."

Abigail looked at Mercy with concern. A horrible grief had come into her dark eyes.

"Perhaps he's just busy?" Abigail suggested carefully.

Mercy shook her head slowly. "The only way Lightless wouldn't come is if he *can't*," she said. Her voice trembled on the words.

"Let's not think the worst right away," Abigail reassured her. "All we know is that he can't answer. Could other things prevent him from doing that?"

Mercy crossed her arms over her chest with a shiver. "Maybe . . . iron could," she said hopefully. "An' we did just run into a whole trap made of iron." She knit her brow in frustration. "But I wish I knew *anything* else about what's goin' on! I'm sure Lightless could've told us somethin' helpful."

Abigail studied Mercy carefully. "We could try another sluagh," she said slowly, "if you happened to know another name."

Mercy closed her eyes with a groan. "I know a few," she said, "but I only know so many who hang around London." Abigail waited patiently, and Mercy opened her eyes again with a wince. "You can try callin' Black Catastrophe. But you'll have to do the talkin'. She doesn't like me much at all."

Black Catastrophe sounded much less friendly than Lightless Moon, on the basis of her name alone. But Abigail nodded anyway. "We need information," she said. "I'll do my best to be polite. Though . . . perhaps you should move back a bit?"

Mercy clambered to her feet, inching back against the wall. She dragged the shadows weakly around herself, obscuring her form. "Good luck," she muttered bitterly.

Abigail returned her attention to the circle and gathered up her magic once again.

"Black Catastrophe!" she called – a bit more cautiously this time. "Black Catastrophe, Black Catastrophe! I'm in need of your counsel, an' I require you to appear!"

This time, the sluagh's name roiled through the air like a dark, sullen cloud. Abigail's magic hooked upon a distant presence, tugging emphatically.

Shadows quickened within the circle, casting back the morning light. Slowly, they coalesced into a rail-thin woman with indigo skin. Her dark clothing hung from her limbs in feather-like rags; her eyes were entirely black and deeply hateful as they stared out from the circle at Abigail.

"Who gave you my name, little magician?" Black Catastrophe hissed. Her voice was harsh and birdlike.

Abigail hid her flinch and forced herself to meet the sluagh's eyes directly. "It doesn't matter who gave me your name," she said. "But you can call me Abby. Girls are dyin' in London, Black Catastrophe, an' now a sluagh has disappeared. Do you know anything about either one?"

Black Catastrophe curled her lip at Abigail. She paced the circle slowly, testing out its edges. Surely enough, the milk and honey seemed to interest her not at all. "I know of both," the sluagh said. "I am not inclined to tell you much of either."

Abigail watched the sluagh pace. As a magician, Abigail *could* command answers from Black Catastrophe using her name . . . but doing so would probably earn her a lifelong enemy. She wondered briefly if that was how Mercy had irritated Black Catastrophe in the first place.

"I don't intend to hold you here, if it makes you feel any better," Abigail said slowly. "I only want to help. Right now, everyone thinks the sluagh are responsible for these murders, an' so Lord Longshadow has been blamed. If you can clear his name—"

"What do I care about Lord Longshadow?" Black Catastrophe sneered. "He is only the first among sluagh because Longshadow loves him for now. It will tire of him someday . . . and then, perhaps *I* shall be Lord Longshadow."

Abigail pressed her lips together. It hadn't occurred to her, somehow, that certain of the sluagh might not be so loyal to their lord. "Lord Longshadow wouldn't say for certain that the sluagh hadn't killed those girls," she observed. "Perhaps he wouldn't say that because he knew that some of you *might* do."

Black Catastrophe lunged at Abigail – but her hands came up short, scratching against the invisible wall that the circle made between them. Her fingernails were long and pointed, like talons.

"What reason do we have to murder you?" Black Catastrophe hissed. "You all die so soon regardless, little mayfly. I have ferried you mortals for centuries now, and never heard a word of gratitude. I will continue to do so without requiring it."

Abigail raised her eyebrows very slowly.

I wonder why no one's ever thanked you for keeping them company if you're always so pleasant, her mind supplied snidely.

But Abigail stifled this idea and thought instead, *Black Catastrophe wants gratitude. She's just told me as much.*

"I know very well how important your work is, Black Catastrophe," Abigail said. She forced a note of false respect into her tone. "It's why I hate to hear you an' the other sluagh so maligned. It's nothin' but nasty gossip, because people don't appreciate you until it's far too late."

Black Catastrophe tilted her head at Abigail. For a moment, the movement made her look more like a raven. "Humans enjoy casting aspersions on everything they do not understand," the sluagh said. Her raspy voice now held a note of grudging agreement.

Abigail forcibly hid her smile. "I would be awful lucky to have you show up an' collect my soul if I was ever in distress," she told Black Catastrophe. "It must be so much work ferryin' all of London's souls where they're meant to go, too."

Black Catastrophe relaxed slowly in place. "Not every soul requires our help," she said. "But those who die painful or unexpected deaths so often linger on afterwards . . . and London has a way of killing in such a manner."

A brief, awful memory floated back to Abigail's mind: she remembered her mother's last laboured breath as she languished in a dirty workhouse bed.

"At least London's souls have someone to keep 'em company," Abigail said softly.

Black Catastrophe settled back upon her heels. She watched Abigail more coolly now, and with less hostility. "We have no reason to murder you," the sluagh repeated. "You should ask instead why so many sluagh have vanished."

Abigail blinked at her. "*Many* sluagh?" she asked. "I'd only heard of one sluagh goin' missin'."

Black Catastrophe shook her head slowly. "I know of three who have not shown their feathers lately," she said. "Lightless has disappeared – but Silent and Never both disappeared before *him*. I cannot help but wonder if I will be next." Her brow furrowed, and her expression grew dark. "Lord Longshadow may be gone as well."

A chill shivered down Abigail's spine at the suggestion. Elias had bound Lord Longshadow from harming anyone with his magic, among other things. If someone *was* abducting sluagh, then the Lord Sorcier might conveniently have handed the first among sluagh over to them on a silver platter.

Abigail forced the thought aside – but it lingered at the back of her mind, worried and uneasy.

"I found a trap made of iron horseshoes on the path through Kensington Gardens to Longshadow," Abigail told Black Catastrophe. "You should warn the other sluagh to stay away from there." She paused, thinking hard. "I don't suppose you know *who* would want to abduct the sluagh?"

Black Catastrophe frowned. "Any who misunderstand us

might wish to harm us," she said. "Otherwise . . . I have heard that the Lord Sorcier bears a grudge against Lord Longshadow. Perhaps he is to blame."

You really know how to make friends, Dad, Abigail thought ruefully. She decided then that she ought to do the very *opposite* of what her father might do in her place, and make sure that Black Catastrophe remembered her fondly.

"I appreciate your counsel," Abigail told Black Catastrophe. She hesitated. "I hear it's customary to give somethin' to a sluagh when they see you off. I know you haven't ferried me anywhere . . . but if it pleases you, you could take the blue from my eyes. I think it'd look good on you."

Black Catastrophe blinked. The offer seemed to both startle and please her. "It is . . . a very pretty blue," she said. "I do like it."

"It's yours, then," Abigail said. "I hope you enjoy it."

Even as she watched, the shining black of the sluagh's eyes bled away, replaced with a clear sky-blue. Black Catastrophe still had no irises – but her new robin's-egg eyes made her seem somewhat less terrifying.

Oh, Abigail thought, *that is rather pretty*. She was surprised to realise that she didn't miss the idea of her blue eyes, even so. She so rarely got to see them, after all – and she suspected that the gift meant more to Black Catastrophe than the blue would ever mean to Abigail.

"You are very polite, little magician," Black Catastrophe said. She pursed her lips consideringly. "If you are ever dying, you should call my name again. I will see you safely to the Other Side."

Abigail smiled at the sluagh. "I don't ever plan to die," she said. "But if I do, you'll be the very first person I call." She glanced down at the chalk circle. "I should let you go; I'm sure you're awful busy. But you should know I'll do my best to clear your name an' stop whoever's snatchin' sluagh." She reached down – very carefully – to smudge the chalk at her feet. "Here . . . let me get the western window for you."

Abigail walked slowly for the window, opening the shutters more fully. As she did, she heard a rustle of wings behind her.

A large indigo raven rushed past her, bolting through the window to the city beyond.

Abigail watched the sluagh go thoughtfully, putting pieces together in her mind.

"You gave her your *eyes*?" Mercy asked from behind Abigail. She sounded aghast.

Abigail turned back towards her. "Well, no," she said. "I gave her the blue from my eyes. I doubt I'll really miss it, an' it seemed to really please her. I think she just wanted someone to give her a gift at all."

Mercy looked into Abigail's eyes, searching them slowly. "I *liked* the blue in your eyes," she said plaintively.

A flush crept up into Abigail's cheeks at the words. It was rare indeed that anyone complimented her features ... and Mercy sounded so genuinely sincere.

"I mean ..." Mercy fumbled awkwardly. "Oh, it was just a bit of a shock. I like your eyes in general. They're a lovely grey now, like the mist in parts of faerie."

Abigail glanced down at the floor. She was suddenly having a hard time looking straight at Mercy. "Thanks," she mumbled. "I suppose I match half of Mum's eyes now. I rather like that."

Mercy bit her lip. "What Black Catastrophe said, though ... I had no idea so many sluagh in London were missin'."

"*Three* sluagh," Abigail said. She forced herself to straighten again. "Three dead girls, an' three missin' sluagh – if we don't count Lord Longshadow, anyway. That can't be a coincidence."

Mercy searched Abigail's face worriedly. "What do you mean by that?" she asked.

Abigail frowned grimly. "I think we've had it backwards all along," she said. "The girls aren't the victims – they're the bait. Someone's goin' after all the sluagh in London."

Chapter Nine

"It has to be a black magician," Elias said, once Mercy and Abigail had rejoined him over breakfast, relating what they'd learned. "I do my best to keep London clear of them, but I'm afraid that new ones show up all the time. All that's really required for black magic is an interest and some knowledge of folk superstitions."

"Outside magic," Abigail mumbled tiredly. "Someone with any talent at magic just needs to find somethin' enough people believe at once, an' use it for themselves." Her eyelids were beginning to droop, however, now that she'd eaten half of the plate in front of her.

"Outside magic?" Elias asked. "I've never heard the term."

"Well, I'm sure it's not in any magicians' books," Mercy said with a yawn. "But Abigail's right – that's how I've always known outside magic to work. Anyway, you didn't *really* think it was the books an' the plants an' the wands that were magic, did you?"

Elias considered this slowly. "I suppose not," he murmured. "But what an unusual theory. I can't help but wonder how you came to it."

Mercy shrugged. "I hate outside magic," she said. "Sometimes you learn the most about the things you don't like."

Abigail smiled sleepily at her. "Sometimes you learn so much about somethin' that you *come* to hate it," she said. "We used to live above a perfume shop. I hate perfume now, but I can tell you what stupid flower someone's wearin' any day of the week." She rubbed at her eyes, and then added, "You smell like lilies. Mostly lye, but a *little* bit of lilies."

Mercy raised her eyebrows. "Longshadow has a lot of lilies," she said. "An' they *aren't* stupid."

Abigail grinned down at her plate. "I guess lilies aren't stupid," she allowed. "They smell nice on *you*, anyway."

"I will have to check with the merchants here who cater to magicians," Elias said slowly. "One *can* become a magician without access to formal materials, but those with an interest just as often end up in a shop. If anyone new has started spending money on magic, then the merchants will know."

"We could watch the path to Longshadow to see if someone comes back to check that trap," Abigail observed.

Mercy pressed her lips together. "If the girls are bait," she said, "then no one will check the trap until another one's died. I'd hope we sort this out *before* that happens."

Elias frowned tiredly. "Which brings us to the matter of Lord Longshadow," he said. "If Lord Longshadow is trapped, then there is little that I can do. But if he is *not* yet trapped, then I have left us both at a disadvantage, all at once." He closed his eyes. "Lord Longshadow truly believes that he would be doing good by stealing away Hollowvale's children – he argued with me over it, even during this dire situation. If I give him back his power, disappearing sluagh will not deter him ... but I also do not know what might happen if Lord Longshadow is abducted."

Mercy picked uncomfortably at one of the bandages on her hands. Finally, in a small voice, she said, "You shouldn't undo the bans."

Elias glanced at her curiously.

"Lord Longshadow is responsible for your mistrust," Mercy said. "An' you're right to have been concerned about

Hollowvale's children." Her voice was heavy with weariness. "You banned Lord Longshadow from harmin' anyone with magic – but you didn't say anything about usin' magic for protection. That ought to be enough to keep a powerful faerie safe."

Mercy's pale face was full of misery and contrition. But the argument surprised Abigail all the same.

"I thought you liked Lord Longshadow," Abigail said slowly.

Mercy swallowed. "Just right now," she said, "I don't know if I do." She looked up at Abigail. "There's somethin' I think you ought to know, for more reasons than one. It's why you shouldn't undo the bans." She sucked in a determined breath. "Lightless wasn't lyin' to Lucy when he said Lord Longshadow could bring her back to life."

Abigail stared at her. "It... had occurred to me that faeries can't lie," she said. "But Lightless only said that in order to convince Lucy to go with him, didn't he? Maybe Lord Longshadow *could* bring someone back to life – but he never *would*."

Mercy bit her lip. "In Longshadow – on the border between faerie an' the Other Side – there's a big silver tree," she said. "Every hundred years, that tree grows an apple that can bring someone back to life. Lord Longshadow's never once let anyone have that apple. But you could undo those bans in exchange for the apple an' bring back ... anyone you liked. You could bring back Hugh, or Lucy, or one of those other girls."

Abigail's heart flipped in her chest. The revelation opened up so many sudden possibilities that she wasn't even sure where to begin. She tried to imagine what it would be like to have Hugh back in the flesh – able to talk to anyone he wanted, hug anyone he wanted, bake all of the apple tarts that he wanted. Her imagination wasn't nearly up to the task ... but it didn't matter. Even if Abigail couldn't envision the idea, she knew that it was something she had to pursue.

"I'm sure Lord Longshadow wouldn't be happy with you for tellin' us this," Abigail observed softly.

Mercy grimaced. "I don't see as that matters either way," she said. "Lord Longshadow's caused you years of trouble. You deserve to know." She looked up at Elias again. "Leave the bans in place. When this is all over, you can trade 'em for that apple."

Elias considered this seriously. Rather than answering the implicit question, however, he glanced at Abigail. "You're going to fall asleep in your food," he told her.

Abigail had slumped forward onto the table in front of her such that her chin was close to touching her plate. She blinked quickly, forcing herself upright once again. "I'm fine," she said.

Elias shook his head. "You should both get some sleep," he said. "This will not be solved within the day." He frowned at Mercy. "I am not best pleased at the idea of letting you stay here. But . . . you don't have a family of your own, do you?"

Mercy crossed her arms over her chest uncomfortably. "The sluagh are the closest thing I have to family," she said. "I could probably stay in Longshadow, but . . ."

"The way is closed," Elias finished for her. There was a sense of pity in his eyes, and Abigail knew that he couldn't help but compare Mercy to his younger self.

"I don't think Mercy is goin' to steal away Hugh at this point," Abigail said softly. "I think she's a good person, even if she *has* been a little dense." She paused and then said to Mercy, "You can stay in my room."

Mercy looked between the two of them. There was surprise on her face; Abigail wondered whether Mercy had truly expected to be thrown out onto the street. The idea miffed her a bit.

"Thank you," Mercy said. It was hard to tell which of them she was addressing, as she glued her eyes back to her lap. "I'll try not to be a bother."

Abigail's bedroom was relatively small compared to Lucy's room – but compared to the workhouse, it was an unprecedented luxury. The narrow bed was fitted with clean sheets and sturdy blankets – and until today, Abigail had always had it entirely to herself.

Normally, Abigail was jealously possessive of her bed. She was willing to share her parents and her food and her time with all of the other children as long as she had her very own bed. She was surprised, therefore, to feel no particular reluctance at sharing the bed with Mercy. In fact, the idea was pleasantly comforting.

Mercy shucked her frock and apron such that she was left in only her shift. The thin cotton emphasised her long limbs and her far-too-skinny frame. Abigail was perfectly used to seeing other people in various states of undress – there had not been much privacy in her early life – but something about the way that Mercy's shift clung to her form made Abigail look away with embarrassment. Perhaps, she thought, it was because she had considered all the other children to be siblings of a sort. But something about Mercy's sly smiles and strange magic precluded Abigail from thinking about her in that way.

Mercy slipped beneath the sheets on the other side of the small bed, curling up beneath them. The heavy curtains blocked out the late-morning sunlight such that they were left in sleepy half-darkness.

Abigail had been sure that they would both fall asleep immediately, given how long they'd been awake. But only a few minutes later, Mercy spoke very quietly.

"I'm worried for my friends," she said.

Abigail turned to face Mercy beneath the covers. Mercy's dark eyes were troubled and fearful. Her oddly expansive presence had disappeared for the moment; she seemed very small and fragile now.

Slowly – before Abigail could think better of it – she reached out to pull Mercy into her arms.

Mercy buried her face in Abigail's shoulder. Now that Abigail had embraced her, she realised that Mercy was shivering with misery. A handful of tears soaked Abigail's shift, and she tightened her arms.

"Lightless an' Silent an' Never could all be dead," Mercy whispered in a choked voice. "I might never see 'em again."

Abigail reached up hesitantly to stroke Mercy's hair. "I'm sorry," she mumbled. "I wish I could fix it."

This only made Mercy hiccup harder. "I'm not supposed to be afraid of death," she said. "I'm not supposed to *want* to fix it."

Abigail scowled. "Everyone's scared of death," she said. "Anyone who wasn't scared, I figure they'd already be on the Other Side. All of this is unfair, Mercy. You *ought* to be scared – an' sad, an' angry."

Mercy swallowed. "You were right about me," she said. "I've been so awful, Abigail. I thought I knew best, tellin' people they ought to accept death – but I never thought any of the people *I* loved would ever die. Now they might be gone, an' I'm just as upset as everyone else. I'm the one who's been stupid an' stuck-up."

Abigail threaded her fingers through Mercy's hair. It was softer than it looked – and Abigail realised belatedly that she had been *wanting* to touch Mercy's hair. She set aside the strange thought, glancing down at Mercy.

"You're not stupid," Abigail told her. "You've been . . . a *little* stuck-up. But so have I. An' so has Dad. We're all just doin' the best that we can." She rubbed soothing circles into Mercy's back. "I appreciate you tellin' us about the apple. I don't know if we can make Lord Longshadow give it to us, even holdin' onto those bans. But at least now we've got the chance to try."

Mercy hesitated. "Lord Longshadow is . . . just like me," she said. "A little stuck-up, I guess. But I really believe you can work things out."

Abigail studied her curiously. "How did you end up in

Longshadow, Mercy?" she asked. "You can't have been abducted like me, if you're so fond of everyone there. Do you remember your original family at all?"

Mercy took a deep, shuddering breath. Gradually, her tears stopped – but she continued clinging to Abigail uncertainly. "I don't know," she said. "I don't think I ever had a family. For a while, Longshadow was all I knew. But I also knew that there were lost people out there who were supposed to walk through Longshadow to the Other Side an' hadn't done it. Longshadow *wanted* me to lead 'em back there."

Abigail frowned distantly. "You've just always been in Longshadow, then," she said. "But aren't you a laundress?"

Mercy shifted in Abigail's arms, suddenly embarrassed. "I, um . . . I saw a laundress to the Other Side," she said. "We talked for such a long time – all about her life, an' her friends, an' her dreams. I thought she was really lovely. When she crossed over, she gave me her cap, an' I kept it. I think she must've given me more than that, though, because I smell like she did now. It's . . . nice."

Abigail blinked. "I never heard anyone call the smell of lye *nice*," she said. The Cleveland Street Workhouse had *always* smelled of lye, and Abigail hadn't been able to stand the scent ever since.

Mercy flushed in the darkness. "I like it," she said. "But only because it was hers. It makes me feel like I've still got a piece of her with me, even though she's gone."

Abigail turned her cheek against the top of Mercy's head. The idea warmed her a little bit – and she thought again about the sluagh, who often received similar gifts from the dead. "That *is* nice," she said quietly. "You know . . . I think I understand why so many ghosts give gifts to the sluagh now. It's just as nice to know you're leavin' somethin' behind you – that someone might remember you from time to time. I'll wager that laundress is happy, wherever she is, whenever you get to thinkin' about her."

Somehow, the idea endeared the smell of lye to Abigail, too. She inhaled softly – and this time, when the acrid scent hit her, it reminded her less of the Cleveland Street Workhouse and more of Mercy's smile.

"They're not gifts," Mercy mumbled. She sounded calmer now, and sleepier. "Well . . . not really. Faeries can't give things away without payment, an' they can't *accept* things without payin' 'em back, either. But it's all right with the ghosts, because the sluagh did 'em a service first."

Abigail smiled dimly. "But the ghosts don't *have* to pay their way," she said. "The sluagh think it's their duty to take 'em to the Other Side. So maybe it's payment . . . but it's still somethin' the ghosts choose to give over."

Mercy thought on that quietly – and for a while, Abigail thought that perhaps she'd fallen asleep. But then Mercy said, "Black Catastrophe will think of you often as well."

"She will," Abigail murmured back. "I think that's nice, too. I told her I don't ever intend to die, an' I meant it. But I'd be happy to leave pieces of myself with everyone else, even while I'm alive."

Mercy tightened her arms on Abigail. "I don't want you to die either, Abigail," she whispered. "I never want to lead you to the Other Side. That'd be . . . it'd be awful."

Abigail wasn't certain just what prompted the gesture, but she found herself leaning down to brush her lips over Mercy's hair. "I wouldn't go even if you tried," she assured Mercy. "I've got too many people to haunt."

Mercy closed her eyes with a tiny smile.

Abigail fell asleep still holding her. In fact, it was probably the best way she had ever fallen asleep.

Chapter Ten

Elias had already left to question the merchants by the time Abigail and Mercy awoke. But he had left a note that Abigail should have full access to the ballroom, and to his existing notes on the current case. Abigail therefore went upstairs to the third floor, settling herself in the large chair before the desk while she read through her father's slightly messy handwriting.

Mercy sat down on the stool nearby, while Hugh – and presumably Lucy – stood behind her.

"People only figured out the pattern by the time Lucy died," Abigail said thoughtfully, "so Dad didn't get a chance to investigate the first two deaths as they happened. But he interviewed people at all three houses who saw the ravens comin' an' goin', which is how he got onto the sluagh. Dad mentioned earlier, remember, that there *might* have been some black magic on Lucy – only, Lucy's mum had a priest visit after she died, an' some of his blessings might've mucked things up."

Hugh frowned. "You think someone killed Lucy with magic?" he asked.

Abigail leaned her chin into her hand, resting her elbow upon the desk. "I think so," she said. "Mostly because of what Black—" Abigail cut herself off quickly before she could say the sluagh's full name aloud, and she amended the statement. "Mostly because of what the sluagh said. Not everyone who dies ought to leave a ghost – but there's been three deaths an' three missin' sluagh, which means that someone made *sure* these girls left ghosts. There's got to be some kind of black magic that could do that, but it'll take time to figure out exactly *which* black magic it is." She turned back towards Mercy. "Would you mind lettin' me talk to Lucy again?"

Mercy nodded. She offered out one of her bandaged hands. Abigail took it very gingerly, aware of the burns still beneath the bandages.

Twilight flooded into view, skittering across the ballroom floor in vivid splashes of colour. Lucy's figure melted into view just behind Mercy. She was still in her nightgown, with her blonde hair spilling over her shoulders and her arms crossed uncomfortably over her chest.

"What were you doin' the day before you died?" Abigail asked Lucy. "Do you remember anyone actin' funny around you? Maybe they sprinkled somethin' on you, or said some gibberish in your direction?"

Lucy looked away. "I was at Lady Lessing's ball," she said.

Abigail quirked an eyebrow. "I didn't know Lady Lessing had thrown a ball," she said.

Lucy pressed her lips together. "You were obviously not invited," she said. Her tone was practical rather than insulting. It was at least an improvement over the way that Lucy had addressed Abigail while she'd been alive. "I don't recall anyone acting strangely around me. But balls in London are always such a crush that I doubt I would have noticed if anyone *had* done."

Abigail nodded slowly. "An' you weren't feelin' ill at all until that night?" she asked. "You didn't ail for weeks an' then get worse?"

"I did not," Lucy said simply. "I was in perfect spirits just before the ball. I was feeling a bit ill when I returned home afterwards – but it was very late, and I had been dancing all evening. I thought I would be fine after a good night's rest."

Abigail took a long breath. "I think that narrows it down, then," she said. "It was someone at that ball who got at you – another noble, or maybe someone's servant they brought with 'em. It'd explain why all the victims have been noble girls our age. They're most likely to be at every possible party, searchin' for husbands."

Lucy's lip trembled at that, and Abigail suddenly felt bad about bringing up the subject. "I danced with Mr Red," Lucy sniffled. "He complimented my dancing and said that he would like to dance with me again another time."

"Mr Red?" Abigail asked.

Lucy let out a frustrated sound. "His real name is Mr James Ruell," she said. "He's Lord Belwether's second son. We call him Mr Red because he always wears that handsome red cravat."

Abigail shrugged. "I can't remember if I ever met him," she admitted. "I suppose Mr Red's compliment was a coup for you?"

Lucy stamped her foot. "It was *everything*!" she said. "I was the envy of every woman in attendance. I was thinking of marrying Mr Red, you know. I could have had him by the end of the Season if I'd wanted. And now I'll never even dance with him again!"

Abigail closed her eyes and gritted her teeth.

All you have to live for is owning people and being envied, she wanted to say. *Can you even hear yourself talking?*

But Abigail knew that she needed Lucy's continued cooperation, and so she said instead, "I'm very sorry for your loss. We're goin' to make sure that whoever did this to you gets what's comin' to 'em."

Lucy quieted at that. She still looked miserable, but she managed a stiff nod at Abigail. "And we're going to find Lord Longshadow," Lucy said, "so that he can bring me back to life, as Lightless said that he would."

Abigail pressed her lips together. It took everything she had not to remind Lucy that Lightless had said nothing of the sort – that Lord Longshadow *could* bring her back to life, but that he surely would not do.

Thank goodness Lucy wasn't there to hear about that apple, Abigail thought. *If we do get our hands on it, then it's definitely going to Hugh.*

"We need to figure out where the other two girls were on the days that they died," Abigail said. "If we're right, then they'll have been at a ball ... or at a smaller gatherin', if we're lucky. Anyone who showed up to all of those events could be our killer – or at least, one of their servants might be the killer."

"How are we goin' to do that?" Hugh asked sceptically. "No one's goin' to give you their guest list, Abby."

Abigail considered this for a long moment. "We'd need someone very well-connected to ask *for* us," she said slowly. "Someone that lots of people like very much."

"Maybe Aunt Vanessa?" Hugh asked.

Abigail shook her head. "People *like* Aunt Vanessa," she said, "but they're always dodgin' her because of the charity these days." Apparently, the worst social crime one could possibly commit among the *ton* was to allow one's interest in charity to develop past the superficial.

Lucy straightened with a look of dawning realisation. "My mother could get those guest lists!" she said. "Everyone is very fond of *her*."

Abigail nodded, trying to look impressed – as though Lucy had come up with the idea entirely on her own, instead of being carefully led to it. "That's true," Abigail said. "Your mother would be perfect." She looked over at Mercy, suddenly hesitant. "I'm almost certain Lady Pinckney would help us if Lucy were the one to ask her," Abigail said, "but she'd have to be able to *hear* Lucy."

Mercy sighed heavily – but she nodded, all the same. "I don't think it's healthy, chattin' up your dead loved ones," she mumbled. "But I've been all wrong before, an' there's people in danger anyway."

Abigail smiled at her. She nearly squeezed Mercy's hand – but she remembered just in time what a poor idea that would be, and she dropped it instead.

Twilight faded from the room, sinking it back into daylight. Abigail stood up from her chair, glancing at Hugh. "I do need to talk to you first, Hugh," she said. "Alone, I mean."

Hugh frowned. "It's nothin' bad?" he asked warily.

"Nothin' bad," Abigail promised. "It's family stuff, is all."

Hugh followed Abigail just outside of the ballroom. She settled herself onto one of the stairs, and he soon followed suit, looking over at her curiously.

"Mercy told me an' Dad somethin' important last night," Abigail addressed Hugh. "Lord Longshadow *can* bring people back to life, Hugh. He's got an apple that'll do it, just once." Abigail leaned her arms onto her knees, sucking in a deep breath. "I don't want to get your hopes up, but I thought you deserved to know. We're goin' to ask Lord Longshadow to trade the apple for his feathers, once we've sorted out these murders."

Hugh glanced up the stairs behind them, at the closed door which led into the ballroom. "You didn't want Lucy to know?" he asked slowly.

Abigail scowled darkly. "Lucy's more interested in findin' Lord Longshadow an' comin' back to life than she is in savin' any other girls," she said. "If I tell Lucy about that apple, Hugh, I guarantee she'll stop helpin' us until we promise it to her, even if it means more people die."

"And . . . you don't want to give Lucy the apple," Hugh said.

Abigail raised her eyebrows at him. "I don't want to, no," she replied. "I feel bad for her bein' dead – an' if I could bring back as many people as I liked, then I *would* bring her back. But if there's only one apple, then I think one of Hollowvale's children ought to have it. Lucy's had a comfy life, with a mum who loved her an' people givin' her everything she ever wanted. All Hollowvale's children died young in a workhouse. If Lucy's death was unfair, then yours was even *more* unfair."

Hugh looked away from Abigail uncomfortably. "It just feels strange, not tellin' her," he mumbled.

Abigail knit her brow. "I thought you'd be excited," she said. "I know we've still got to talk to the other children in Hollowvale, but you're the youngest, an' there's a fair chance they'll all agree to give you that apple. I thought you had tarts to bake, Hugh."

Hugh only looked more glum at this for some reason. He hunched his shoulders. "I don't know why I'm not excited," he admitted. "I guess . . . I don't want to get my hopes up. There's an awful lot of dead people, an' only one of me. An' almost every other dead person is probably more important than I am."

Abigail clenched her jaw. She suddenly wished, harder than she had ever wished before, that she could hug Hugh. "You *are* important," she told him. "Other people called you less important an' put you in a workhouse – but they weren't *right* to do that, Hugh."

"How could I be important?" Hugh scoffed. "I didn't even live long enough to do much. All I know how to do is pick oakum."

Abigail took another long, deep breath. She knew why Hugh was being so obtuse, of course: he was having trouble imagining something nice happening to him, in the same way that Abigail had trouble imagining anything at all.

"People think Lucy is important," Abigail said, "but she'd never be caught dead makin' tarts for someone else. All she'll ever do is eat everyone else's tarts, Hugh. You understand what I mean?"

Hugh nodded listlessly – but Abigail was sure that he did *not* understand. Frustrated as she was, she knew that Hugh had stopped listening entirely, and that she would need to figure out a different approach.

"Well, we've got murders to sort out before we ever get to askin' who gets this apple," Abigail sighed. She pushed back up to her feet. "Let's go an' get those guest lists."

Chapter Eleven

It was far too late in the day for visiting – but Abigail had never had a reputation to ruin in the first place, and so she took them all to Lord Pinckney's townhouse, even as the sun began to decline behind London's western skyline.

The butler, Mr Swinton, was not at all pleased to see Abigail again.

"I know it's late," Abigail told him, in her best attempt at an upper-class accent. "I do need to see Lady Pinckney urgently, though. If she doesn't like what I have to say, I promise I'll leave immediately."

Abigail and Mercy *were* led inside to wait in the entryway – though they were left to share only one hard stool between them.

"You can have the stool," Abigail muttered to Mercy.

Mercy arched an eyebrow at her. "I don't want it," she said. "*You* have it."

Abigail narrowed her eyes. "You're injured," she said. "I insist."

Hugh groaned audibly. "You're both bein' stupid," he said. "I'm goin' to go spy on Lady Pinckney with Lucy."

Abigail gave him a sharp look. "That isn't polite, Hugh—" she started. But Hugh had already turned to vanish through one of the townhouse walls.

Silence stretched between Abigail and Mercy.

"I can't sit while a lady's standin'," Mercy said. Abigail knew that she was only saying it in order to be contrary.

"What luck," Abigail said. "I'm not a lady."

"You're *dressed* as a lady," Mercy pointed out.

"An' you're dressed as a laundress," Abigail said. "But neither of us is actually what we appear to be, are we?"

Mercy grimaced at that and crossed her arms. "We're both just standin' here until the butler comes back, then?" she asked.

"I suppose we are," Abigail said stubbornly.

Thankfully, Mr Swinton reappeared much more quickly than he had done the first time Abigail had visited. He cast one last withering glance at Abigail and Mercy before saying, "Lady Pinckney will see you in the drawing room."

Lady Pinckney was seated at the same table as before when they entered. She was still wearing black – but her stern family Bible was missing, which made the whole atmosphere seem a bit more at ease. Hugh had seated himself on a distant divan, though his eyes rested on a space just *next* to Lady Pinckney.

"Your mum still can't hear you," Hugh told the empty air, in a long-suffering tone. "You'll have to wait until Mercy does her inside magic."

"This is a very unusual visit," Lady Pinckney informed Abigail. Her eyes flickered towards Mercy, and a hint of distaste showed in her gaze.

"I know," Abigail said. She had to work to ignore the obvious condescension in Lady Pinckney's manner. It was such a perfect, eerie reflection of Lucy's own habits that there was little mistaking the relation between them. "I found out some things about Lucy," Abigail added. "Actually, I found . . . well, Lucy's ghost."

Abigail hadn't expected to feel so uncomfortable saying the words aloud. But a series of wild, raw emotions crossed Lady Pinckney's face as Abigail spoke, and she couldn't help a wince.

"I thought . . . I thought I felt her just now," Lady Pinckney whispered. "Is she here? Can I speak to her?"

Abigail took in a deep breath. "I brought Lucy back here with me," she said. "She can hear you just fine. But Mercy will have to do some magic if you want to see and hear Lucy in return."

Lady Pinckney frowned at Abigail. "Mercy?" she asked. She looked behind Abigail, as though expecting to find yet another person in tow.

Abigail raised her eyebrows. "*This* is Mercy, Lady Pinckney," she said. She gestured just next to her, where Mercy still stood.

Lady Pinckney focused on Mercy again with a slight frown, as though trying to reconcile two impossible ideas. Belatedly, Abigail realised that Lady Pinckney simply could not imagine that someone so poor-looking might have a rare skill which she required.

Mercy, for her part, did not seem to take offence. In fact, there was a hint of bemusement in her manner. For the first time, Abigail identified it for what it was: Mercy was not *actually* a laundress, and she was tickled at being mistaken for something she was not. After leading the rich and the poor and the powerful alike all to the Other Side, Abigail imagined that it must be difficult to consider them nearly as consequential as they all considered *themselves* to be. After all, they would all eventually *come around*, as Mercy had previously observed, once they had everything taken away from them.

"I can help you see Lucy if you like, Lady Pinckney," Mercy told her. "You might find it more painful than you expect, talkin' to her again. But I've been thinkin', an' I've decided I can't make that choice for you." Mercy spoke with the same lower-class accent which she had always used before – and for a moment, Abigail envied her stark confidence.

The offer overwhelmed Lady Pinckney's decorum, such that she seemed to forget that she was speaking to a woman dressed as a laundress. "Of course I want to see my daughter again!" Lady Pinckney said desperately. "I never even got to say goodbye!" Tears wavered in her voice, and Abigail looked away uncomfortably.

Mercy nodded grimly. "If you're sure, then," she said. She glanced sideways at Abigail. "I'll hold your hand too if you want."

Abigail nodded wordlessly. Lady Pinckney's grief had wormed its way past her hard feelings against Lucy, no matter how she tried to resist it. But she went to sit at the table next to Lady Pinckney and took Mercy's hand very carefully. Lady Pinckney did not hesitate to take Mercy's other hand, though the bandages there were starting to look a bit sorry.

The twilight that filtered into the drawing room was soft and subdued. It was particularly strange, given that there was barely any light from the windows there in the first place.

As Lucy's figure faded into view once more, Abigail saw that she was crying.

" . . . I'm here, Mama!" Lucy was saying. "I'm so sorry for leaving you all alone; *please* don't look so upset."

Lady Pinckney stared at her daughter. Slowly, she brought her other hand up to her mouth. Her tears spilled over, and she sucked in a shuddering breath. Lady Pinckney lurched to her feet, reaching for Lucy – but Mercy tugged her back, with a slight wince about the pain in her hand.

"You can't touch her," Mercy said apologetically. "It doesn't work that way. I'm sorry."

Lucy's lip trembled. "I have tried to hug you so many times, Mama," she said.

Out of the corner of her eye, Abigail saw Hugh shrink down into the divan. The expression on his face was miserably upset.

"I should have taken better care of you, Lucy," Lady Pinckney sobbed. "I used to check on you every night when you went to bed. Why did I ever stop checking on you, darling?"

"It's not at all your fault, Mama," Lucy assured her tearfully. "How should you have known that someone would curse me? You did nothing wrong, I promise."

Lady Pinckney shook her head in confusion. "Someone cursed you?" she asked. "But the faeries—"

"Oh, no," Lucy said quickly. "The faeries did not kill me, Mama. There was a very handsome gentleman with stars in his eyes, but he only came to hold my hand and keep me company. He said that he could bring me to Lord Longshadow, and—"

Abigail knew instinctively that Lucy was about to tell her mother all about how Lord Longshadow would supposedly bring her back to life. She interjected quickly. "Lucy," she said. "Don't make promises you can't keep. We don't know if Lord Longshadow is even still alive."

Lucy opened her mouth to protest – but her eyes flickered towards Lady Pinckney, and she swallowed the words she'd been about to say. She must have realised on some level that the idea could badly hurt her mother once again.

Lucy looked down at her feet, suddenly far more subdued. "Well, that is true," she said quietly. "I may not ever meet Lord Longshadow now. But Abigail and her father seem very certain that it was a black magician who cursed me, and so I am helping them to find the person responsible. I do not see that they could possibly do so without me."

Abigail closed her eyes and breathed in patiently. Even in the throes of grief, Lucy had managed to find a way to stroke her own ego. But it was helpful to their cause for now, and so Abigail managed somehow to stay silent.

Lady Pinckney whirled upon Abigail. "A black magician?" she demanded. "But the Lord Sorcier is supposed to protect England against black magicians! Are you saying that three girls have now died to black magic right beneath his nose?"

Abigail worked consciously not to tighten her hand on Mercy's. She opened her eyes again, forcing herself to stay calm. "No one had brought the matter to his attention until Lucy," Abigail said. "We are all working as quickly as we can now to make sure that this doesn't happen again. I know that isn't as much of a comfort as it might be, but my father cannot be expected to divine the future."

This was only *mostly* correct – for Abigail's mother, at least, could sometimes divine the past or the future when she looked into mirrors. But the practice was woefully unreliable, and you could never actually be certain what it was that you would see. Predicting black magicians on purpose was truly beyond any diviner's capabilities, as far as Abigail knew.

Lucy sighed. "Oh, maybe the Lord Sorcier is competent and maybe he is not," she said. "But we must still find my killer either way. I was at Lady Lessing's ball on the day that I died, and Abigail thinks that I was cursed there. You are good friends with Lady Lessing, aren't you, Mama? Surely, you could ask her for the list of guests who were there."

Lady Pinckney was still staring at Abigail with great fury. But she calmed somewhat as she looked back towards her daughter's ghost. "I can, of course," Lady Pinckney said. "Lady Lessing visited in order to offer her condolences. She said that if there was anything she could do for me, then I had only to ask her. I do not imagine that a guest list was what she had in mind – but I shall insist regardless, if you think that it would help."

Lucy nodded in satisfaction. "There were two other girls, you remember – Miss Edwards, who was about to be engaged, and Miss Hancock, the girl with the unfortunate nose. I don't recall whether either of them attended any balls before they died, but the killer surely found them at a social event as well." Lucy spoke with great confidence, as though she had deduced all of this entirely on her own. "I know that it has been some weeks, but I am sure that your other friends could find out where the other girls had been and who else was at those events."

Lady Pinckney dabbed at her eyes with her handkerchief. "I will find out everything I can," she promised. "Whoever did this to you will regret it very soon, Lucy."

Abigail glanced at Lady Pinckney. "You should be careful who you speak to," she warned. "If Lucy's killer finds out that you are searching for them, they could try and curse you next.

We don't know which exact curse they are using yet, and I won't be able to protect you until we have narrowed it down."

Lady Pinckney waved her off tiredly. "I do not care," she said. "Truly, I don't. I could die tonight and it would not matter."

Lucy gave a stricken gasp. "No!" she said. "Please don't say that, Mama. I don't want you to die. You must be careful, so you can live a very long time more."

Lady Pinckney attempted a weary smile at her daughter. It was not very convincing. "I will . . . try," she said. Lady Pinckney looked at Mercy then, from beneath her eyelashes. "I would like to engage your services," she said. "I can pay any price you like, if you will only let me see my daughter each day."

Mercy sighed heavily, as though she had been expecting the offer. "You must not make offers like that," Mercy advised Lady Pinckney. "I am friends with faeries, you know. I could take your smile, or your happiness, or even your soul." She paused. "But I won't – because my services aren't for hire. I've been questionin' some things lately, but one thing I *do* know is that there'll always be ghosts who are scared an' confused an' need a guide to the Other Side. I can't help those ghosts if I'm here usin' my magic for just one person."

This was clearly not the answer that Lady Pinckney wished to hear. Her brows drew together, and she looked deeply stricken. "I can convince you, surely," she said. "I will find something that you want—"

"You will not," Mercy told her gently. "You aren't even the first person who's tried. Some things are not for sale, Lady Pinckney. I'm sorry." Her pale features softened, though, and she asked, "Would your husband want to see his daughter while I'm here?"

Lady Pinckney stared at Mercy, still trying to digest her response.

"No," Lucy said quietly. "My father won't wish to see me. And I don't wish to see *him*. I only wanted to see my mother . . .

and now I have." Lucy turned back to her mother. "You will be happy again one day," she said softly. "Please don't be sad on my account. I am going to go and find the faerie with the stars in his eyes – so I will not be alone, Mama. He is excellent company, and I will be just fine."

Lady Pinckney glanced between Mercy and her daughter's ghost. Abigail thought that the lady was still trying to come up with a clever way to force Mercy to stay. But finally, she looked away again. "I love you very much, Lucy," Lady Pinckney said. "I am sorry that I did not say it often enough."

"I love you too, Mama," Lucy said softly.

Mercy tugged her hands back. The twilight faded but did not disappear – and it took Abigail a moment to understand that it was now real twilight filtering through the window of the drawing room.

The emotion on Lady Pinckney's features remained keen and cutting. She continued staring with obvious longing at the place where Lucy had been.

"It's nearing dark," Abigail said quietly. "I think we must leave. Thank you for seeing me again, Lady Pinckney." She took Mercy's arm gently in hers and started them towards the door.

Lady Pinckney pressed her lips together. She wasn't crying any longer, but her eyes still shone with unshed tears. "You will be back, surely?" she asked Mercy. "At least once more?"

Mercy did not pause them on their way to the door. "I truly don't know," she said. "I don't think you should expect as much." Her tone was firm, though not unkind.

Hugh rose from the divan to walk behind them. His posture was still slumped, as though someone had drained all of the energy from him.

They left Lady Pinckney at the table in her drawing room, cast in the hazy pink twilight of London.

Chapter Twelve

"It's not wrong to be upset," Mercy said, as they climbed the steps up to the House. "A bad thing happened, an' lots of people got hurt. But that isn't my fault, Lucy – I didn't kill you. An' what you're askin' isn't fair to me, or to anyone else. I don't exist to serve you."

Lucy and Mercy had been talking nearly the entire way back, though Abigail could only hear Mercy's side of the conversation. Mercy sounded very tired of it all, though she had somehow managed to maintain her patience so far.

"Lucy is still tryin' to convince Mercy to work for Lady Pinckney, I guess?" Abigail muttered to Hugh.

"She is," Hugh mumbled back. "I understand why. Her mum was awful upset. It was terrible to see."

Abigail sighed heavily. "I understand now why Mercy doesn't like lettin' people talk to their dead loved ones," she said. "It's like takin' someone away for a second time. But I didn't realise how much danger it might put Mercy into. Lady Pinckney is desperate, an' she thinks she can have anything she wants. I don't *think* she'd try an' abduct Mercy, but—"

Abigail stopped cold, with her foot partway lifted for the next stair.

Hugh looked up at her questioningly.

"Mercy," Abigail said, "I think I know why someone might be abductin' sluagh."

Mercy turned, just before the door that led into the ballroom. "You've got a theory?" she asked.

Abigail picked up the pace again, hurrying to join Mercy at the top of the stairs. "Imagine if Lady Pinckney could trap her very own sluagh," she said. "I'm not at all sure that she'd hesitate." Abigail winced as she remembered that Lucy was nearby, and added, "I'm sorry, Lucy, but you know your mum is very upset right now, an' maybe not thinkin' straight."

Mercy frowned. "But why capture *three* sluagh in that case?" she asked.

Abigail shook her head. "I don't know that part," she said. "But I think this must be in the right general direction. It *feels* right. The sluagh speak to the dead – an' they can probably touch the dead too, if their magic is anything like yours. Someone's tryin' to bridge that gap, an' they know the sluagh can help 'em do it."

Mercy grimaced. "There's outside magic for some of those things," she said.

"There is," Abigail agreed. "But it's hard to do, an' not very reliable. I didn't ask Dad's help when I made Hugh's locket – I asked Other Mum. An' let's say you're a magician with very few resources. Why *wouldn't* you take a shortcut an' just abduct an expert?"

Abigail opened the door into the ballroom, letting them inside. The sky had truly grown dark now, and she was just thinking that she ought to run back downstairs with one of the lamps to find a light – but even as she picked up the lamp on the desk, it sprang to life of its own accord, burning with a bright golden flame.

"I see that we have all spent the day quite fully," Elias observed from the doorway to the stairs. He had come up behind them somehow, without so much as a sound. Dark circles had started beneath his eyes, and Abigail suspected that he had not slept nearly as much as she and Mercy had done.

"I thought your magic was all tied up in those bans," Abigail said, with a glance at the lamp.

Elias closed the door behind him, tugging wearily at his already-mussed cravat. "I should hope that I can still do something as simple as lighting a lamp," he said.

Abigail could *not* light a lamp with her magic, even at her best. But then, Hollowvale was fond of the damp and the cold, and she had to imagine that Swiftburn was the opposite. She nodded at her father. "Thank you for the light, then," she said. "We *have* been out all day. Did you find anything helpful on your end?"

Elias walked for one of the tall, heavy bookshelves on the wall, glancing over the tomes there. "I did, and I did not," he said. "Could you please bring that lamp over here for a moment?"

Abigail carried the lamp over to Elias, and she saw that he was searching the shelves for a specific title.

"I have a list of several people who have purchased books of interest in the last few months," Elias said, as he hunted through the shelf. "But even more interesting is this: when I went to John's magic shop on Berkeley Square, I asked him to check through his stock. Two books in particular came up missing. No one has bought them, as far as he knows – and so, they were likely stolen. I find it more likely than not that the magician we are searching for is to blame."

Elias pulled a book from the shelf and handed it over to Abigail. She looked down and saw that it was *Debrett's Peerage of Faerie*.

"Our edition is older than the one that was stolen," Elias said, "but it might still help us understand what it is our thief was looking for."

Abigail tucked the tome beneath her arm. "And the other book?" she asked. "You said that there were two books missing."

"*A Cunning Grimoire of Plants*," Elias replied. "I am afraid that I do not own it, and I was unable to find a copy of it today."

Abigail frowned. "We have plenty of other books on plants an' magic," she said. "I could go through 'em an' see if somethin' jumps out. We're waitin' on Lady Pinckney to get some guest lists, so I'll need somethin' useful to do anyway."

Elias nodded wearily. "I will require some sleep," he admitted. "But before I go, I should ask what you have learned today."

Abigail dutifully updated him on the day's events as best she could, trying not to leave anything out. As she spoke, Elias sat down at the desk and picked up a quill pen, and Abigail was pleased to see him taking notes. There was something very satisfying about seeing her work set to paper right next to his own.

"I believe that you are on the right track, searching out those guest lists," Elias said, when Abigail was done. "I will go one step further and suggest that we should only consider aristocrats and upper servants. Lower servants do not generally walk into John's magic shop; they would stick out very noticeably."

Abigail nodded slowly. "Do *you* happen to know how our magician might be guaranteein' ghosts?" she asked. "I can't imagine there are many spells that do that."

Elias shook his head. "I do not know *yet*," he said. "But that is why I have a library. Perhaps while you are reading through the peerage book and the witchery with plants, you can keep an eye out for curses to do with ghosts."

Mercy groaned softly. "Outside magic," she muttered. "I *hate* outside magic."

Abigail shot Mercy a bemused glance. "You don't have to help," she said, "but it *would* go faster if you did."

Elias rose to his feet, a bit unsteady. "There will be a decent bit of French in there," he said. "I don't believe you've learned any, Abigail. Dora is always pleased to help with research – especially the French – but I do not think she will be available until tomorrow."

Abigail thought about this for a second. "I'll wager that Lucy knows French," she said. "She can read any French books over Mercy's shoulder, if she's feelin' amenable."

Mercy glanced behind her, and then nodded. "Lucy can help with the French," she confirmed.

Abigail looked back towards her father. "That's settled, then," she said. "Now go an' rest, Dad. We'll probably still be here in the morning."

"I am not certain that I have a choice," Elias said. "I already feel as though I am sleepwalking." He trapped a yawn behind one hand and headed for the door to the stairs. On his way there, he dropped an absent kiss atop Abigail's head, which made her blush with embarrassment.

Once Elias had left, Abigail cleared her throat. "I suppose we ought to make a pile of books," she said. "Are you all right at readin', Mercy?" Abigail considered this a terribly relevant question, given that she had only learned to read herself once she had left the workhouses behind.

"I'm fine at readin'," Mercy muttered crossly. She looked for a moment as though she would have preferred being illiterate.

"I can't read much at all," Hugh admitted. "I guess I couldn't turn the pages, anyhow."

"You'll just have to cheer us on as we go," Abigail told him.

Abigail turned her attention back to the bookshelves and started pulling down the most promising volumes. By the time she was done, she found herself grimly considering a very sizeable pile.

"I suppose I'll start with *Debrett's Peerage of Faeries*," Abigail said.

Mercy blinked. "Why shouldn't I read that one?" she asked. "I'm sure I'm more familiar with faeries than you are."

Abigail nodded. "That's exactly why I ought to read it," she said. "Our magician was searchin' through this book for somethin' they *didn't* know. I think you know too much about faeries already to guess what they were lookin' for."

Mercy acknowledged this with a slight bob of her head. "I'll start on the plant books, then," she said grudgingly.

There was only one lamp, and plenty of books to get through – and so, Mercy and Abigail sat down together against one of the bookshelves, each with their own research. As the evening wore on, Abigail found herself leaning against Mercy in order to soak up the slight heat she gave off. To her surprise, the scent of lye and lilies that clung to Mercy's clothing had become comforting; each time Abigail breathed it in, her body relaxed a bit more, despite the importance of their work.

Around the time the oil in the lamp had burned down halfway, Abigail sat up against Mercy, looking down at the page in *Debrett's Peerage of Faeries* to which she had just turned.

"Listen to this," Abigail said. And she read:

"LORD LONGSHADOW, Earl of LONGSHADOW. True name unknown. Titles include: The Last Sigh, The Final Usher, The First Among Sluagh, The Keeper of Life and Death, The Raven with a Thousand Faces. *Heir Apparent* – Several speculated, among them the sluagh known as Lightless."

Mercy listened intently as Abigail spoke – but just as Abigail had expected, she did not look at all surprised by this information.

"Were you goin' to mention any of this?" Abigail asked Mercy with a hint of exasperation.

Mercy blinked. "I didn't realise it was relevant," she said. "Which parts did you find interestin'?"

Abigail rubbed at the bridge of her nose. "Oh, *plenty*," she said. "But let's start with 'The Keeper of Life and Death'. That seems to reference – well, what Lightless told Lucy. That Lord Longshadow could bring someone back to life if he chose to do so." Abigail had nearly said something about the apple in Longshadow, but she had remembered just in time that Lucy was probably sitting next to Mercy too.

Mercy nodded slowly. "But we already knew that," she said. "It's not new."

Abigail let out a short breath. "It's not new to *us*," she said. "But it's in this book for anyone to read! Imagine that our killer got a look at this. I'll tell you what: there's one thing no magician has *ever* managed to do with outside magic, an' that's bringin' someone back to life. In fact, I don't think anyone *except* for Lord Longshadow can do it."

Mercy set down the book she was reading in order to stretch her shoulders. Slow concern had started to spread across her features. "But why abduct all the *other* sluagh if it's Lord Longshadow the killer was after all along?" she asked.

Abigail narrowed her eyes. "I suppose the killer could've summoned Lord Longshadow directly," she said. "But even Dad had trouble *holdin'* Lord Longshadow, an' he's the most powerful magician I know." She glanced back at the page, ruminating grimly. "I've got a theory, I think. But I'm not sure about it."

Mercy had now leaned in over the book next to Abigail, reading and re-reading the words there intently. A stray lock of her long black hair brushed against Abigail's cheek, and Abigail found herself thinking again how soft and pleasant it had been against her hand the night before.

"Abigail?" Mercy asked. "What's your theory?" Abigail realised that Mercy had repeated the question more than once now, and she blinked away her thoughts.

"I think our killer is trappin' whatever sluagh they can get their hands on," Abigail said. "I think they're hopin' one of those sluagh will know Lord Longshadow's weakness so that they can use that weakness to trap *him*."

Mercy stared at the book with growing unease. "Oh," she murmured. "That's . . . awful."

Abigail tapped at the *heir apparent* section of the entry. "This is the real problem, though," she said. "If Lightless really is set to inherit, that means he must be close to Lord Longshadow – an' maybe close in power? Do you think Lightless could overcome Lord Longshadow if he was bound to do so?"

Mercy bit her lip. "That's an even more awful idea," she said. "But no, Lightless isn't . . . *powerful*, exactly. The realm Longshadow just likes Lightless enough that everyone assumes he'd be next in line if somethin' were to happen to the current Lord Longshadow. Lightless an' Lord Longshadow both know each other's real names, but Lord Longshadow is stronger, so if it ever came to a fight—"

"They *what*?" Abigail asked. Horror leaked into her voice, and Mercy frowned in confusion.

"Some faeries *do* use their real names with each other," Mercy said. "If it's a faerie they trust, it means they can easily call upon one another."

Abigail pressed her face into her hands. "Dad said that he could have *commanded* Lord Longshadow if he'd had his real name," she said. "If our killer has Lightless, then that means they only have to convince Lightless to give up Lord Longshadow's name, an' then . . . well, they could do all *sorts* of terrible things!"

Mercy was already very pale in the lamplight – but at this, she blanched even further. "I didn't . . . I didn't think of that," she whispered. A moment later, however, she looked sharply to her right. "Is that *really* what concerns you most right now?" Mercy demanded.

Abigail groaned softly. "What's Lucy sayin', then?" she asked – though she knew she would likely regret the question.

"She's sayin' Lightless is even better than Mr Red, since he's very nearly an earl of faerie," Mercy gritted through her teeth. She narrowed her eyes at the empty air where Lucy was. "Do you *ever* think of people as people 'stead of thinkin' of how important they are an' what they can do for you?"

Mercy's normally endless patience had clearly run up against her growing distress. Abigail had never heard her speak with quite so much anger before. Mercy soon shoved to her feet; her twilight eyes had darkened to a furious, unearthly shadow.

"Lord Longshadow is *not* goin' to bring you back to life, Lucy Kendall!" Mercy hissed. "Just imagine you thinkin' you're more special than every single other person who's died before! I've met a hundred hundred ladies just like you, all of 'em always talkin' about themselves an' what they think they deserve – an' they *all* think they're the most unique, the most important people ever! All hundred hundred of 'em! You just blend in with all the others, Lucy Kendall, with the very same arrogance an' the very same tone of voice. You're so foolishly common an' so stupidly oblivious about it that in only a year or so, *none* of the sluagh will even remember your name."

The lamp's long, flickering shadows coiled around Mercy as she spoke until her silhouette rose menacingly against the far wall. There was a cold, terrible finality to her pronouncement – as though someone had rung a deep church bell and let it hang upon the air.

Abigail quailed against the bookshelf, staring at Mercy. In that moment, she caught a glimpse of the piece of Longshadow that Mercy carried with her, loosened from Mercy's own veil of mortality. Longshadow had seemed oddly kind, or whimsical, or merciful at times . . . but it was also dark and final and terrible in a way that little else could be.

Abigail was not even the direct target of Mercy's ire – but even so, she found that she could not bring herself to move.

Hugh had been lounging in the chair next to the desk – but now, he sprang up to his feet. "Stop that!" Hugh said. "You're scarin' everyone." He stalked across the distance that separated him from Mercy and grabbed at her arm.

Mercy glanced sharply back at Hugh. As she did, the blackness in her eyes retreated somewhat . . . and, very slowly, the dread silhouette upon the wall bled away its darkness, shrinking back to a more natural size.

"An' now Lucy's cryin'," Hugh said furiously. "You're just bein' cruel now because you're scared."

Mercy took a deep, shaky breath. The dark razor-edge of Longshadow had yet to entirely depart her form. "I *am* scared," Mercy said, "but I didn't say any of that *because* I'm scared. I said it because I was angry, an' because it's all true. I'll wager no one ever told Lucy the truth in life, so I've gone an' done it now before it's too late. We all know I'm right, an' I won't take back any of it – not even a little bit."

Hugh looked past Mercy at something Abigail couldn't see. His brow knit with worry, and Mercy turned away from him.

"Go after her an' comfort her if you want," Mercy told him. "But Lucy wouldn't do the same for you, Hugh. An' I won't pretend that she deserves it."

Hugh released Mercy's arm with a sharp, sullen huff. He stalked away towards the door that led to the stairs, and disappeared through it.

Chapter Thirteen

Mercy was still trying to calm herself a full minute after Hugh had disappeared. Abigail, for her part, was still trying to recover her voice; leftover fear weighed upon her throat, stifling her words.

Finally, Mercy cast a subdued glance at Abigail. Her eyes flickered once again with pink and blue twilight rather than with darkness. Her pallid skin was stark against the shadows in the room so that she nearly looked like a ghost herself. Mercy must have seen some measure of the fear in Abigail's eyes because a hint of shame crossed her features, and the last remnants of Longshadow's ire faded from her manner.

"I'm sorry," Mercy said softly. "I didn't mean to scare you."

Abigail swallowed. "I didn't mean to be scared," she said.

Mercy walked slowly back towards Abigail like she was approaching a trapped animal. She sat down next to her and slumped her shoulders as though she could shrink herself to something less frightening if only she caved her posture enough.

"I don't want you to be scared of me," Mercy said quietly. "I don't like it at all."

Abigail took a deep breath, steadying her pulse. She reached out to place her hand on top of Mercy's. Again, Abigail was struck by how long and fine Mercy's fingers were, and by how much she enjoyed holding her hand. It was a helpful reminder that Mercy was many things at once – for while she *could* be frightening, she could also be very kind and caring when she was of a mind.

Mercy glanced down at Abigail's hand. Gradually, she curled their fingers together, rasping ragged bandages against Abigail's skin.

"I am scared of you," Abigail said quietly. "You're powerful, an' you don't always appreciate that."

Mercy pressed her lips together miserably. "I can't help bein' powerful," she mumbled. "I just am. I try not to do bad things with it . . . but I guess I don't always manage." Mercy stared down into her lap. "I thought Lucy should hear the truth. But now I'm not so sure. Do you think Hugh was right, Abigail?"

Abigail leaned herself back against Mercy, as she had done earlier. She sighed heavily. "Hugh's still a kid," Abigail said. "Kids think bein' mean is always bad. An' they think that if you're nice to people, then they'll be nice back."

Mercy released Abigail's hand to wind an arm around her back. Mercy was warm and comfortable – and while the scent of lilies that she carried with her was sweet, it was the smell of lye that reminded Abigail that she was human. "That isn't an answer, exactly," Mercy observed warily.

Abigail dared to lay her head against Mercy's shoulder. Somehow, it was easier to talk about difficult things while Mercy was holding onto her.

"You've never *needed* anything from a ghost until you met Hugh – and now Lucy," Abigail told Mercy. "You just accepted 'em as they were because you knew they were movin' on soon anyway. Honestly, I always treated Lucy that way, even while she was alive. She's never goin' to change because she doesn't *want* to be a good person – she just wants to be praised an' petted an' given treats. She'll pretend to be good if you dangle those for her sometimes, but it's still just an act."

Mercy huffed slightly. "That's your lack of imagination

talkin'," she said. "You can't imagine Lucy ever bein' a better person, so you don't even want to give her the chance?"

Abigail grimaced. "I think it's easier to imagine things when you don't have to live in the real world with real people," she said. "I've figured out why my imagination's broken, Mercy – I have to deal with things as they are, an' not as I wish they were. I don't believe that things are ever really goin' to change, because they so often don't. That doesn't mean I won't *try* an' change things anyway sometimes, but I don't think it's a bad thing to be ready for how hard that is."

Abigail craned her head to look up at Mercy, putting on a serious expression. "There's a time an' a place for ignorin' all your past experience with someone an' gamblin' that they might change anyway. I don't think that time an' place is in the middle of tryin' to save other people's lives."

Mercy looked down at Abigail for a long moment. Twilight glimmered in her eyes, strange and confused. "So you believe I shouldn't have told Lucy what we all think of her," Mercy murmured. "Even though it's the truth."

Abigail shook her head. "I don't know," she sighed. "I just know that *I* wouldn't have told her. Lucy isn't worth the truth to me any more. But maybe she's still worth it to you."

Mercy tightened her arm around Abigail. "Lucy wasn't very kind to you when she was alive," she observed. Mercy sounded pained now, and offended on Abigail's behalf.

Abigail closed her eyes. "That's not worth thinkin' about any more either," she said softly. "I'd rather spend what imagination I've got on somethin' nicer." Abigail slid her arms around Mercy, holding her in return.

Thoughts had started chasing themselves around Abigail's mind ever since she had danced with Mercy on the Round Pond. It had taken an awful long time, at least by Abigail's standards, for those thoughts to make any sense. But Abigail was nearly certain now that the way she'd felt while dancing with Mercy was the way that she was *supposed* to feel when dancing with a handsome gentleman.

The realisation was nearly as annoying as it was relieving. On the one hand, Abigail was terribly peeved that no one had *told* her that she might find another woman to be interesting and lovely and deserving of sideways glances from beneath her eyelashes. But on the other hand, the understanding that she was *attracted* to Mercy freed Abigail from a nameless, confused anxiety which had plagued her for so many years – a feeling that something was not quite right, that she would never be able to relate to the way that other women sometimes wrote soppy love poems and sighed with heavy longing.

Abigail did not necessarily want to write a love poem. But she did let out a heavy sigh as she pressed her cheek to Mercy's shoulder. A new frustration replaced the old one as a fresh thought occurred to Abigail: Mercy probably considered her to be a possible friend, rather than anything more. Abigail had known close female friends to dance together, and sleep in the same bed together, and even to kiss each other while declaring their undying love and friendship.

How on earth *did* one woman express romantic interest in another woman?

"I'm imaginin' somethin' right now," Abigail mumbled.

"An' what's that?" Mercy asked distantly. She pressed one hand very gently to Abigail's hair, and Abigail nearly lost her train of thought entirely. Her skin flushed, and her heart stuttered annoyingly in her chest.

"I'm imaginin' . . ." Abigail trailed off, thinking on what she *wanted* to say, and on what she really *ought* to say.

She thought, *I'm imagining that your heart might do funny things when you look at my smile, or at my eyes, or at my hands, the same way that my heart does when I look at you.*

But she discarded that thought and tried another: *I'm*

imagining that if I kissed you, perhaps you would kiss me back, and that would be so wonderful that I'm not sure what I would do.

In the end, Abigail said neither of these things. What she said was, "I'm imaginin' that maybe two women might fall in love the way that men an' women normally do. Wouldn't that be somethin'? Two women courtin' an' gettin' married an' livin' their lives together like it was nothin' special."

Mercy's hand was featherlight on Abigail's hair. Her bandages had snagged at the strands here and there, but just the idea of her touch was delightful enough that Abigail didn't care.

"Well . . . that's not very imaginative," Mercy mumbled apologetically. "Generally, when you're tryin' to exercise your imagination, you ought to come up with things that haven't happened before."

Abigail blinked. "I'm sorry?" she said.

Mercy threaded her fingers through Abigail's hair now, tattered bandages and all. "I've met women who married women," Mercy said. "Oh! I guess you wouldn't know. Ghosts are so much more honest once they've got nothin' left to lose. There's women who just went off an' lived together, an' told everyone they were bosom friends. There's women who dressed as men so they could marry their sweethearts. I met a lady adventurer once who travelled all across the Continent seducin' women. She was interestin' enough, even if she wasn't all that kind."

Abigail required a very long moment to digest this information. Mercy's revelation was so straightforward and matter-of-fact that Abigail wasn't at all certain whether she should take it as a hopeful sign. Clearly, Mercy was *aware* that women could care for other women in that way – but if that were so then surely Mercy would have mentioned if she *herself* was one of those women.

"Can you imagine if there were trees that grew things other'n fruit?" Mercy mused, perfectly oblivious to Abigail's sudden agony. "A tree full of books would be helpful right now, for certain."

Abigail made an exasperated noise. "You're so dense," she muttered beneath her breath.

"You're mumblin', Abigail," Mercy said helpfully. "I can't hear you."

Abigail resettled herself against Mercy's shoulder. "You're very warm," she said more loudly. "An' I'm gettin' tired. Sorry."

Mercy patted her softly on the head. "Well, you can sleep for a bit, then," she said. "Hugh an' Lucy will come back eventually. An' I've got plenty of awful books on outside magic to keep me company until then."

Abigail smiled dimly at that. And though she hadn't quite admitted it aloud yet, it was nice to know that the fond twinge in her heart was actually called *affection*.

"Psst. Abigail."

Mercy was whispering to Abigail – but Abigail was very warm, and she didn't particularly wish to wake up. Her back ached a bit, as she was lying on the floor, but Mercy had pillowed Abigail's head in her lap and settled her hand absently upon her head. It was somehow both very comfortable and very uncomfortable all at the same time.

"Abigail," Mercy murmured again, "you should really wake up an' see this."

Abigail groaned softly – but she shifted in Mercy's lap and forced herself upright, blinking away the morning.

Mercy had a small book open on her knee, just next to where Abigail's head had once been. Mercy was looking at an illustration on one of the pages which showed a flower with a five-pointed blossom and a dark clutch of berries. Her sly smile held an unusual tinge of pride.

"I've found it," Mercy said. "I know how our magician is makin' ghosts."

Abigail rubbed her eyes and looked down at the book.

"Is that nightshade?" Abigail asked.

Mercy nodded and read out loud, "Nightshade can be used to wake the sleeping dead. The determined magician may use it to summon spirits and request their wisdom."

Abigail knit her brow. "Well, that's ... admittedly clever," she muttered. "Our magician's just summonin' the dead right after they die." She straightened with an abrupt thought. "Nightshade – belladonna – it's poisonous. The perfume shop we used to live over sold belladonna perfume. Dad always said it was goin' to get someone killed."

Mercy frowned. "Why would people put somethin' poisonous on their skin?" she asked. "That seems awful silly."

Abigail snorted. "People don't just put it on their skin," she said. "Some ladies put it in their *eyes*. Makes 'em look all dark-eyed an' mysterious. I don't think any of it is good for you, but belladonna only kills you right away if you eat it."

Mercy shook her head incredulously. "That's got to be the poorest reason I ever heard of to die," she said. "Imagine slowly killin' yourself to make your eyes darker."

Abigail shot Mercy a bemused look. "That's not very imaginative," she said. "Generally, when you're tryin' to exercise your imagination, you ought to come up with things that haven't happened before."

Mercy winced. "I'll admit," she said, "I never met a ghost who poisoned 'emselves with eyedrops. Or else, I guess I wouldn't know if I *had* met one, would I? I'm sure they'd have died just like Lucy, without ever knowin' why they fell asleep an' never woke up."

Abigail frowned at that. "Speakin' of which – where *are* Hugh an' Lucy?"

Mercy sighed heavily. "They're downstairs," she said. "Lucy won't talk to me directly any more. She's doin' this thing where I have to talk to Hugh, who talks to her *for* me."

Abigail shrugged. "Lucy could've stormed away entirely, I guess," she said. "At least we can handle her havin' a tantrum for a while." Abigail pushed herself up to her feet, wincing against her body's stiffness, and she offered Mercy a hand up in turn.

Downstairs, Dora was sitting at the dining table with her pocket mirror in front of her and Hugh at her side. Abigail had to assume that Lucy was present, though she couldn't see her.

"I've got good news an' bad news," Abigail announced as they entered the dining room. "The good news is Mercy might've figured out how our magician is killin' people an' makin' sure they leave ghosts behind. If we've found the right information, then it means that someone's done a spell usin' belladonna an' used it to poison those girls." She glanced at Hugh. "That means someone must have slipped belladonna to Lucy at that ball – an' probably near the end of the party, since she didn't die in the ballroom."

Mercy looked at the chair just next to Hugh. "Do you remember anyone givin' you somethin' to eat, perhaps—?" she started saying.

But Lucy had clearly turned up her nose in some obvious way. Mercy cut herself off with a sigh and turned to Hugh instead. "Could you please ask Lucy whether someone gave her somethin' to eat or drink at the ball?" she requested.

Hugh gave Mercy a faintly reproving look, but he turned to repeat the question to Lucy all the same. A moment later, Hugh replied, "There were little treats an' punch at the ball, but Lucy doesn't remember if anyone *gave* her any."

Abigail chewed at the inside of her cheek. "I think someone must have poisoned Lucy's punch," she said. "It's easier'n poisonin' a little sandwich – an' the flavour wouldn't have changed all that much. You'd barely need a moment with someone's punch to slip some poison into it, I'd wager."

Dora turned her even-tempered gaze upon Abigail. "But you mentioned that you had good news and bad news," she said. "What is the bad news, Abigail?"

Abigail sighed. "The bad news is I don't know how to protect against belladonna," she admitted. "I think I could find a spell to protect against the necromancy part – the turnin' someone into a ghost – but then whoever it was would still be poisoned like normal. The only magical antidotes I know of are things like theriac an' bezoars, an' we're not goin' to find any of *those* in a hurry."

Dora considered this for a long moment. "I believe that Lady Hollowvale might be able to help," she said.

Abigail blinked. "Other Mum?" she asked.

Dora nodded slightly. "Lady Hollowvale still has half of my soul. I dream of her sometimes, you know – and I am sure that she also dreams of me. The longer that this business with the dead girls has gone on, the more convinced I have become that she wishes to see you, Abigail."

Abigail shifted on her feet. It had occurred to her more than once that her Other Mum might have helpful insight into the current situation . . . but Hollowvale was not so very close that she could wander there and back whenever she pleased. "It could take days to go an' see her," Abigail said. "I'm not sure I can leave for that long."

Dora nodded serenely. "I thought as much," she said. "Lady Hollowvale seems to know that as well. That is why she has risked leaving Hollowvale. I believe that she will join the other faeries in Kensington Gardens tonight."

Abigail felt a faint spike of alarm at that. "But that means Other Mum's left the children alone in Hollowvale?" she asked.

Dora frowned distractedly. "I cannot say what all Lady Hollowvale has done," she admitted. "But I am sure that if she is here, then it must be important enough for her to have left."

Abigail wanted to ask for more explanation – but Dora clearly had no further explanation to offer. She sighed instead. "I suppose I'll be headed to Kensington Gardens again tonight, then," Abigail said.

Chapter Fourteen

Abigail spent the rest of the afternoon reading through her father's library, in case there was some other magical antidote to be found there – but she still had not found anything useful by the time the sun had started trending downwards. She therefore set aside the books she had been searching through and started preparing herself to visit the gardens once again.

Mercy had slept part of the afternoon away herself, but she had eventually joined Abigail in the ballroom once again to assist with the research. As Abigail set aside the book she had been reading, Mercy reached out to pull it into her lap.

"Are you not comin' with me to the gardens?" Abigail asked Mercy.

A flicker of uncertainty crossed Mercy's pale features. "I hadn't intended to join you," Mercy admitted. "I don't imagine Lady Hollowvale would be very happy to see me, since I'm carryin' Longshadow with me."

Abigail clasped her hands nervously behind her back. "But you've been nothin' but helpful," she said. "I promise I'll tell her as much. I just think you should meet her, is all."

Mercy blinked. "Why?" she asked. The question was sincere, and slightly baffled.

Abigail twisted her hands behind her. It was very important

to her that Mercy should meet her Other Mum – and it was furthermore very important to her that Lady Hollowvale should *like* Mercy. "I'd just . . . like to keep seein' you when this is all over," Abigail said to Mercy. "An' that seems more likely if everyone in the family knows you. I'm sure you normally come an' go from faerie very often. Maybe next time I go to Hollowvale, we could go together."

Mercy widened her eyes with alarm at this suggestion, and Abigail cringed. "Never mind," Abigail said. "It isn't necessary—"

"I didn't mean to upset you," Mercy said hastily. "I just . . . I really don't think we'll get on, Abigail. Lady Hollowvale's so notorious for not likin' the sluagh, or anything to do with Longshadow. I can't imagine her ever lettin' me visit."

Abigail looked down at her feet. "We *will* still see each other when this is over, though?" she asked in a small voice.

Mercy considered this question. As she did, Abigail saw many strange emotions flicker across her face in turn – so quickly that she couldn't quite pick them apart. "I would *like* to see you," Mercy said finally. "But I . . . well, dependin' what happens, I don't know if that'll be possible. I don't know how things will all fall out with Lord Longshadow an' those bans, an' the rest of your family."

Abigail bit at her lip. "You think . . . Lord Longshadow might stop you from visitin' any more?" she asked worriedly.

Mercy shook her head. "No," she said. "That's not what I think. I just . . ." She sighed heavily. "It's so complicated. I've thought more'n once I should try an' explain it, but . . . you said there's a time an' a place for hard talks. An' I guess that's true. We have so much else to focus on, an' I've already made things more difficult with Lucy. I don't want to do somethin' like that again by accident, when it could just as easily wait until we've saved everyone who needs savin'."

Abigail's throat tightened with worry. "You have something bad to talk about, then," she said quietly.

Mercy winced. "I don't *know* if it's bad," she replied. "It could be, I guess. But it's my problem an' not yours, an' I don't want to distract us."

Abigail didn't mean to look heartbroken – but the idea that she might never see Mercy again once they were done felt abrupt and overwhelming. Abigail had only just figured out that she might like to kiss Mercy someday – and some small part of her had admittedly been trying to figure out how to make that more likely. But the way that Mercy now spoke made it seem as though Abigail might not even get to remain friends with her.

Mercy must have seen something of Abigail's distress on her face. Guilt curled at the corners of her mouth, and she set aside the book in her lap. "I . . . I guess I could come with you to the gardens," Mercy said. "If you're really sure that you want me there."

A ribbon of relief fluttered through Abigail's chest. Mercy's talk of later discussions still bothered her – but Abigail was *sure* that if her Other Mum took a liking to Mercy, then everything would be just a little more likely to turn out all right.

"I do want you there," Abigail assured Mercy softly. "I think you're . . . well, you're . . . I like you plenty, is all. An' I'd like us to be friends."

Mercy parted her lips in surprise. The idea had caught her utterly off-guard. "You want to be friends?" she repeated.

Abigail knit her brow. "Is that bad?" she asked. The words came out slightly cross, and Mercy held her hands up quickly.

"Not bad!" Mercy assured her. In fact, she looked deeply touched. A faint pink flush spread across her cheeks, and she glanced away from Abigail in embarrassment. "I like you plenty, too. I just never thought . . . well, you an' your family have been awful kind to me, in spite of everything."

Mercy hesitated, trying to put words to thoughts. She struggled for a moment before she said, "I'd like to be your friend, Abigail. I *will* be your friend, even if things fall out badly. An' if you do want to see me, you can always come an' visit Longshadow. I'd love to show you the lilies that grow silver there, an' the hill where you can see all the way to the Other Side."

Abigail smiled. "I *will* come visit," she said. "Now that you've made the invitation, you can't take it back." She offered her hand out to Mercy to help her up to her feet. Abigail found herself savouring the way that Mercy's long fingers curled around her hand. She dared to dream, just for an instant, that there *would* come a day when she kissed Mercy. Maybe it would be among the lilies in Longshadow, as they glimmered in the faerie moonlight.

Oh! Abigail thought suddenly. *I just imagined something.*

Mercy's hand lingered in Abigail's. They were standing very close now – and so, when Mercy glanced up at Abigail and gave her that sly smile, it was even more devastating than usual.

"You look like someone hit you over the head just now," Mercy observed. She sounded deeply amused.

Abigail searched Mercy's twilight eyes. "I imagined somethin'," she said. "Somethin' good. I saw it in my head for a second, clear as day. That doesn't happen very often at all."

Mercy's sly smile softened at that, and she squeezed Abigail's hand. "Would you tell me about it?" she asked.

Blood rushed swiftly to Abigail's face. She had to look away from those dark, glimmering eyes. "Not right now," Abigail mumbled self-consciously. "But . . . maybe someday."

Abigail imagined herself picking up that delicate dream, gingerly folding it up and tucking it away within herself for safekeeping. It didn't seem safe, somehow, to look at it for too long at once. But she knew that she would take that dream back out again – probably more than once – whenever she wanted to long for something nice.

Abigail had expected Hugh to accompany her to see their Other Mum since she had his locket with her – but she was surprised when Dora also appeared downstairs, in her bonnet and her pelisse, and volunteered to come with them.

"I don't particularly need to speak to my other half," Dora said, "but I would rather be there in case you find any other iron. I suspect that I will also need to impose upon the grounds-keeper to let you out before dawn."

Lucy must have said something about going as well – but Mercy and Hugh both turned upon her at once with an emphatic and resounding "No!"

Had Abigail been able to hear Lucy, she was sure she would have offered exactly the same reaction. Lady Hollowvale might have had half an English soul – but she had still partially come of age in faerie, and she could be quite wicked when she was of a mind. That Lady Hollowvale mostly directed her wickedness against cruel people did not much improve the situation; Lucy's usual attitude was exactly the sort of thing which would normally stir her ire.

Hugh flushed and floundered to explain the matter to Lucy in a gentle way. "Other Mum isn't . . . she's nice to *us* because she's our Other Mum," he said. "But she's not obliged to be nice to you, an' I don't think she would be."

Abigail sidled up next to Mercy, smiling at her with faint amusement. "You haven't even met our Other Mum yet," she murmured. "You're just as dead set as Hugh against introducin' Lucy to her, though."

"I've met plenty of *faeries*," Mercy muttered back. "The sluagh are positively patient, since they've got to be. But the way that Lucy talks, she'd get herself cursed or torn apart only five seconds after meetin' most faeries."

Abigail sighed. "I almost want to see it," she said ruefully. She turned back towards Hugh and Lucy and raised her voice to the empty air. "Other Mum is unpredictable, an' she *could* hurt you even though you're a ghost, Lucy," Abigail said. "If you ever want a chance of comin' back to life, you'd best stay here while we're out. The House is one of the safest places in London, as long as you're a welcomed guest."

Abigail couldn't see or hear Lucy at the moment – but she knew that this was the proper thing to say. Lucy might have been petty and foolish at the best of times, but she was *also* understandably obsessed with coming back to life.

Surely enough, Hugh relaxed in relief and reached up to pat the air where Lucy's shoulder should have been. "We won't be long," he assured her.

The four of them left the House, retracing the walk which they had taken only a few days ago. Abigail's best muslin was beginning to look a bit sorry for a proper walk in Kensington Gardens, and Mercy still looked every bit the out-of-place laundress – but as they came closer to the gate, Mercy took Abigail's arm, and the creeping shadows of the early evening swept over them, hiding them from view. Longshadow's darkness was cool and pleasant against Abigail's skin . . . but some part of her still recalled the seed of dark finality that lurked within it, and she shivered slightly against Mercy's arm.

"No wonder I keep findin' you in places you ought not to be," Abigail murmured to Mercy as they slipped through the gate. "I'm not sure as anyone could *stop* you from goin' where you please."

Mercy gave Abigail one of her sly smiles. Within the shade that covered them, that smile had a dark and dangerous edge – but the danger within it was still magnetic in a way that made Abigail's heart twinge with excitement. Again, Abigail had the thought that the world and everything in it had been created merely to bow before Mercy when she was like this – all dark and deliciously haughty. Abigail, too, would have given much for the chance to reward that arrogant smirk with a kiss.

But the enchantment of Mercy's dark smile crested and

passed like a wave, and Abigail regained control of herself before she could do something too foolish.

Hugh still walked behind them, Abigail realised, following the tug of his locket; she was barely cognisant of him in the shadow of Mercy's presence. But Dora had paused herself at the gate behind them, speaking quietly with a man there. She had the posture of a woman who intended to remain right where she was.

"I wonder if Other Mum left someone behind to keep an eye on the kids in Hollowvale," Hugh muttered worriedly.

The shadows fell away from Abigail and Mercy as they left the gate behind, and Abigail glanced behind them at Hugh. "Other Mum is a little flighty," she said dubiously, "but I can't see her leavin' the other children in danger."

Hugh nodded uncertainly.

Abigail led them slowly towards the Round Pond, since she knew that her Other Mum did enjoy the occasional dance. Again, she found herself passing other mortal couples on the Broad Walk, scurrying their way towards the exits – but Mercy held onto Abigail's arm the entire time, and Abigail couldn't help a small smile at the thought.

As the sky darkened further and the human population of the gardens disappeared, however, Abigail became aware that Kensington Gardens had gone a bit *too* dark *too* quickly. In fact, a familiar, cloying mist had started swirling about their feet as they approached the Round Pond.

"Oh," Abigail said.

"Oh my," Mercy murmured, with a hint of disapproval.

Hugh looked at them both askance. "What is it?" he asked.

Abigail waved a thread of wet mist away from her face. It curled around her hand as though in greeting, and she felt an answering tug from within her soul.

"Other Mum didn't leave Hollowvale at all," Abigail said. "I think she brought Hollowvale *with* her."

"Faerie realms don't belong in England," Mercy muttered distastefully. "This could be a real disaster."

Abigail shook her head. "Best we go find out what she has to say, then," she said. "I'm sure Other Mum will leave an' put Hollowvale back where it belongs once she's said her piece."

The mist soon grew so thick that Abigail nearly stumbled straight into the Round Pond. Mercy caught her by the waist just before she could tumble in – and Abigail stared ahead in confusion.

The shrill, piping flute music from a few nights ago was playing again – but the flowered faeries were not dancing upon the Round Pond this time. Instead, a young girl in a ruffled, highly embroidered white dress and a lacy blindfold was chasing two faerie ladies dressed like daisies across the surface of the water.

"I'll catch you!" the little girl shrieked. "Ooh, stay still!"

One of the daisy faeries giggled – and the little girl lurched forward, throwing her arms out. She caught the faerie by the arm with a triumphant yell. "A daisy!" she yelled. "I've caught a daisy, haven't I?"

"I am caught!" the daisy acknowledged. "I shall be a blind flower next!"

The little girl tore off the blindfold – but as she did, she caught sight of Abigail and blinked.

"Abby!" she said with a broad, partially toothless smile. "An' Hugh, too! You've come to visit!"

"Fanny," Abigail said blankly. "You're . . . *here*. An' I can see you an' everything."

Abigail looked out over the pond. It did not take much effort this time for her to imagine stepping onto the water as though it were solid ground – for Hollowvale welcomed her back with every step, assuring her that it would support her. A trickle of cool power flooded Abigail's veins, and she released Mercy's arm to stroll quickly across the water.

At thirteen years old, Fanny was one of the older ghosts in

Hollowvale, and she rarely let anyone forget it. Her brown hair was shorn nearly to her scalp – she had only just survived a fever in the workhouse before a faerie had finally killed her for good. Like Abigail, Fanny was a bit too skinny, and the physical impact of the workhouses showed on her blemished skin – but the faeries in Hollowvale had greatly enjoyed pampering her ever since Other Mum had taken over, and so Fanny was never seen now without a lovely gown.

"Ah, more blind men!" the daisy observed cheerfully, as Abigail approached. "Will you be joining us tonight? I am about to take my turn."

Abigail blinked a few more times, trying to get her bearings. "I suppose I might eventually," she said carefully. "But I'm here to see Other Mum – er, Lady Hollowvale. I suppose if all of Hollowvale is here, then she *must* be around somewhere."

"Oh yes, Mum's about," said Fanny. "She brought us all out to see the gardens – aren't they grand? No one ever would've let me into Kensington when I was alive. An' there's all these other faeries about as well. They barely know how to play Blind Man's Bluff, but we're teachin' 'em all the same." So saying, Fanny handed the lacy blindfold off to the daisy, who pulled it over her eyes with bemusement.

Mercy and Hugh caught up to Abigail then, and Hugh lit up as he saw the blindfold. "Ooh," he said, "I want to play! There is room, isn't there?"

"The whole pond is playing," the daisy replied helpfully, from behind her blindfold. "You mustn't use magic if you join us, though – it spoils the fun."

"Of course," Hugh said seriously. "I promise not to use any magic."

Fanny shot him a bemused grin and took him by the arm. But before they could start sneaking away, a man's voice called out across the fog.

"Fanny!" The voice was high-pitched and refined – and quite

familiar. "You are not wandering too far, I hope! Remember that you must not leave the mist!"

A tall, dark-haired man in a black velvet jacket soon appeared out of the murk. At first glance, he might easily have been mistaken for a human being – but any sort of closer look quickly dispelled that impression. His eyes were a bright, uncanny green; his cheekbones were far too sharp and his ears were gently pointed at the ends.

The green-eyed elf paused as he saw Abigail. They considered each other with a brief, puzzled silence.

"Lord Blackthorn?" Abigail asked. "I thought you were bein' a butler these days."

"Oh, it is Mr Jubilee now," the elf reminded Abigail cheerfully. "I unbecame a lord years and years ago. But how kind of you to remember – I *did* secure a job as a butler! I was having great fun at it, but the lady of the house eventually grew tired of being cursed, and she begged me to leave – er, perhaps that is a story for another time. All of that is just to say: I have volunteered to be a governess tonight. I hope that I am doing a halfway proper job of it."

"You're doin' fine, Mr Jubilee," Fanny informed the elf gravely.

Mr Jubilee beamed with pride, and Abigail shook her head. "I'm shocked your wife let you out of her sight," she said. "*Is* Effie here tonight?"

"She is," Mr Jubilee said. "She is taking tea with Lady Hollowvale right now—"

But Mr Jubilee cut himself off suddenly, and Abigail saw that he had gone terribly pale, staring at something just over her shoulder. She turned and saw that he had fixed his eyes upon Mercy.

"You should not be here," Mr Jubilee said worriedly. "Lady Hollowvale would not be pleased at *all*."

Mercy shrank down into herself very slightly. "I didn't mean to walk into Hollowvale," she said. "I thought I was walkin' into Kensington Gardens. How was I to know she'd picked up all of Hollowvale and brought it here?"

Abigail glanced between the two of them. "You know Mr Jubilee?" she asked Mercy.

Mercy nodded minutely. "I've been to Blackthorn more'n once," she said. "Mr Jubilee's always been a real fine fellow."

Abigail looked back to Mr Jubilee, pressing her lips together. "I invited Mercy to come here with me," she said. "I know Other Mum doesn't want anyone from Longshadow here, but it's my fault an' not Mercy's. She isn't goin' to abduct anyone."

Mr Jubilee continued staring at Mercy, still deeply anxious. "Oh," he murmured. "And you have given Abigail your real first name. I had thought I should keep that to myself, but Lady Hollowvale will surely learn it now. In any case, I cannot help but think . . . Well, it might still be best if you were to . . ."

Mercy sighed. "I'm here already," she said. "I promised I would come, an' so I have. If Lady Hollowvale wants me gone, then I'll leave the moment that she tells me to do it."

Mr Jubilee took a deep breath. "If you are . . . *quite* certain," he said. "In which case, I suppose that I will show you back to the Hollow House."

Hugh glanced at Mercy warily. "Should I come with you?" he asked. "I can tell Other Mum how nice you've been."

Mercy shook her head. "Enjoy your game," she said. "I can take care of myself."

"I won't let Other Mum hurt Mercy," Abigail assured Hugh. She took Mercy's arm again, with perhaps a hint of possessiveness. "Lead on, Mr Jubilee. We could all use some tea, I expect."

Chapter Fifteen

The Round Pond should not have been big enough to contain the Hollow House. But somehow, as they walked through the mist to the centre of the pond, the old faerie mansion rose from the fog all the same.

The Hollow House was much as Abigail remembered it: a huge grey manor in the style of an English country estate. Ivy covered much of the architecture – though since the Hollow House was suddenly sitting atop the surface of a lake, Abigail wasn't now entirely certain where the ivy was growing from.

Normally, the ever-present mists of Hollowvale stopped at the entryway of the Hollow House – but today, fog roiled through its corridors, leaving the marble floors dangerously slick. The piece of Hollowvale which Abigail carried within her twinged with confused delight, and she wondered if Hollowvale itself had any sense that it had been messily relocated to England.

Though the Hollow House had several sitting rooms within its labyrinthine halls, Abigail was not at all surprised when Mr Jubilee led their small party towards the ballroom at the centre of the manor. Lady Hollowvale expected guests to meet her wherever she happened to be at the time of their visit, and she often frequented the ballroom.

The great doors which led into the ballroom had been thrown open – indeed, they were rarely ever closed. Beyond them was an impossibly large room with a black and white chequered marble floor. The last bit of twilight outside diffused weakly through Hollowvale's fog before trickling in through the upper windows; this twilight was not nearly enough to light the room, which was why hundreds of eerie blue-lit candles currently floated about the area. The flickering blue light reflected off the polished floor as though it were a mirror, highlighting the large pianoforte at the centre of the room.

Lady Hollowvale currently sat upon the back of the piano, prim and proper, with a cup of tea in hand. She looked very much like Dora, even from a distance, but she kept her rusted red hair much longer in a single braid down her back, and Abigail knew that Lady Hollowvale's left eye was grey rather than her right one. Still, no one with any sense would ever have mistaken Lady Hollowvale for Lady Theodora Wilder: Lady Hollowvale's features were always animated with one intense emotion or another, and while the ragged grey gown she wore was strangely dignified, it would have been utterly improper at any real society event. There was, as well, a wild and faintly predatory air to everything which Lady Hollowvale did. She was, in short, everything which a terrifying faerie lady *ought* to be.

Mrs Euphemia Jubilee had settled herself onto the piano bench with her own cup of tea. Euphemia was nearly as plain and nondescript as Lady Hollowvale was wild and dangerous: her brown hair was kept back in a neat working bun, and she was dressed only slightly better than Mercy in a faded, cast-off gown, speckled with bright bursts of lovely embroidery. Euphemia had a warm smile on her face, however, and Abigail heard Mr Jubilee heave a heavy, lovestruck sigh as he saw her.

As they entered the ballroom, Lady Hollowvale glanced their way. A broad, overly joyous grin lit up her features, and she leapt from the back of the piano, tossing her teacup aside to shatter against the marble floor. She sprinted for the doorway, shooing candles hurriedly out of her way as she went. Eventually, she reached Abigail, sweeping her up into an excited embrace.

"My lovely daughter!" Lady Hollowvale cried. "I've missed you so much – and here you are again! The other children have missed you terribly as well, you know. We shall have a feast now that you are here!" Her voice should have been utterly identical to Dora's – but the manic emotion within it changed its tenor so much that she might as well have been another woman.

Abigail embraced her Other Mum back with a wry smile. "I'm not sure we need a feast, Mum," she said. "There's already tea, an' that'll do just fine."

Euphemia set down her own teacup much more calmly, stepping over broken crockery to join them. "Careful what you say in front of all those faeries outside," she advised Lady Hollowvale. "First you mention feasts, an' then one of 'em will decide there ought to be a *tournament*, an' you won't find even five minutes to talk to your daughter."

Mr Jubilee's green eyes lit up with excitement. "A tournament!" he said. "Why, that's a marvellous idea, darling. The delphiniums are excellent jousters, I can go and speak to them now—"

"You're a governess tonight, Mr Jubilee," Euphemia reminded him with bemused patience. "Governesses don't set up tournaments."

Mr Jubilee's excitement wilted into a frown. "Er . . . not even tournaments for children?" he asked hopefully.

"*Certainly* not tournaments for children," Euphemia confirmed. She stepped forward and leaned up onto her toes to press a fond kiss to his cheek, all the same. "There's still tea on the piano, though. Why don't we all sit down and have a cup?"

Lady Hollowvale had released Abigail from her embrace, however – and as Abigail's Other Mum turned her uncanny gaze to Mercy, a sudden, chilling fury overcame her joy, like a black cloud passing before the sun.

"*You.*"

The word was dark and cold in more ways than one. Blue flames flickered frenetically, casting angry shadows across the marble floor. Frost crackled at Lady Hollowvale's feet, spiralling out from her figure to climb the surrounding walls.

"You are barred from my realm," Lady Hollowvale hissed. Alien rage danced within her mismatched eyes. "How dare you walk where you are not wanted?"

Abigail stepped instinctively between Mercy and her Other Mum, holding up her hands. Had Abigail been anyone else, she was sure that she would have cowered beneath Lady Hollowvale's gaze – but the piece of Hollowvale that Abigail carried reassured her that no power born from this faerie realm would ever harm her.

"An' here I thought I was goin' to have to introduce you," Abigail said softly. Her breath misted in front of her in the sudden cold of the room.

"Ah," Mr Jubilee mumbled, a few feet to Abigail's right. "No, introductions are unnecessary. I keep forgetting that humans cannot see souls as we faeries can do."

"I've got Longshadow all over my soul," Mercy agreed quietly. "Lady Hollowvale might have half an English soul ... but she's more faerie than not these days. She can see the Longshadow in me just fine." Somehow, Mercy had not bowed beneath the weight of that otherworldly fury ... but she did wear a faintly apologetic expression upon her face.

"You *know* what she is?" Lady Hollowvale asked Abigail incredulously. "And you still brought her to Hollowvale?"

"I invited Mercy to come with me to Kensington Gardens, Mum," Abigail sighed. "We didn't know you'd brought all of Hollowvale with you. I wouldn't have put everyone in such an awful position if I *had* known."

Mercy pressed her lips together. "I'm aware that I've trespassed, Lady Hollowvale," she said, "an' I apologise for it. But on my word, I'm not here to cause any trouble."

Lady Hollowvale flexed her fingers with agitation, staring past Abigail at Mercy. It was clear that she was struggling with the problem of how best to attack Mercy with her own daughter in the way. Abigail was taken aback by the sheer hatred in Lady Hollowvale's mismatched gaze. She should have expected as much, given that Lady Hollowvale's half a soul did not possess much patience or moderation – those attributes had mostly gone to Dora – but Abigail had so rarely seen her Other Mum truly angry at anything before.

"I dreamed that Longshadow had snared my daughter," Lady Hollowvale said to Mercy, with a hint of soft menace. "I saw her walking in *your* shadow, didn't I? Well, you will not have her. You must have believed that I could not leave Hollowvale in order to protect her, but I have outsmarted you."

Abigail shifted uneasily. "You came here to protect me from Longshadow?" she asked her Other Mum. "But I don't need protectin' from Mercy, Mum. She hasn't *snared* me. She's been helpin' me."

Lady Hollowvale narrowed her eyes. "You would believe that, of course," she said. "Lord Longshadow helped your father once – but payment came due, Abigail. It will come due again."

Mercy winced and pressed her fingers to the bridge of her nose. Shame and embarrassment showed on her features. "That is . . . well, much of that is true, I'm sad to say," she mumbled. "But the last part *isn't* true, Lady Hollowvale. There won't be payment this time – because as much as I'm helpin' Abigail, she's also helpin' *me*. The Lord Sorcier is obliged to solve this matter, but so am I. It's my friends that are missin'. As such, there's no debts to be had on either side."

Lady Hollowvale's anger and suspicion did not cool – but Mr Jubilee cleared his throat delicately. "I am . . . very fond of everyone here," he said, with a hint of apology. "I know that I am a governess today, but perhaps I might still help with a solution?" He pulled his handkerchief from his jacket, looking down at it with an expression of deep concentration. "You have every right to be angry with Longshadow, Lady Hollowvale. But . . . we must think about how our decisions today will affect things tomorrow, must we not?"

Mr Jubilee glanced at Lady Hollowvale with a questioning expression as he said this, as though searching for her approval. Lady Hollowvale looked back at Mr Jubilee – and all at once, she sighed heavily, slumping her shoulders.

"I wish you wouldn't remember my advice sometimes, Mr Jubilee," Lady Hollowvale muttered. "Don't you forget most everything *else* that I say?"

Mr Jubilee did not seem at all insulted by this statement – instead, he proudly held out his handkerchief for Lady Hollowvale to see. Upon the handkerchief was embroidered the words: *Think about tomorrow.*

"I knew that I would forget your advice," Mr Jubilee assured Lady Hollowvale. "That is why I tucked it away in my pocket, so that I could carry it around with me all the time."

"Ah," Lady Hollowvale said simply. "I see. Very clever of you, Mr Jubilee." She crossed her arms – and while the frost on the walls had yet to fade, the chill in the air at least grew less oppressive. "Well. Speak your piece, Mr Jubilee. I am listening."

Mr Jubilee cast his gaze across the tense gathering. There was fresh worry in his manner as he realised that he had indeed been offered the opportunity to help solve the issue. Mr Jubilee had a terrible history of making problems worse whenever he tried to solve them – a fact of which he was painfully well aware. "Well, I . . ." Mr Jubilee took a deep breath and glanced at his wife. Euphemia smiled wryly at him and nodded in encouragement.

Mr Jubilee straightened. "If it is potential debts which worry you, Lady Hollowvale," he said, "then Mercy can simply swear before us all that Abigail shall owe nothing for her help until they are finished working together."

"I would swear that if it would make you feel better, Lady Hollowvale," Mercy assured her.

It was a sensible suggestion; in fact, Lady Hollowvale now seemed upset at *how* sensible the suggestion was, since she could find little fault with it. She tapped her foot on the chequered marble, fighting against her obvious hatred of Longshadow.

"I know all about what's happened with Longshadow up until now, Mum," Abigail said softly. "But I like Mercy, an' so does Hugh. We're friends, an' I like to think that at least *we'll* talk things out from now on." It took most of Abigail's willpower just to hold her Other Mum's eyes – but somehow, she managed it. "I'd like it if you both could get along. I know that's a bit of an ask."

Lady Hollowvale knit her brow with obvious distress. Abigail suspected that her Other Mum still thought they were all being tricked. But Mercy stepped out carefully from behind Abigail, placing a hand on her shoulder.

"You're the injured party," Mercy told Lady Hollowvale quietly. "It's on me to fix things, an' not on you. So I'll swear this: Abigail won't pick up any debts to me until we've saved my friends. An' I'll swear this too, Lady Hollowvale: I will never try an' take any ghosts from you, even if the piece of Longshadow I've got disagrees with me on that. That's what I really wanted to tell you while I'm here."

Lady Hollowvale stared at Mercy, as though reluctant to believe what she was hearing. "You will disagree with Longshadow itself?" Lady Hollowvale asked slowly.

Mercy shrugged ruefully. "I hear *you* don't always do what Hollowvale tells you to do," she pointed out.

"Well yes," Lady Hollowvale said. "But I pride myself on being very contrary."

Mercy chuckled. "Well, maybe Longshadow will get sick of me," she said. "I know at least one sluagh who'd be real happy about that." She looked away. "You'll have no trouble from me, at least. I can't promise anything more'n that, I'm afraid. I know there's still sluagh out there who feel different."

Lady Hollowvale smiled abruptly – and all at once, the ominous weight upon the air vanished. Her mood had shifted jarringly, so that she was suddenly a joyful, gracious host once more. "You are a guest here, then!" Lady Hollowvale said. "How wonderful! We must all sit down to tea together."

Euphemia coughed with amusement. "I'm afraid we've only got one teacup left," she said. "You broke the other one, Lady Hollowvale."

"Oh," Lady Hollowvale said absently. "Yes, I did do that. Do you mind if we all share your teacup, Mrs Jubilee?"

"I was prepared to offer," Euphemia agreed. They started back towards the piano – but Euphemia frowned at Mercy as they walked. "Mr Jubilee knows you," she said, "but I can't seem to place you. Have we met?"

Mercy let out a long breath. It was clear now that she'd been far more anxious than she'd appeared while facing Lady Hollowvale's fury. She reached out for Abigail's arm, clinging to it with relief, and glanced at Euphemia. "I went to your weddin' in Blackthorn, Mrs Jubilee," Mercy said. "But that was years ago, before I was even a bit of a laundress, so you might not recognise me."

"The cap suits you wonderfully," Mr Jubilee offered agreeably.

Mercy smiled shyly. "I *am* very fond of it," she said. "Did you notice I even smell like lye?"

Mr Jubilee seemed suitably impressed by this. "How delightful!" he declared. "You know, I have yet to try being a laundress. Have you done any real laundry?"

"I tried," Mercy said, "but I think I ruined it."

Abigail shot her a bemused look. "You *want* to learn to do laundry?" she asked Mercy. "I'm sure you can help next laundry day at the House, if you really want."

Mercy blushed. "I would like that, actually," she mumbled. "It was so much more difficult than I thought it'd be."

It took more than a bit of doing for them to situate themselves around the piano for tea, as there was not nearly enough room for four people to sit upon it. Lady Hollowvale picked Abigail up by the waist, settling her upon the top, while Euphemia took up her spot on the piano bench again. Abigail helped Mercy onto the piano next to her, but Mr Jubilee insisted on standing, as he was a governess today.

Lady Hollowvale took up the teapot from the back of the piano and refilled Euphemia's cup, passing it to Mercy. "My goodness," Lady Hollowvale observed, as she saw the fraying bandages around Mercy's fingers. "Your hands! Whatever happened to them?"

Mercy took a long sip of tea. "I tried to magic some iron," she said. "I can't recommend it."

Both Lady Hollowvale and Mr Jubilee shuddered at the idea. Mercy passed the teacup to Abigail, who lingered over it for a long moment.

"Mum," Abigail said slowly, "I meant to ask you while I was here – I don't suppose you know how to protect someone from bein' poisoned with nightshade?"

Lady Hollowvale frowned. "I fear I do *not* know," she said. "But even if Mr Jubilee is not Lord Blackthorn any more, I believe that the realm Blackthorn still owns him, and Blackthorn grows flowers of all kinds. Do you have any advice regarding nightshade, Mr Jubilee?"

Mr Jubilee looked faintly offended at the subject of conversation. "Nightshade!" he said. "What an awful, temperamental flower. Blackthorn does not allow nightshade to grow within its borders at all."

Euphemia considered Mr Jubilee thoughtfully. "Blackthorn's very clever, though," she said. "I'm sure it could grow an antidote to nightshade if it wanted to?"

Mr Jubilee knit his brow. "Yes," he said slowly. "Blackthorn surely *could* grow an antidote. I could ask the realm for a nightshade remedy – but it will not offer up such an antidote without payment."

Abigail opened her mouth to reply that of *course* she would find some form of payment – but to her surprise, Mercy responded first. "I'll pay for the antidote, Mr Jubilee," Mercy said. "You can tell Blackthorn that I'll bring it some of the silver lilies from Longshadow as soon as we've rescued my friends. Those lilies would grow just fine in Blackthorn, as long as they're kept in starlight."

Mr Jubilee brightened. "Why, that's perfect," he said. "I shall go and ask Blackthorn as soon as I am free to return there. I am only a governess for tonight, after all, so I am sure that I can manage something by tomorrow."

Mr Jubilee, of course, was prone to forgetting even very important things – but Euphemia looked over at Abigail and silently mouthed the words, *I'll remind him.*

Abigail could not curtsy while on top of the piano – but she bowed her head to the two of them nevertheless. "Thank you very much, Mr Jubilee," she said. "I greatly appreciate it."

"I wonder now which flowers grow on the Other Side," Mercy mused absently. "Maybe the silver lilies grow there as well? Or maybe there's special flowers that the living never see at all."

This, it seemed, was a conversational cue for the faeries there – for both Mr Jubilee and Lady Hollowvale soon began enthusiastically exercising their imaginations on the subject.

"Surely there are flowers there that smell of pleasant memories," Mr Jubilee said.

"There could be flowers that sing when the wind blows through them," Lady Hollowvale said dreamily.

Abigail passed the teacup to Euphemia, who sipped at it placidly. "I don't know about any of those strange things,"

Euphemia said, "but there ought to be roses on the Other Side – or else it's not much of a place to retire, is it?"

Abigail tried to imagine up a strange flower that might be found on the Other Side – or really, any image of the Other Side at all – but her imagination failed her once again. She had no interest, she found, in speculating about the Other Side since there were so many things yet for her to see on *this* side. But she didn't wish to ruin everyone else's fun, and so she stayed quiet and listened to the conversation instead.

Eventually, they emptied the teapot, and the discussion tapered off. Mr Jubilee insisted that he ought to get back to watching the children, and Euphemia went with him to take a turn at Blind Man's Bluff. Lady Hollowvale saw them all to the entryway of the Hollow House – but she asked for Abigail to stay behind for a moment as Mercy went ahead.

"I am glad that you came," Lady Hollowvale said. "I *was* concerned about Longshadow, Abigail. But I know that you are facing other dangers, and I wanted to offer you what help I can."

Abigail considered her Other Mum. "You said you couldn't protect me against nightshade," she said.

"I cannot protect you from nightshade," Lady Hollowvale agreed, "though I am heartened that Blackthorn may be able to provide you a remedy. I *can* offer you my love, though – and hopefully, that will be of use." So saying, she tore an edge from the sleeve of her tattered grey gown. Before Abigail could fully react, Lady Hollowvale bit her thumb just hard enough to draw blood; she allowed three drops of that blood to fall into the rag, and then she folded it into quarters, offering it over to Abigail.

Abigail took the rag in confusion. "I'm afraid I still don't understand," she admitted.

Lady Hollowvale pressed her bleeding finger against her chest. "Keep my love close to you," she said. "I cannot protect you from danger – but I can warn you, at least, when danger comes near. I thought it best to give this to you where no one else can hear of it."

Abigail closed her hand around the makeshift handkerchief. It was surprisingly light, even for a scrap of cloth – and something about it made Abigail remember her first mother in sudden, vivid detail. Abigail had forgotten almost all of her early memories involving her first mother, except for those last, very awful memories – Abigail had even forgotten her first mother's name, since she had always simply called her *Mum*.

But right now, as Abigail held her Other Mum's love, she found that she could picture her first mother's smile very clearly for the first time in a very long while. The memory made her heart twinge with both happiness and longing.

Abigail held the ragged handkerchief tightly to her heart. She looked up at her Other Mum. "Is this love really for me?" Abigail asked softly. "I'm not even your real daughter."

"How silly!" Lady Hollowvale laughed. "Of course you are my real daughter. You are standing right in front of me. I am certain that I did not dream you up."

Abigail smiled up at her. "You didn't dream me up," she agreed – though that hadn't been her original point at all. "Thank you, Mum. I promise I'll keep it close."

Lady Hollowvale embraced her once more – and Abigail walked out from the Hollow House, through the fog that clung to her like a friend.

Chapter Sixteen

Though night had now fallen, no stars shone over Kensington Gardens. Hollowvale's mists leaned upon the Round Pond, shot through with shafts of sourceless moonlight.

It was easy to spot Mercy's dark figure, walking ahead. Even in the heavy fog, her form seemed to drink in the moonlight, draining it from the world around her. She was an otherworldly shadow in the mist – both unnerving and comforting all at once.

Abigail tucked the ragged handkerchief hurriedly into her décolletage and quickened her steps to catch up with Mercy. Mercy's black hair was loose around her shoulders now, and her eyes gleamed with twilight more vividly than ever before. She smiled as she saw Abigail, and she slowed so that they might fall into step next to one another.

"I'm glad you came," Abigail told Mercy softly. "I know it wasn't easy."

Mercy looked down at her feet. Once again, Abigail's steps had left ripples upon the water where she walked, while Mercy passed without trace – like a ghost, stepping sideways through the world. "I'm glad I came too," Mercy said. "I had things I needed to say. An' it *was* a very pleasant tea. Mr Jubilee's always wished I could come here with him to visit, an' now I have."

Abigail bit at her lip. "You could come to tea again, in that case," she said. "If you wanted, I mean. It only seems fair, since I'll be goin' to Longshadow to see those lilies."

Mercy paused upon the water, and Abigail stopped with her. For a moment, it felt as though they were utterly alone in the quiet of the mist. Mercy turned to look at Abigail – and there was something soft and hopeful behind the setting sun in her eyes as she did.

"I *would* like to come to tea again," Mercy said. "Here in Hollowvale, an' maybe at the House. I've got a little cottage in Longshadow too, where I could put on a kettle."

Abigail had not imagined much of anything for the entire time they had been in Hollowvale – but this suggestion inspired a wonderful series of images in her mind. She could see Mercy sitting down to tea with everyone in the House, wrinkling her nose as Abigail discussed outside magic with her father. And though Abigail had never seen Longshadow, nor the cottage of which Mercy spoke, she imagined them all the same. The cottage was probably very small, with lacy curtains and open windows; it had a little stove full of flickering coals, and it smelled entirely of lilies and fresh laundry.

"I don't know how you do that," Abigail said softly. "Sometimes, when you talk about things like that, I can almost see 'em in my head. Am I borrowin' your imagination somehow – like the first time you helped me walk on the lake?"

Mercy tilted her head. "I'm not lendin' you anything," she said. "You must really be comin' up with it all on your own." She studied Abigail's face, as though searching for something in particular. "You said you've got to deal with things as they are. I know it's hard for you to imagine things that seem unreal, so … I've started tryin' to figure out how to make the good things more real for you. I thought that if I came to Hollowvale an' sorted things out with your Other Mum, it might help. So maybe it *did* help?"

Tears pricked abruptly at Abigail's eyes. They were warm

tears, and not sad ones. "It did help," she said. "I'm imaginin' all sorts of nice things right now. I've imagined more things since I met you than I have in years an' years."

Mercy reached out to take Abigail's hand. Her long, delicate fingers were still covered in bandages, but Abigail now imagined that those fingers would eventually heal, and that they would eventually hold hands again in that way which a chaperone might find inappropriate.

"I want to make more good things real for you, Abigail," Mercy said. "I'm imaginin' all sorts of ways to do that lately. It's a nice way to pass the time when I'm feelin' down."

Abigail wasn't at all sure how to respond to this at first. The suggestion that Mercy spent her spare thoughts upon Abigail's happiness was a wonderful surprise. Abigail was at once both deeply grateful for it and pained at the thought that the overwhelming affection which it inspired within her might not be entirely welcome.

Abigail reached up to wipe at her tears. "I am . . . really fond of you, Mercy," she managed. "I think you ought to know that."

Mercy released Abigail's hand. A moment later, though, she had thrown her arms around Abigail's neck and pressed her cheek to her shoulder.

"I'm fond of you too," Mercy mumbled. "We'll have all sorts of adventures together when this is over, I'm sure. Look forward to 'em, won't you?"

Abigail closed her arms around Mercy. She couldn't help but think how very well they fit together that way. The embrace lingered for quite a while, as Abigail tried to work up the courage to express the *other* things she kept imagining. But just as she had settled the butterflies in her stomach and steeled her spine, a small form stumbled blindly out of the mist, barrelling straight into them.

All three of them went sprawling upon the water. Abigail clambered up to her knees with a very unladylike word and saw that Fanny had taken them all to the ground. She was wearing the lace blindfold again – though now, she tugged it up to reveal her eyes, looking confused.

"I got two people?" Fanny said. "Oh! Well, there you are again, Abby. But you weren't actually playin', so I guess I'll have to put back on the blindfold."

Abigail pushed back up to her feet, brushing herself off with her very last scrap of dignity. "I'd stay an' play, but I really think I've got to be off," she said, as she turned next to help Mercy back to her feet. "Do you know where Hugh is, Fanny?"

Fanny frowned. "Hugh's back at the shore," she said. "He got real serious after the talk we all had."

Abigail paused. "The talk you *all* had?" she asked.

Fanny twisted the blindfold slowly in her hands, looking anxious. "Hugh . . . told the lot of us about the apple in Longshadow. I think he expected we'd tell him to bring it back to Hollowvale so one of us could have it, but . . ." She glanced away. "Everyone agreed he ought to keep that apple for himself if he can get it. We told him that none of us would take it from him, even if he offered."

Abigail let out a long breath. "Oh," she said.

Mercy crossed her arms. The soft look in her eyes was gone, replaced by sudden thoughtfulness. "Do you know," Mercy said, "I think Hugh's got the same problem you do, Abigail. I don't think he'll believe in that apple till you throw it at his head."

Abigail managed a rueful smile at that. For just a moment, she managed to conjure up the image of Hugh's surprised expression as she tossed a magical apple at his head. It was getting easier and easier to imagine things, she found, the more that good things happened to her.

"I'll take care of him, Fanny," Abigail promised.

Fanny twisted her lips into a sour expression. "Well, he needs it," she said. "He's still a kid, you know."

Abigail tried and failed to hide a grin. She declined to point out that Fanny wasn't that much older than Hugh herself. Instead, she said, "Come give me another hug before you blind yourself again."

Fanny wasn't yet so mature that she was willing to turn down hugs. She squeezed Abigail around the midsection as tightly as she could manage. Because they were in Hollowvale, she felt very nearly solid. "You'll be back soon?" Fanny asked Abigail.

"As soon as I can," Abigail assured her. "Me an' Mercy are goin' to come for tea, after Hollowvale's gone back where it belongs."

Fanny's eyes sparked with mischief. "Once Hugh's alive again," she said, "you tell him he's got to bake us all tarts an' send 'em along with you."

"I won't come back without Hugh's tarts," Abigail said solemnly.

They left Fanny behind them, still wiggling the blindfold back over her eyes. Sure enough, as the fog gave way to reveal the shore, Abigail saw Hugh sitting at the edge of the water with his elbows on top of his knees.

"Did you catch any flowers tonight, Hugh?" Abigail asked him lightly.

Hugh looked up at her and forced a smile. "No flowers," he said, "but I got Robert an' Fanny at least once each."

Abigail offered Hugh a hand up. His skin was a bit too cool, and his hand seemed hazy and ephemeral – but it was good to be able to touch him, even briefly.

Abigail continued holding onto Hugh's hand as they walked away from the Round Pond. By the time they reached the edge of Hollowvale's mists, however, the moon reappeared in the sky above them, even as Hugh's grip disappeared.

Dora had indeed kept the groundskeeper late so that Mercy, Abigail and Hugh could leave the gardens. As they all walked back to the House, Abigail noted that the sky was far darker than it should have been based on the time that they had spent at tea – but this was not entirely a surprise, as time often moved strangely in faerie.

Abigail was a bit disappointed to find out that one of the maids had cleared off a bed for Mercy while they were gone – but this did make it easier, at least, for Abigail to stash her Other Mum's handkerchief beneath her pillow without eliciting strange questions.

Just as Abigail did not often imagine things, neither did she often dream. But that night, she dreamed of a little cottage in Longshadow, with a fresh pot of tea upon the table and a lovely view of the silver lilies outside.

Abigail woke to late-morning sunlight, and to a gentle nudge at her shoulder. When she opened her eyes, she saw Mercy standing over her. There was a bemused, affectionate look on Mercy's face that suggested Abigail was not a graceful-looking sleeper.

"Abigail," Mercy murmured, "Lady Pinckney is visitin' downstairs. She asked to see me, but I expect you'll want to be there too."

Abigail stretched and yawned, nudging her mind back into motion. "I will, yes," she said. "I hope she's not here just to bully you into lettin her chat with Lucy again."

Mercy grimaced. "I don't think that's the *only* reason she's here," she said, "but what do you want to wager it comes up at least once durin' our visit?"

Abigail shook her head. "I wouldn't wager *against* it," she said ruefully. She stumbled out of bed, searching for her cream muslin. The gown had seen far too much use in the last few days, by Abigail's reckoning – she would be only too happy to hide it away for a few weeks, once everything was sorted.

Mercy's cheeks flushed slightly as Abigail started getting dressed, and she turned her head. "I'll see you downstairs, then," Mercy mumbled.

Abigail rushed to make herself barely presentable. She nearly hurried out the door without the handkerchief beneath her pillow – but at the last moment, she remembered it, and she tucked it down the front of her gown before heading downstairs.

The House had exactly one small drawing room, mostly used for meeting those dignitaries whom Elias could not dodge for ever. As with most of the House, the drawing room was furnished in a way befitting the dignity of England's court magician – but said furnishings were well out of date and fraying at the edges. The room's single window let in both a waxy bit of sunlight and all of the noises from the street below. All in all, it was a very cramped, uncomfortable sort of drawing room. Happily, this meant that formal visitations rarely lasted long.

Lady Pinckney had settled herself at the main table, dressed all in black. Dora sat with her, sipping tea in silence, while Hugh sat invisible in another chair. At first, Mercy was nowhere to be seen – but as Abigail entered, the shadows in the corner of the room slipped away to reveal her, and Abigail realised that Mercy had been hiding from Lady Pinckney.

Lady Pinckney glanced over as Abigail arrived – and her brow furrowed. "Surely that isn't the *only* gown you own?" she asked.

Surely, that isn't a proper way to greet someone in their own home, Abigail was tempted to reply.

But Abigail smothered the response beneath a brittle smile. What she said aloud was: "I am at home, and it is simple to wear. I didn't wish to keep you waiting, Lady Pinckney."

Abigail was careful once again to round out her accent, lingering over every syllable.

Lady Pinckney let out an irritated sound. "Well, you cannot wear *that* to the ball tonight," she said. "I hope that you have something else available to you."

Abigail paused just behind Hugh's chair. "The . . . ball?" she asked carefully.

"The ball," Hugh repeated sourly. "Lucy's been upset ever since it came up, since she won't be able to go an' dance."

Dora had been regarding Lady Pinckney with the same blank, careful expression she normally used when trying to decide on a proper conversational reply – but she took her cue from Abigail and abandoned whatever clever retort had been upon her lips. "Lady Pinckney has acquired the three guest lists for which you were searching," Dora told Abigail. "There is another ball tonight, and most of the same guests will be attending."

Abigail struggled to keep the instinctive horror from her face. She had barely survived her only Season – the idea of attending even one more ball with the *ton* made her feel sick to her stomach. "And you thought I should attend this ball?" she asked Lady Pinckney.

Lady Pinckney's expression darkened. "Some other girl may die this evening," she said. "You implied that you could prevent such a thing from happening."

Abigail's heart sank down into her stomach. For a brief, terrible moment, she thought, *I could simply let them die.* It was an awful, unworthy thought, and she knew it. But Abigail knew deep down in her bones that no one would want her at the ball, and that those in attendance would make things as difficult as possible for her, even while she tried to protect them.

"I am certain that I am not invited to this ball," Abigail said slowly. "I am rarely invited to anything."

Lady Pinckney pulled a small envelope from her reticule, and Abigail suppressed a sigh of defeat.

"Lord Breckart's sister is throwing a ball tonight," Lady Pinckney said. "I have requested an invitation for you, as a personal favour. It was the most taxing favour I have ever asked, in fact." Her eyes narrowed. "But you *cannot* wear that gown."

Hugh sighed heavily. "I always knew toffs were somethin' else," he said, "but they'd really rather risk dyin' than bein' seen with someone in an old gown."

Abigail bit her lip. She had no other quality gowns, of course – and there was no way she was going to be able to find a new one in time for the ball. But before she could formulate a polite way of saying so, Mercy interrupted.

"Gowns won't be a problem," Mercy said. "We'll just wear midnight."

Lady Pinckney startled and nearly dropped her teacup. She glanced over at Mercy sharply, noticing her presence for the very first time. "We?" she asked.

Mercy shrugged. "This is my problem, too," she said. "Obviously, I'll be goin' with Abigail."

Lady Pinckney did not grimace, but her disgust was palpable, nevertheless. "This invitation is for the Lord Sorcier, his family and his ward. It will not suffice for . . ." Lady Pinckney trailed off as she realised she did not know just *what* Mercy was.

Mercy smiled coldly. "And just what do you think I am, Lady Pinckney?" she asked.

Her accent was suddenly cool and refined in a way that could not possibly be faked. Mercy's shadow lengthened subtly behind her once again, twisting lazily against the morning sunlight.

Abigail stared at Mercy in confusion.

"Never mind," Mercy said. Her accent had reverted to the one which Abigail found more familiar. Mercy looked past Lady Pinckney towards Abigail. "I don't need an invitation. I go where I please. An' I don't mind sortin' out some gowns. I'm hardly an expert tailor, but midnight hides an awful lot of sins."

Lady Pinckney kept her eyes fixed upon Mercy. Desperate longing rose once more within her gaze, and Abigail knew exactly what she was about to say even before she said it.

"I have gone far out of my way for you," Lady Pinckney said. "I would like to see my daughter now."

The repetition did not surprise Abigail at all. Some part of her had known that Lady Pinckney could not – *would* not – accept another person's decision which was contrary to her desires. Like Lucy, her sense of entitlement was so strong that all things must inevitably bend to it: neither courtesy, nor reality, nor even her own promises to the contrary would ever prevent her from demanding what she wanted, over and over.

Mercy shook her head. "You weren't listenin' at all last time," she told Lady Pinckney. "I told you my services weren't for sale, an' they're not. I didn't offer to use my magic for you again if you did somethin' helpful – I said the opposite, in fact. You went out of your way so we could find Lucy's killer . . . or at least, that's what you *said*."

Hugh sank down into his chair, suddenly weary. "You won't even talk to Mercy!" he told the air next to him. "Why d'you think she'd go out of her way for you?"

Abigail could only assume that both Lucy *and* Lady Pinckney had decided to lean upon Mercy at the same time.

Lady Pinckney straightened coldly in her chair. "If that is truly how you feel," she said to Mercy, "then I can always speak again to Lord Breckart's sister and have the invitation rescinded."

"You've got everything all backwards," Mercy said. "I'm helpin' people I care about – but I don't need your invitation to do that. *Abigail* needs the invitation so she can go an' risk her life to protect you an' your lot. I'd be only too happy if she stayed safe at home instead."

Abigail pressed her fingers to her forehead. Everything that Mercy said was true, of course. In fact, Abigail was frighteningly tempted to let Lady Pinckney do as she'd threatened – in which case, she wouldn't be *allowed* at the ball, and perhaps that much would soothe her conscience.

But of course, Abigail's conscience was not soothed at all. If another girl were to die tonight, she knew that she would never forgive herself.

"Mercy," Abigail said quietly, "I think you should let Lady Pinckney speak to Lucy."

Mercy glanced sharply at Abigail – the suggestion seemed to mortally offend her. Her twilight eyes had darkened with black shadows again, seething with indignation. But Mercy must have read something of Abigail's weariness – for she took a deep breath and crossed her arms. "Why?" Mercy asked.

Abigail looked at Lady Pinckney. "I understand that you're hurt and that you think this will help you," she said to the older woman. "I don't think that it *will* help – and you're going about it all the wrong way, ordering people around. But if another girl dies tonight, you *will* regret it. I want to save us both from that."

Abigail pressed her lips together and turned back to Mercy. "No one could ever pay you enough to do this," she said, "so I'm not offering you payment. I'm asking because we're friends: let Lady Pinckney see her daughter one more time. For her part, she must swear never to ask you again." Abigail met Mercy's eyes carefully. "There's a time and a place for this," she said.

What Abigail did not dare say was, *You have already alienated Lucy with the truth. Please don't do the same with her mother, or else we will be short on help.*

Lady Pinckney's promise not to ask again would mean nothing, of course. But they would not require her aid for ever.

Mercy considered these words very carefully. The shadows in her eyes did not recede – but her expression lost some of its hardness, and Abigail thought that perhaps Mercy had understood her message.

Slowly, Mercy inclined her head.

"Once more, Lady Pinckney," Mercy said. "I'll trade my services this time only – for friendship, which is priceless, an' somethin' which I'm not sure you know how to pay." Mercy's shadow shivered again, and she narrowed her eyes. "This will be the last time that you ask. Swear that to me, Lady Pinckney. An' know when you make that oath that somethin' terrible will befall you if you break it. Argue with me any further, even once, an' you'll have nothin' at all."

Abigail glanced at Mercy's shadow with a dim surprise. Belatedly, she remembered that promises carried far more import when one made them to faeries and their associates. Just this once – whether she willed it or not – Lady Pinckney *would* be bound by her word.

Lady Pinckney stared at Mercy. It was clear that she *did* wish to argue. But the piece of Longshadow which Mercy carried had leaned its weight upon the room around them, lengthening their silhouettes and deepening the silences. It was like catching a glimpse of cold, impartial doom.

In that moment, even Lady Pinckney knew to be afraid.

"I swear," Lady Pinckney whispered. "I will not ask again."

Mercy nodded curtly. "Then you'll have again what no one else is ever offered at all," she said. "You'll see your daughter one more time – but only in spite of yourself, an' only because Abigail asked it."

Abigail looked away. She should have been relieved at the outcome – but all she felt was drained. She had often felt that way after dealing with the *ton*. It occurred to her now that this was because, like Lucy, they only knew how to take things that they wanted. It was deeply tiring to always be the one giving, even when giving seemed to be the only reasonable choice.

Dora had listened silently to this exchange, with her hand on her teacup. But now, she rose from her chair and looked at Mercy. "I am feeling faint," Dora announced. "I will need Abigail to help me retire. This is my home, and you are my guest; I trust that you will not harm anyone in my absence."

Mercy knit her brow at Dora. "I . . . will not," she said slowly.

Dora smiled dimly and then turned to Abigail. "Would you please help me back upstairs?" she asked.

Hugh swivelled his head sharply, glancing at Dora with worry. "Somethin' wrong, Mum?" he asked, as he hopped from his chair.

Dora could not hear him, of course – but Abigail moved to offer out her arm, and Dora leaned lightly upon her, heading for the exit of the room. Hugh followed them out, hovering with concern.

Dora straightened again once they had closed the door behind them.

"Mum?" Abigail asked softly. "What's goin' on?"

Dora managed an apologetic smile. "I do not normally entertain people like Lady Pinckney," she said. "I would have asked her to leave almost instantly, except that I knew you had need of her." She sighed. "I have been worried about saying the wrong thing and foiling whatever you are after. But I fear that my silence has reached its limit, and I am not sure how much longer I can let her speak down to you. I thought I would remove us both from the room, since your business seems complete."

Abigail relaxed with relief; out of the corner of her eye, she saw Hugh do the same. "Thank you, Mum," Abigail said. "For keepin' quiet *and* for helpin' me leave."

Dora wound her arm around Abigail's shoulders. "I think that perhaps now is an appropriate time to tell you how marvellous you are," Dora said seriously.

Abigail knit her brow. "Is it?" she asked. "An' how's that?"

"Everything always seems very straightforward to me," Dora told her, "but you are so good at knowing when things are actually complicated. I have become passably good at staying silent . . . but you are good at coming up with things to say once the silence is over. You are an excellent liar, Abigail. You always have been, ever since the day I met you."

Abigail raised her eyebrows. "I can tell that's supposed to be a compliment," she said, "but I'm fairly sure most mums aren't proud of their children for bein' liars."

Dora beamed gently at Abigail. "But I *am* proud," she said. "You lied to save me from Lord Hollowvale – and now, you are lying in order to save more girls from dying."

Hugh glanced between Dora and Abigail. His brows knit together. "What were you lyin' about just now?" he asked.

Abigail blinked. "I wasn't aware I *was* lyin' just now," she admitted. She addressed both Hugh and Dora at the same time.

Dora tilted her head. "You said that you believed the best of Lady Pinckney – that she would feel regret if another girl died from her stubbornness. I thought that you were lying just then. Lady Pinckney probably would not feel guilty for very long, if at all. She has already changed her own memories to suit herself once, it would seem."

Abigail considered this seriously. Twice now, she had implied that Lady Pinckney *did* have good intentions, if only she would take a moment to recognise them. Both times, Abigail thought, she had been lying. No part of her truly believed that Lady Pinckney was capable of moving past her own self-serving nature. She was not capable of imagining such a thing.

"I've been flatterin' her," Abigail observed aloud. "Lady Pinckney wants to believe she's a good person. She won't listen even if anyone tells her different, so I may as well *pretend* that she's good when I ask her to do things."

Dora nodded reasonably. "You see?" she said. "I would never have thought of it like that. But I remember now – you pretended to believe that Lord Hollowvale was a good person too, all those years ago. It is part of why he believed you when you lied to him and protected us."

Hugh shifted uncomfortably on his feet. Abigail could tell that he didn't much like the topic of conversation.

"There are plenty of faerie tales full of clever liars who do good things," Dora told Abigail. "Faeries are wicked – Lady Hollowvale is always the first to say so – and Mr Jubilee once told me that trickery is almost as good a weapon against faeries as iron is. I think that people can be even more wicked than faeries, though. So I am glad that you are better at lying to all of them than I am, Abigail. And I am glad that you seem to know when to do it and when not to do it, for the most part."

Abigail chewed on this slowly. "I lied to you an' Dad

about goin' back to Hollowvale," she observed. "Doesn't *that* upset you?"

Dora thought on this. "It does not," she admitted – and she sounded very surprised as she said it. "It does seem that your father was wrong to send you away, even if he meant for the best. And I am glad that you have been here to help him." She squeezed Abigail's shoulder. "I would not like for you to make a habit of lying to either of us. But I am determined that you should never feel the need to do so again."

Abigail looked down at her feet. It was a strange thing to be admired for something so shameful. But Abigail knew that her mother was not nearly a good enough liar to fool her; Dora must have really believed in everything she'd said.

"I am proud because you are a good liar *and* a good person," Dora added softly. "I must not forget to mention the latter part."

Abigail smiled wryly. "I'll trust your judgement on the matter, I guess," she replied.

Dora glanced suddenly towards the stairs. "Oh," she murmured. "I shall have to tell Elias that we are attending a ball this evening."

Hugh coughed on a laugh for the first time since they'd come out into the hallway. "Oh, Dad will love *that*," he chortled.

Abigail hid a small smile. "I'll let you break the news to him," she told her mother. "I'll just . . . wait out here, until Mercy an' Lady Pinckney are done."

Dora gave her a knowing look. "I will let you hide down here since you have endured enough today," she said. "That is how you know that I love you."

Abigail smirked, thinking of the handkerchief she'd hidden in her gown. "I know, Mum," she said. "I love you too."

Chapter Seventeen

Mercy and Lady Pinckney did eventually emerge from the drawing room. Abigail thought that Mercy had stayed behind as she saw Lady Pinckney off at the front door – but when Abigail turned to head back up the stairs, Mercy was suddenly there again behind her, standing halfway within a little pool of shadows.

"You're awful good at sneakin' up on people," Abigail admitted to Mercy. "You really do give me a fright sometimes."

Mercy smiled wanly. "It's just petty vengeance," she said. "I hated every minute I had to spend with Lucy an' Lady Pinckney." She hunched her shoulders against the thought. "Anyway . . . at least it's over an' done with. An' Lucy's talkin' to me again, so there's that."

Abigail nodded uncertainly. "I didn't like puttin' you on the spot," she said. "But if tonight doesn't go well, then we might still need Lucy an' Lady Pinckney's help."

Mercy grimaced. "It still stings," she muttered. "I just hate rewardin' bad behaviour."

Abigail sighed. "I know," she said. "I do feel the same way. But at least now it won't come up again. Either Lady Pinckney will keep her oath, or else . . ." She frowned. "What *would* happen if Lady Pinckney broke her oath, anyway?"

Mercy shrugged. "Longshadow would do somethin' to

her," she said. "I don't know *what* it'd do exactly . . . but it sure wouldn't be pretty. She'll just have to deal with the consequences in that case. I warned her outright, as much as I was able to do."

Abigail nodded grimly. "Lady Pinckney chose to swear that oath," she said. "I won't hold it against you if she breaks her word an' somethin' bad happens to her."

Mercy relaxed a bit at that. "Well . . . let's stop talkin' about her, then," she said. "Let's get to your room so I can dress you up for a ball. I'm lookin' forward to it." Mercy offered out her arm, and Abigail took it, before they both started up the stairs. "I think you'd look good dressed all in midnight."

Abigail glanced sideways at Mercy. "I've never seen a gown made of midnight," she said, "but I guess it'll get a better reaction than what I'm wearin' now?"

Mercy rolled her eyes. "I don't have a problem with what you're wearin' now," she said, "but I think you look good in everything. Anyway, it's more about how people will treat you. Most people think midnight is scary an' mysterious an' beautiful. So maybe everyone will stop talkin' down to you if you're wearin' it."

Abigail smiled at that. "I appreciate the thought," she said. "I'm *not* lookin' forward to goin' to a ball again. It never ended well before. But if we're both wearin' midnight, an' I get the chance to dance with you just once, then I promise I'll look forward to it just a little bit."

Mercy looked away shyly. "I *would* like to dance with you again," she said. "We had all that fun, didn't we, on the Round Pond? But I guess we can't play with the shadows this time. None of these nobs has got even an inch of humour or imagination."

They came to Abigail's room soon enough, and Mercy closed the door behind them. She turned to consider Abigail thoughtfully, raking her eyes up and down her form in a way that made Abigail blush.

"You'll have to take off what you're wearin'," Mercy said. A little impish smile crossed her features for some reason, and Abigail blushed harder. She fidgeted for a second – but eventually, she reached for the buttons on the back of her gown, craning her arm to loosen them.

Mercy stepped behind her – and a moment later, her long fingers found the buttons on the back of Abigail's gown.

Abigail froze. Her face was burning hot now, and she knew that it would be painfully visible if Mercy bothered to look. She was, as always, acutely aware of those lovely fingers, now slipping loose the buttons on her gown one by one.

"You haven't got bandages on your hands today," Abigail observed breathlessly. She stared at the floor, willing Mercy to stay focused on her clothing and not on her face or her voice.

"I'm almost good as new," Mercy agreed. She flicked open another button, and Abigail shivered. "It's good to feel things when I touch 'em again. Though I guess we'll both be wearin' gloves tonight."

Abigail suppressed a dim sense of disappointment. *Your hands are so pretty, though*, she wanted to say. This was a strange thing to say, of course, and so she thought about keeping it to herself.

But Mercy opened another button on Abigail's gown – and for some reason, this gave her the courage to say it anyway.

"Your hands are so pretty," Abigail mumbled. "It's just a shame to cover 'em up."

Mercy paused. At first Abigail was terrified that she'd gone too far and said something out loud which she couldn't take back. But – very slowly – Mercy reached out to run one finger across Abigail's bare back. "Your ... *everything* ... is pretty," Mercy murmured. "Shame to cover it up."

Abigail's nerves jangled at the statement. If a man had said those words, she would have been absolutely certain of his intentions. But there was still just enough doubt – just enough fear – to hold her back from assuming that Mercy had the same intentions.

Abigail's throat was dry. But she cast about for something to say anyway. Finally – a bit hoarsely – she said, "I was worried you might get bullied too . . . but that accent was perfect. If we put you in midnight, then I'm sure that everyone will think you're a lady."

Mercy let out a soft *hm*. "Well . . . I've helped more'n just laundresses over to the Other Side," she admitted. "I helped a noble lady right here in London, maybe half a year ago. She asked if I wanted anything, and I figured a good noble accent might come in handy someday."

Something about this bothered briefly at Abigail – but she was *very* distracted by Mercy's fingers, which had now travelled all the way down to the buttons at the small of her back.

"But you'd rather be a laundress?" Abigail mumbled.

"I'd *much* rather be a laundress," Mercy confirmed. "An' don't lie – you prefer me as a laundress too, don't you?"

Abigail smiled down at her toes. "I've grown a bit attached to your cap," she admitted. "But I wouldn't throw you over if you suddenly sounded like a lady or looked like a solicitor."

The words struck Mercy oddly for some reason. She was quiet for a long moment, with her hand paused at the small of Abigail's back.

"What if . . .?" Mercy struggled with an idea – but she trailed off worriedly rather than finishing the question.

Abigail turned to look at her quizzically. "What if?" she asked.

It was Mercy's turn to avert her gaze, though. She swallowed, unable to meet Abigail's eyes. "What if the gamekeeper on the moon was breedin' those stars like fishes? New stars would show up every night, wouldn't they? D'you think anyone would even notice?"

Abigail was *certain* that Mercy had been about to say

something completely different. She reached out to take her hand, threading their fingers together. It was particularly nice feeling Mercy's skin against hers again, and she savoured the sensation.

"You can tell me if you want," Abigail said softly. "Or not. I won't *make* you do it."

Mercy looked up at Abigail. The shadows in her eyes had utterly gone now, washed away by wistful twilight. "I want to tell you," she whispered. "I . . . I *will* tell you. Eventually."

Abigail nodded – but she didn't let go of Mercy's hand. Rather, she tightened her grip reassuringly. "I'll wait," she said. "It's all right."

Mercy closed her hands briefly on Abigail's – but then, she loosened her grip and stepped back, clearing her throat. "Lose the gown," Mercy said authoritatively. "I'm makin' you a better one. All those toffs are goin' to go green with envy when they see you."

Abigail shot Mercy a half-smile – but she turned away and pulled the handkerchief free from its hiding place before letting her gown slip obediently to the floor. "You're soundin' like Lucy," Abigail said. "I don't want everyone to envy me. I just want to get through tonight without anyone dyin'."

Mercy scoffed. "Lucy wants everyone to envy her because she's greedy," she said. "*I* want everyone to envy you out of vengeance, since they've all treated you so badly. You'll never convince me to give up my vengeance, so don't even try."

The shadows in the corners of the room darkened again as she spoke. Abigail flinched a bit, expecting to feel that cold, awful doom – but instead, there was only a sense of soft, pleasant calm. Slowly, the blackest parts of those shadows coiled together, wafting towards her on some invisible breeze. They caught against her skin like strands of spider's silk, sticking where they touched.

The gown that slowly formed around Abigail was so dark

that it drew in the light around them. It wasn't black in the way that Lady Pinckney's mourning gown had been black – rather, the black of the gown was a complete absence of light and colour. Surely, there were details to the high waist and short sleeves . . . but none of those details were visible enough to make them out. There was instead a broad sense of sweeping skirts and a kind of dark majesty which sank into Abigail's heart, whispering to her that she was far more beautiful and mysterious than she believed herself to be.

The feeling dazed Abigail for a long moment – but as Mercy stepped around to inspect her work, Abigail remembered just in time to tuck her Other Mum's handkerchief back into the gown.

"My best work yet!" Mercy declared, as she looked over the gown. She trailed her fingers along the gown's skirt with a deeply satisfied expression; the shadowy material rippled beneath her fingers as though preening at her touch.

Abigail smiled sheepishly. "I appreciate it," she said. "I don't know where I'd have found a gown up to Lady Pinckney's standards, otherwise."

Mercy pursed her lips. "If Lady Pinckney isn't satisfied with a gown made of midnight, then her an' her sense of fashion are a fraud," she said. "Other materials might come in an' out of style in faerie, but midnight is *always* a classic."

Abigail considered this. "Where did you get midnight from, though?" she asked. "It's late morning. I can't imagine there's much midnight to be found right now."

Mercy glanced up at Abigail, and a flicker of uncertainty crossed her features. She seemed to think very hard on her response – but finally, she said, "I always have midnight with me. It's . . . the name I chose. I'm Mercy Midnight."

Abigail blinked. Mercy's wary manner suggested that this was indeed her real name – and there was something about that name which lingered upon the air, dark and heavy and thrilling.

A name was a terrible thing to offer, especially to a magician. Abigail couldn't imagine at first just what had prompted Mercy to trust her with such dangerous and personal knowledge.

But Mercy had *wanted* to tell Abigail something else earlier – something even more dire, it seemed. It occurred to Abigail now that there was a hint of guilt on Mercy's face; Abigail thought that perhaps this was Mercy's way of assuring her that she still had her trust.

"That's a really lovely name," Abigail said softly. "An' you chose it yourself? I think it suits you."

Mercy had looked down to the floor, unable to meet Abigail's eyes. A light blush crept into her pale cheeks. "It's a sad thing, keepin' my name all secret," Mercy said quietly. "I really like it, an' I like tellin' it to people. If it wasn't so dangerous, you know, I'd tell the whole world."

Abigail reached out to take Mercy's hand again. "But you've told it to me," she said. "I know I'm not the whole world . . . but I think your name is beautiful. An' I'll try an' treasure it enough to make up for everyone else who doesn't know it."

Mercy tightened her hand on Abigail's. "That matters," she said. "I hope you know how much it matters to me."

Abigail nodded slowly. "I'm Abigail Wilder," she murmured. "There's some middle names in there too, so you know. But that last part means the world to me. I chose to be a Wilder, an' I got chosen back. Names matter. It's why they're so powerful, I figure."

Mercy smiled in a misty sort of way. She looked down at Abigail's hand again and cleared her throat. "Well," she said. "Look at me, declarin' victory before we're even done. You still need gloves an' slippers – an' I want to do up your hair as well."

There was real enthusiasm in Mercy's voice – as though she were talking about dressing up her favourite doll. It warmed Abigail's heart so much that she forgot all of her worst misgivings about going to a ball once again. Horrible aristocrats and hidden murderers fell away from her mind for just a moment, replaced by the simple pleasure of Mercy's company and her enjoyment of Abigail's company in return.

"By all means," Abigail said, "turn me into a midnight princess."

Mercy's vengeance was a terribly pleasant thing, at least where Abigail was concerned. She spent quite some time playing with the shadows of the gown, shortening and lengthening them, spinning gloves and slippers from thin air. Mercy even added bits of midnight to Abigail's ragged blonde hair, smoothing out its harsh ends. Something about all of that midnight seemed to soften all the imperfections of which Abigail was always so acutely aware – as though the darkness had washed away the up-close details and left behind only the *idea* of Abigail, as she might appear to someone in the middle of the night.

Eventually, however, Abigail insisted that Mercy should make herself a gown as well. Mercy agreed – with great reluctance – but the gown that she fashioned for herself was clearly an afterthought compared to the masterpiece which she had laboured over for Abigail.

It didn't really matter. Mercy had been *made* to wear midnight. Abigail knew it deep down in her soul, with only the barest glance. The dark, beautiful sense of command which Mercy carried with her was only further revealed by the shadows that surrounded her. Midnight loved Mercy; it was clear in the way that it clung to her form, shifting with her steps.

More than ever, Abigail wanted to beg Mercy for . . . something. It was a strange feeling – as though Abigail *needed* Mercy's presence, even though she was already there.

"You'll really have to dance with me tonight," Abigail breathed helplessly. "You won't forget?"

Mercy smiled slyly over at Abigail, and her heart thudded strangely in her chest.

"Why would I forget?" Mercy asked. "It's top of my list."

Abigail realised then the nature of the unearthly feeling she'd kept having around Mercy. She wanted Mercy's attention – but more importantly, she wanted to *belong* to Mercy, to have the privilege of her possessiveness.

It would have been a dangerous feeling all on its own. But Abigail had discovered another stubborn feeling, right next to the first one: she wanted Mercy to belong to her as well. A mutual belonging, she thought, would do very nicely.

Chapter Eighteen

Elias Wilder was dressed for a ball – and he was not very happy about it.

"Perhaps we could simply pass a ban upon balls in general," he muttered, as their carriage approached Lord Breckart's town house. He tugged uncomfortably at his silver cravat. "No one can be poisoned at a ball if there are no balls being thrown."

Dora smiled at him indulgently, reaching up to fix his cravat once more. She was wearing a green silk gown tonight, in a very outdated style – but the colour matched one of her eyes, and something about her dress made her seem a bit warmer and more approachable than usual. "That is true, of course," she said to Elias. "But one expects that someone would then be poisoned *elsewhere*. For once, you must admit, we are fortunate to have a ball. It means that everyone of concern is in one place and feeling sociable."

Abigail snorted. "Like any of these people would give up their parties even if you asked," she said. "Anyway – we'll want to find out who's been dabblin' in magic lately. I'll handle the marriage mart crowd, since they're right around my age. That leaves the older people for you an' Mum."

Hugh had sat himself in Mercy's lap, right next to Abigail, since the carriage was so small. "Me an' Mercy an' Lucy will listen in on conversations," he said. "I wanted to go watch the cook downstairs anyway, an' the servants always talk while they're workin'."

"Ah!" Dora said suddenly, digging into her own reticule. "I made certain to bring my pocket mirror, Hugh. I will check it religiously in case you require anything." She soon produced the small mirror, displaying it helpfully towards Abigail.

"Hugh's over there, Mum," Abigail said, with a helpful jerk of her chin at Mercy.

Dora now smiled dimly in Mercy's direction. "Of course," she said, as though the mistake had been entirely hers. "My apologies, Hugh. I am so scatter-brained sometimes."

Hugh smiled back, though Dora couldn't see it. "Thanks for tryin', Mum," he said softly. Perhaps it was Abigail's imagination, but she thought she saw Mercy squeeze Hugh's hand silently.

The carriage rolled to a stop outside the townhouse, and their family descended the steps. Lord Breckart's townhouse was a somewhat unfortunate affair: the tall building had probably once been white, but London's atmosphere had long since stained it a sooty grey. As a footman directed them up the stairs to the ballroom, Abigail noted that the inside of the townhouse matched its outside in many ways; though it had been recently cleaned, there were signs of sullen, ongoing neglect. Fairly or not, Abigail generally assumed that neglected homes were a sign of unhappy servants – happy servants could make even a shabby home feel somewhat welcoming – and her opinion of Lord Breckart adjusted itself accordingly.

Any more recent efforts had clearly been directed towards the ballroom, which was lit with candles in every corner. Idle music trickled over the air, though at least one flute sounded as though it was being played by someone's inept cousin. The press of people already inside the ballroom looked positively stifling, and –

– and Abigail realised that she was searching for things with which to take issue. With each step closer to the ballroom, her body had coiled with growing dread, and her hands had clutched more tightly at the reticule of magician's tools which she held to her chest.

I don't want to be here, Abigail thought dizzily. *But I am here. I chose to attend this ball. It's best I get on with it.*

Mercy squeezed Abigail's arm – and for a moment, at least, Abigail was pulled from her dread. She glanced over and saw that sly, knowing smile on Mercy's lips. The twilight in her eyes was even more vivid in the darkness of the stairwell; her black hair was pooled atop her head in a way that lengthened the pale column of her neck. The midnight that she wore shifted in and out of the flickering shadows which surrounded them.

"You've faced down worse'n this," Mercy murmured to Abigail. "You're a magician, an' a faerie friend. What's a lot of empty-headed toffs goin' to do to you?"

Abigail smiled wryly at that. "I know that I *shouldn't* be afraid," she said softly. "But I am. I don't belong here. Stickin' yourself where you don't belong is always painful."

Abigail had only meant for Mercy to hear this – but Elias paused just in front of them and turned his head with a dark expression. "I knew you didn't really enjoy your Season," he accused Abigail. "I asked whether I ought to turn anyone into a toad, and you said no."

Abigail winced. "An' that's *exactly* why I didn't tell you," she said, with a hint of apology. Privately, she thought it was probably for the best that Elias had used up so much of his magic on the bans against Lord Longshadow before coming to this specific party. Their investigation would *certainly* be derailed if a tactless lady started croaking in the middle of the ball.

Mercy shook her head in bemusement. "I gave you my midnight this time," she said. "No one ought to *dare* be awful to you." She released Abigail's arm, however, and glanced up at the front of the line into the ballroom, where a footman was calling out introductions. "It'll be fine – you'll see. I'll meet you inside."

Abigail nodded tightly. In the next moment, Mercy had fully disappeared into the shadows.

Soon enough, Abigail's family reached the footman in the doorway. The poor man's expression turned instantly wary as he saw them – there was no mistaking their otherworldly nature, given Elias's uncanny bearing, Dora's mismatched eyes and Abigail's resplendent dress made of midnight. The footman took their invitation with a hint of trepidation and spoke to Elias in quiet tones. He turned then, and announced to the ballroom:

"Lord Elias Wilder, Lady Theodora Wilder and their daughter, Miss Abigail Wilder."

At that, Abigail had to hide a smile. Technically speaking, society saw her as the Lord Sorcier's ward, and not as his daughter. But Elias had clearly taken her worries to heart and insisted that she be introduced as such regardless. Few people would be courageous enough to insult the Lord Sorcier's daughter while he was present in the room to register his displeasure.

As they headed into the ball, however, Abigail could not help but notice the way in which people's eyes slipped uneasily past her mother and father to settle upon her. At first, the muted whispers set a sick churning in her stomach . . . but guests inclined their heads to Abigail as she passed, and she slowly became aware that the stares, this time, possessed a kind of mingled awe and fear.

"*There is danger, darling*," Lady Hollowvale's voice whispered in her ear.

Abigail startled, glancing around the room. She brought her hand up to her chest, where the handkerchief was hidden. But her Other Mum's voice faded away again, replaced by the furore of the ballroom. It was hard to tell just what had caused the whisper.

Abigail pulled the silver flask from her reticule and sipped at her eyebright tea. The candlelight took on a strange sort of too-bright haze . . . but nothing hidden leapt out at her, and she tucked the flask back into her reticule with a frown.

A man in a blue waistcoat with salt-and-pepper hair excused himself from his current conversation, striding out towards Elias. Elias in turn set his jaw as though he were about to deal with something very unpleasant.

"Blast it," he muttered, disturbing Abigail's thoughts. "Lord Breckart is headed over to give his personal regards. Well, there's no need for all of us to suffer at once."

"I can see Lady Mulgrew from here," Dora observed idly. "She is certain to spend the entire evening gossiping. I will go and encourage her for a bit."

Abigail thought about bringing up her Other Mum's whisper . . . but admittedly, she wasn't certain what to say about it. They suspected already that someone dangerous was in attendance, and she could not yet offer any more specific information on the subject.

Abigail's parents both slipped away into the crowd, even as Hugh looked around, wrinkling his nose. "So many people," he muttered. "I'm goin' to have to walk through 'em. Always feels funny."

Abigail brushed away her uncertainty, shooting him a sympathetic look. "You can stick to the corners if you want," she said. "I think most of the unsavoury talk happens there anyway."

Hugh nodded. "Lucy says she knows just who to go listen in on. I think she's a little excited about it, actually."

Abigail stifled an annoyed response – *of course Lucy would love being able to eavesdrop on everyone* – and nodded her head instead. "I'd be obliged if you could point Hugh in a helpful direction then, Lucy," she said. "Well. We all know where I'm headed. I suppose I'll go pretend to join the husband huntin'."

Hugh chortled to himself at that as he strolled away with his hands in his pockets. Abigail glanced about the room, searching for her targets. She found them soon enough – for the young women of the marriage mart always seemed to congregate together in a flock. This evening, they were huddled together with their punch and their fans, waiting for the hostess to officially open the dance floor.

Abigail picked up her skirts – conscious, this time, not to flash any bit of her ankles – and started towards the marriage corner. Previous experience led her to expect that she would be hard-pressed to shove her way through the other guests; this time, though, people moved instantly out of her way, watching after her as she passed.

Miss Bridget Gillingham was the first to assess Abigail's approach. Abigail did not have much of a head for social details, but she seemed to recall that Miss Gillingham was considered to be possessed of both an average appearance and an average dowry. Miss Gillingham had made up for both by cleaving closely to Lucy's company, showering her regularly with the compliments that she so clearly desired. For her part, Abigail found nothing off-putting about Miss Gillingham's appearance – she had always chosen simple, flattering gowns which went well with her brown eyes and chestnut hair. Rather, it was Miss Gillingham's ruthless, mercenary personality which bothered Abigail the most.

Miss Gillingham was, Abigail thought, the most likely young lady to give her the cut and to encourage the other ladies to do the same. But tonight, Miss Gillingham pasted on a pleased sort of smile as she saw Abigail, and she gestured her over to join the group.

Privately, Abigail reminded herself to thank Mercy later. It was amazing, really, what a little bit of midnight could do for one's social standing.

"And here we thought we would never see you again!" Miss Gillingham declared, as Abigail came within speaking distance. "It has been *far* too long, Abigail. I hope that you and your parents are doing well?"

Abigail had to work not to flinch at the use of her first name. Lucy and the others had always called her 'Abigail' as a point of disrespect. Miss Gillingham now used the name as though it had always been a sign of affectionate familiarity rather than scorn. But there was no point in correcting her, Abigail decided. This suddenly warm welcome could only work to her advantage.

"We are doing well," Abigail said, rounding out her accent with care. "We have been very busy, of course, and so our social commitments fell sadly by the wayside."

"Of course, naturally," Miss Gillingham agreed sympathetically. "Service to one's country must come first. We are all so grateful to the Lord Sorcier for his diligent protection."

Miss Phoebe Haddington – a blonde young woman with self-consciously crooked teeth – shot Abigail a close-lipped smile. "But perhaps you have been attending balls in faerie instead?" Miss Haddington suggested. "I always said that you were surely a faerie princess in disguise. And now I am proven correct! Please tell us, Abigail – is there a faerie lord pining over your return as we speak?"

Abigail blinked slowly. The flattery was nearly outrageous enough to be insulting. It reminded her, in fact, of the way in which ladies had once spoken to Lucy. The idea left such a sour taste in her mouth that she struggled to keep it from her face.

That's exactly the sort of ridiculous flattery that would work on Lucy, Abigail thought. *They're only doing what they know best.*

"There are no faerie lords pining over me, as far as I know," Abigail said carefully. She wondered whether she ought to confirm the idea that she had been to faerie balls before – Lady Hollowvale held bizarre parties for the children and the other faeries every so often – but Abigail was certain that the admission would derail the conversation entirely. Instead, she said, "Miss Lucy Kendall is missing, I notice. I had nearly forgotten about that tragedy."

Miss Gillingham and Miss Haddington exchanged suddenly wary looks. The other ladies behind them shifted in discomfort.

"Yes, er . . . a terrible tragedy," Miss Haddington said.

"Truly awful," Miss Gillingham agreed. "One cannot help but feel that it should never happen to anyone. But . . ."

"But," Miss Haddington agreed, with a wince.

Miss Gillingham leaned forward conspiratorially, speaking from behind her fan. "One must admit that things have been somewhat more pleasant without Lucy, God rest her soul. She treated us all so abominably. And the way in which she spoke of you in particular – oh, forgive me, but there ought to be limits to performing grief. Lucy really was nothing but a bully."

Abigail stared at Miss Gillingham for a long moment. The obvious callousness did not bother her – Abigail had shared the very same sentiment with Hugh after all. But the implication that every terrible thing said about Abigail had been Lucy's fault – the idea that the other young women had just handed off all their own previous nasty behaviour to a dead woman – seemed so utterly beyond the pale that Abigail could not immediately manage a coherent response.

"I remember when you called Miss Wilder a pockmarked hag, Miss Gillingham," said a quiet voice. "I am sure that she remembers it as well."

Abigail glanced sharply towards the voice in question. Miss Esther Fernside was short and unassuming, with her mousy hair and her downcast gaze; it had been terribly easy to miss her among the other ladies. She was wearing a pale yellow ball gown tonight which looked as though it had been packed away for some time.

Miss Gillingham flushed brightly. "I . . . I don't recall that at all," she floundered. "Your memory has failed you entirely, Miss Fernside. I know that your father is our host, but that certainly does not give you leave to slander your own guests."

Abigail stifled a wince. She hadn't intended to waste time

defending herself – but she could hardly allow Miss Fernside to be harassed for sticking up for her in turn.

"I do distinctly remember hearing that comment from your lips, Miss Gillingham," Abigail said. "But I understand the difficult position that you were in at the time. I am sure that Lucy encouraged you to speak that way."

Miss Fernside cast a sharp look at Abigail – and Abigail knew then that they were both aware that she was lying. Abigail did *not* understand the mindset necessary to insult someone else so callously. And, against all implications, she did not forgive Miss Gillingham in the slightest for her previous behaviour.

Still, Miss Gillingham relaxed, now looking only mildly embarrassed. "I truly cannot remember ever having made such a remark," she said. "But . . . if I ever *did*, of course, you have my deepest apologies. As you say, I was not always myself around Lucy."

Now that Abigail was aware that she could find women attractive, she could not help but think, *This is why I never fell in love at any balls. So many of you aristocrats are all so terrible.*

Abigail smiled gratefully at Miss Fernside nevertheless. Had she ever *noticed* Miss Esther Fernside before now, she thought, they might have got on very well.

"I'm sure that you saw Lucy on the night of Lady Lessing's ball," Abigail observed to Miss Gillingham. "I heard that Lucy danced with Mr Red, in fact."

Miss Gillingham waved a hand quickly. "Oh, Lucy rather threw herself at him until he had no choice," she said. "Mr Red is always such a gentleman that he probably felt obliged."

Abigail bit back a frustrated comment. She had been hoping, at least, to find out who had been hovering around Lucy on the night that she had died – but so far, all of the ladies present had been far too focused on minimising their friendships with Lucy to offer any useful information on the matter.

"But you are not interested in Mr Red, of course," Miss

Haddington said quickly. "He must seem so very *normal* to you, Abigail. The Lord Sorcier's daughter must surely require a magician for a beau, at the very least."

I am not interested in men at all, Abigail thought sourly. *Your own designs on Mr Red are perfectly safe, Miss Haddington.* But she seized quickly on the last comment. "I expect that I *would* need to marry a magician," Abigail said. "Or at least someone who has dabbled enough to discuss the subject. I don't suppose you know of anyone present tonight who might fit that description?"

Miss Haddington looked very much as though she *wished* she could offer some names to that effect. But it was Miss Fernside who smiled wryly at Abigail and said, "I do hope that you don't intend to court my father, Miss Wilder. He is far too old for you, and I cannot recommend his personality."

Abigail worked desperately to hide her surprise. She thought back on the rest of the conversation and remembered that their host, Lord Breckart, was Miss Fernside's father. "I, er . . . cannot say that it has crossed my mind," Abigail assured Miss Fernside. "I wasn't aware that your father was a magician."

Miss Fernside sighed. "He likes to *call* himself a magician," she murmured. "He has probably cornered your father already in order to discuss magic with him with great seriousness."

Several of the ladies laughed nervously at this forthright observation. Miss Fernside, Abigail thought, had foregone almost all tact tonight. There was a kind of rebellious desperation to her manner for some reason, which Abigail could not quite pin down.

"Miss Wilder." The voice came from behind Abigail. It took a second for her to place it, given the refined accent – but as she turned, she saw that Mercy had approached her from behind. Her own midnight gown was resplendent in the candlelight, shifting against the darkness like a sigh. She was so utterly, breathtakingly beautiful that Abigail could not help but think,

You may all have your Mr Red. I am very nearly in love with Miss Midnight.

"What a lovely gown you are wearing," Mercy observed, without a hint of irony. "I do hope that you will do me the honour of joining me for a dance soon, before the floor opens and you are cornered by a dozen gentlemen."

Abigail's cheeks heated slightly at the sentiment. Ladies *did* often dance together before the floor opened – but they rarely invited each other to do so with such flowery language.

Miss Fernside stared at Mercy. "I don't . . ." She trailed off uncertainly. "I feel like I might know you, miss. But I can't seem to remember your name. Were you on the guest list tonight?"

Abigail stifled a wince. Mercy couldn't have known that she'd just made herself plain in front of the host's own daughter. "Mercy and I are acquaintances," Abigail said swiftly. "I'm sure she's meant to be here. There must have been some strange oversight, is all." Abigail took Mercy's hand quickly and added, "Perhaps we should have that dance now."

"I will hold your reticule if you like," Miss Gillingham volunteered. She seemed entirely too eager to please after having her previous comments brought to light.

Abigail bit her lip. It did not seem a terribly good idea to hand her magician's tools over to Miss Gillingham. But the lady had a desperately stubborn expression on her face, and Miss Fernside was still looking at Mercy as though she were a puzzle to be solved – and so, Abigail shoved the reticule hurriedly into Miss Gillingham's hands.

"Do be careful with it," Abigail said. "My father has cursed it against thieves, and terrible things might happen if it were to fall open."

Miss Gillingham widened her eyes at this. But Miss Fernside was just opening her mouth to address them again, and so Abigail spun away with Mercy, hurrying onto the dance floor.

"That was surprisingly illuminating," Abigail murmured.

"Our host, Lord Breckart, fancies himself to be a magician. He'll have told my father by now."

Mercy frowned. "Well, that makes for one suspect, at least," she murmured. "Should *we* tell your father?"

Abigail searched the room for Elias. He was, however, no longer speaking to Lord Breckart. The crowd was far too large for the size of the ballroom, and she let out a soft noise of frustration. "I don't know where he's gone," she said. "But he must know about Lord Breckart's interest by now, if he was cornered into a conversation."

Mercy considered this. "*Would* a black magician dare talk magical theory with the Lord Sorcier?" she mused.

Abigail shot Mercy a dry look. "I wouldn't credit black magicians with an overabundance of either intelligence or caution," she said. "Imagine this, instead of your sky full of star fishes: what would Lucy be like if she learned black magic? She'd just have to show it off in *some* way, no matter how ill-advised it was."

The questionable flautist hit a shrill note, and Abigail winced. "I'm sorry," she said. "I don't think we'll get the chance for a proper dance tonight. I really wanted one, but this is all too much."

Mercy smiled knowingly. "It's a shame I can't claim any debts from you right now, Abigail Wilder," she murmured. "Because I'd say you owe me a dance later, if I could."

Abigail smiled back wearily. "You'll just have to trust that I *want* one later," she said.

Lord Breckart's sister interrupted them then, calling the floor to attention, and Abigail heaved a heavy sigh. She was about to flee the dance floor entirely, in fact, when her Other Mum's voice whispered in her ear once again.

"*There is danger, darling,*" Lady Hollowvale breathed.

A moment later, someone pressed a hand to her elbow, hesitant.

"Miss Wilder?" a young man said. "Please forgive the forwardness – it's so hard to get anyone's attention in here. I was hoping that you might join me for the first dance?"

Abigail turned with a frown. The man who had just touched her elbow was a good head taller than she was; he had dark hair and a strong jaw, with a classically handsome smile.

He was wearing a deep red cravat.

"Mr Red, was it?" Abigail said.

The young man gave Abigail a quizzical look, and she corrected herself quickly. "Mr James Ruell," she said. "Apologies. The ladies all call you Mr Red, and it seems to have stuck in my head."

"*There is danger, darling*," Lady Hollowvale insisted.

"Oh," Mr Ruell said sheepishly. "I suppose that I am overly attached to this cravat, aren't I? I always mean to wear something else, but it *is* my favourite."

Abigail narrowed her eyes. Part of her was tempted to put off Mr Ruell as swiftly as possible in order that she might get back to searching for her father. But Lady Hollowvale's warning had inspired within her the very opposite of wariness: in fact, Abigail was now absolutely certain that she would learn something of interest if she *did* dance with Mr Ruell.

"I would be delighted to dance with you, Mr Ruell," Abigail said, as politely as she could manage.

Mercy shot Abigail an injured look – but Abigail winked at her quickly. "You were searching for my father, I think?" Abigail said to Mercy. "I do hope that you find him soon. I'll be right here with Mr Ruell, either way."

Mercy knit her brow . . . but Abigail must have managed to convey *something* useful, for she nodded slowly. "I do think that I will go continue searching for him," she said. "Enjoy your dance, Miss Wilder."

Abigail turned back to take Mr Ruell's hand. Out of the corner of her eye, she saw that the marriage mart crowd had turned its full attention upon her.

"*There is danger, darling*," Lady Hollowvale said again, more urgently than before.

Aha, thought Abigail. *So there is.*

Chapter Nineteen

The floor opened with a quadrille, which was not terribly conducive to private conversation. Still, Abigail managed bits and snatches in between movements, distinctly aware the entire time of her Other Mum's voice whispering of danger in her ear.

"You are an excellent dance partner, Mr Ruell," Abigail said, though she kept her tone measured. "I am certain that you must be in high demand."

Mr Ruell beamed at the compliment. "I greatly enjoy dancing," he said. "I know that it is fashionable to talk of how tedious all of these balls are, but I would dance every evening from dusk until dawn if I could."

Abigail studied him carefully. "Be careful what you say, Mr Ruell," she said. "One never knows who might be listening. The faeries in Whisperlake hold balls which last for weeks at a time. I have heard that their mortal guests sometimes die of exhaustion."

Mr Ruell blinked at the grim observation. "Oh," he said. "How, er . . . how terrible."

Abigail had already started to suspect that Mr Red was not at all aware of his place at the middle of this murderous problem. But she was now utterly convinced that he was exactly as he seemed: a handsome but oblivious nobleman with little to no understanding of either magic or faeries.

"I heard that you danced with Miss Lucy Kendall the evening that she passed away," Abigail said. "I was wondering if you also danced with Miss Edwards and Miss Hancock relatively recently." The subject of conversation was not at all appropriate, and Abigail knew that if she *had* been angling for marriage, it would surely have spoiled her chances with the man in front of her.

Mr Ruell looked suddenly torn. The midnight gown that Abigail was wearing had clearly piqued his interest, but her insistence on this macabre topic of conversation was probably making him regret that interest the longer that they spoke. "I . . . I think that I must have done, yes," he said uncomfortably. "I have done an awful lot of dancing, Miss Wilder."

"*There is danger, darling—*"

This time, the last bit of Lady Hollowvale's whisper was drowned out by someone's scream.

Abigail whirled – but it was difficult to pick out the source of the scream among the great press of guests. Worse, of course, was the fact that all those people had begun to panic. The dance floor soon erupted into chaos as couples blindly backpedalled.

Mr Ruell, to his credit, took Abigail about the waist and tugged her sharply back, just before a wave of stampeding guests shoved past them. Delicate jewellery snapped, and decorative feathers fell loose, mingling with discarded shawls on the floor.

One of those discarded shawls – a light pink bit of fabric – marched its way across the dance floor with determination, as though chasing the mob of people.

"Oh no," Abigail groaned.

"What on earth is going on?" Mr Ruell gasped.

Slowly, the pink shawl fell away to reveal a tiny straw man with a soldierlike stride.

Midnight rippled at the corner of Abigail's eye. Mr Hayes turned towards it, narrowing the eyes which he did not possess. Abigail knew, somehow, that if she'd had a swallow of her eyebright tea, she would have seen Mercy's form, fleeing through the shadows.

Why is Mr Hayes going after Mercy? Abigail wondered. *He's only supposed to frighten birds.*

Mr Hayes was not at all deterred by Mercy's darkness. He marched after her with unerring precision, scattering terrified aristocrats in his wake.

"Black magic!" someone gasped.

"Where is the Lord Sorcier?" a man demanded.

Abigail pried herself free of Mr Ruell's grip, forcing her way through the crowd. "Mr Hayes!" she hissed. "Stand down, Mr Hayes!"

But the crowd was far too loud, and Abigail knew that the little straw man had not heard her. He continued his stubborn chase, hunting down his invisible opponent.

Abigail decided that enough was quite enough. She elbowed her way past a shrieking lady, hiking up her midnight skirts to an indecent length. Then, all at once, she launched herself forward to tackle the little straw doll.

"Stand down, Mr Hayes!" Abigail snarled.

Mr Hayes turned his head to look up at her, as though to plead his case. But a moment later, he heaved a great straw sigh and went limp in her hands.

Abigail shoved back up to her feet, clinging to the doll with a dark expression. Several of the guests had stopped to stare at her openly.

"It's a doll," she said. "A *doll.* It's no danger to any of you."

Abigail glanced around for her reticule ... and found it sitting open on a chair. She stalked over towards it, and – with a furious breath – shoved Mr Hayes back inside where he had been before.

Abigail quickly searched through her bag, going through her magician's tools. But even after several counts, nothing came up missing.

"Did you break out of there all on your own?" Abigail muttered at Mr Hayes.

The little straw doll, of course, did not respond.

Abigail sighed heavily. *We'll talk about you abandoning my bag later, Miss Gillingham*, she thought. For now, she pulled out her little silver flask and took another swallow of eyebright tea.

A bright haze enveloped the ballroom once again. It took Abigail some searching – but she soon picked out a small, blurry figure, shivering upon the balcony.

Abigail's shock had now given way to resigned understanding. There could be only one reason, after all, for Mr Hayes to chase after Mercy.

Abigail tucked the flask back into her reticule and shoved the bag beneath her arm. She headed towards the balcony with such obvious purpose that even the guests who were clearly angling her way in search of gossip material stepped out of her path.

Mercy had huddled herself within the shadows of the evening; scraps of her midnight gown still clung to her, but the material had started unravelling into a wispy haze. Abigail's gown, too, had started coming undone . . . but this was not at all her primary concern.

Abigail strode purposefully onto the balcony, and Mercy glanced up at her sharply. Her eyes had gone utterly black again – and this time, Abigail could not help but notice how much they looked like a raven's eyes.

"I don't understand," Mercy said, in a trembling voice. "Why am I so frightened of a doll?"

Abigail closed her arms around herself, fighting back the evening chill. Her gown was ragged now, though it still clung to solidity. "Because scarecrows are meant to frighten birds," Abigail said quietly. "And you *are* a bird in at least one sense. You're actually a sluagh, Mercy . . . aren't you?"

Mercy pressed her lips together, and Abigail knew that it was true.

"You never told me that you were a ward of faerie," Abigail said. "I only assumed that you were . . . and you let me believe it."

Mercy looked away, and her gown melted further into the night. Flashes of her too-pale skin appeared, stark against the evening. "When we first met," Mercy said miserably, "I only knew that you were a magician. I turned into the most harmless person I could think of so that you might leave me be an' let me go. But you kept followin' after me. An' after a while, I . . . I *did* want to tell you. But I was so frightened you'd be angry, an' maybe you'd stop lettin' me help."

Abigail sighed heavily. "I'm not angry," she said. "You lied for a good reason. An' after all the lies I've told lately, I can hardly blame someone *else* for tellin' one or two."

Mercy closed her black, birdlike eyes. There was something tight and pained about her expression. "There's so much more to it," she said, "but I'm afraid I don't have the time to explain."

Midnight wavered around them again, and Abigail realised that there was something very *wrong* with Mercy.

"I've made such a terrible mistake," Mercy whispered. "I'm sorry, Abigail. For everything."

All it took was a blink. Somehow, by the time Abigail opened her eyes again, Mercy was simply . . . gone. All of her midnight had gone with her; Abigail was now standing alone on the balcony in only her shift.

"Blast it!" Abigail hissed. She fumbled for the silver flask in her reticule and took another swallow of eyebright tea – but Mercy was not hiding behind her magic. The balcony was truly empty.

"Abby!" Hugh gasped. Abigail turned, and saw that he had sprinted *through* the wall, onto the balcony. The silk kerchief over his eye had slid somewhat askew, and he fixed it hurriedly as he continued babbling. "What're you doin' in your underthings? Wait, it doesn't matter! Abby, I heard one of the maids say somethin' about Miss Fernside's mum. She passed away half a year ago in her bedroom, Abby, with the western window open!"

Abigail looked at Hugh sharply. "Miss Fernside must have only just come out of mourning, then," she said. "That explains why she's only been at the latest charity teas. And . . ." A horrible thought occurred to Abigail. "The girls have only been dyin' for the last few weeks. Ever since Miss Fernside started attendin' balls again."

Hugh nodded emphatically. "What do you want to wager Lucy was just as horrible to Miss Fernside as she was to you?" he asked. "An' get this: the maids aren't allowed to clean Miss Fernside's bedroom. She keeps it locked up tight when she isn't in there."

Abigail hissed in frustration. "Miss Fernside's father fancies himself a magician!" she said. "She's probably heard him go on an' on about it. An' she *was* far too interested in faerie tales, wasn't she? Why didn't I suspect her?"

Abigail knew even as she said the words, however, why she hadn't suspected Miss Fernside. In truth, Abigail hadn't *wanted* to suspect Miss Fernside; the other woman had hated all of the same people that Abigail hated, and so Abigail had imagined them to be allies.

"Stupid," Abigail muttered. "The enemy of my enemy isn't always my friend. Sometimes they're just awful in a different way." She reached down to hike her skirts up – and remembered belatedly that she *had* no skirts.

Hugh looked Abigail up and down. "You can't go back in like that," he said. "They'll throw you right out."

Abigail clenched her jaw. "Do you think you could possibly get Mum's attention an' get her out here, Hugh?" she asked.

Hugh nodded seriously. "Mum's still got her pocket mirror out," he said. "I'll do what I can. Just . . . don't catch a cold or anything."

He whirled around then, and vanished back through the wall.

Abigail waited for several minutes, painfully aware of each passing moment. She had nearly resolved herself to march back into the ball regardless when the door to the balcony opened and Dora slipped outside, with Hugh close upon her heels.

"Oh," Dora said, blinking. "Did you decide to launder your gown, Abigail?"

Abigail shivered violently. "I – no, Mum, I did not," she said. "I'm not sure how you'd launder midnight, anyhow. But that's neither here nor there, is it? Somethin's really wrong with Mercy, an' I'm almost positive Miss Fernside is our black magician. Where's Dad?"

Dora considered Abigail calmly. Then – just as calmly – she turned around to gesture at her gown's buttons. "I cannot reach these on my own," she said. "Would you mind?"

Hugh coughed and turned away, blushing.

Abigail knit her brow – but she caught the implication a moment later, and quickly started undoing the buttons along the back of her mother's green silk gown.

"Lord Breckart has an interest in magic," Dora continued, as though they were having a perfectly normal conversation. "Elias has slipped away to investigate his library while I cover for him. He is hoping to find one of the stolen books there in order to confirm Lord Breckart's involvement in these deaths. But if what you say is true, then he might find those books in the library either way. Miss Fernside likely has access to it, after all."

Dora tugged the gown from her arms and stepped free of it. Now in her own underthings, she turned to offer the gown to Abigail. "It is hardly a gown made of midnight," Dora said apologetically, "and I do not know how well it will fit you. But it should be presentable enough for you to walk through the ball and reach your father."

Abigail stepped into the gown and spun around to let her mother do up the buttons for her. "I'm hardly goin' to complain about you givin' me the gown off your back, Mum," she said. "What're you goin' to do out here in your underthings, anyway?"

Dora shrugged. "I suppose that I will climb down from the balcony and retrieve my pelisse from the carriage," she said. "There is a very sturdy tree here, and it does not look like a difficult descent."

Abigail shook her head. *Thank goodness I don't have a normal mum*, she thought to herself. "Thanks, Mum," she said. "Good luck with the tree."

Dora smiled dimly. "Good luck with the black magician," she said.

"Are you decent?" Hugh demanded, with his back still turned to them both.

"I'm decent, Hugh," Abigail said wryly. "Mum's not – but that's never stopped her before." She stepped past Hugh for the door back into the ballroom, slipping back inside.

Heads turned here and there as Abigail entered, and she quickly became conscious of the overly large gown that she wore. In particular, its hem was a few inches longer than she was used to, and it dragged uncomfortably upon the floor as she walked. The obvious strangeness made people murmur around her – but Abigail had far more important things to worry about than her already dubious reputation.

"D'you know where the library is, Hugh?" Abigail asked. She rubbed at her arms uncomfortably; the warmth of the crowd had dashed the cold that lingered from outside, but her body still wouldn't stop shivering. And now, on top of that, her stomach was feeling slightly queasy.

"I've only been down to the servants' area," Hugh said. "Lucy says it's probably on the second floor, though, just underneath us."

"Oh?" Abigail muttered beneath her breath. "Lucy is with us too, is she?"

"She's, er . . . very upset with Miss Fernside right now," Hugh said. Though he was still an eight-year-old boy, he said this with a surprisingly diplomatic tone.

"And where *is* Miss Fernside?" Abigail asked grimly. She cast her gaze around the room – but if Miss Fernside was indeed present, then she had faded most effectively into the crowd.

I need to find Dad, Abigail decided. *I'll deal with Miss Fernside once I've got his help.*

Abigail strode across the ballroom as swiftly as she could, pushing through guests in order to make her way for the stairs. She halfway expected someone to try and stop her – but the voice which called out her name surprised her enough that she turned her head rather than barrelling onwards.

"Miss Wilder!" Mr Ruell called breathlessly. "Please wait!"

Abigail caught the flash of Mr Ruell's deep red cravat just before he caught up to her. He was waving something in his hand – a familiar bit of tattered grey fabric.

Abigail widened her eyes as she recognised her Other Mum's handkerchief.

"Miss Wilder," Mr Ruell gasped again, as he paused for breath just in front of her. "You dropped this earlier, when you were, er . . . during that business with the . . . doll?"

Abigail forced a nervous smile. "Thank you very much, Mr Ruell," she said. "I hadn't even noticed."

Abigail reached out to take the handkerchief from him. She found it oddly difficult to do so, for her fingers had started shaking.

As Abigail took the handkerchief, her Other Mum's voice whispered again in her ear – but her urgent murmur had changed.

"*Alas, darling,*" Lady Hollowvale lamented. "*Alas. It is too late for warnings.*"

Chapter Twenty

Abigail stared at Mr Ruell. There was no guile in his eyes; in fact, he looked so sheepish and uncomfortable that Abigail had to assume that he knew where she had been keeping the handkerchief in the first place.

"*Alas*," Lady Hollowvale sighed again. "*Alas*."

Abigail nodded curtly at Mr Ruell. "Thank you for returning my handkerchief to me, Mr Ruell," she said. "I'm afraid that I'm not feeling very well. I really must go back to my carriage."

Abigail turned back towards the stairs once more, cutting off any possible reply. As she did, she realised that she was not entirely lying: she did *not* feel very well at all. Her legs had started to shake. Her heart raced uncomfortably in her chest and her mouth was strangely dry. A terrible headache had come upon her all at once.

Abigail stumbled onto the stairs, stepping out of sight of the ballroom. *I've been poisoned*, she thought with sudden horror. *But how? I didn't drink anything—*

Oh, but she had. Abigail had taken several swallows of her eyebright tea tonight. She had taken at least two, in fact, since discovering her reticule lying open on a chair, entirely unattended.

"Abby?" Hugh asked warily. "You don't look well."

"I think Miss Fernside got to my reticule," Abigail rasped. "My eyebright tea's been poisoned."

Hugh straightened with alarm. "How much did you drink?" he asked urgently. "It can't be enough to kill you, can it?"

The shaking in Abigail's hands had intensified. She stuffed the ragged handkerchief back down the front of her borrowed gown, trying to ignore her Other Mum's continued lamentations. "I don't know, Hugh," Abigail said. "I wish I did. Either way, I've got to find Dad. No one at the ball is goin' to be able to help me, that's for sure."

Abigail considered the stairs bleakly. Had she been in normal health, it would have been a simple matter to descend one floor and search out the library. But her entire body now felt sick and unsteady, and her heart was somehow racing even faster by the second.

She stumbled down the steps, gritting her teeth against her own growing weakness. *I danced with Mr Red*, Abigail thought. *That was my real crime, wasn't it? Miss Fernside might well be trying to bring someone back to life, but she's sacrificing people that she doesn't care for in order to carry out her plan.*

Abigail had nearly made it to the second-floor entrance when her foot slipped out from beneath her. She tumbled down the last few stairs and landed with a painful wince. It briefly occurred to her that she would have terrible bruises later, before she remembered that this was the least of her worries.

Abigail struggled back to her feet, breathing hard. Her vision had started to slant, as though the entire world had slipped sideways. Thankfully, the door to the second floor was unlocked, and it soon gave way before her, leading her into an empty, darkened drawing room.

"I just have to find Dad," Abigail mumbled. "He'll have some idea what to do."

Hugh hovered around her, looking more and more worried by the second. "Where's Mercy?" he asked. "Why isn't she here helpin' you?"

Abigail gritted her teeth, leaning momentarily upon a chair.

"Mercy's really a sluagh," she said. "Her magic started doin' funny things, an' then she disappeared." Belatedly, it occurred to Abigail that she had Mercy's name – in theory, she thought, she could probably summon Mercy just as she would summon any other sluagh. Abigail had no circle to *contain* Mercy, of course, and no milk or honey, but she suspected that Mercy would not grudge her the missing food.

"Mercy Midnight," Abigail muttered, as quietly as she could. "Mercy Midnight, Mercy Midnight. I need you, please."

Silence echoed in the drawing room, broken only by the distant sounds of the ball from upstairs.

"What're you mumblin'?" Hugh asked warily.

Abigail let out a desperate breath. "Mercy can't come," she said. "She's trapped, Hugh – just like all the other sluagh. I don't know how, but Miss Fernside caught her."

Hugh swallowed fearfully. "This isn't good," he said. "Stop an' rest for a second, Abby. I'll go ahead an' try to find Dad so you don't waste time searchin' around for the library."

Abigail nodded. The simple movement required far more energy than she preferred. She half collapsed into the chair in front of her, breathing hard. The world continued spinning around her, no matter how carefully still she kept herself. Every inch of her still trembled violently, and her skin was flushed and burning.

Hugh flitted down the hallway in front of her, stepping through doors one by one. As he walked through one door in particular, Abigail heard the raucous noise of several birds squawking in unison.

Hugh stumbled quickly back through the door, backpedalling in a panic.

"I think I found the sluagh!" he said in surprise.

Hope surged through Abigail. Somehow, it gave her the strength to get back up to her feet. The dizziness and the nausea had passed, and she suddenly found it far easier to stride towards Hugh.

"I think this must be Miss Fernside's room," Hugh said. "It's locked, isn't it?"

"Why on earth would Miss Fernside have her bedroom down here?" Lucy demanded. "Surely, her room ought to be *above* the ballroom?"

Abigail stared at Lucy, confused. The other girl was now perfectly visible, standing behind Hugh in her thin white nightgown, with her arms crossed over her chest.

"Why can I see you, Lucy?" Abigail asked. "Why can I *hear* you?"

A terrible thought occurred to Abigail, then. She turned around – and saw herself still sitting in the drawing room chair, slumped over the table.

Oh, Abigail thought wearily. *Well. That's that.*

Perhaps Abigail should have been more upset about being dead. After all, she had been telling the truth when she'd said she intended never to die. But Abigail had always had a rather pessimistic understanding of the world, and so it did not terribly surprise her that she had died anyway.

Hugh stared at Abigail, looking horrified. "But – no!" he said. "No, it's all right, Abby. We'll ... we'll get Lord Longshadow's apple, an' we'll bring *you* back instead. It's all right, really."

Lucy whirled on Hugh with a furious sound. "We will *not*!" she said. "You promised that you would give that apple to me!"

Abigail clenched her jaw. "You promised Lucy *what* now, Hugh?" she demanded. But after another moment's thought, she realised that this did not terribly surprise her either. "No. It doesn't matter. We can't waste time arguin' about this. Mercy's in danger, an' who knows who else might be in danger *with* her. We don't even have an apple to talk about yet, so let it be."

Abigail turned to face the door to Miss Fernside's room – and walked right through it. Her body tingled slightly as she passed through the solid door.

The bedroom beyond was surprisingly large, and Abigail thought that it must be a second master bedroom. Perhaps, she thought, it had once belonged to Miss Fernside's mother. Moonlight poured through a western window, casting the entire room in weak illumination.

There was a four-poster bed, unmade, with very tousled sheets. Abigail's eye caught upon a dressing table in the corner; most of the brushes and cosmetics had been stashed elsewhere or else swept aside in order to make way for a large stack of books. An empty glass bottle that looked to have once held eyedrops had spilled over onto its side next to one of those books. And there, just next to the dressing table, was a large wrought-iron birdcage.

Three huge ravens turned their eyes towards Abigail as she entered the room.

"So many ghosts!" one of the ravens murmured in a deep, rolling voice. It had, Abigail noticed, four wings instead of just two.

"We are helpless now," another raven sighed, "just like them." It was a perfectly white raven with pinkish eyes.

The last raven looked at Abigail, and she saw that its black eyes sparkled with thousands of tiny stars. "Why have you come here, spirit?" it asked. It had a soft, pleasant voice which struck Abigail as faintly masculine. "You should be wary. Our captor can see ghosts. She uses those eyedrops just over there. She is a necromancer; she will bind you if she catches you here."

Abigail filed this information away for later, but she did not comment on it; she had far more pressing concerns at the moment. "Lightless?" Abigail guessed. "Is that you?"

The other two ravens shuffled and murmured to one another, and Abigail knew that she had guessed correctly.

"That is part of my name, yes," Lightless said. He inclined his head to her stiffly. "But how did you know?"

"Oh, it *is* Lightless!" Lucy and Hugh had stepped in behind

Abigail – and now, Lucy clasped her hands to her chest with delight. "I was terribly worried, you know! But here you are, all safe and sound! As soon as we have freed you, we can be off again, and you can introduce me to Lord Longshadow!"

Lightless glanced past Abigail at the other two. He cocked his head, just as a normal raven would do. "I know you, I think," he said to Lucy.

Lucy's mouth dropped open. "I should think that you do!" she huffed. "I'm Miss Lucy Kendall! You found me several nights ago, and you held my hand and led me into faerie so that I could talk to your lord!"

"Did I?" Lightless murmured. "Yes, that seems likely. My apologies, Miss Lucy Kendall. I have been in this cage for so long. The iron wearies me terribly."

Abigail pressed her lips together. "I was hopin' to see Mercy here," she said. "Why isn't she in the cage with you?"

"Mercy?" said the raven with four wings. "Oh dear. You've done it now, Lightless, haven't you? I told you not to give the girl what she wanted."

Abigail knitted her brow. "What does that mean?" she asked. "It *was* Miss Esther Fernside who trapped you here, wasn't it? What was it that Miss Fernside asked from you?"

Lightless heaved a terrible sigh. "Our captor met Lord Longshadow by chance several months ago when he came to collect her mother's soul," the raven said. "She begged him not to take her mother – but what else was he to do? She has since captured us each, one by one, in order to demand Lord Longshadow's real name from us. She believes that she can command him to give her mother back to her."

Abigail swallowed slowly. "But what has that got to do with Mercy?" she asked. "She isn't . . ."

The stars in Lightless Moon's eyes banked their embers. "I gave our captor the second half of Lord Longshadow's name, in return for letting us leave," he said. "But I was a fool – she never specified just *when* it was that she would let us leave. By some method I do not know, you have learned the first half of Lord Longshadow's name. Has our captor also learned it?"

Abigail closed her eyes, with a fresh sinking feeling in her stomach.

The Raven with a Thousand Faces, she thought. *That was one of Lord Longshadow's names, wasn't it? Silly me. Why did I never think that some of those faces were women?*

"I told Miss Fernside Mercy's first name," Abigail said softly. "I didn't realise that Mercy was Lord Longshadow. And I didn't . . . I didn't know that Miss Fernside was your captor at the time. I'm the one who gave Miss Fernside what she needed."

But *how* had Miss Fernside recognised Lord Longshadow? Even Elias, who had placed several bans upon Mercy, hadn't recognised her at all.

The answer came to Abigail far too quickly, and she groaned.

I helped a noble lady right here in London, maybe half a year ago, Mercy had said. *She asked if I wanted anything, and I figured a good noble accent might come in handy someday.*

Surely any daughter would recognise her own mother's accent. No wonder Miss Fernside had looked at Mercy with such surprise.

"This is awful," Abigail muttered miserably. "I'm so stupid. Mercy's been stupid too, but I have to take at least some of the credit." She rubbed her face. "But if Miss Fernside has Mercy's full name, and Mercy isn't *here* . . . well, where is she?"

Lightless gazed at Abigail heavily. Somehow, he managed to look troubled, even as a bird. "Our captor will have summoned Lord Longshadow, I expect," he said. "If neither of them is here, then they have probably gone to Longshadow by a path which only Lord Longshadow knows. There is a tree, you see, at the border between Longshadow and the Other Side—"

"Yes, of course," Abigail sighed. "Curse it all. What an inconvenient time to be dead. I need to catch up with them somehow.

I don't know what on earth I'll *do* if I catch up to them, but I've got to try *somethin'*—"

Abigail stopped herself suddenly.

"Abby?" Hugh asked. "What is it?"

Abigail sucked in a deep breath.

"Black Catastrophe," she whispered. "Black Catastrophe, Black Catastrophe. I am dead, an' I need you to take me to the Other Side as fast as you possibly can."

There was no real sense of fanfare or transition. At first, there were three ghosts and three sluagh in the room. A moment later, there were three ghosts and *four* sluagh, as Black Catastrophe melted from the shadows behind Abigail with her indigo skin and tattered clothing.

"Well," said Black Catastrophe, as she fixed her robin's-egg eyes upon the iron cage. "That is something, isn't it?"

Abigail turned to look at Black Catastrophe. "I did say that I would find the missing sluagh," she said weakly. "I'm afraid I died right before I found 'em, though, an' now a black magician's abducted Mercy."

"What a dolt he is," Black Catastrophe sneered. "And always looking down on the rest of us, isn't he?"

Abigail held back her instinctive protest. Instead, she said, "It's she. Mercy is a woman right now."

"Well, fine," said Black Catastrophe. "What a dolt she is." She glanced at the iron cage again. "And aren't all of you in a fine predicament? I'd help you out of your cage, but I can't touch iron either."

Abigail looked down. "Someone needs to tell Dad about all of this," she said to Black Catastrophe quietly. "I can't talk to him now, but . . . I think *you* could, couldn't you?"

Black Catastrophe pursed her lips. "I could," she said. "I might. But first, I'll need to kill you."

Abigail blinked. "What?" she asked. "But I'm already dead!"

Black Catastrophe raised her eyebrows. "You are not," she

said. "I can tell. You are *dying*, certainly – but something has knocked your spirit loose before its time."

Abigail widened her eyes. "The nightshade!" she said. "Miss Fernside enchanted it to create ghosts. It's made me into a ghost too early, hasn't it?" She looked back towards the hallway. "I'm not dead yet, then. If Mum an' Dad can find me, then maybe they can save me. Mr Jubilee is supposed to be bringin' a nightshade remedy any moment now, assumin' he hasn't forgotten."

Black Catastrophe tilted her head in much the same way that Lightless had done. "Where *is* your body, then?" she asked. Abigail shot her a wary look, and she sighed heavily. "I won't kill you if you don't wish it. I have *some* class, you know."

Abigail looked back at the caged sluagh. "Hold on for just a little while longer," she said. "I'll try an' find you help."

Abigail took a deep breath – and walked back through the door all at once.

Hugh and Lucy followed curiously as Abigail headed back towards her own body, slumped over at the table. Black Catastrophe appeared from the shadows a moment later, looking at Abigail's sleeping form.

"Dying, but not dead," Black Catastrophe confirmed. "You haven't got very long at all, though. A minute or two, perhaps. I could probably stave off the poison – but I cannot offer gifts freely. That's very powerful magic, and you'd have to trade me something equally powerful. I'm not certain that you can trade me something like that right now."

Abigail's heart dropped into her stomach. "So there isn't any hope after all," she said. "Mr Jubilee will arrive too late."

Black Catastrophe frowned. Thoughts flickered behind her borrowed blue eyes. Finally, she turned towards Abigail and scowled.

"You forgot to offer me milk and honey," Black Catastrophe said.

Abigail blinked. "I . . . I didn't have any on hand," she said. "I was dead. Or sort of dead. Besides, I thought faeries didn't actually *like* milk an' honey?"

Black Catastrophe rolled her eyes. "That was the least polite summoning I've ever seen," she insisted. "In fact, I'm thinking I ought to curse you for it. I can't have magicians summoning me up all the time whenever they feel like it. There are rules of decorum, you know."

Abigail knit her brow. "You told me to call you when—" But she stopped as she saw the cunning look in Black Catastrophe's eyes. "Oh. Well . . . perhaps you *ought* to curse me. It would certainly learn me a thing or two."

Black Catastrophe straightened haughtily. "I think I'll curse you to sleep like the dead, for . . ." She frowned consideringly. "A hundred years?"

Abigail widened her eyes. "Oh," she said. "Um. I'm deservin' of punishment – but perhaps that's too much?"

Black Catastrophe cleared her throat. "Well then," she said. "A year and a day ought to do it. Just to be safe. Or rather – because you've insulted me so terribly."

Abigail nodded slowly. "That seems like an appropriate punishment," she agreed. "I'll definitely have milk an' honey waitin' for you next time, that's for certain."

Black Catastrophe waved one taloned indigo hand. The shadows around Abigail's body flickered frenetically, closing in upon her. They coiled sinuously around her form, slipping between her parted lips.

Abigail had not noticed before that her body had still been breathing – but she certainly noticed now, as her body *ceased* breathing entirely.

For just a moment, Abigail was worried that Black Catastrophe had killed her after all. But the shadows that still clung to her body shivered as she watched . . . and slowly, Abigail realised that they seemed to be breathing *for* her.

"I don't do that very often, you know," Black Catastrophe said. "Powerful curses really are a chore to pull off."

"I understand," Abigail said, with a great sense of relief. "That was very kind – er, terrible of you. I appreciate the gesture."

"Abby's goin' to live, then?" Hugh asked softly.

"That's unfair!" Lucy declared. "Do you mean to say Lightless could have put *me* to sleep instead of taking me to the Other Side?"

Abigail pressed her fingers to her forehead. *I'm getting a fresh new headache, and I'm not even alive any more*, she thought to herself. But Abigail was so used to Lucy making everything about herself by now that she merely sighed and ignored her.

"Let us find your father, then," Black Catastrophe said. "Where is he?"

"I think he's in the library, somewhere on this floor," Abigail said.

Even as Abigail said the words, a door opened quietly just down the hall. It was a simple matter to identify Elias as he slipped back towards them – for though it was very dark, Abigail had always thought that he had a tall, noble bearing which other *real* aristocrats only wished they possessed. His golden eyes burned strangely in the shadows; Abigail was especially disconcerted to have those eyes glance straight past her to settle upon Black Catastrophe.

"Oh," said Black Catastrophe. "Well, isn't that a strangeness. Good evening, Lord Sorcier. Your daughter is in trouble. It's a good thing she's so much more polite than you are."

Elias glanced sharply at Abigail's sleeping form. His eyes flashed with fury. "Undo your curse, sluagh," he said. "You will not like what happens otherwise."

Black Catastrophe snorted. "*You* won't like what happens if I fulfil your request," she replied. "In any case, Lord Longshadow has been abducted – because of course she has – so I ought to keep this short. I'm certain that your daughter's spirit can explain it all if you don't mind holding my hand."

Black Catastrophe offered out one wicked-looking talon towards Elias. He gave the hand a withering look, and Abigail worried briefly that he might not take it. But Elias glanced once more at Abigail's sleeping body, and she saw a terrible fear in his eyes, growing steadily in tenor.

He reached out to take Black Catastrophe's hand ... and then, he looked directly at Abigail.

"You're all here," Elias said with surprise. He looked between Lucy, Abigail and Hugh. "What on earth is going on? Why has this sluagh cursed you, Abigail?"

Abigail sucked in a deep breath. "I, um ... I'm afraid I got myself poisoned," she admitted. "Mr Jubilee is supposed to be arrivin' with a nightshade remedy at some point, but I can't be sure just when. Anyway, I summoned up this sluagh very impolitely, an' so she's cursed me to sleep like the dead. I'll have to finish off that punishment before I can get back to dyin', I expect."

"It was very nice of her," Hugh added helpfully. "And ... well, hullo, Dad! I don't ever get to talk to you like this unless you visit Hollowvale. It's really somethin'." He smiled mistily. "I wish we had more time. But we really do need to get to Longshadow."

Abigail glanced at Hugh. "We?" she asked. "You're comin' with me?"

Hugh rolled his eyes. "Of course I'm comin' with you," he said. "Didn't you listen the first time around, Abby? I'm still here because *you're* here, an' I want to stick with you. If you head off to Longshadow, then you won't be here any more – so I'm not stayin' here either."

"I am coming too," Lucy said hotly. "I was promised an audience with Lord Longshadow, and I will *have* an audience with Lord Longshadow."

No one, Abigail thought, had promised Lucy anything of the sort. And in fact, she realised, Lucy had technically *had* her audience with Lord Longshadow already. But there was little point in debating the matter.

"Miss Esther Fernside is our black magician," Abigail told her father. "She's tryin' to bully Lord Longshadow into bringin' her mother back to life. That is . . ." She trailed off uncomfortably. "*Mercy* is Lord Longshadow. She has been, all along. But I don't understand it – why would Mercy tell us about the apple herself? An' why would she tell us not to destroy the bans you placed on her?"

Elias blinked in surprise. "I . . . none of that makes the least bit of sense," he said. "But do you really mean to say that Lord Longshadow has been sleeping in my *home*, and I never noticed?"

Black Catastrophe shrugged. "Lord Longshadow *does* have a thousand faces," she said bitterly. "All of those ghosts just love giving her bits of themselves."

Abigail gasped. "Gifts!" she said. "Faeries can't give gifts, Dad! Mercy told us to keep the bans because she has to trade the apple for something just as valuable!"

Elias scowled. "Everything to do with faeries is so convoluted," he muttered. "Not that I was thinking of destroying the bans in any case. If Miss Fernside knows Lord Longshadow's real name, then she could order him – *her* – to do all manner of terrible things. Those bans will prevent the worst of it, at least for now."

Abigail looked back towards the locked bedroom door. "There are three sluagh trapped in an iron cage in Miss Fernside's bedroom," she said. "Mum could surely let them out as soon as she comes back in her pelisse. But you'll have to tell her where they are."

Elias narrowed his eyes. "I will not be letting you walk into Longshadow alone," he said. "You cannot even use your magic in your current state."

Black Catastrophe turned her bright blue eyes upon him. "You do not have a choice," she said. "The Kensington path to Longshadow is blocked – and that path would take too long in any case. Mercy will have taken her captor by a special way which only Lord Longshadow can open. There is one other path which we may take – and it is open only to ghosts and to sluagh. Even magicians may not walk this path, unless they ride the edge of their own death."

Elias opened his mouth – and Abigail knew that he was about to suggest one of *several* methods which could induce a deathlike trance – but she cut him off.

"You haven't got much of your magic right now," Abigail told him quietly. "Don't try an' throw together some half-baked ritual on the spur of the moment. I don't know how I'm goin' to save Mercy ... but I *will* save her. Trust me this time, won't you?"

Elias stared at her for another long moment ... and then, he sighed heavily. "I will trust you," he said softly. "I must find Mr Jubilee, in any case, if we are going to save you. Do not dare walk over to the Other Side, Abigail. I will come after you if you do."

Abigail grinned at him. "Some sluagh would have to drag me there by force," she said. "An' I hear that they don't do that." She turned back to Black Catastrophe. "Where is this path we're takin', then?"

"Lucy an' I are comin', too," Hugh added quickly. "Don't forget us."

Black Catastrophe looked them all over grimly. "We shall walk the path of the dark night," she informed them. "Some call it *annwfyn*; others call it stranger things. It is a path for ghosts who seek to understand their own mortality. The path is very close, for it lives within your soul. I will take you if you ask me – but know that you may lose yourself upon the path for ever."

Abigail pressed her lips together. "I'm goin'," she said. "I'm happy to go alone. But I won't stop anyone else from comin' with me if they really want."

Lucy shrank into herself visibly. "I . . . perhaps I had better stay here," she amended quickly.

Hugh crossed his arms. "I'm goin'," he repeated. "Take me with you."

"As you like," said Black Catastrophe. "It is part of my duty to bring you there if you wish it. I cannot turn you down."

The sluagh released Elias's hand, and his golden eyes slid away from Abigail, searching for her anew.

"You will have to come back," Elias warned her, though he could not see her any longer. "We will be waiting, Abigail." He paused, and then added, more softly, "I love you."

"I love you too," Abigail whispered back. After that, she couldn't bear to look at him any longer. She rested her gaze instead upon Black Catastrophe's indigo skin and bright blue eyes. "Please take me to *annwfyn*," she said. "I'm ready to leave."

Chapter Twenty-One

Before Abigail had even finished the words, the shadows in the room surged forward, crawling over her. For a moment, she was dimly aware of Hugh next to her, fighting off the black tendrils – but then, Abigail's awareness of him disappeared, and she was suddenly alone in the darkness.

She wasn't quite certain what she was expecting. Black Catastrophe's tone as she described *annwfyn* had been chilling . . . but there was nothing particularly frightening about this darkness. Rather, it felt warm and still – like being cocooned in a soft blanket in the middle of the night.

The longer that Abigail stayed still, however, the more tempting that softness became – like a mental quicksand, tugging gently at her thoughts. It would have been a simple matter just to lie down in the darkness and fall asleep right where she was. And so, she started blindly forward, taking each step warily.

Thankfully, the further that Abigail walked, the more the darkness lifted. A soft silver light started in at the corner of her eye, defining the details around her.

Annwfyn looked an awful lot like a workhouse.

The warm, comforting closeness of the darkness had evaporated, replaced by simple claustrophobia. Dirty straw beds clustered against the walls, each with far too many people – all sick, or injured, or else just tired and desperate. The air was thick with the stench of unwashed bodies . . . and, of course, the pungent scent of lye.

Anyone else might have been horrified by the scene. But Abigail had lived it – and so, to her, the sight was simply tiring.

Somewhere underneath the growing din of murmurs, however, Abigail heard a young girl crying . . . and this, for some reason, gave her terrible pause.

Near one bed, in a little corner of the room, a little girl with blonde hair and pockmarked skin sobbed over her mother.

"You'll be fine, Mum," Abigail heard her younger self whisper. "You just need to fight it. You'll get better."

The woman in the bed was blonde, too – but her hair was plastered to her forehead, and her eyes were barely open. If she heard her daughter pleading, then no sign of it registered on her expression.

"Well," Abigail said flatly. "That's just a low blow, isn't it?" Her voice trembled on the words, though, and she found herself staring at her first mother, struck by the sight of her obvious suffering.

"I am the Last Sigh." The words came from behind Abigail, and she whirled to face the woman who spoke. "I am the Final Usher. I am the Calm and the Dark Night."

The figure that stood behind Abigail *looked* like Mercy. Her hair was long and black, and her skin was far too pale. Her eyes were full of darkness, though, and she wore no cap – instead, she was clad entirely in heavy folds of midnight.

Her eyes fixed upon Abigail with a terrible, inhuman kindness. "Let me take her with me, Abigail," the woman said softly. "I will spirit her away from here and give her peace."

Abigail looked back at her mother. It was clear to her now, in a way that it had not been clear when she was young, that her mother had held on for far too long – that she had indeed listened to her daughter's pleas and tried to survive the illness which had taken her.

"She doesn't want to go with you," Abigail said. "She knows her own sufferin', an' she still doesn't want to go. Can't you understand that?"

The false Mercy considered Abigail seriously. "Your mother is staying for you," she said. "But you have the power to let her go."

Abigail swallowed hard. She took a hesitant step towards the dirty straw bed, kneeling down in front of it.

"Please don't die," the younger Abigail begged. "Don't leave me all alone here, Mum."

Tears pricked at Abigail's eyes. Slowly, she reached out to take her mother's other hand. Her skin was warm and dry – she had already sweated most of her water away.

"You won't leave me all alone," Abigail told her, with great difficulty. "There are other people who'll take care of me. If you want to live, then you should fight. But you shouldn't stay here just for me. Do you understand? It has to be your choice, Mum."

For just a moment, Abigail thought she saw her mother's distant eyes fix upon her. A quiet sigh escaped the woman in the bed – so soft that it was barely perceptible.

And Abigail's first mother died.

"Your mother required no guide to the Other Side," said the false Mercy, "because you told her not to wait for you."

Abigail dropped her mother's hand to swipe at her eyes. "Is this real?" she asked in a choked voice. "Am I really here?"

"You are," said the false Mercy. "And you are not. It is very complicated." Her voice was flat and toneless. It was nothing like the voice that Abigail had come to love. "It is not your time to die, Abigail Wilder. But there will come a time when you are tired. And when that time does come, I will take away your pain."

Fury sparked within Abigail's throat. She shoved to her feet, turning upon the spectre that had Mercy's face. She knew, suddenly, exactly whom – or rather, exactly *what* – she was talking to. It was bigger than Mercy, and darker, and far more implacable. She had seen it sometimes in terrible glimpses, on those occasions when Mercy used her power.

"You will not have my pain, Longshadow," Abigail said. "I haven't *offered* you my pain. You will not have *me*, not ever." She clenched her fingers into fists at her sides. "You look around at this, an' all you see is suffering. But I see *unfairness* – a whole awful heap of it! I won't take your stupid peace, no matter how many times you offer it to me."

Longshadow frowned dimly. "That is silly," she said. "Death is inevitable. There is both peace and virtue in accepting that."

Abigail scoffed. "*Peace*, I'll grant you," she said. "But there's no virtue in layin' down an' dyin'. It just is what it is. Why should anyone accept that if they don't want to accept it? I won't let death take me quietly. I'll linger as a ghost if I have to. I'll find some magician who wants advice, an' I'll make 'em spin me up a locket. I'll fight you for every spare second of my existence."

Longshadow glanced towards the woman in the bed – and Abigail clenched her jaw at the implication.

"My mum made her choice," Abigail said. "I won't grudge her that, an' I won't grudge anyone else who wants to go on. But you won't make *my* choice for me. As long as death is unfair, then I'm not ever goin' to the Other Side. I'm stayin' here with my sufferin', an' I'm stoppin' unfair deaths – people who would starve, an' people who'd die sick, an' people who'd be murdered, like Lucy an' Hugh. An' I'll even figure out how to bring 'em back if I can. I'll give out that apple to someone – an' then, I'll wait a hundred years, an' I'll give *another* apple out, until that tree finally withers an' dies."

Longshadow shook her head. "I don't understand," she said. "You *cannot* live for ever, Abigail Wilder. It is not done."

"I will do it," Abigail said. "So watch me." She met the false Mercy's deep black eyes. "I know what you are. You think you an' Mercy are the same – but you're not. You're just a piece of land in faerie. She's . . . more. She's got a thousand faces that you don't – a thousand stories – an' she's learned to care about 'em all. She's learned how to give people their choices. I hope you learn that someday too."

Abigail breathed in deeply, summoning up her anger and her courage. "You've offered me a gift, Longshadow – but you don't understand gifts, do you? I don't have to take a gift just because you've offered it. Next time, offer me fairness an' not peace, an' I'll consider it."

Longshadow did not offer a reply this time. But slowly – very slowly – the workhouse faded from view, melding into darkness.

Twilight rose upon the horizon. Abigail turned and saw the rosy light glimmering upon a tall hill, carpeted by silver lilies.

"Oh!" said Hugh. "You *are* here!"

He and Black Catastrophe had appeared just behind Abigail. Hugh looked tired but determined, while Black Catastrophe simply looked thoughtful.

"Did you learn something from the dark night?" Black Catastrophe asked Abigail.

Abigail considered that. "I did," she said, with a hint of surprise. "Though . . . I'm not sure that I learned what it *wanted* me to learn, if I'm goin' to be honest."

Black Catastrophe studied Abigail carefully. Then, she said, "I promised to lead you to the Other Side. I will take you there now. It is up to you whether you cross or not."

Abigail nodded. "Miss Fernside will have gone to the tree which grows on the border," she said. "I want to go there too, if you don't mind."

Black Catastrophe pointed one taloned finger at the hill in the distance. "There," she said. "From the top of that hill, you can see the tree and the Other Side. It will not take us long. I hope you are prepared."

Abigail looked at Hugh – and offered him her hand. He threaded his fingers through hers with a wry smile.

Abigail thought, *I still have no idea what I'm going to do.*

But this was a useless thought, and so what she said out loud was, "I think we're prepared."

~

The climb up the hill of silver lilies took much longer than it should have done – but Abigail was used to this since she had travelled through faerie so many times before.

The hill never seemed to get any taller, nor did the sky come any closer. But the further they trudged up its slope, the more the twilight sky darkened into evening. There was no moon and no stars in faerie ... which was how Abigail knew when they had reached the top of the hill.

As they finally came to the summit, Abigail saw stars.

They were sprinkled all across a midnight sky, far in the distance. There was a clear delineation, Abigail thought, between the empty sky of faerie and the brilliant cascade of stars which overlooked the Other Side. In fact, she discovered, the Other Side was truly the other side of the hill itself – a land washed in wistful starlight.

A tall silver tree grew at the top of the hill, taking up most of the space there. It was wildly large for an apple tree; half of its huge, winding limbs reached up into the faerie sky, and the other half reached for the Other Side – as though to knit the two realms together.

Before the tree stood Miss Fernside in her light yellow ball gown. With her was a pale, white-haired man even shorter than Miss Fernside was – dignified and dressed all in midnight, with the twilight of Longshadow flickering in his eyes.

"You *will* bring her back, Mercy Midnight!" Miss Fernside choked out. "After everything I have done – after all of the suffering you have caused me – you *will* bring my mother back to me. You have no choice in the matter."

Abigail studied the man next to Miss Fernside with a strange, hollow feeling in her chest. There were traces of the Mercy that she knew within him; his skin and his eyes were the same, though his hair was far different. The alien majesty which he carried was familiar. But Lord Longshadow, Abigail thought, was deeply *uncomfortable* in a way which Mercy had not been, and he held himself in a stiff and miserable manner.

The man that Abigail was looking upon now was, in some way, a false form. He was a kind of forced performance – an empty mask for Mercy to wear.

You are not really a lord at all, Mercy, Abigail thought sympathetically. *You were so much more comfortable as a laundress, weren't you?*

"I cannot give you what you ask," the lord in front of Miss Fernside said quietly. "Your mother has passed on to the Other Side. None may return from that land – not even the sluagh."

Miss Fernside stared at Lord Longshadow with tear-stained cheeks. "You are lying," she whispered. "You are the Keeper of Life and Death. You *can* bring people back to life."

Lord Longshadow winced. "But faeries cannot lie, Miss Fernside," he said. "I swear to you: your mother is beyond my power."

Abigail drew in a deep breath, clutching to Hugh's hand more tightly.

I can't use my normal magic, Abigail thought. *What can I do?*

"Sluagh can kill people," Abigail observed slowly to Black Catastrophe. "In theory – couldn't *you* kill Miss Fernside?"

Black Catastrophe regarded her grimly. "I could," she said. "I could kill her with a mere touch. Normally, of course, I would *not* do so. But she has abducted my friends and dishonoured Lord Longshadow. I am therefore owed my vengeance."

Abigail raised an eyebrow at Black Catastrophe. "I thought you weren't too fond of Lord Longshadow," she said.

Black Catastrophe smiled sharply. "I am not," she said.

"But while *I* may dishonour Lord Longshadow with impunity, no mere mortal should deign to do the same." She paused. "Unfortunately, Miss Fernside has Lord Longshadow's name, and the Last Sigh is more powerful than I am. As long as Miss Fernside is wary, I will never manage to reach her; she'll simply order Lord Longshadow to stop me."

Abigail nodded slowly, thinking hard. Lightless had said that Miss Fernside used eyedrops to see ghosts; hopefully, Abigail thought, Miss Fernside had used her eyedrops very recently. "You should watch for your chance," Abigail told Black Catastrophe. "I'll do my best to give you one."

She turned then, and stepped forward, levelling her voice at Miss Fernside.

"Mercy isn't lyin'," Abigail said. "You've read enough faerie tales yourself, Miss Fernside."

Lord Longshadow glanced sharply towards Abigail. A series of terrible emotions flickered through those familiar eyes: shame, Abigail thought, and a deep sense of awful worry.

Miss Fernside turned to consider Abigail, wiping at her eyes. "I thought you would be dead by now," she observed warily.

Abigail suppressed her relief, trying to keep it from her face. *Miss Fernside can see me*, she thought, *but she doesn't realise yet that I'm a ghost.*

"Did you really think you'd trick me so easily?" Abigail asked, with more bravado than she felt. "I had a faerie charm, an' it warned me off your poison." It was a plausible lie: Abigail *had* possessed exactly such a faerie charm, after all. Had she not lost it at precisely the wrong moment, in fact, she was certain that it *would* have warned her about the poison in her flask.

Miss Fernside hardened her jaw, and Abigail added, "I wasn't dancin' with Mr Ruell because I wanted to marry him, you know. I just thought that he might be the one poisonin' people. I'm afraid your stunt *did* confuse me, though. I told my father Mr Ruell was responsible. He'll be tried as a black magician soon enough."

Miss Fernside widened her eyes. "What?" she asked. "No! But Mr Ruell didn't kill anyone!"

Hugh fixed Miss Fernside with a perfectly naive expression. "I heard Abby say it," he agreed. "It all made sense at the time."

Out of the corner of her eye, Abigail saw Black Catastrophe's shadow flickering along the ground.

"Mr Ruell danced with every lady who died," Abigail continued blandly. "I realise now that those ladies died because *you* wanted to marry him—"

"I did not! I mean – I *do* not!" Miss Fernside was now flushed with distress. "Mr Ruell is my friend! I only hated the way that all those women talk about him. Mr Red, they call him! Even *you* called him that – as though he isn't a real person at all, but a very handsome cravat!"

Abigail shook her head. "So those women deserved to die?" she asked. "That seems extreme, doesn't it?"

Miss Fernside pressed her lips together. "No one deserves to die," she said. "But I had to *choose* people to die, all the same. So I chose awful people."

"And me," Abigail added sceptically.

"And you," Miss Fernside agreed worriedly. "I thought that you were investigating me – and I was correct. But you are *not* dead, and so it's immaterial." She glanced quickly between Abigail and Lord Longshadow. "When my business here is done, I will turn myself in and save poor Mr Ruell. I don't care, as long as I have my mother back."

Abigail looked away. It was hard, seeing the look on Miss Fernside's face – not because she felt *bad* for Miss Fernside, but because she seemed so self-righteously certain of her cause.

"You would do anything you had to, as well," Miss Fernside said. "You would. If it was *your* mother."

Abigail remembered very clearly the feel of her mother's hand in hers.

I did learn something from Longshadow, after all, she thought.

"I would not," Abigail said. "I know that for a fact." She raised her eyes back to Miss Fernside. "Lots of people die, Miss Fernside. An' I'd bring 'em all back if I could – if they *wanted* to come back. But I wouldn't kill another person in order to do it."

There was a harsh croak, and a sudden flutter of wings. Black Catastrophe – now a vicious-looking indigo raven – dived from the sky, reaching out her talons for Miss Fernside's face.

Lord Longshadow whirled, fixing his twilight eyes upon the other sluagh.

Shadows moved like water, flinging themselves against Black Catastrophe. The indigo raven tumbled to the base of the silver tree, still thrashing against its bonds.

Miss Fernside clutched at her chest, breathing hard. She let out a soft, nervous laugh. "Oh, how clever," she said. "You nearly had me, Miss Wilder. But Lord Longshadow is bound to protect me. And now – I think that I will have him kill you, after all." She turned towards Lord Longshadow. "Mercy Midnight, I command you: kill Miss Abigail Wilder."

Lord Longshadow blinked very slowly. A slow, sly smile crossed his lips.

"I cannot," he said.

Miss Fernside raised her eyebrows. "What?" she demanded. "You are the Keeper of Life and Death—"

"I am bound by several bans," Lord Longshadow informed Miss Fernside. "I cannot harm anyone with magic."

Abigail glanced at Black Catastrophe, still seething in her shadow trap. Lord Longshadow had not harmed the other sluagh at all, she saw now . . . but he *had* stopped her from harming Miss Fernside. Soon enough, Abigail knew, Miss Fernside would realise that Lord Longshadow could trap Abigail too, if she asked in the right way.

Abigail closed her eyes. The piece of Hollowvale which she normally carried with her was gone . . . but the entirety of Longshadow stretched out beneath her feet, quiet and wary. It was a land that could touch ghosts . . . and so, Abigail thought, it was a land whose magic she could use.

"Give me what I need, Longshadow," Abigail whispered to it. "I know that you can."

A tiny tendril of cold, black power wound about her feet. Abigail took hold of it with her mind, willing her imagination to turn it into something real.

Abigail's imagination was as lacking as ever. Certainly, she would never be able to imagine up anything as fantastic as Lord Longshadow could, in his very own realm. But she did not really need to imagine anything fantastic; she only needed something small.

Abigail imagined her body becoming solid, just as Hollowvale often made Hugh solid when he visited it. The image was not a difficult stretch, for Abigail had seen it happen before.

Slowly, Abigail's form strengthened into solidity . . . and she opened her eyes once more.

"I need you to run for Black over there," Abigail whispered to Hugh. "Make it seem as though you're tryin' to let her free."

Hugh frowned. "I don't have any magic," he said dubiously. "I couldn't do that even if I was still alive."

"Miss Fernside doesn't know that," Abigail hissed. "Will you do it, Hugh?"

Hugh grinned obligingly. "Should be easy," he said. "I'm not even wearin' a blindfold." He met Abigail's eyes. "On three?"

"On two," Abigail said. "One. Two!"

Hugh took off sprinting for the base of the silver tree, where Black Catastrophe still struggled.

"Mercy Midnight – stop him too!" Miss Fernside commanded swiftly. A look of confused fear had entered into her eyes, and Abigail knew that Miss Fernside was far less certain of her plans than she had let on so far.

Abigail broke into a run too, in the split-second that Miss Fernside had focused on Hugh. Miss Fernside glanced towards her with alarm and opened her mouth – but Abigail spoke first.

"Mercy Midnight!" Abigail commanded. "Take your true form!"

Lord Longshadow stumbled, caught halfway between reaching out for Hugh and listening to Abigail's command.

But Abigail knew Mercy's real name, just as much as Miss Fernside did. And more – Abigail was certain that she had just commanded Mercy to do something that she truly *desired* to do.

Abigail collided with Miss Fernside. The two of them hit the ground with a hard *thud*. Soon, they were rolling end-over-end, down the other side of the tall hill – towards the starry curtain that led to the Other Side.

Miss Fernside struggled violently against Abigail as they tumbled away ... but Abigail had endured far worse than a noble lady's thrashings in her time. She held stubbornly to Miss Fernside, ignoring the scratches that raked along her arms and face.

"Stop!" Miss Fernside cried dizzily. "We'll both be lost for ever!"

"You will," Abigail told her fiercely, squeezing her eyes closed. "But I *won't*."

Stars spun at the corners of her eyes, swiftly growing ever closer. Soon, the Other Side was right *there*, shining through her eyelids with the brilliance of a thousand stars—

But Abigail's descent halted abruptly, and she carefully opened her eyes ... just as the last of Miss Fernside's yellow gown disappeared, swallowed up by the curtain of starlight at the very base of the hill.

There was a land beyond that curtain – dark and shadowy and strange. As Abigail narrowed her eyes against the bright starlight, she could barely make out the world beyond it. But while she could see the distant outline of dark hills and beautiful lilies, she could *not* see any sign of Miss Fernside.

The lady and her yellow gown were simply gone.

"You're not allowed to go there yet," Mercy told Abigail. "You said you wouldn't go, remember?"

Mercy Midnight – pale-skinned, black-haired Mercy Midnight, with her twilight eyes and her laundress cap – held Abigail tightly in her arms. Shadows still clung to Abigail's skin, straining to keep her from falling forward. The Other Side shimmered peacefully, a mere inch away from Abigail's nose.

"I knew you wouldn't let it happen," Abigail lied, with more confidence than she really felt. In truth, she hadn't known anything of the sort. She'd simply *hoped*.

Mercy helped Abigail carefully back to her feet. The worry and shame had yet to leave her eyes. "I suppose you know now," she said softly.

Abigail tilted her head. "What do I know?" she asked curiously. She reached out to take Mercy's hand in hers, threading their fingers together.

Mercy looked down at their hands in surprise. "Well, that . . . that I'm not a woman. Or even a man, really. I guess I'm actually nothin' at all."

Abigail smiled slowly. "I beg to differ, Mercy Midnight," she said. "I commanded you to take your true form. And this is what you picked."

Mercy glanced at Abigail from beneath her hair as they turned to climb the hill once again. A vaguely hopeful expression had dawned upon her features. "I . . . I guess you're right," she said. "You know – I never really *had* a true form before. I didn't know there was such a thing. I just kept turnin' into whatever I thought people expected me to be."

Abigail smiled warmly. "But you have one now," she said. "An' I'm very fond of it, you know."

"I know," Mercy said softly. "I was so worried that you wouldn't like me any more if I was someone else. But I'm *not* someone else. That's so wonderful to know."

"I would have grown fond of anything you chose, eventually," Abigail told her shyly. "But I do think you make an awfully pretty laundress."

The silver lilies glinted on the hillside, in the starlight of the Other Side. Abigail looked around and decided that this was even better than her imagination had suggested it would be.

She wrapped her arms around Mercy's neck and leaned down to kiss her.

Mercy blinked her twilight eyes – but she leaned up at the last moment to press her lips to Abigail's.

Mercy's lips were soft and warm. All of her was soft and warm, Abigail thought. She was somehow even smaller than Abigail was, and though Abigail knew that it was probably the other way around entirely, she enjoyed the idea that she could protect the woman in her arms.

Slowly, Abigail wound her fingers in Mercy's long black hair, tugging more of it free from her cap. Mercy smiled blissfully against her, and Abigail's heart swelled with affection and relief.

Finally, Abigail pulled away – though she leaned in again to touch her nose against Mercy's.

"I have decided to fall in love with you, Mercy Midnight," Abigail announced seriously.

Mercy reached up to press her palm fondly against Abigail's cheek.

"I have decided that sounds lovely, Abigail Wilder," Mercy replied. "Why don't I return the favour?"

Chapter Twenty-Two

Abigail did her best to explain the events that had led her to Longshadow as she and Mercy walked back up the hill. They walked for far longer than they should have needed to do, before they managed to reach the top once again. Abigail held Mercy's hand the entire way, watching the silver lilies sway in an unseen wind as they passed.

Hugh and Black Catastrophe were sitting at the foot of the silver tree, staring down the hill at them. Black Catastrophe was an indigo faerie once again – though a few of her feathers still littered the ground around them.

"I'm surprised to see Black here," Mercy said to Abigail. "An' grateful, too. I wouldn't have thought she'd come an' help me."

Black Catastrophe rolled her eyes. "What sort of gratitude is that?" she asked. "You won't even thank me directly?"

Abigail smiled sheepishly. "Mercy's been under a ban," she explained to Black Catastrophe. "She can't speak to any other sluagh directly. But hopefully we'll fix that soon."

Black Catastrophe made a soft sound of consideration at this. She tilted her head at Mercy. " . . .you are a fool," she said. "But we are still siblings, of a sort. I will always help you, if you are truly in need."

Hugh smiled over at Black Catastrophe. "That's what I told

the dark night," he said. "I had to yell it over an' over an' *over*, but it finally let me through."

"You told the dark night that I was a fool?" Abigail asked, bemused.

Hugh snorted. "I said somethin' like that," he told her. "You are sometimes, you know. It's why I have to stick around an' help you out so much."

Mercy looked out over the Other Side of the hill, watching the stars wistfully. "It is a lovely view, isn't it?" she asked Abigail. "Even if you don't intend to go there."

"It is," Abigail agreed softly. "I don't mind just *lookin'* at it."

Mercy took a long breath. "Well," she said, "it looks like I've got company. If I've learned anything at all from pretendin' to be English, it's that I ought to put a kettle on."

"And what are you going to put the kettle *on*?" Black Catastrophe asked with confusion.

Mercy shook her head and offered out her other hand to help Black Catastrophe to her feet. Though she wasn't able to respond directly, her amusement was clear upon her face.

Mercy led them down the faerie side of the hill, back into the pink and blue twilight of Longshadow. This time, there was a little stone cottage which had not been there the first time they had passed. The cottage was mostly overgrown with ivy and wisteria, but a few shuttered windows peeked out from the greenery. It was on the whole a very cosy, welcoming sort of home.

"I expect we'll have further company soon enough," Mercy told them, as she opened the door and let them inside. "We may as well wait until they arrive." She threw open each shuttered window in turn, letting in the half-light from outside. The inside of the cottage had only a small kitchen, a table and chairs, and a single bed with a comfortable-looking quilt. There was indeed a stove in the kitchen, so close to Abigail's imaginings that she had to stop and marvel for a moment.

Two faeries and two ghosts settled in for tea, as though nothing strange had just occurred at all. True to Mercy's predictions, however, there was soon a knock at the cottage door, and she rose to greet their guests.

The man at the door was tall and thin, with a tatty-looking coat and an overly dignified bearing. His skin was as black as Mercy's midnight – but endless stars glittered in the depths of his dark eyes.

Mercy threw her arms around the man with a happy cry – though whatever she might have said to him seemed to lodge in her throat.

"Oh!" Abigail said. "Is that Lightless, all safe an' sound?"

Lightless embraced Mercy in return. He looked past her shoulder at Abigail. "And none the worse for the wear," he replied, in the same voice which Abigail had heard from the raven in the cage. "Though I must confess a terrible thing, Lord Longshadow. For I have divulged the latter half of your name—"

"She can't talk to you yet," Abigail said, with an apologetic smile. "But I did tell her everything already, an' I think she's just happy to see you."

Mercy squeezed Lightless emphatically, as though to signal her agreement. She stepped back and glanced past him at several other people behind him. "I thought I'd have guests!" she said. "Well, you're all welcome in for tea – though it'll be a cosy fit, I'm sure."

A veritable parade of people soon entered Mercy's cottage. First, of course, there was Lightless Moon. Lightless was followed by two other sluagh – one was a ghostly-looking figure, pale and genderless, while the other was a spidery woman with far too many fingers on her hands. Lucy – still wearing her nightgown – insisted on entering directly behind them. Dora followed Lucy, carrying Abigail's reticule beneath her arm – and Abigail immediately realised that her mother must have marched into faerie directly from the ball, for she was wearing only her shift and her pelisse.

Last of all, Elias Wilder entered the cottage, gently carrying Abigail's sleeping form in his arms. The other Abigail was still wearing Dora's green silk gown – though a journey through the thorny areas of faerie had clearly nipped it at the edges.

"This is the dread Lord Longshadow's lair, then," Elias observed dryly. "I must admit, my imagination failed to prepare me for it." He was smiling with obvious relief, though, as he took in the sight of Abigail sitting at the table, and the expression took the sting from his words.

Lucy looked around the cottage with a blatantly bewildered expression. "What on earth is this dingy place?" she asked. "Do you mean to tell me that this is what passes for an earl's home in faerie?"

Mercy sighed heavily. "Maybe I shouldn't have invited *everyone* inside," she muttered. "Me an' my big mouth." She glanced at Elias. "You can set the other Abigail down on the bed if you like."

Elias deposited Abigail very gently upon the quilted bed. "I notice that Miss Fernside is not among our company," he observed. "I take it I will not be bringing her back to England to face the king's justice?"

Abigail looked down at her teacup. "Miss Fernside has gone on to the Other Side," she said quietly. "She will not be coming back."

"Good," sniffed Lucy. "It's only what she deserved, isn't it?" She had paused herself at the little table, looking around at the empty chairs. Abigail wondered for a moment just *what* Lucy was waiting for – until Mercy gave another heavy sigh and gestured with her hand. One of the chairs pulled itself out for Lucy – whereupon she settled herself into the chair with a mildly gratified expression.

"We met Mr Jubilee on our way here," Dora said, as she

glanced around the cottage with detached interest. "I have his nightshade remedy with me. He has suggested that we should all make a visit to Blackthorn later, in order to bring him the lilies. I thought that you would not mind, Miss Mercy?"

Mercy smiled at that. "I'll be delighted," she said.

Dora rummaged inside Abigail's reticule. As she did, a little straw arm wriggled stubbornly free.

Mercy froze, staring at the bag. Lightless backpedalled for the open door, with the two other sluagh hiding behind him. Black Catastrophe disappeared, suddenly replaced by the indigo raven – the bird flashed for the window, cowering with an angry hiss.

Dora shot the straw arm's owner a look of mild reproval . . . and it disappeared grumpily into the reticule once more.

The sluagh in the cottage slowly relaxed once more. Black Catastrophe scrabbled her way down from the window with a last suspicious croak at the reticule. She cleaned her feathers briefly, as though to prove how little the straw doll had frightened her, before transforming back into an indigo faerie.

"Aha," Dora said, as she found what she was searching for in the bag. She closed the reticule firmly and offered something out to Mercy, who considered it quizzically.

"A bean?" Mercy asked.

"So it would seem," Dora agreed. "Mr Jubilee has advised that Abigail should grind it up and take it with tea. And so, we are already halfway there."

Lucy had begun to tap her toe impatiently during this particular exchange. Her face grew darker and darker – and finally, she burst out, "I have waited long enough! I am here in Longshadow, precisely where I was advised to come. I would like my formal audience now."

Mercy blinked at Lucy. "You what?" she asked incredulously.

Abigail pressed her fingers to her forehead. "Were you not listenin' at all, Lucy?" she asked. "Mercy *is* Lord Longshadow. You've talked to her a dozen times now."

Lucy narrowed her eyes. "I have not made my formal petition," she said. "I was *promised* that I would have a chance to plead my case to Lord Longshadow."

Lightless glanced over at Lucy with a look of such serene patience that Abigail *knew* he could not possibly be human. "But I did not promise you anything of the sort," he told her. "I said that you *might* have an audience with Lord Longshadow, and that you *might* have the chance to plead your case."

Lucy crossed her arms furiously. "You *implied*—"

"Oh yes, I certainly implied," Lightless agreed pleasantly. "But implications are not binding contracts."

"You'll sit down an' have your tea an' be quiet," Mercy advised Lucy shortly. "I won't hear a word from you until Abigail's safe an' sound."

Lucy opened her mouth hotly – but though her lips moved, no sound came out. She blinked in shock.

"Oh, good," Black Catastrophe sighed. "I was about to remove her tongue."

Lucy shut her mouth again with a terrified snap.

Dora headed to one of the counters with Mercy. The two of them chatted amiably in quiet tones while they ground up the strange bean. Elias settled himself at the table directly between Hugh and Abigail, openly checking them over for injuries. They did not *have* any injuries, of course, being ghosts, but Abigail allowed him to do so all the same.

Eventually, Mercy mixed the powdered bean with a fresh cup of tea and brought it over to the bed. Abigail had the most peculiar sensation of heat along her throat – followed by a strange, chalky taste. She winced and tried to wash away the flavour with the tea just in front of her . . . but it did nothing to dispel the taste upon her real body's tongue.

"Is it working?" Dora asked.

Mercy tilted her head at Abigail's body, considering. "I think it is," she said. "She was minutes from death before, but it's startin' to look more like hours. Oh! She's not dyin' at all now. I should have expected as much. Blackthorn knows its business when it comes to plants."

Abigail sighed with relief. "Well, I suppose I'm just a bit cursed now," she said. "I won't complain about sleepin' for a year, instead of dyin'."

Mercy shot Abigail a bemused look. "Psh," she said. "You weren't ever goin' to sleep for a whole year. True love's kiss breaks most faerie curses – an' you've got far too many people who love you."

"Oh yes," Dora said. "I had nearly forgotten about that." So saying, Dora leaned down to brush her lips across Abigail's forehead . . .

. . .and Abigail woke up.

Abigail blinked a few times, feeling bleary. Her head still hurt, and her tongue still tasted as though it had been coated in chalk . . . but the awful shivers and the nausea had gone entirely.

Mercy offered Abigail a hand off the bed. Abigail took it gratefully, dragging herself back to her feet.

"What a relief," Dora said. And though her voice was flat and toneless as always, Abigail knew that she meant it.

"I'd have kissed you myself, you know," Mercy told Abigail seriously, "but I'm more powerful than Black, an' I could break any curse of hers, so it wouldn't prove much."

Black Catastrophe scoffed and crossed her arms. "You could *not*," she said. "You were clearly too scared to try, so you cheated instead."

Lucy thumped her hand emphatically on the table. Her face had now gone red with frustration.

Mercy shook her head. "Annoyin' as she is," she observed, "Miss Kendall *has* reminded me . . ."

Mercy reached into the pocket of her laundress's apron. When she pulled her hand out again, there was a small silver apple sitting in the hollow of her palm. Longshadow's twilight glimmered upon its surface, in shifting hues of pink and blue. Abigail stared at it for a moment, unable to speak.

"This is the apple of life," Mercy said. "I am a woman of my word. I will trade it now, in return for an end to the bans which still bind me."

Elias watched her with a careful, closed-off expression. Abigail noticed then that he had yet to touch his tea.

"After all of this time," he said softly, "I am loath to trust you. You have not ever given me much reason to do so."

Mercy looked away from him. "I know," she said. "An' I am . . . truly sorry for that. There were things which I never understood before – things which you yourself left faerie in order to find." She hesitated. "But I have led a thousand lost souls to the Other Side. I have heard all of their stories, an' accepted all of their payments. An' I think . . . that bein' a laundress, an' losin' my friends, an' losin' my power were all things that I needed in order to learn the last important bits about bein' human. By takin' my power from me, Lord Sorcier, you gave me a gift – whether you meant to do it or not. An' now, in return for that, I must give you somethin' which is equally priceless."

Elias watched Mercy's face as she spoke. His own near-ageless features betrayed very little. But finally, he glanced at Abigail and Hugh.

Abigail inclined her head. "I'm very fond of Mercy," she said softly. "I would like to give her feathers back to her."

Hugh nodded too – though that old, lacklustre weariness was back in his manner. Abigail knew that Hugh was thinking again how unlikely it was that he should get another chance at life, no matter how close at hand it seemed to be.

Elias reached slowly into his jacket to retrieve three long black feathers.

"I will release you from your bans, then, Lord Longshadow," he said, "in return for the apple of life."

A reddish-golden flame flickered along the feathers in Elias's hand, licking at their edges. Slowly, the feathers withered away into a fine white ash, which drifted away to the floor.

Mercy sighed with visible relief. Elias closed his eyes, and Abigail saw a similar sentiment reflected in his manner as his magic finally returned to him.

Mercy offered out the silver apple to Elias . . . but as he opened his eyes, he shook his head slowly. "That goes to Hugh," Elias said quietly. "We are all agreed."

Mercy turned to offer the apple to Hugh instead. He took it tremulously, with a worried glance at Lucy – and Abigail remembered far too late that Hugh had promised the apple to her instead.

"No," Abigail said shortly. "Don't you *dare*, Hugh. That apple is yours."

"I know," Hugh said, in that familiar, weary tone. He slumped his shoulders. "It's mine. An' I'm givin' it to Lucy so that her an' her mum don't have to be sad any more."

At this, Dora turned her mismatched eyes upon Hugh.

"Oh," Dora said softly. "Oh dear. I am so badly suited to being a mother." There was a distant grief in her eyes as she considered Hugh. "Did you think that I was not sad, Hugh? I am so sorry if I have not shown it before now. I have such trouble crying, as a normal mother might."

Hugh cast a suddenly stricken look upon his mother. "What?" he said. "No, I . . . Of course not, Mum. You've always been wonderful. An' I . . . well, I know you must be sad, but at least you get to *see* me sometimes. It's just that Lucy's mum won't *ever* see her again. An' doesn't that seem . . . well, unfair?"

Elias looked away. "I would love to see you regularly too, Hugh," he said, in a pained tone. "You deserve to grow up with us as the other children do."

Hugh wavered uncertainly – and at first, Abigail was hopeful that their parents had swayed him. But after a moment, Hugh took a deep breath and set his jaw, and he said, "You all told me I was allowed to make my choices. Didn't you mean that?"

Abigail clenched her fingers into her palms. There was, she thought, very little that she could say to that. Oh, there was plenty that she *wanted* to say to it, certainly: that Lucy was using Hugh's goodness against him; that Lucy would not have done the same for him in return in a hundred years, if she were ever given the chance. But Abigail knew in her bones that none of these things would sway Hugh at all. He *had* made his decision – as terrible as it was.

Lucy still could not speak – but she shot Abigail a look of silent triumph. There was no gratitude on Lucy's face, Abigail thought; her eyes glittered with spite, and with deep satisfaction at having got her way.

Hugh offered the apple out to Lucy, who reached out to take it . . .

. . . but as she touched it, there was a cold flicker of shadow.

Lucy dropped the apple with a silent cry, clutching her hands to her chest. The very edges of her ghostly fingertips were blue with frostbite.

Abigail glanced towards Mercy. A cold, inhuman smile had appeared upon her lips.

"Miss Lucy Kendall," Mercy said softly, "you had your audience with me – in fact, you had several. But you thought I was a laundress then, an' you treated me accordingly. Had you ever read a faerie tale in your life, you might've known better." Midnight gathered in Mercy's eyes – and for just a moment, the twilight in the cottage turned to evening. "I rendered my judgement upon you, though you didn't notice it. I said that Lord Longshadow would not bring you back to life. An' since I cannot lie, I also cannot let you have that apple."

Hugh turned a furious look upon Mercy. "You said you'd let me make my own choices!" he accused her. "Why are you stickin' your nose in the middle of this?"

Mercy's pale face was calm and terrible as she looked back at Hugh. "You have made your choice, Hugh Wilder," she said gently. "But Lucy has made her choices, too. An' now, she must pay the consequences for them."

Hugh stared at Mercy helplessly. Just behind him, Lucy lunged for the apple on the floor once again, as though another attempt might end differently from the first. But she could not seem to grasp the apple, no matter how many times she tried. Shadows crawled all the way up her arms, leaving painful blue welts in their wake.

Finally, pained and defeated, Lucy sat down on the floor and cried.

Hugh's face took on a heartbroken expression as he watched Lucy's tears. But Mercy's countenance remained perfectly unmoved.

"That is a consequence too, Miss Kendall," Mercy advised her. "I wish I could say that someday you will learn *how* consequences work. But I'm not sure that you ever will – an' I haven't the time to teach you."

Mercy leaned down to pick the silver apple back up, brushing it off with her long, delicate fingers.

She offered it out to Hugh once again.

Hugh took the apple listlessly. After a moment, he sighed and stuffed it into his pocket.

"I won't eat it," Hugh said stubbornly. "You're doin' this for nothin'."

"I'm doin' this for my own reasons," Mercy corrected him. "Eat it or not. My business with you is done – except for the tea, that is."

And with that, Mercy Midnight poured them all a fresh cup.

Epilogue

Abigail knew without having to ask that her reputation among the *ton* was in tatters – or rather, that it was even more in tatters than it had been before. It hardly mattered that Abigail had risked her life to catch a black magician, given the crimes that she had otherwise committed by wearing her mother's oversized gown and chasing after a little straw doll in the middle of a party.

This tattered reputation, however, did not bother Abigail in the least, for she had earned herself *quite* the reputation in faerie. Faeries of all shapes and sizes and titles had begun to whisper that the Lord Sorcier's daughter was an even more powerful magician than he – and besides which, they said, she was far more polite. Abigail did little to disabuse the faeries of this notion, for she continued watching her words very carefully – and often outright lying – such that she made new friends out of dangerous acquaintances wherever she went. More often than not, of course, Abigail travelled with her best friend and lady love, Miss Midnight, who had a habit of glaring down any other faeries who thought to pull one over on the Lady Sorcière.

Abigail did return to England on occasion in order to see her family. And while she never did entirely warm up to her Aunt Vanessa's charity teas, neither did she ever fail to attend them – for though Abigail herself found it difficult to imagine a better world, she was always grateful to lend her presence to those who *could* imagine one.

And perhaps you will find it surprising to know that eventually, Abigail walked into one of these charity teas to discover a black-clad Lady Pinckney at Aunt Vanessa's right-hand side, calmly calling the tea ladies to order and chastening them for their gossip. And while Abigail and Lady Pinckney never did learn to get on very well, Abigail still found it strangely reassuring to know that certain people *could* change, even just a little bit.

Sadly, Miss Lucy Kendall did not change at all. Rather, she lingered on and on, sitting stubbornly beneath the silver tree in Longshadow, waiting for another apple to grow. Mercy often noted to Abigail when she visited that someday Lucy would surely grow roots and turn into a tree herself. But one day, when Abigail glanced out the window of Mercy's cottage, she saw that Lucy was no longer sitting at the base of the tree. Perhaps, as Mercy had surmised, Lucy had finally grown into the tree and become a part of it . . . or more likely, Abigail thought, Lucy had decided that being so roundly ignored was simply intolerable, and she had crossed to the Other Side in pursuit of other people to give her their attention.

Hugh Wilder kept the apple of life, fully intent on giving it away to one of the other children in Hollowvale. But while he had managed to endure his mother and father's sadness, Hugh could *not* endure his Other Mum's wild tears when she heard that he would not be coming back to life after all. Thus, after many difficult arguments, did Hugh Wilder give up the last of his fear and uncertainty and finally eat the silver apple that he had been given.

Hugh Wilder grew up in a loving home with wonderfully affectionate parents, surrounded by other children. For the first few weeks of his life, he baked several batches of tarts. Many of these, he took to the workhouses to hand out to the other children there. But upon one of these visits, Hugh happened by chance to meet a charitable physician named Mr Albert Lowe – and while Hugh had never imagined that he might give up his dream of baking tarts, he soon asked for an apprenticeship with the good doctor. Years later, Mr Hugh Wilder became a physician himself. He did not bake very many tarts after that – but he did fix several bruises and save several lives, which otherwise would not ever have been saved.

As for Abigail Wilder: regardless of what the dark night had claimed, she did not ever die. Rather, Abigail still wanders both faerie and the mortal world, using her magic to fight unfairnesses both large and small. And behind her, death shall always follow, for Abigail walks in the loving shadow of Mercy Midnight, who will never leave her side.

Afterword

I am not fond of death. I feel strange that I even have to write those words, but apparently, I do. For some reason, we are surrounded by stories which romanticise death, and which imply that people who refuse to accept death are doing the world some sort of moral disservice.

Obviously, I do not think that accepting death is a virtue. Rather, I think that it is simply a choice. And so, I decided that if I was going to write a faerie tale about death, then I wanted to write a *truly* fantastical story – one which glorifies life and stubbornness and attempts to accomplish the impossible. Death, in the form of Mercy Midnight, was not a villain . . . but she *did* need to learn that people are allowed to fight until the bitter end, if they so choose it.

Which brings me to a small historical footnote known as the Hays Code.

For the longest time, American cinema had an informal code regarding queer characters: they were allowed on-screen, but only if they were eventually punished by the story in some way. Queer characters were not allowed to live happily ever after; at the very least, they were required to die tragically. If you asked most people today, they wouldn't know what the Hays Code is – but it has endured beneath the surface of our media, even in stories with otherwise excellent representation.

If there is one thing which I *do* think should die a horrible, final death, it is definitely the Hays Code. And so, dear readers, while most faerie tales end with a euphemistic sort of death by apotheosis ("they travelled off to faerie and were never seen again") or a journey into legend ("they became a part of every unionisation effort in England for evermore"), you may rest assured that Abigail Wilder's further journeys are *not* a euphemism. Rather, Abigail is quite literally a stubborn, immortal lesbian – and she and her transgender faerie girlfriend will live together happily for ever and ever in perfect defiance of the Hays Code.

There are, as usual, many people who deserve thanks for their help with this book. An endless thank you to my husband, Mr Atwater; without his help, this book would surely not exist – and it would also have at least one less pun. Thank you to Dr Heather Rose Jones for the detailed breakdown of queer Regency history. Thank you to my alpha readers, Laura Elizabeth and Julie Golick, for their unceasing encouragement. A special thank you to Cullen McHael for fielding the strangest questions about British folklore at odd hours of the day. Thank you to my fellow authors from the Lamplighter's Guild, Jacquelyn Benson, Rosalie Oaks and Suzannah Rowntree, for their support and suggestions. And of course, many thanks to Tamlin Thomas for the historical nitpicks and for believing that I could do this book justice; this book is for many people, but it is really primarily for you.

Lord Elias Wilder, Regency England's court magician, regularly performs three impossible things before breakfast – but the one thing he cannot do is raise a daughter. As Theodora Wilder continues taking children under their roof, however, Elias is finally forced to confront his dark familial past and the matter of his dubious faerie father.

This short, exclusive novella, written from Lord Elias Wilder's perspective, takes place just after the events of *Half a Soul* and includes glimpses of the Lord Sorcier's childhood in faerie. Visit the link below to subscribe to *The Atwater Scandal Sheets*, and read *The Latch Key* today!

https://oliviaatwater.com/newsletter

extras

meet the author

Olivia Atwater writes whimsical historical fantasy with a hint of satire. She lives in Montreal, Quebec, with her fantastic, prose-inspiring husband and her two cats. When she told her second-grade history teacher that she wanted to work with history someday, she is fairly certain this isn't what either party had in mind. She has been, at various times, a historical reenactor, a professional witch at a metaphysical supply store, a web developer and a vending machine repairperson.

Find out more about Olivia Atwater and other Orbit authors by registering for the free monthly newsletter at orbitbooks.net.

if you enjoyed LONGSHADOW

look out for

FOR THE WOLF

Book One of The Wilderwood

by

Hannah Whitten

The first daughter is for the Throne.
The second daughter is for the Wolf.

An instant New York Times *bestseller and word-of-mouth sensation, this dark, romantic debut fantasy weaves the unforgettable tale of a young woman who must be sacrificed to the legendary Wolf of the Wilderwood to save her kingdom. But not all legends are true, and the Wolf isn't the only danger lurking in the Wilderwood.*

As the only Second Daughter born in centuries, Red has one purpose: to be sacrificed to the Wolf in the Wilderwood in the hope he'll return the world's captured gods.

Red is almost relieved to go. Plagued by a dangerous power she can't control, she knows that at least in the Wilderwood, she can't hurt those she loves. Again.

But the legends lie. The Wolf is a man, not a monster. Her magic is a calling, not a curse. And if she doesn't learn how to use it, the monsters the gods have become will swallow the Wilderwood—and her world—whole.

Chapter One

Two nights before she was sent to the Wolf, Red wore a dress the color of blood.

It cast Neve's face in crimson behind her as she straightened her twin's train. The smile her sister summoned was tentative and thin. "You look lovely, Red."

Red's lips were raw from biting, and when she tried to return the smile, her skin pulled. Copper tasted sharp on her tongue.

Neve didn't notice her bleeding. She wore white, like everyone else would tonight, the band of silver marking her as the First Daughter holding back her black hair. Emotions flickered across her pale features as she fussed with the folds of Red's gown—apprehension, anger, bone-deep sadness. Red could read each one. Always could, with Neve. She'd been an easy cipher since the womb they'd shared.

Finally, Neve settled on a blankly pleasant expression designed to reveal nothing at all. She picked up the half-full wine bottle on the floor, tilted it toward Red. "Might as well finish it off."

Red drank directly from the neck. Crimson lip paint smeared the back of her hand when she wiped her mouth.

"Good?" Neve took back the bottle, voice bright even as she rolled it nervously in her palms. "It's Meducian. A gift for the Temple from Raffe's father, a little extra on top of the prayer-tax for good sailing weather. Raffe filched it, said he thought the regular tax should be more than enough for pleasant seas." A halfhearted laugh, brittle and dry. "He said if anything would get you through tonight, this will."

Red's skirt crinkled as she sank into one of the chairs by the window, propping her head on her fist. "There's not enough wine in the world for this."

Neve's false mask of brightness splintered, fell. They sat in silence.

"You could still run," Neve whispered, lips barely moving, eyes on the empty bottle. "We'll cover for you, Raffe and I. Tonight, while everyone—"

"I can't." Red said it quick, and she said it sharp, hand falling to slap against the armrest. Endless repetition had worn all the polish off her voice.

"Of course you can." Neve's fingers tightened on the bottle. "You don't even have the Mark yet, and your birthday is the day after tomorrow."

Red's hand strayed to her scarlet sleeve, hiding white, unblemished skin. Every day since she turned nineteen, she'd checked her arms for the Mark. Kaldenore's had come immediately after her birthday, Sayetha's halfway through her nineteenth year, Merra's merely days before she turned twenty. Red's had yet to appear, but she was a Second Daughter—bound to the Wilderwood, bound to the Wolf, bound to an ancient bargain. Mark or no Mark, in two days, she was gone.

"Is it the monster stories? Really, Red, those are fairy tales to frighten children, no matter what the Order says." Neve's voice had edges now, going from cajoling to something sharper. "They're nonsense. No one has seen them in nearly two hundred years—there were none before Sayetha, none before Merra."

"But there were before Kaldenore." There was no heat in Red's voice, no ice, either. Neutral and expressionless. She was so tired of this fight.

"Yes, two damn centuries ago, a storm of monsters left the Wilderwood and terrorized the northern territories for ten years, until Kaldenore entered and they disappeared. Monsters we have no real historical record of, monsters that seemed to take whatever shape pleased the person telling the tale." If Red's voice had been placid autumn, Neve's was wrecking winter, all cold and jagged. "But even if they were real, there's been *nothing* since, Red. No hint of anything coming from the forest, not for any of the other Second Daughters, and not for you." A pause, words gathered from a deep place neither of them touched. "If there were monsters in the woods, we would've seen them when we—"

"Neve." Red sat still, eyes on the swipe of wound-lurid lip paint across her knuckles, but her voice knifed through the room.

The plea for silence went ignored. "Once you go to him, it's over. He won't let you back out. You can never leave the forest again, not like... not like last time."

"I don't want to talk about that." Neutrality lost its footing, slipping into something hoarse and desperate. "Please, Neve."

For a moment, she thought Neve might ignore her again, might keep pushing this conversation past the careful parameters Red allowed for it. Instead she sighed, eyes shining as bright as the silver in her hair. "You could at least pretend," she murmured, turning to the window. "You could at least pretend to care."

"I care." Red's fingers tensed on her knees. "It just doesn't make a difference."

She'd done her screaming, her railing, her rebellion. She'd done all of it, everything Neve wanted from her now, back before she turned sixteen. Four years ago, when everything changed, when she realized the Wilderwood was the only place for her.

That feeling was mounting in her middle again. Something blooming, climbing up through her bones. Something *growing.*

A fern sat on the windowsill, incongruously verdant against the backdrop of frost. The leaves shuddered, tendrils stretching gently toward Red's shoulder, movements too deft and deliberate to be caused by a passing breeze. Beneath her sleeve, green brushed the network of veins in her wrist, made them stand out against her pale skin like branches. Her mouth tasted of earth.

No. Red clenched her fists until her knuckles blanched. Gradually, that *growing* feeling faded, a vine cut loose and coiling back into its hiding place. The dirt taste left her tongue, but she still grabbed the wine bottle again, tipping up the last of the dregs. "It's not just the monsters," she said when the wine was gone. "There's the matter of me being enough to convince the Wolf to release the Kings."

Alcohol made her bold, bold enough that she didn't try to hide the sneer in her voice. If there was ever going to be a sacrifice worthy enough to placate the Wolf and make him free the Five Kings from wherever he'd hidden them for centuries, it wasn't going to be her.

Not that she believed any of that, anyway.

"The Kings aren't coming back," Neve said, giving voice to their mutual nonbelief. "The Order has sent three Second Daughters to the Wolf, and he's never let them go before. He won't now." She crossed her arms tightly over her white gown, staring at the window glass as if her eyes could bore a hole into it. "I don't think the Kings *can* come back."

Neither did Red. Red thought it was likely that their gods were dead. Her dedication to her path into the forest had nothing to do with belief in Kings or monsters or anything else that might come out of it.

"It doesn't matter." They'd rehearsed this to perfection by now. Red flexed her fingers back and forth, now blue-veined, counting the beats of this endless, circling conversation. "I'm going to the Wilderwood, Neve. It's done. Just... let it be done."

Mouth a resolute line, Neve stepped forward, closing the distance between them with a whisper of silk across marble. Red didn't look up, angling her head so a fall of honey-colored hair hid her face.

"Red," Neve breathed, and Red flinched at her tone, the same she'd use with a frightened animal. "I *wanted* to go with you, that day we went to the Wilderwood. It wasn't your fault that—"

The door creaked open. For the first time in a long time, Red was happy to see her mother.

While white and silver suited Neve, it made Queen Isla look frozen, cold as the frost on the windowpane. Dark brows drew over darker eyes, the only feature she had in common with both her daughters. No servants followed as she stepped into the room, closing the heavy wooden door behind her. "Neverah." She inclined her head to Neve before turning those dark, unreadable eyes on Red. "Redarys."

Neither of them returned a greeting. For a moment that seemed hours, the three of them were mired in silence.

Isla turned to Neve. "Guests are arriving. Greet them, please."

Neve's fists closed on her skirts. She stared at Isla under lowered brows, her dark eyes fierce and simmering. But a fight was pointless, and everyone in this room knew it. As she moved toward the door, Neve glanced at Red over her shoulder, a command in her gaze—*Courage.*

Courageous was the last thing Red felt in the presence of her mother.

She didn't bother to stand as Isla took stock of her. The careful curls coaxed into Red's hair were already falling out, her dress wrinkled. Isla's eyes hesitated a moment on the smear of lip color marking the back of her hand, but even that wasn't enough to elicit a response. This was more proof of sacrifice than a ball, an event for dignitaries from all over the continent to attend and see the woman meant for the Wolf. Maybe it was fitting she looked half feral.

"That shade suits you." The Queen nodded to Red's skirts. "Red for Redarys."

A quip, but it made Red's teeth clench halfway to cracking. Neve used to say that when they were young. Before they both realized the implications. By then, her nickname had already stuck, and Red wouldn't have changed it anyway. There was a fierceness in it, a claiming of who and what she was.

"Haven't heard that one since I was a child," she said instead, and saw Isla's lips flatten. Mention of Red's childhood—that she'd been a child, once, that she was *her* child, that she was sending her child to the forest—always seemed to unsettle her mother.

Red gestured to her skirt. "Scarlet for a sacrifice."

A moment, then Isla cleared her throat. "The Florish

delegation arrived this afternoon, and the Karseckan Re's emissary. The Meducian Prime Councilor sends her regrets, but a number of other Councilors are making an appearance. Order priestesses from all over the continent have been arriving throughout the day, praying in the Shrine in shifts." All this in a prim, quiet voice, a recitation of a rather boring list. "The Three Dukes of Alpera and their retinues should arrive before the procession—"

"Oh, good." Red addressed her hands, still and white as a corpse's. "They wouldn't want to miss that."

Isla's fingers twitched. Her tone, though strained, remained queenly. "The High Priestess is hopeful," she said, eyes everywhere but on her daughter. "Since there's been a longer stretch between you and... and the others, she thinks the Wolf might finally return the Kings."

"I'm sure she does. How embarrassing for her when I go into that forest and absolutely nothing happens."

"Keep your blasphemies to yourself," Isla chided, but it was mild. Red never quite managed to wring emotion from her mother. She'd tried, when she was younger—giving gifts, picking flowers. As she got older, she'd pulled down curtains and wrecked dinners with drunkenness, trying for anger if she couldn't have something warmer. Even that earned her nothing more than a sigh or an eye roll.

You had to be a whole person to be worth mourning. She'd never been that to her mother. Never been anything more than a relic.

"Do *you* think they'll come back?" A bald question, one she wouldn't dare ask if she didn't have one foot in the Wilderwood already. Still, Red couldn't quite make it sound sincere, couldn't quite smooth the barb from her voice. "Do you think if the Wolf finds me *acceptable*, he'll return the Kings to you?"

Silence in the room, colder than the air outside. Red had nothing like faith, but she wanted that answer like it could be absolution. For her mother. For *her.*

Isla held her gaze for a moment that stretched, spun into strange proportions. There were years in it, and years' worth of things unsaid. But when she spoke, her dark eyes turned away. "I hardly see how it matters."

And that was that.

Red stood, shaking back the heavy curtain of her loose hair, wiping the lip paint from her hand onto her skirt. "Then by all means, Your Majesty, let's show everyone their sacrifice is bound and ready."

Red made quick calculations in her head as she swept toward the ballroom. Her presence needed to be marked—all those visiting dignitaries weren't just here for dancing and wine. They wanted to see *her*, scarlet proof that Valleyda was prepared to send its sacrificial Second Daughter.

The Order priestesses were taking turns in the Shrine, praying to the shards of the white trees allegedly cut from the Wilderwood itself. For those from out of the country, this was a religious pilgrimage, a once-in-many-lifetimes chance not only to pray in the famed Valleydan Shrine but also to see a Second Daughter sent to the Wolf.

They might be praying, but they'd have eyes here. Eyes measuring her up, seeing if they agreed with the Valleydan High Priestess. If they, too, thought her *acceptable.*

A dance or two, a glass of wine or four. Red could stay long enough for everyone to judge the mettle of their sacrifice, and then she'd leave.

Technically, it was very early summertime, but Valleydan

temperatures never rose much past freezing in any season. Hearths lined the ballroom, flickering orange and yellow light. Courtiers spun in a panoply of different cuts and styles from kingdoms all over the continent, every scrap of fabric lunar-pale. As Red stepped into the ballroom, all those myriad gazes fixed on her, a drop of blood in a snowdrift.

She froze like a rabbit in a fox's eye. For a moment, they all stared at one another, the gathered faithful and their prepared offering.

Jaw set tight, Red sank into a deep, exaggerated curtsy.

A brief stutter in the dance's rhythm. Then the courtiers started up again, sweeping past her without making eye contact.

Small favors.

A familiar form stood in the corner, next to a profusion of hothouse roses and casks of wine. Raffe ran a hand over close-shorn black hair, his fingers the color of mahogany against the gold of his goblet. For the moment, he stood alone, but it wouldn't be that way for long. The son of a Meducian Councilor and a rather accomplished dancer, Raffe never wanted for attention at balls.

Red slid beside him, taking his goblet and draining it with practiced efficiency. Raffe's lip quirked. "Hello to you, too."

"There's plenty where that came from." Red handed back the goblet and crossed her arms, staring resolutely at the wall rather than the crowd. Their gazes needled the back of her neck.

"Quite true." Raffe refilled his glass. "I'm surprised you're staying, honestly. The people who needed to see you certainly have."

She chewed the corner of her lip. "*I'm* hoping to see someone." It was an admittance to herself as much as to Raffe. She shouldn't *want* to see Arick. She should let this be a clean break, let him go easily...

But Red was a selfish creature at heart.

Raffe nodded once, understanding in the bare lift of his brow. He handed her the full wineglass before getting another for himself.

She'd known Raffe since she was fourteen—when his father took the position as a Councilor, he had to pass on his booming wine trade to his son, and there was no better place to learn about trade routes than with Valleydan tutors. Not much grew here, a tiny, cold country at the very top of the continent, notable only for the Wilderwood on its northern border and its occasional tithe of Second Daughters. Valleyda relied almost entirely on imports to keep the people fed, imports and prayer-taxes to their Temple, where the most potent entreaties to the Kings could be made.

They'd all grown up together, these past six years, years full of realizing just how different Red was from the rest of them. Years spent realizing her time was swiftly running out. But as long as she'd known him, Raffe had never treated her as anything more than a friend—not a martyr, not an effigy to burn.

Raffe's eyes softened, gaze pitched over her head. Red followed it to Neve, sitting alone on a raised dais at the front of the room, eyes slightly bloodshot. Isla's seat was still empty. Red didn't have one.

Red tipped her wine toward her twin. "Ask her to dance, Raffe."

"Can't." The answer came quick and clipped from behind his glass. He drained it in one swallow.

Red didn't press.

A tap on her shoulder sent her whirling. The young lord behind her took a quick step away, eyes wide and fearful. "Uh, my…my lady—no, Princess—"

He clearly expected sharpness, but Red was suddenly too tired to give it to him. It was exhausting, keeping those knife-edges. "Redarys."

"Redarys." He nodded nervously. A blush crept up his white neck, making the spots on his face stand out. "Would you dance with me?"

Red found herself shrugging, Meducian wine muddling her thoughts into shapeless warmth. This wasn't who she was hoping to see, but why not dance with someone brave enough to ask? She wasn't dead yet.

The lordling swept her up into a waltz, barely touching the curve of her waist. Red could've laughed if her throat didn't feel so raw. They were all so afraid to touch something that belonged to the Wolf.

"You're to meet him in the alcove," he whispered, voice wavering on the edge of a break. "The First Daughter said so."

Red snapped out of wine-warmth, eyes narrowing on the young lord's face. Her stomach churned, alcohol and shining hope. "Meet who?"

"The Consort Elect," the boy stammered. "Lord Arick."

He was here. He'd come.

The waltz ended with her and her unlikely partner near the alcove he'd referenced, the train of her gown almost touching the brocade curtain. "Thank you." Red curtsied to the lordling, scarlet now from the roots of his hair to the back of his neck. He stammered something incomprehensible and took off, coltish legs a second away from running.

She took a moment to steady her hands. This was Neve's doing, and Red knew her sister well enough to guess what she intended. Neve couldn't convince her to run, and thought maybe Arick could.

Red would let him try.

She slipped through the curtain, and his arms were around her waist before the ball was gone from view.

"Red," he murmured into her hair. His lips moved to hers, fingers tightening on her hips to pull her closer. "Red, I've missed you."

Her mouth was too occupied to say it back, though she made it clear she shared the sentiment. Arick's duties as the Consort Elect and Duke of Floriane kept him often out of court. He was only here now because of Neve.

Neve had been as shocked as Red when Arick was announced as Neve's future husband, cementing the fragile treaty that made Floriane a Valleydan province. She knew what lay between Arick and Red, but they never talked about it, unable to find the right words for one more small tragedy. Arick was a blade that drew blood two different ways, and the wounds left were best tended to alone.

Red broke away, resting her forehead against Arick's shoulder. He smelled the same, like mint and expensive tobacco. She breathed it in until her lungs ached.

Arick held her there a moment, hands in her hair. "I love you," he whispered against her ear.

He always said it. She never said it back. Once, she'd thought it was because she was doing him a favor, denying herself to make it easier on him when her twenty years were up and the forest's tithe came due. But that wasn't quite right. Red never said it because she didn't feel it. She loved Arick, in a way, but not a way that matched his love for her. It was simpler to let the words pass without remark.

He'd never seemed upset about it before, but tonight, she could feel the way his muscles tensed beneath her cheek, hear the clench of teeth in his jaw. "Still, Red?" It came quiet, in a way that seemed like he already knew the answer.

She stayed silent.

A moment, then he tilted a pale finger under her chin, tipped it up to search her face. No candles burned in the alcove, but the moonlight through the window reflected in his eyes, as green as the ferns on the sill. "You know why I'm here."

"And you know what I'll say."

"Neve was asking the wrong question," he breathed, desperation feathering at the edges. "Just wanting you to run, not thinking about what comes next. I have. It's *all* I've thought of." He paused, hand tightening in her hair. "Run away *with* me, Red."

Her eyes, half closed by kissing and moonlight, opened wide. Red pulled away, quickly enough to leave strands of gold woven around his fingers. "What?"

Arick gathered her hands, pulled her close again. "Run away with me," he repeated, chafing his thumbs over her palms. "We'll go south, to Karsecka or Elkyrath, find some backwater town where no one cares about religion or the Kings coming back, too far away from the forest to worry about any monsters. I'll find work doing... doing *something*, and—"

"We can't do that." Red tugged out of his grip. The pleasant numbness of wine was rapidly giving over to a dull ache, and she pressed her fingers into her temples as she turned away. "You have responsibilities. To Floriane, to Neve..."

"None of that matters." His hands framed her waist. "Red, I can't let you go to the Wilderwood."

She felt it again, the awakening in her veins. The ferns shuddered on the sill.

For a moment, she thought about telling him.

Telling him about the stray splinter of magic the Wilderwood left in her the night she and Neve ran to the forest's edge. Telling him of the destruction it wrought, the blood and the violence. Telling him how every day was an exercise in fighting it down, keeping it contained, making sure it never hurt anyone again.

But the words wouldn't come.

Red wasn't going to the Wilderwood to bring back gods. She wasn't going as insurance against monsters. It was an ancient and esoteric web she'd been born tangled in, but her reasons for not fighting free of it had nothing to do with piety, nothing to do with a religion she'd never truly believed in.

She was going to the Wilderwood to save everyone she loved from *herself.*

"It doesn't have to be this way." Arick gripped her shoulders. "We could have a *life*, Red. We could be just *us*."

"I'm the Second Daughter. You're the Consort Elect." Red shook her head. "*That* is who we are."

Silence. "I could make you go."

Red's eyes narrowed, half confusion and half wariness.

His hands slid from her shoulders, closed around her wrists. "I could take you somewhere he couldn't get to you." A pause, laden with sharp hurt. "Where *you* couldn't get to *him*."

Arick's grip was just shy of bruising, and with an angry surge like leaves caught in a cyclone, Red's shard of magic broke free.

It clawed its way out of her bones, unspooling from the spaces between her ribs like ivy climbing ruins. The ferns on the sill arched toward her, called by some strange magnetism, and she felt the quickening of earth beneath her feet even through layers of marble, roots running like currents, *reaching* for her—

Red wrestled the power under control just before the ferns touched Arick's shoulder, the fronds grown long and jagged in seconds. She shoved him away instead, harder than she meant to. Arick stumbled as the ferns retracted, slinking back to normal shapes.

"You can't *make* me do anything, Arick." Her hands trembled; her voice was thin. "I can't stay here."

"Why?" All fire, angry and low.

Red turned, picking up the edge of the brocaded curtain in a hand she hoped didn't shake. Her mouth worked, but no words seemed right, so the quiet grew heavy and was her answer.

"This is about what happened with Neve, isn't it?" It was an accusation, and he threw it like one. "When you went to the Wilderwood?"

Red's heart slammed against her ribs. She ducked under the curtain and dropped it behind her, muffling Arick's words, hiding his face. Her gown whispered over the marble as she walked down the corridor, toward the double doors of the north-facing balcony. Distantly, she wondered what the priestesses' informants might make of her mussed hair and swollen lips.

Well. If they wanted an untouched sacrifice, that ship had long since sailed.

The cold was bracing after the hearths in the ballroom, but Red was Valleydan, and gooseflesh on her arms still felt like summer. Sweat dried in her hair, now hopelessly straight, careful curls loosened by heat and hands.

Breathe in, breathe out, steady her shaking shoulders, blink away the burn in her eyes. She could count the number of people who loved her on one hand, and they all kept begging for the only thing she couldn't give them.

The night air froze the tears into her lashes before they could fall. She'd been damned from the moment she was born—a Second Daughter, meant for the Wolf and the Wilderwood, as etched into the bark in the Shrine—but still, sometimes, she wondered. Wondered if the damning was her own fault for what she'd done four years ago.

Reckless courage got the best of them after that disastrous ball, reckless courage and too much wine. They stole horses, rode north, two girls against a monster and an endless forest with nothing but rocks and matches and a fierce love for each other.

That love burned so brightly, it almost seemed like the power that took root in Red was a deliberate mockery. The Wilderwood, proving that it was stronger. That her ties to the forest and its waiting Wolf would always be stronger.

Red swallowed against a tight throat. Biting irony, that if it hadn't been for that night and what it wrought, she might've done what Neve wanted. She might've run.

She looked to the north, squinting against cold wind. Somewhere, beyond the mist and the hazy lights of the capital, was the Wilderwood. The Wolf. Their long wait was almost ended.

"I'm coming," she murmured. "Damn you, I'm coming."

She turned in a sweep of crimson skirts and went back inside.

orbit